THE CHINESE SEAMEN'S CHILDREN

Wayne Ward

Published by

MELROSE BOOKS

An Imprint of Melrose Press Limited
St Thomas Place, Ely
Cambridgeshire
CB7 4GG, UK
www.melrosebooks.co.uk

FIRST EDITION

Copyright © Wayne Ward 2012

The Author asserts his moral right to
be identified as the author of this work

Cover designed by Hannah Belcher

ISBN 978-1-907732-94-2

All rights reserved. No part of this publication may be reproduced, stored in a retrieval system, or transmitted, in any form or by any means electronic, mechanical, photocopying, recording or otherwise, without the prior permission of the publishers.

This book is sold subject to the condition that it shall not, by way of trade or otherwise, be lent, re-sold, hired out or otherwise circulated without the publisher's prior consent in any form of binding or cover other than that in which it is published and without a similar condition including this condition being imposed on the subsequent purchaser.

Printed and bound in Great Britain by:
CPI Antony Rowe, Chippenham, Wiltshire

reflection ...

"The Merchant Navy, with Allied comrades, night and day, in weather fair or foul, faces not only the ordinary perils on the sea, but the sudden assaults of war beneath the waters or from the sky."

Winston Churchill, July 1941. A few months later Britain's wartime prime minister added:
"But for the Merchant Navy who bring us our food and munitions of war, Britain would be in a perilous state and the Army, Navy and Air Force could not operate."

Winston Churchill ebullient in victory:
"We must ensure the maintenance of a large, modern and highly efficient Merchant Navy. This country must never forget the debt she owes to her merchant seamen. The men who sailed the convoys to Britain, to Malta, to Russia and all over the world must be sure of steady employment, ships designed to give them good living conditions, good standards of food and proper provision for their welfare."

1

June 1978

OLD AND JAUNDICED EYES peered from under thick bone ledges thatched in wiry grey hair; so deeply sunken the men's eyes it seemed as if the mirrors into their souls peered out upon the world from dark tunnels. Eight men wrapped in thin army blankets sat around the fire, warm and comforted in the approaching chill of winter's night air, their emaciated bodies cushioned by shell grit and coarse sand of their temporary beach camp.

Among the older men a sprinkling of younger, the elder content to stare in the glowing embers of the fire while the young's attention focused on the two ships berthed opposite each other alongside the wooden wharf jutting into the still waters of Spencer Gulf. From a distance the naked eye found it difficult to discern the bulky accommodation blocks of the ships shrouded in a dense cloud of thick white dust, the talc-like phosphate particulates shimmering like snowflakes in the combined glare of their deck floodlighting.

One ship's funnel, illuminated by boat deck spotlights, highlighted its owner's crowned blue seahorse and trident through ingrained phosphate residue. The ship opposite given a casual glance could be mistaken for a sister ship, similar accommodation block aft, deck cranes, her funnel also with a crowned seahorse and trident.

The *Baron Maclay* and *Cape Otway,* owned by Scottish Ship

The Chinese Seamen's Children

Management, an amalgamation of H Hogarth & Sons and Lyle Shipping Company, discharged phosphate from Nauru and Christmas Island under charter to the British Phosphate Commission. BPC, a tripartite of Australian, British and New Zealand agricultural interests and governments, assumed control of phosphate rising in Nauru after the defeat of Germany and the confiscation of its colony in 1918. Christmas Island and its phosphate reserves, administered by the Singaporean government until 1957, sold sovereign territorial rights to Australia for a payment of almost £3 million.

As a colonial master, BPC show little bounteousness with royalty payments struck at a halfpenny a ton, increasing in the late 1920's to seven pence halfpenny a ton. BPC's grand largesse not only decreed Nauru's eventual bankruptcy under a benign Australian version of colonialism, the Commissioners with little regard to fragile environmental balances and checks, also set about with grim determination to extract the finite reserves of phosphate from Christmas Island and Ocean Island with the ruthlessness of an economic mercenary.

Three phosphate rich islands, Nauru, Ocean Island, Christmas Island, two straddling the equator in the Pacific Ocean, the other in the Indian Ocean northwest of Western Australia, experienced the full brunt of exploitation of their only natural resource. Nauru, with independence in 1967, its heart torn out, crushed and loaded into ships drifting offshore, managed to negotiate a higher royalty, though still a pittance which led to ultimate sovereign impoverishment.

Ocean Island, west of Nauru, became the first of the three islands to be depleted of its phosphate reserves, the others following a few years later, their inevitable pathway to destitution ordained by their unfortunate colonial history.

Both ships flew the red duster on their blunt sterns, port of registry Ardrossan, but there all similarities ended. The ship on the southern side of the wharf Australian manned, the ship opposite, British.

The *Baron Maclay,* 21,950 tons, a year out of the United Kingdom, her decks and bulkheads ravaged by the acidic scouring of phosphate residues, her once grey hull bleached almost white, accommodation scuppers visible as wide swathes of rust. Futile efforts to combat the corrosive nature of her cargo appeared to be in progress, a few selected deckheads and superstructure mottled with splotches of what might have been a yellow primer now faded and barely visible. Four fifteen-ton cranes with their purchase and luffing wires wire rope oiled, seemingly applied by the bucketful; tropical heat had melted the tar-like substance, the resultant sludge smearing the crane housings, their original buff paintwork unrecognisable.

The *Cape Otway*'s four eighteen-ton cranes serviced five hatches, idle grabs landed on the outboard side with discharge ceased for the day. Bare bottomed chartered by BPC, third world crewing never far from the collective minds of the Australian maritime unions; the Commissioners were forced to man ships trading exclusively to Australia with Australian crews, Christmas Island an Australian territory and under the jurisdiction of the Australian navigation act and cabotage.

Silence on the wharf, the dust slowly settling as a cold inversion layer of air surged up the Gulf from the deep reaches of the Southern Ocean. The men on the beach huddled closer to their fire; without exception in all of them long extinguished the gene which gave their ancient forebears the ability to survive and prosper in a land reluctant to give up its bounty. Fresh wood, a borer riddled remnant of boat planking, rekindled the fire in a shower of sparks and crackling embers.

Soon someone from the ship would come and appease what gnawed in their bellies.

Shattering the stillness, a shrill feminine shriek, the cry not of anguish but of relief to breathe fresh air after the stifling, sickly sweet fuel oil stench of the accommodation. The girl high-stepped ungainly over the portside stormstep onto the poop; regaining her momentum she staggered aft while she tugged at her mini skirt so short it barely

The Chinese Seamen's Children

covered the rounded globes of her bare bottom, not overly concerned at the loss of her underwear.

Challenging the foulness of the accommodation, a forty-four-gallon oil drum hung from a tackle over the side by the ensign staff, a writhing mass of maggots and oozing putrescence from a spike reamed hole in the base to attach a tripping line. Hanging limply on its ensign staff in non-observance of sunset, the red duster despoiled with grease, its fly shredded.

Shoeless, her dress caught around hips exposing twig-like legs, dark as chocolate, a happy round face and a flat nose crowned by a mass of glistening black curls, she thought she might hide behind a ventilator. Her years more a guess, school age certainly, a slender body yet to surrender to the rapid ravages of ageing predominant of her race.

Railings greasy with evening dew steadied her as she sucked biting air into her lungs, hunching her shoulders and quivering with barely suppressed excitement; Chrissie played a game with Freddie the deck boy, hide-and-seek, which might have been a true indication of both their ages. She thought Freddie a naughty boy and in need of a good talking to, after doing it doggy-fashion against the standard compass binnacle on the monkey island clipping her panties to the starboard inside halyard to fly beside the courtesy flag.

Freddie, drunk and staggering with a near empty flagon of sweet sherry in one hand found her, a remarkable feat in the darkness to which she blended perfectly, possibly her flashing teeth and the whites of her eyes beacons.

Large and furry a tongue filled her mouth and she gagged, giggling as she pulled away to suck in a deep breath. Freddie, more in need of relieving his bladder, swallowed the remainder of the flagon, dropped his shorts and emptied into the scupper. Finished, he turned her around and pressed his flaccid organ against her satiny buttocks. She felt him grinding against her, some grunted expletives as he freed up one hand by throwing the empty flagon on the wharf to smash on the railway lines.

It didn't matter if he couldn't achieve an erection, he thought, having skewered her anyway on the monkey island, a couple of hours earlier her cousin in the spare cabin where he could hide undetected. Then again he should be able to get it up, this darkie prettier than the others fortunate to escape the clutches of the bosun and the prowling ABs.

She turned serious, something else on her mind. "Did that awful man take wine down to the beach?"

"What awful man? There's not one of them on deck that ain't awful. Pack of mongrel dogs the lot of them. Work ya to death."

"That big ugly one in the dirty singlet and underpants, always shouting," she said with an involuntary shiver. "Promised he did to take some flagons down to them camped on the beach when we came on the ship."

"Bosun you mean? No way would that bastard give bloody darkies a sniff of his grog, don't ever believe anything he says. Definitely the bastard wouldn't be giving darky blokes booze, no way."

"Said he would, he's not a nice man," she said; she seemed mesmerised by the glow of the fire on the beach, her family waiting for the bosun to give them their promised reward. Of course the bosun didn't want them on the ship, only herself, her older sister and four cousins. She felt Freddie stirring against her bottom, a nervous reaction tightening her buttocks as she remembered the bosun's huge paws and blackened, broken fingernails. Slobbering obscenities of his carnal intentions when he spread her skinny black legs. Lucky for her the brute staggering in the messroom in his soiled underpants found it more erotic watching sister Angie spread-eagled on the messroom table with a furiously humping motorman on top of her.

Freddie's youthful endurance gave him just enough firmness to slip inside her wet sheaf and she hoped he would finish quickly so she could have a cigarette. Her wish granted a few seconds later when he lost interest, digging in his top pocket for a packet of Silk Cut cigarettes and matches.

The Chinese Seamen's Children

Unusual for ships discharging opposite each other, neither had initiated reciprocal visits, exchange library books and magazines. Again not immediately evident from a distance, both ships worlds apart even with their mutual ownership.

Work on the Wallaroo wharf commenced at 8:00 am and ceased with completion of extended day shift at 7:00 pm. Occupying the middle of the old wooden wharf with about ten feet clearance either side stood two small hoppers with the capacity to hold two grabs from the *Cape Otway* and *Baron Maclay*. These ancient contraptions were laboriously emptied by gripping a chain attached to a counterweight which when pulled opened a chute to cascade phosphate into a truck backed underneath. Outdated, rusted and warped, only a miracle of surviving rivets and gussets caused both to remain somewhat upright on their spindly latticed legs.

The *Cape Otway's* discharge of 4000 tons in the shallow draft port made only possible after lightening 10,000 tons in Albany, Western Australia. The remaining 18,000 tons allocated for discharge in Geelong where the ship would backload crated machine parts, general cargo and reefers for Christmas Island. The Wallaroo discharge exceptionally slow because of hopper constraints, the *Cape Otway* with a discharge capacity to dump on open wharfage 8000 tons in a single shift, a rate achieved on her last trip to Portland, Victoria.

Alex Nielsen, duty watchman, sipped his strong black coffee, the warm mug held firmly in both hands; a glance down No. 5 hatch proved little progress in the discharge, like all the men due to sign off on leave after a double Christmas Island swing, wishing to see exposed ceilings if not crater-like holes. Thoughts of home, Frankston, a beachside suburb south of Melbourne. No more a well kept local secret, discovered by discerning buyers fleeing the rat race of Melbourne, so spruiked the voracious real estate agents fighting for exposure along the Nepean Highway which faithfully followed the Frankston-Melbourne railway corridor.

Some years ago he had mentioned to his father buying a home, something in need of renovation, relatively cheap and on the beach side of the railway. His parents would decree otherwise.

Remembrance of his first kiss in this home perched on a steep hillside with a magnificent view of Port Phillip Bay, the South Channel to Hovell Pile; a clumsy hand on her budding chest, rebuffed for no reason he could understand in his youthfulness eagerness. He never got to unbutton her blouse again, her fickle attention drawn to a more athletic type, a tousled head boy recruited to train with a Melbourne football club.

From this home he had joined his first ship, a hastily packed suitcase secured with a belt when called by the shipping office to join the *Bundaleer* berthed at the Yarraville sugar refinery. His distraught mother wrung her hands and cried for the loss of a son as she watched a rusty old tramp with dense clouds of black smoke roiling from its tall yellow and black funnel, spewing ash and clinker over a forest of derricks, a smudge in the South Channel on passage to North Queensland to load sugar.

With engineering expertise his father had built this home from foundations to finials, the onset of age, retirement and weary joints greatly influencing a decision after long family deliberations, moving to a smaller and more accessible home. Another decision, arrived at with minimum thought, rare in families, the signing over of the deeds to their son for the cost of stamp duty and conveyance. The home came with no righteously imposed parental conditions to vindicate the impact of their overwhelming generosity, a simple act of sharing, of family, of love for a son.

At thirty reaching a crossroads in life, when a man not so young anymore worried of life passing him by without the trappings of a permanent relationship, he thought more often of comfortable domestication and sense of community. Joining an environmental group, weeding and mowing lawns, chasing off neighbourhood dogs with unsociable habits. Fire up the barbeque and invite neighbours for steaks and cold beers.

From his eyrie on bitterly cold winter mornings when an icy southwesterly whipped off Port Phillip Bay mercilessly assailed all who rushed frantically to catch trains further strengthened his belief being a seaman placed him on a special pedestal. Especially on leave when able to pull a fluffy blanket up around chilled ears and occasionally anticipate the stirring of someone soft and warm.

Not one of the seamen of the *Baron Maclay* had bothered to make contact with the *Cape Otway*, even only to exchange gripes about a common enemy, mates, engineers and shipowners. Then again why when earlier in the day five ABs led by the bosun roaring obscenities and shaking his fist at anyone who met his enraged gaze staggered back from the Wallaroo Hotel with mind numbing booty.

Known for depositing his reproductive fluids in any convenient portal, the bosun saw an opportunity not to be missed. Roaring at the top of his voice to a group of Aboriginal men camped on the beach close to the wharf, an open invitation to the nubile members of the tribe to engage in meaningful and social discourse aboard the *Baron Maclay*, the men offered copious amounts of wine for passing the word back to the permanent domicile. To tempt the taste buds, a flagon on deposit perhaps?

Wheat sacks slung over their shoulders clinking glass, a cheer rose from those hanging about the gangway awaiting their fellow shipmates return. Another oddity about the *Baron Maclay*, a rare officer presence on deck, but then by the look of what gathered by the gangway, unshaven, battered and scarred heads, tattoos close to mutilation, grease stained clothes that might have been used to mop bilges, could well be a deterrent to a mate or engineer wanting a fair day's work.

Being an intrepid leader of men not to be denied, the bosun took up a compulsory collection from the sub paid on arrival, $300, the money immediately proffered to the delighted publican of the Wallaroo Hotel. Not overly bright with finances, he banked the money with the obliging and trusting publican, withdrawing funds in wine, spirits and beer. For his financial acumen and infantile trust, a complimentary bottle of vintage wine from the stock the publican kept under the bar for sale to the local Aboriginal community. The bosun's arrangement with the publican simplicity itself and evidence of his organisational skills, the deck boy doing a daily runner, the bosun taking delight imbecile Freddie's back might break under the weight of his burden. Then of course he would have to make his own bunk, disturbing the comely lubra occupying it, empty the rosy and generally clean up the mess of the cabin.

Piercing shrieks and giggles, wild dancing and copulation of Bacchanalian proportions, no wonder these revellers avoided the sterile *Cape Otway*, the only thing on the crew's mind paying off in Geelong after a swing of two months. The men across the way sailed from the United Kingdom a year ago!

Alex thought about the bosun at the head of his men leading them down the wharf and smiled. What mate would be game enough to ask a simple question of where his men might be working? The bosun's breath would peel paint, his fists and mental reasoning the battering rams of an alcohol fuelled wet brain. He might be able to define day from night but barely capable of any other rational thought.

Sanitary *Cape Otway*, he thought about that, too. Three men on the gear working grabs, completion of cargo two men stood down, one on duty until 8:00 am as watchman. Simple, easy, well organised. After work a comfortable barstool with an icy pint of Melbourne beer on tap, a selection of spirits, soft drink and duty free cigarettes in an unlocked glass cabinet. Walport Marine based in the United Kingdom supplied an aluminium suitcase plastered with shipping stickers of documentaries, movies, British drama and comedy. Stocked with 700 books, a wide-ranging library, cabinets and drawers packed with board games, playing cards, social club videos, magazines and in port television and local newspapers.

On social occasions the two cooks baked sausage rolls, party pies, cocktail frankfurts, deep fried potato crisps for bingo nights. Cribbage and euchre tournament winners received pewter mugs inscribed with the ship's name and date. Barbeques abaft the funnel, free beer dispensed from a portable temprite unit when the ship drifted off Christmas Island and Nauru waiting for the swell to abate.

The Chinese Seamen's Children

Achieved through union and company negotiations a leave system of two swings on and one swing off, followed by one swing on, one swing off to balance leave accruals. On standby a private jet, first class air travel, five star hotels, a limousine service door to door swinging off and joining. Aggregate wage and industrial clothing, general purpose manning, restaurant food and working conditions guaranteeing adequate rest periods. Single accommodation, three quarter bunks and duck down doonas, toilet and shower, refrigerator and piped music, settee and wall-to-wall carpet.

The *Baron Maclay* with a full British crew manned under the British Board of Trade unfortunately signed articles with history against them. A maritime past though grand not favourable to British seamen forced to eat swill and embalmed meat, live in open focastles on straw mattresses, beg for wages, bashed and driven, strict segregation, a life of deprivation and hardship with few exceptions. Some cynics of a mind the lot of British seamen in sail little changed in modern times.

No more apparent when the United Kingdom struggled to survive in a war seemingly lost on land and at sea. With seamen dying in their thousands, British shipowners partitioned with plywood bulkheads the single messing arrangements standard on North American built Liberty and Victory ships. Saloons and white tablecloths for officers, messrooms and laminate for seamen. Even more contempt for the lower ranks followed with gangways landing on the wharf in the first British ports, the removal of generously donated libraries from North American benevolent societies, curtains, coffee urns, mats and common menus, anything that might make the life of a seaman in dread of his life every waking moment a little more bearable.

Alex walked forward to check the lines, then from the focastle head a slow amble down the starboard side to the accommodation aft. Time to check the various decks and communal spaces, finally the after lines. Coffee and a grilled cheese and ham sandwich, and unlike the ship opposite, a long and lonely night in front of him.

In the afternoon the *Baron Maclay* decided to entertain the wharf with a cassette player blaring Rolling Stones music as loud as the cheap and battered instrument could blast. On the poop deck a party raged, non-caring the tribal dancing of the girls stirred choking dust devils of phosphate. Who cared with plentiful amounts of restocked wine and beer to wash it down, Freddie having made a morning trip to the Wallaroo Hotel, a kindly wharf labourer lending the struggling deck boy a handcart.

There emerged even louder voices than the bosun's, singing and senseless chortling. Counting heads of those cavorting on the poop proved the agent correct, informing the *Cape Otway's* purser the ship sailed from her last Australian port four men down, replacements arriving from London that afternoon.

Welcoming the new lads from home? Alex with his watch mate and co-delegate, Paul Toomey, and motorman Trevor Snell, stood by the gangway ready to go ashore when a deafening silence descended on the wharf, so intense the sound of a grab slamming shut amplified tenfold. The music and dancing ceased abruptly, the girls and their panting partners crowding around the gangway now hoisted almost horizontal.

"What are those bloody drunks up to? One minute a party of which I am all envy, now all hands lifting the gangway," Paul said, shaking his head.

"Could be the old man's read the riot act," Trevor said. "Or maybe shifting ship?"

"No, she's still discharging. Something's going on, look." Alex indicated the agent's car parked by the stern of the *Baron Maclay*. Accompanying the agent four men with suitcases and bags, one Chinese, three so black their faces shone purple.

As if possessed by a mechanical demon the *Baron Maclay's* gangway performed a wild and erratic dance, a seaman with a jeering girl on his arm stabbing the control buttons of the power lead draped around his neck. Egged on by the bosun, the gangway lowered a few turns of wire before jerking to a bridle shaking halt, then hoisting

The Chinese Seamen's Children

parallel with the fishplate. To give leadership and encouragement to his men, the bosun shouted hoarsely through cupped hands: "Fuck off chink! Fuck off niggers! Hear me, we got no chinks and niggers on this ship! We's Brits!"

Bouncing off the bulkheads, the chant echoed around the poop. Giving his unconditional support to his drinking mates, a drunken steward threw rotten fruit he had scraped from the deck of the chill room at whatever moved on the wharf. One enterprising AB with the deck boy hauled in the garbage bin hanging over the stern and spilled its meagre but potent contents on deck, globules of fat and putrid sludge crawling with maggots flowing into the scuppers. Gagging, the seaman handed the deck boy a shovel, indicating the targets who edged closer to the safety of the *Cape Otway*.

Freddie, exhausted having serviced the unconscious girl in the bosun's bunk after giving up the idea of making it, blinked rapidly to bring his fuzzy vision into focus. The shovel weighed heavily in his hand, as did the quivering jellified putrescence of rotten meat, potatoes and cabbage. His first effort at finding the direction indicated went over his shoulder, rebounding off the accommodation bulkhead, splattering on those gathered by the gangway. Freddie's rear became a point of interest, the bosun's boot finding its mark and a whelp of pain as the deck boy went sprawling in the foulness spreading over the poop.

Standing beside Alex the *Cape Otway*'s bosun, Ben Anderson, scowled at the melee across the divide, then the agent and men on the wharf. "Am I seeing this correctly, those dusky young maidens of our sunburned land are calling those men on the wharf niggers? Jesus, I hate that word."

"Yeah, and the other one a chink," Alex said. "Doesn't take much figuring out those men on the wharf are the replacement ABs the agent told our purser about. Have a look at those three, are those blokes black!"

"Might be Scottish Ship Management is changing flags," Ben said.

"Wouldn't the agent have a busload of them, an empty one with bars for the white raving lunatics?" Paul said.

An assortment of crockery and mugs thrown with lethal intent caused the party on the wharf to move even closer to the *Cape Otway*, the distance enough for Alex to call out to the harried agent raking his hands through his hair: "What the hell's going on?"

Apprehension etched in the wan face of the agent. "Telling you this, if bloody Horrie the publican of the Wallaroo Hotel would put these bastards on the coal we might get some sense here. Okay, British ships change white crews for coloured, but not in Wallaroo. Not in bloody Wallaroo!"

"Are you sure?"

"Four seamen off a plane from England a crew? No way!" the agent bleated, edging another nervous step closer to the *Cape Otway* as an erratically aimed loaf of brick hard stale bread from the steward run out of rotten fruit landed close to his feet. "These men come from London! These men were engaged by Scottish Ship Management!"

"Union pool?"

"How the damn hell would I know something like that? All I know is these four are to replace four that went missing in Geraldton."

More abuse hurled down on the wharf, the bosun's voice reclaiming the distinction of being the loudest: "We told the old man you ain't signing on them taking our jobs, hear that! We're a crew of Brits! That's the way we're stayin'!"

This rallying statement brought a rousing cheer from the gangway, sneers and shrills from the girls, the bottom platform roller bouncing off the apron before it became airborne again. For a few seconds a brief respite as the dull witted AB on the controls forgot which buttons to punch before the bottom platform landed on the apron, this time with a resounding thud, kinked wire on the winch drum a tangle of loose and riding turns.

At that moment the agent's courage overcame his fear, leaping forward with his briefcase tucked under his chin to grab the slack bridle chains; his youthful days as an agile wingman for the Wallaroo Kangaroos came to the fore, bouncing up the gangway three steps at

The Chinese Seamen's Children

a time. Almost in sight of his objective, an open door, a huge hand grabbed him by the back of the collar and lifted him off the deck; an almost inhuman face devoid of any compassion glared nose to nose.

"Where do you think you're going?" the bosun snarled, his breath causing the agent to gag. "We know what your orders are! Replacing us Brits with chinks and niggers!"

"I don't know what you're talking about!" the agent cried, now in fear for his life. "These men were picked up at Adelaide airport and sent to the ship from your company. From England! Every one of them speaks like you lot do, I swear!"

"What's that mean? You sayin' something about the way we speak?"

Praying not to embarrass himself with a bodily function, he cried: "It's imperative I speak to the master! Please!"

"Those niggers on the wharf come from Nigeria, the chink from Hong Kong! We know what the company's up to! Wants us Brits off their fucking ship and chinks and niggers in our place!"

"You're shorthanded four men! My information from the master is your company is obligated under your articles of agreement to maintain full manning!"

"Oh, is that right?" spittle from the bosun's breath flecked the agent's face. "Their obligation is to feed us shit and work us to death, then sign on chinks and niggers."

Able to lift his head, his chest gripped in a vice-like clamp, the agent would have seen four heads peering over the bridge taffrail; a nervous voice from above: "Release that man immediately." If its tone represented authority it mattered not to the bosun; persisting, the voice said: "Agent, come to the bridge immediately. It is imperative we to ring London urgently."

Slowly and menacingly the bosun raised his eyes aloft, bloodshot and crazed, releasing his victim. His bemused brain though painfully slow to react to changing circumstances did register the fact the master's voice penetrated the cauliflower gristle either side of his head. With his gangway guarded and secure from threats of incursion he should take time to savour the spoils of success, a comely black bitch asleep in his bunk dreaming of what bulged in his underpants. Most assuredly he needed a recharge.

Drink stirred something in the back of his clouded mind; he would have to send the cretin deck boy back to the pub for more booze, a flagon of port thrown to the Abos on the beach. No problem with stores, the bank buoyant from two breast wires run off their reels and twenty gallons of topside paint flogged last night which the tractor driver on the wharf agreed to pick up around midnight in his boat.

Watching the agent disappear in a frantic tangle of arms and legs through the accommodation door, those standing at the *Cape Otway*'s gangway changed their mind about going ashore, calling down to the wharf for the four seamen to come onboard.

Around his own age, Alex thought, surprised when he said thirty-eight; his lineage though faint still unmistakable Chinese; he introduced himself as Edward Huang.

Alex returned the introduction, shaking hands with the others of indisputable African ancestry. The three black ABs exchanged names which brought smiles to the faces of their hosts, broad and deep South Shields accents; Otis Worthington, Clyde Potter and Gavin Newbury. Born and raised in Hull, all financial members of the National Union of Seamen.

"Which of course those running the asylum across the way have no idea of," Paul said, at the bar ordering four pints.

"Strange, I don't blame them. No one can condone their behaviour, but their suspicions I can well understand. Our shipowners supported by government are flagging out ships in increasing numbers, manned with low wage foreign crews without leave or conditions," Edward said, taking a tentative sip of his beer; a beaming smile filled his face. "Good. Thank you."

"So the drunks of the *Baron Maclay* reckon you're a replacement crew of a shade favourable to shipowners worldwide," Alex said. "Could be if some of them sobered up the true facts would become obvious. Then being four down and four men on the wharf with their gear, even for drunks you'd reckon the arithmetic would be fairly simple."

"Three black, one Chinese," Edward said resignedly. "Maybe in their minds there are others behind us? It's happened in the past and without a doubt will happen again in the future."

"Your father or mother Chinese?" Paul said.

"Singaporean on my father's side. My mother's from Liverpool, Merseyside working class."

Tensions quickly dissipated in the comfort of chintz covered lounge chairs set around a small table, two other chairs drawn up for Alex and Paul. On the table the peggy cleared a space for a small raffia basket of freshly baked scones, tubs of strawberry conserve and whipped cream.

Edward glanced up quizzically.

"Whatever takes the two cooks fancy, muffins, scones, cupcakes or shortbreads," the peggy said offhandedly, placing by each man a small side plate and a knife.

Otis wolfed down his scone, his mouth plastered with cream and jam. "Hey man, I see a seahorse on the funnel and two ships almost identical. Also both British, but here I am eating warm scones and cream. Can I ask you what is for dinner?"

"Mushroom soup, roast pork, baked vegetables and greens. Cold roast chicken salad. Dessert, bread and butter pudding," he said, thinking he might have to return to the pantry for more scones. "We enjoy our conditions but never take them for granted. What we have won is only because of our union, the Seamen's Union of Australia."

Alex agreed. "If not for cabotage the crazies across the wharf would be having their party on this ship, or a crowd of third world seamen under a flag of convenience working for fish heads and rice. Our shipowners are not a benevolent society for seamen, far from it. Every condition we enjoy we fought for through award struggles, strikes and a one-sided battle against an arbitration system which rarely rules in favour of the unions. We take pleasure in our scones and cream, but never forget for one moment where those little extras came from."

Edward looked around the bar; barstools, lounge chairs, television and video player in one corner, full glassed library cases, cabinets of magazines and games in the other. Behind the bar mounted on the laminated deckhead spirit dispensers of whisky, brandy, rum, ouzo, vodka and gin. Another glass cabinet stocked with cigarettes and tobacco.

"How does this all work?" Edward said, visibly awed. "It just doesn't seem possible for a working ship."

"Simple," Paul said. "Honesty and allegiance to our union. Now the social side is a little different and it is left to us to police our members and keep them on course. For instance on this swing the beer is free because when we swing on we each buy a nine gallon keg for nine dollars, our meal money joining the ship, and place the keg in a queue. Company has a rigid alcohol policy of one keg for the two bars every second day, ours and catering. Stewards' bar is dry and used for videos and television. Spirits twenty cents a nip, cigarettes I wouldn't know because I don't smoke, but duty free and cheap."

Indicating a framed photograph and certificate on the bulkhead of a group of small children with two young women in the background, a note of pride filled the peggy's voice. "That's an orphanage outside of Port Adelaide where a percentage of the profits from the bar go. The rest to the members, the peace council and political donations condoned by the union."

Otis's eyes widened; he looked at his companions, overwhelmed. "Many times I have heard you Aussies brag in the pubs back home about how good it is on your coast, which no one ever believed. My apologies, I take it all back."

"Not so fast." Alex held both hands up. "We have some horrors on the coast, skippers and mates who would gnaw the leg off a junkyard dog. Underpowered rust buckets and notoriously bad feeders. When

The Chinese Seamen's Children

we worked for overtime the amount dictated by the master's whim. This ship and BPC is an exception when you compare her against BHP where their officers are set in concrete-like company dogma which relates in reality to crushing unionised dissent. Officers who have sold their souls to the company in the misguided belief their jobs and promotions are safe for life."

"Our conditions took a turn for the better in 1955 with an award handed down by Judge Foster of the arbitration court," Paul said. "Granted, only a sea lawyer could understand the green book it came in, but it gave us oilskins and seaboots. Overtime and leave that would later be admitted with mortification by the good judge an error of judgement on his part. He would at a later date remove the anomaly with weekend penalties slashed to a point of having the farthing reintroduction into the currency. We accepted begrudgingly, later awards giving us industrial clothing and longer leave accruals. We have done well with our union and we never forget it."

"Without fear of contradiction, a union held in fear by shipowners all over the world," Edward concurred and his three companions nodded agreement.

In a quandary, the agent frantically searched his mind to where his replacements might have disappeared, again reverting to prayer, not the Wallaroo Hotel preparing retribution against him. His answer obvious by suitcases and bags stacked at the foot of the *Cape Otway*'s gangway. Thank God! He needed a double Captain Morgan badly, even a triple.

"Seen it with my own eyes, behind locked doors the officers are in sheer terror of the crew, especially the bosun," the agent said, slumping in a lounge chair, a huge sigh of thanks when handed a neat double overproof rum. "Mad, the bloody lot of them, the bosun locked up and the key thrown over the side. Master couldn't guarantee the safety of the four replacements and he will be coming ashore with me to ring London in two hours. "That's of course if he can get past the gang at the gangway, excuse the derogatory term as it's not mine, guarding the gangway on nigger watch." His eyebrows almost met as he tried to calculate time zones.

Ben with family in Manchester glanced at the bar clock. "Reckon the London office staff would be catching their trains or buses right now. 7:25 am."

"Thanks." The rum stirring his stomach juices commenced working its magic; he too looked at the clock, thoughts of driving the master to his closed office. Arrange accommodation for the four seamen now relaxed and at ease, even smiling which he most certainly could not. What a contrast, the two ships. One that stunk like an open sewer, no, a whorehouse with more Aboriginal girls from Port Adelaide onboard, if he recognised correctly the battered old Sixties Ford Falcon nose first in a ditch adjacent the wharf. Same car, easily recognised by its red, yellow and black body panels, that followed a Swede from Port Adelaide loading grain for Europe a few weeks ago. Word got around.

"What about these men?" Alex asked.

"I'll have to put them up at the pub. Then maybe the master will have matters in hand after he contacts his owners. He wants police protection for his officers going ashore. Jesus Christ!"

"What did you say to that?"

"No way! Our local police! I know them too well. We play bowls on the weekend. Our kids go to school together. I've seen those bloody heads close up, riot squad from Adelaide armed with tear gas and truncheons."

"Fine role model for our lofty profession," Paul said with a broad grin. "Gotta admit though, she must be a good job. None of them turn to and there's not a sight of a mate on deck. With of course delectable young female company to fill in the long hours of boredom."

Retrieving the empty glasses, the peggy's raised eyebrows questioned refills; four heads nodded eagerly. "By what I have observed a man would have to be truly desperate to poke around between their legs," he said.

The Chinese Seamen's Children

Offering his empty glass to anyone who would take it, the agent almost begged. "One more with the same potency as the last, please. God, I need it. This is going to be a long night."

Alex caught Paul's attention. "Shouldn't we do something as delegates? These are four comrades and that lot across the wharf are no more than a bunch of racist thugs. Wouldn't even call them waterfront rats in fear of demeaning that much-maligned vermin."

"Not so sure about that. Look at it from another angle, a mob of white maniacs replaced with imagined third world seamen. How would we react if the same happened to us in Wallaroo?"

"I'm certain not like that lot. Anyway, no one is replacing them. Four jumped and the ship is shorthanded. The company has replaced them with British nationals." Alex took the agent's glass and tossed it to the peggy who refilled it to the brim. "You don't have to be Einstein to know how Scottish Ship Management is going to react, we've supplied men and flown them to Australia. Get them onboard using the log book and whatever threats of local intervention can scare the hell out of them. Or even worse, maybe the crowd has given the owners a trigger to get rid of them and flag out."

"My God, spare me that! Whole crew of Africans and Chinese on the wharf and that mob howling on the ship! Nightmares are made from what you've just said!"

2

TORRENTIAL RAIN REDUCED TO intermittent showers deferred the commencement of discharge, the hatches of both ships still closed since cessation of cargo the previous evening. The *Cape Otway*'s bosun pondered a dilemma, excluding the standby gearmen, where to work his spare men, finally settling on cleaning out and painting the bridge store adjacent the battery room. Agreement with the mate work in such a confined space should be classified a job-of-finish appeasing some disgruntled comments.

Onboard were the replacements for the *Baron Maclay*, dropped on the wharf by the agent with advice to seek protection on the *Cape Otway*.

On a large white plate three thin pork sausages, onion gravy, bacon and a fluffy cheese omelette; Alex's breakfast. "Accommodation in the pub okay?" he said, with his knife and fork indicating the vacant table opposite.

All four stared at the food on Alex's white enamel plate, then the typed menu the peggy placed on their table. "Beef sausages, onion gravy, sauté mushrooms, bacon, eggs-to-order, toast, chips, fruit juice, yoghurt, fresh fruit and choice of breakfast cereals," Otis said, awed. "With one leg shorter than the other an ancient waitress at the pub served us cold baked beans on a single slice of burned toast!"

The Chinese Seamen's Children

"We won a common menu years ago, sending shipowners into a frenzy of impending bankruptcies," Paul said, sitting beside Alex with fried eggs, bacon and four slices of toast.

"Can you imagine how a British shipowner would react to a menu such as this?" Edward said. "Though some companies are better feeders than others, especially tankers."

"What did the agent have to say about the master contacting England last night?"

"Not much except the old man went silent and turned as white as snow. Told the agent to bring us down in the morning to sign on. In the interim the agent requested we wait on the *Cape Otway*, I don't think he's overly confident about our safety though there's no one by the gangway we could see. Made mention also the wharf delegates being concerned about the tomfoolery going at the gangway, impeding safe access or something like that."

"There's been no activity over there for awhile. Maybe it's squeezing-up time with a bit of added remorse."

"Agent said something about London not wanting the local authorities involved, afraid of having the crowd thrown in jail and the ship held without a crew."

"So where do you fellows stand now?"

"What we have heard from the agent we'll be signed on today, but I am not so sure. Wondering if baked beans on toast constituted an Aussie breakfast in the glossy tourist brochures, we talked a few things over. Telling them all to go to hell and request a flight home, but what would that solve? Nothing except expose four others to a similar situation, though we are pissed off being the brunt of racial intolerance and refused what is our right as members of the union to join our ship."

"Well, you aren't going onboard by yourselves, that's for sure. You've got two delegates, Paul here as big as an ox our battering ram and me standing a few feet behind him. So much for Aussie courage in the field."

"Thanks for your support," Edward said; he looked around the messroom and added despondently: "That it has come to this, having to have an escort to join our ship. Sad."

"Edward, those pack of drunks are not your typical seamen, British or otherwise. Seamen have no racial barriers, Irish, Pom, Yank, Chinese, Greek, Fin, Swede, Dane, Dutch, Maltese, French, Russian, Filipino and all those I have forgotten. Seamen, one simple word encapsulating what each and every one of us is. We also have one important bond in common, we fight a single enemy of no known or admitted nationality, the shipowner."

"Over our baked beans on toast we talked of empathy, just a little I'll admit, for the crowd of the *Baron Maclay*, their concerns the same as ours in respect of third world crews manning British ships. From the ship looking down on the wharf, Otis, Clyde, Gavin and yours truly look exactly like what these blokes dread."

"We're painting a bridge store which doesn't exactly strike a chord with any of us, reckon though we can arrange with the bosun some time off for union business. Then if good sense fails to prevail we'll call the union in Adelaide. First though, order yourself a decent breakfast."

Overpowering, a cloying odour of rancid fat saturated with sickly sweet fuel oil hung in a thick pall about the accommodation, access surprisingly without incident, the gangway deserted. One reason quickly to mind, seamen and two officers gathered around No. 4 crane.

Three accommodation alleyways were accessed through dark and claustrophobic port and starboard alcoves, an athwartships alleyway joined by two fore and aft dimly illuminated by overhead fluorescent lighting. Similar to the alcoves, the alleyways were coated with a thick sheen of phosphate dust, the deck imprinted with footprints akin to a cattle holding pen. Six closed doors faced forward, three aft; of the doors aft two accessed steep companionways leading to the

The Chinese Seamen's Children

messroom, recreation room, galley, stores, freezers and chill rooms. Opening the amidships door revealed a pantry, stainless steel sink, cupboards, disconnected electric coffee percolator and hot water urn, standard fittings when the ship left her Norwegian builder's yard, but now used to store mops, buckets, brooms and deck stores in transit.

Likened to the *Cape Otway*, the similarities between the ships ended with its state of neglect and poor overhead lighting, fluorescent tubes burned out and others flickering.

Paul sniffed. "Christ, is that coming from the galley?"

"God, I hope not," Edward groaned.

Every door in the ship closed made Alex wonder if a fire drill might be in progress; behind a door came muffled voices mixed with high pitched feminine laughter.

Messroom?

Bare of curtains a row of portholes followed the curvature of the stern; what little bleached light managed to seep through encrusted phosphate and salt into the alleyway silhouetted the threatening bulk of a man standing in the doorway. Recognised as the bosun he smelled of stale booze, dressed in a pair of grease ingrained bib-and-brace khaki overalls polished shiny and caked with grime and paint. Tall as Alex but at least six inches shorter than Paul, an advantage in their favour if he decided to attack.

"Youse off the Aussie ship across the ways?" the bosun slurred, cocking his head to see around Alex, squinting first at Edward and the indistinct dark figures beside him, behind them a mass of hard breathing bone and muscle.

Alex regulated his breathing, tensed for a frontal assault, more so a head-butt which the likes of this man held as a preferred method of assault in his arsenal of violence. "Yes, and with us four British seamen, financial members of your union and replacements for four who jumped ship."

Almost entirely covered in glistening black curls, a tiny head appeared under the bosun's left armpit and spat. So large the span of the bosun's right hand it fully covered her head, with a grunt pushing her behind him. "Fuck off, bitch!"

With a parting sneer and a wiggle of her miniature buttocks, she rejoined five others in various states of undress sitting at a corner settee table strewn with empty bottles, overflowing ashtrays and crushed cigarette packs floating in beer and wine slop.

Added to the smell from the galley and engine room, sour sweat and unwashed bodies, only the desperate would stake their lives taking a meal in the messroom. That aside, the bosun's clothing and the crowd turned to possibly signalled a return to normalcy.

"So what you want?" he growled, a gurgling sound in the base of his throat as he swayed unsteadily on his feet.

Certain the man no longer posed an immediate threat, Alex relaxed. "Can we talk seaman to seaman?" he said, aware of Paul who wanted to settle the matter in a more forceful manner. Play it cool, play it simple. "No master, no agent, no union. Just us and the four men who are not a third world crew picked up to replace you."

"So says you. Tellin' ya we ain't having chinks and niggers taking our jobs," the bosun said, his roar now no more than a whimper.

"No one is taking your jobs! You're four men down and there are four replacements! Four men standing right here!" Paul said, clenching his fists and about to push Alex aside.

Alex continued to block his path, still confident of his assessment of the man's intent. "We want to talk to you, or have you delegates we can get some sense out of?"

"Talk to anyone, you talk to me."

About as useful as entering into meaningful dialogue with the village idiot, Alex thought, then lost patience and pushed him aside to enter the messroom. Ignoring taunts and sniggers from the girls, he sat at a table. "Sit down and we'll make some sense of this fiasco."

No effort had been made to return encrusted and greasy dishes and mugs to the sink, or to clear away the remnants of a drunken orgy. By the pantry door a slide accessed the galley, framing a face crowned with a shock of fair hair restrained with a red bandana.

"Hamish Wallace," the cheerful announced in a broad Scottish

The Chinese Seamen's Children

brogue. "Chief cook and you'll get nothing but gibberish out of Reese Boyle's pickled brain, or that of a baboon's implanted in the bonehead at birth."

If the bosun heard the insult he showed no reaction, shuffling from the door to slump in a chair. In his stupor he took offense at the stack of plates on the table, using his elbow to sweep them on the deck. "Make a good peggy," Paul remarked. "Might be Maltese Joe's brother, another who uses the same mop he cleans toilet bowls with to swab messroom tables."

"Don't go away, I'm coming around," Hamish said. "This ship needs some Aussie clout."

Quivering on a slender thread, a blob of saliva clung precariously to the bosun's bottom lip, Alex wondering if the man's brain still had a functioning purpose. Close up his battered face appeared to be the result of a lifetime of fists and upended barstools, exuding from him a barely suppressed brutality that would make any mate extremely wary of him. No wonder chaos ruled on the ship, though a hopeful sign of a return to sanity with seamen on deck.

"We kind of got off on the wrong foot which does not excuse your bigotry to your fellow seamen," Alex said. Preaching when he had no right to moralize, but this occasion called for righteous indignation, to stand on a soapbox and lambast a fellow seaman. "Okay, four seamen who happen to be of an unacceptable colour to you lot turn up on the wharf, seen as a threat to your current manning. Understandable when you consider the past form of your shipowners, the bastards can't wait to sack you in favour of those who will work day and night without a murmur, no leave, no medical, food you wouldn't feed a mangy dog, and a few dollars a month to send home to the village. About the food I take that back, throw them a few fishing lines."

Alex passed his hand across the bosun's eyes, glanced at Paul and Edward and shook his head. "Got to hand it to them, the lunatics really do run the asylum. Congratulations, a state of affairs most of us on the coast aspire to but rarely ever succeed."

Inside the bosun's head drove a ruthless pile driver, the relentless pounding causing his temples to pulsate and his ears throb. Strangers all around him spoke in a strange dialect, their indistinct images shifting continuously and structuring new body shapes with no reality to the human form. He thought them not a threat, unlike the ones who tried to tear his brain apart last night, demons.

Earlier with a full mug of brandy he regained some control over the trembling of his limbs, a sense of responsibility returning through the miasma of dread contained within those deep, dark and threatening shadows. Other senses returned when the last of the brandy burned its way into his gut. Sense of smell, yeasty genitalia, the state of his cabin. When he found the worthless deck boy his arse would be sore for a month for not changing his linen and making his bunk.

Those that did not pose an immediate threat to his being spoke among themselves because he could see their mouths moving, their voices irritating and indistinct. Repeat of this morning? No, not as threatening. Orders for all hands to change No. 4 crane purchase. Loggings, demotion, the master and chief officer in full uniform standing over his bunk, his naked bitch squashed hard against the bulkhead.

Gripped with terror the young gin wet herself, cringing from the bars of gold braid, gold leaf and insignia, black suits, black ties, white shirts. She should have been in school, now fearing for her life, a pair of hanging judges about to sentence her, the unforgiving face of absolute authority with orders from London. Control the men without interruption to the sailing schedule of the ship or explain to the marine superintendent *in person* why the position of master and mate should not come under review.

Alone he wondered what happened, why he felt remorse so profound and debilitating death might be preferred to living. He tried hard to gain the motivation to go on deck, succeeding in the gruelling task of pulling on his overalls, staggering to the poop and grabbing the forward accommodation railing for support.

Through other competing images he saw what he thought were his men working on a crane, flaking out a replacement purchase and

The Chinese Seamen's Children

marrying it to the damaged wire. If his brain retained any practical purpose what he witnessed might well have been mindless beings stumbling and high-stepping to the shouts and abuse of the second and third officers. His men, physically dragged from their bunks, falling over bights of large diameter wire, colliding with buckets of tools, tangling gantlines, bruised and bloodied. Even so his men would not fail him.

Something dropped out of his mouth that might have been an order, a mumbled remnant of his past authority to hurry up and finish the job. Seamanship changing a purchase wire in chaos, the second officer shouting loud enough to carry to the *Cape Otway*. Setting up the job, almost apoplectic, ordering with shoves and threats his benumbed charges to the bosun's store for a sock to join the old and new purchases. More orders, burning gear from the engine room, find the elusive electrician to bypass the crane's limits.

Another mug of brandy might be what he needed to clear the fog in his brain; the job would run smoothly without him for awhile. Well done, lads. He needed sweet elixir to rid his mind of a foam flecked mouth, flaring nostrils and flint-like eyes filled with loathing. Damnation, at a time of the master's choosing selecting a new bosun, if not the senior cadet possibly one of the four new men. Then again he might have imagined it, the voices in his head wrong.

Hamish bounded into the messroom, a cheerful smile or a cheeky grin never far from his round, florid face. "Are you lads connected to the Seamen's Union?" he inquired; seeing the bosun slumped at the table staring into space he advanced a couple of steps and punched him in the side of the head, the effect minimal as the bosun's thick skull supported by an even more expansive neck absorbed the force. Rubbing his right fist vigorously he said: "Delegates, perhaps?"

"We are. Edward, Otis, Clyde and Gavin are your new ABs," Alex said.

With a wince and rubbing his knuckles, he offered his hand all round. "Now you lads wouldn't be privy to the latest happenings on this heap of shit, but the bosun's been demoted and the mates are running things. Even a rumour the old man is going to put the snot-nosed senior cadet in charge of the deck mob. Painfully observing what this lot know or are capable of, a retarded ape on crutches could run the job better. About that I couldn't give a damn, but it does a belly-robber chief steward who learned his profession in an Ethiopian refugee camp."

"She feed badly?" Edward said, memories of the *Cape Otway*'s fare vivid in his mind.

"That probably goes without saying," Paul interrupted. "You burn breakfast this morning?"

Hamish frowned, at a loss.

"There is a distinct smell in the accommodation."

"Changed the fat in the deep fryer which might have been there since she left the builder's dockyard. Did get a bit overheated when I turned it on full to break away the crud." Hamish, with the skill of a Scottish football player, kicked broken crockery from under his feet, pulled a chair out from the table, spun it around and sat on it.

"Did you cook a better breakfast than cold baked beans on burned toast?" Edward said, not really wanting an answer.

Hamish rocked his chair closer to the comatose bosun, changing his mind about throwing another punch, instead kicking him in the shin. "Breakfast, you ask, quite a repast this morning with a choice of burgoo, standard roughage for the British merchant marine to maintain satisfactory bowel movements. Bubble-and-squeak, sufficient to feed maybe half the crowd which joyfully for the chief steward you could count the takers on one hand, so tomorrow with a couple of handfuls of flour golden pan fried vegetable fritters."

"If the steward's mean with his victualling on you blokes, what's left for the girls?" Paul said, trying not to laugh.

"None of them get fed through the slide! Good God, that munificence would put the rate through the roof and the chief steward in a straitjacket."

Alex watched the six young Aboriginal girls huddled in a tight group on the settee; their eyes met his, filled with hostility, one even screwing her face up and sticking her finger in her nose to flick something in his direction.

"Good old Board of Trade bubble-and-squeak of course being leftovers from the day before, even a week, two weeks ago. What I don't scrape in the rosy, the rosy of course thoroughly inspected by the chief steward's trained nose in high hopes of salvage. Haven't got proof, but I reckon maybe a couple of desperate stewards are feeding the girls stuff you wouldn't even want to think about lurking in the back of the chill room, except for putting a crust on as ordered by the chief steward."

"You're joking!" Paul said, aghast.

"I kid you not. Now about eggs, haven't seen a fresh egg for a year. Those protein rich items according to the chief steward are a dollar a dozen in your money, thus in the luxury bracket and henceforth struck from a sparse list of items available to yours truly. Of course I have my old backup, powered egg with a distinct odour."

"Have you any idea what the two cooks on the *Cape Otway* prepared for breakfast this morning?" Edward said, anger rising in his voice.

"Enough to send Scottish Ship Management shares crashing, a fatal twinge in that cavity where a heart should beat in every British chief steward. Yes, I do know what *Cape Otway*'s cooks prepared for breakfast and I hang my head in shame!"

"Surely your union and shipboard action can force the chief steward to victual the ship with decent food, sufficient without waste the same as the Aussie coast," Alex said, waving a finger at Paul, about to interrupt. "I know, I know, homeboat fare is written in maritime lore as sufficient to maintain life while extracting the maximum amount of work."

"Dollar a dozen for fresh eggs in your money," Hamish repeated, a mental calculation spinning in his head. "Now if each man has one egg a week which he might be entitled to under the articles of agreement that would cause an increase in the rate of more than three cents a man per day. Chief steward would immediately resign in shame, a figure of ridicule in his profession. Made to explain why when he can get powered egg from God knows what country of origin for a backhander to some waterfront purveyor of donkey and vermin bait."

"Without the union we'd be fed the same," Paul grumbled bitterly.

Hamish thought back to when the bosun hoisted him from the deck and spat in the face in addition to a vicious kick in the shin with a steel-capped boot; payback a carefully aimed punch in the twisted flesh of the bosun's right ear. "How I envy your cooks and their union. Me, the brunt of constant verbal and physical abuse, crushed and hardened to the slander to my profession."

Hamish kicked the bosun in the shin again, this time for dragging him through the slide when his dinner consisted of one lamb chop nothing but bone and fat, a spoonful of peas and an ice cream scoop of suspect mashed potatoes.

"Chief Steward never misses a thing, always skulking around alleyways and ears to closed doors. Hovering around the bosun's cabin when the old man and mate read the riot act. He reckons when it fell in a stupor out of its bunk the mongrel babbled turn to, you bastards. Though that didn't matter because the mates had already turned the mob to with loggings, threats and a few well aimed kicks."

"So it would seem everything is back to normal, but I think we should approach the old man just to be certain," Alex said.

Though sceptical, the four seamen agreed.

Paul smiled when Hamish settled another grievance, a high kick to the kneecap for threatening to throw him over the side in Nauru.

"When you get back I want to see you in the galley," Hamish said. "Well, it is a galley though not much is cooked in the place."

"Endeavouring to be polite and correct, what is the procedure to seek an audience with the master of a British ship?" Alex said. "On an Aussie ship I knock once on the bulkhead, pull aside his door curtain and kick off my work boots."

The Chinese Seamen's Children

"Pretty much the same." Edward, relieved to be out of the oppressive atmosphere of the messroom, suppressed a mounting anger at the state of the ship. No excuses on the crew allowing the accommodation to become an extension of the deck with phosphate dust and rubbish, the *Cape Otway* rolls of heavy duty tar paper laid bulkhead to bulkhead in all working alleyways to protect the waxed green linoleum beneath.

Forewarned by the agent, the master expected a visit from across the wharf, fellow seamen of similar inclination supporting each other. Sipping a cup of tea from his breakfast, he cleared his throat. "Have you authority from your Australian union to speak on behalf of matters pertaining to this ship? If not I have no desire to speak with you and would request you leave the vessel immediately."

Alex felt the blood rise in his face; pompous bastard in his accoutrements of petty authority, his refined accent noxious to his ears. "My delegate's authority is conferred upon me by my fellow Seamen's Union members of the *Cape Otway*. A rank-and-file vote acknowledged by officials of the Seamen's Union with powers to act on behalf of the union and its members, and that goes for all those of the seagoing profession who seek the union's help. Captain, act we surely will after witnessing the vilification of four ABs forced to stand on the wharf victims of racial bigotry and abuse."

Leftwing Australian upstart. Parasitic relic of lingering British militancy. Festering pustule bred in the darkest years of the Industrial Revolution and perfected during the Great Depression. The gall to stand in his dayroom and preach his Bolshevik doctrine. "It is no business of yours and my only communication with you is to inform you a distasteful matter has been concluded. These men will turn to immediately or suffer the consequences."

"Suffer what consequences?" Paul, about to explode, slapped both fists together menacingly. "You lot cowered in your cabins like beaten curs while a maniac racist and his mob ran riot! Suffer what consequences? If there are any ramifications against these men it will be you who will suffer the consequences. Remember this well, we are a phone call from our union in Port Adelaide who will take a great interest in how you and your officers dealt with the situation of four ABs fearing for their safety, if not their lives, joining your ship."

Alex took Edward aside. "Turn to quickly when you find a cabin and get your gear on. Never let them get anything on you. Jesus, I'm glad it's you joining this heap of garbage. Then again I would love to take them on, for starters sacking the chief steward and ordering a fleet of stores trucks on the wharf."

Hamish, a bubbling font of knowledge with an endearing brogue to deliver his torrent of information, performed a guided tour of his galley. Designed by Norwegians in stainless steel and equipped with every food preparation device a cook could wish for, deep fryers, mixers, sinks, preparation tables, bread making troughs, hotplates, grillers and two large ovens. Wedged between a bread proving cabinet and a sink, a small holding refrigerator received withering invective from Hamish.

"Hinges broke off six weeks ago and the engineer soldered them, but the pair came apart a day later." Rolling a loose a cigarette, he lit it with a match; in a cloud of smoke his voice took on a reminiscent tone. "Though I should not complain, on the *Baron Renfrew* the cooks made do with an icebox on the boat deck. Believe that in this day and age?"

"What's for dinner?" Edward asked forlornly.

"Our chief steward should write fairytales how he types the menus for the saloon. Soup of the day, fresh fruits in season, cheese board, coffee, tea, biscuits. Unashamedly the fresh fruits in season are rat baits and the cheese board so old and mouldy even the cockroaches give it a wide berth. For dinner you ask? Curried lamb neck chops and stockpot soup. Chief steward and agent made a deal with a desperate farmer in Geraldton whose sheep died of hunger, also the beef which I know for a fact is a scrub bull pumped full of red dye. Even the blowflies turn their noses up. Did I tell you about the freezer and chill room? No human dare go inside unless wearing a breathing apparatus."

When his admonishment received looks of horror, he shrugged and grinned. "Possibly a slight exaggeration, but I do use a lot of curry powder, a dipper or two, and if the meat's really off a full dipper of salt."

"Ever thought about sailing on the Australian coast?" Paul said.

"Sometimes among my delusions I dream of heaven, yes. Your cooks have invited me onboard for a drink. Know what I'm going to do, tip their galley rosy into a baking dish, trowel a layer of potatoes on top and call it cottage pie and serve it up as dinner. This mob will think it's Christmas come early. My stocks will soar in their rheumy eyes, what repast! Cheering until their throats are hoarse and carried around the foredeck on their shoulders."

Returning to the messroom the bosun remained in the same upright position, frozen in time, his dribbling mouth hanging loose, his tongue like a green paddle fastened to his chin. Six girls still squeezed on the corner settee, playing grab with a soggy pack of card; Freddie, sent to the engine room for a ratchet spanner, detoured and offered one an apple pilfered from the saloon as bait for later.

At No. 4 crane a differing of opinions between the second and third officers became agitated, the junior in rank concerned about the dependability of a sock with strained and missing strands. Safe working formulas applied to stranded wires, why not an important tool such as a wire mesh sock for marrying two wires? The third officer, his alternative method based on a Taiwanese pirated seamanship manual, condemned the sock, ordering the cadets to search for a roll of seizing wire and a serving mallet in the forward bosun's store.

Old and new purchase wires now married by at least a dozen parts of seizing wire tightly frapped, the second officer with complete faith in his fellow officer's seamanship, ordered the hung-over ABs to stand clear while he rotated a finger above his head for the electrician to take up the slack.

With comely company sharing his bunk, blacker than old sump oil and shaped like a beach ball, a denizen from the Globe Hotel in Port Adelaide, the electrician dreamed of a quick return to his cabin. In his field of vision in the cramped crane cabin, reflected in the multi-paned front window, he imagined her huge bosom with nipples like overripe plums, a large quivering sexual organ full of tricks that would put a veteran Hong Kong waterfront whore to shame.

Far below the squabbling beasties on deck held no interest for him, a passing thought he must remember to remove the limit bypass key in case a wharf labourer got his hands on it and luffed lower than the working limits permitted. Better things to do like burying his head between Cleopatra's thunderous black thighs, biting and suckling, fighting to keep the contents in his stomach down but so overcome with lust her musky odour added greater dimensions to his passion.

On slow heave the bulky seizing jammed as it came in contact with the head sheave distance piece, the electrician breathing heavily through his nose and caressing his genitals, oblivious in his comfortable cabin to the shouting and frantic gesticulation below. He never heard a final panic stricken cry of stand-from-under as the seizing parted and a ton of wire came crashing to the deck.

3

OMINIOUS, A HUMAN SILENCE befell the lower accommodation block of the *Baron Maclay*, the master's full frontal assault at the source of rebellion a successful foray born of desperation. Undertaken with decisive intent a single pronged attack supported by his executive officer with a single objective the demotion of the bosun, the progenitor of dissent and anarchy. Rule of authority restored, the ship hierarchy in firm control.

Stupefied, a past leader of men waited with his head buried in his arms on a messroom table to be turned to by a smug third officer. Cocky, hands thrust on hips, white overalls and peak cap a perfect stereotype of a competent young officer rising rapidly through the ranks, his orders relayed with relish. "Boyle, you've got two choices. Turn to or proceed directly to the bridge!"

With the spirit of the rebellion finally extinguished, its fuel now only sour dregs sucked from empty bottles, the girls parted with no passionate farewells or tears, returning home to the dusty outskirts of Wallaroo. Imbued with righteous indignity the chief steward abhorred by the disgraceful cavorting of the lower ranks with even more debased female specimens, condoning the presence of three ladies in the engineers accommodation with bows and smiles, proffered a theory the day of the white rating at sea had drawn nearer and good riddance. British shipping would only survive and prosper in the modern era when manned with obedient and submissive ratings selected from the old colonies, of course strictly controlled by carefully chosen senior officers and catering staff.

Edward, Otis, Clyde and Gavin without a murmur from the crew absorbed into the work on the foredeck, punishment for all hands, pneumatic needle guns scaling coamings under a snowstorm of phosphate caused by the grab discharging the adjacent hatch. Not of this world the bosun amazingly managed to remain in an upright position with his body parts shaking violently as high pressure air drove his needle gun.

Lucid he may have thought about the oddity of his new role on deck, day worker, not trusted to stand a watch. Also his smaller cabin in the athwartships alleyway, a spare cabin reeking with a distinct stale and musky odour used by Freddie for opportunist encounters. He did wonder, but only briefly, why the idiot deck boy cleaning his cabin threw his clothes and personal effects in the alleyway; he would kill the little bastard when he got his hands around its scrawny throat.

Freddie took full advantage of the bosun's humbling, playing a game of football with his clothes, a grin of sheer pleasure on his acne pocked face. "Stuff you, Reese. Mate might even give me your job, you steaming pile of wet dog shit."

For the master assigning an officer the role of bosun further strengthened a line of thought prominent among his kind, an additional mate should be signed on articles, an officer a far better seaman than mindless riffraff dredged from the waterfront. Without reservation none of the old crew even considered capable of performing the menial role of bosun. Of course the four new ABs of unknown quality, the senior cadet not fully ruled out. Soon though a choice would be pending, discharge scheduled for completion in thirty-six hours, sailing for Christmas Island to load for Calcutta.

The Chinese Seamen's Children

Edward and Hamish came onboard for dinner, the cook in a frantic rush to strap up the galley after dishing up three kits of heavily salted and curried lamb neck chops and boiled potatoes for the saloon and messroom. Hamish, with a tray of pints and double Captain Morgan's, disappeared in the stewards' bar to have meaningful discussions with the cooks.

Alex and Edward decided to go to the pub. Pausing at the end of the wharf both men looked at the remains of the beach camp, cold ash and partly burned lengths of dunnage, heaps of rubbish, beer bottles and flagons. Gone the Ford Falcon, with great effort dug out of the sand, now parked by the gangway of a Greek loading scrap metal in Port Adelaide.

"How did your day go?"

"Enlightening to say the least," Edward said, then chuckled with a wry shake of his head. "Changing a crane wire yesterday a fiasco beyond description. Blamed of course on the crowd which is not far from the truth, though the officers could put their hands also. Seems the master is keeping a secret who the next bosun will be. I did hear he favours the senior cadet."

"How would the crowd accept that?"

"Well, I wouldn't and I would have something to say. Then again by gauging my fellow shipmates I wouldn't put them in charge of the workboat. Bosun's struck dumb, not an utterance of a sane word for the last two days. Shuffles about like an old man heading for the grave, muttering to himself in his own world, so bad his shaking I reckon his limbs might break off. Being on a needle gun hasn't helped either. What sweet, sweet revenge."

Competing voices of farmers, truck drivers, grain elevator men and a sprinkling of even louder wharf labourers, the public bar of the Wallaroo Hotel hummed, smoke filled and standing room only. Indicating a relatively free space by the toilet door, Alex worked his way to the bar and ordered two schooners; clearing a return passage, he raised his glass and toasted: "To the crushing of the *Baron Maclay*'s revolt. To British officialdom, your intrepid master and his fellow officers."

"Rough headed mob if ever I sailed with one, the mates though fairly abusive still keeping their distance. We took on stores, or at least part of them I hope, this afternoon." Edward raised his glass in return. "Christmas Island and Calcutta and probably back to Christmas Island for an Aussie port. Hamish reckons the chief steward's had a mental breakdown and ordered far too much. Jesus, the lot hardly covered a pallet!"

"We load ours in twenty-ton reefers."

"Don't tell me! Don't tell me! I know, I know!"

"Not boasting, but a sobering fact to think about in the darkest graveyard hours of the twelve to four watch, the huge differences we seamen experience sailing under different flags. We join a Greek, okay we accept the Greek way of doing things and try hard to win better conditions. Same with Scandinavian ships, accept their hard work ethic and absolute cleanliness, but probably not their insanity in port."

"Plainly obvious the United Kingdom is a waning maritime power, but even at its height with unimaginable profits from thousands of ships overflowing their coffers, there still remained a British shipowner policy of depriving their crews of decent food and accommodation, of fighting the unions to the bitter end any condition beneficial to life at sea."

"Spoken like a true militant of the Seamen's Union of Australia, you're a natural, Edward," Alex said. "There anyone back home who might decide your future doing battle with shipowners?"

Momentarily his mind escaped his smoky surroundings. "Oh yes. Someone I miss with all my heart, and here I am only gone a few days. Of course my mother, too."

"My family moved to Whittlesea outside of Melbourne when my civil engineer father retired from his consultancy. You would have to see where I live to understand why he decided a flat environment conducive to a longer life free of aching limbs."

"Not married?"

"No, not married. Once I could have taken a step to a more permanent relationship, the girl in question deciding, probably wisely, the

The Chinese Seamen's Children

lonely life of a seaman's wife not an ideal arrangement. I'm not a complete free spirit with women like some shipmates I'm envious of. Suppose most women might see me as dull, and of course being a nomad doesn't help. Seamen it seems to most women have a licentious reputation, this fallacy of a girl in every port. Wouldn't it be something if true?"

"Ah, but you forget the frolicking on the good old *Baron Maclay*."

"Yes, an orgy of epic proportions with our sweet indigenous maidens."

"Some are having second thoughts."

"Hazard of the job, like long separations from families. Sailing from Newcastle steelworks midday one Saturday on the focastle head a home-porter with a young wife and kids watching a stream of traffic just knocked off from the State Dockyard in Carrington. Workers rushing home to the pub, planning dinner in a club that night. Next day reading the Sunday papers or breakfast in bed served by the kids. Seaman from deck boy to AB, a five week trip to Yampi Sound for iron ore with a lump of despair like a closed fist in his gut, a human being with all the frailties of separation from family."

Edward stared in the foam flecked dregs of his glass. "Loneliness of the sea," he said, his voice barely audible. "It affects all seamen and their families. My father went to sea."

"Edward, we probably will never see each other again, but you never know in this crazy world we seamen inhabit. I'm getting two coasters and a pencil. We need to exchange addresses."

From the foredeck a continuous dull and metallic clang of metal landing on coamings sounded as the *Baron Maclay* squared up. Grabs landed heavily in their deck cradles, cranes in crutches secured with flanges and bolts. Like all ships after a bulk discharge her decks strewn with rubbish, drifts of fine dust and phosphate rock heaped against the coamings and in recesses.

Bridge and accommodation washed down, a section by No. 6 hatch an obstacle course with the pilot ladder spread and checked preparatory to rigging. Then a period of quietness common to ships battened down and prepared for sea after a frenzy of noise and voices raised over the hum of deck machinery.

With the pilot flag hoisted, the whistle tested with four short blasts, the after gang stripped the gangway net, side nets and manropes, the forward gang rigging the pilot ladder.

Alex, working with the gearmen at No.1 hatch changing grab to hook, looked for Edward amongst the men walking forward. When he saw him he waved, experiencing a sense of loss difficult to explain.

Edward paused on the lower rung of the focastle head ladder, turned his head and saw Alex; he grinned and patted his left shoulder. Alex walked to the rail with the haul down gantline gripped firmly in both hands to hear better.

Through cupped hands he shouted: "Someone on the bridge with obvious limited intelligence reckoned a sailor like me better suited among this rabble for a leadership role. Bosun! I've put your coaster in the frame of my girl friend's picture."

4

January 1940

WAR ONLY WEEKS OLD Alfred Holt's Calchus class *Menelaus* sailed from Merseyside loaded to her marks for Far East ports. Four months out of the United Kingdom and passing through the Red Sea northbound, eating away in everyone's mind a dread of what lay ahead, the Kriegsmarine. So early in hostilities, a portent of a bleak and horrendous war at sea, with a huge loss of life British and neutral shipping suffered sixty-four ships sunk, 355,000 tons.

The *Menelaus* might have that day departed her Dundee birthplace, her selected delivery crew standing proudly fore and aft before the admiring eyes of management and dockyard personal. From the very first days of her life a meticulously planned system of maintenance assured the ship would be immaculate for her arrivals in Liverpool, her owner's critical eye waiting to pass judgement upon her master and officers.

Sailing in mostly fine weather for the southbound passage, a programme of chipping and scaling rust and the application of multiple primers spotted the ship's superstructure, winches, goalposts, derricks, ventilators, decks and deckheads.

Men on deck and in the engine room worked bell-to-bell, every minute of every day accounted for. Nothing escaped the attention of those who supervised and urged greater effort, no more so than the serang who took it as personal affront to his seamanship shoddy work, slacking and those who dared grumble of exhaustion.

Many years ago Alfred Holt's marine superintendents, themselves ships masters of the old traditional school with long service to the company, devised the means to combat the scourge of the marine environment. Not only did chipping hammers, wire brushes and liberally applied primers and gloss paints ensure a long and profitable life, it also gave the ship and its company its distinctive signature the shipping world gave due accolade.

Identifying Blue Funnel ships on distant horizons for the seamen's watchful eye posed no difficulty, aesthetically not graceful and void of fashion plates, twenty-four derricks set on goalposts, masts and cowled sampson posts servicing six hatches. Abnormally tall funnels rose from boat decks, no nonsense of rake, painted vivid blue with a black top. Workhorses of the sea, pride of the British merchant marine, exporting without fanfare the manufacturing might of the United Kingdom, returning from the Far East with the treasures of commerce extracted from Asian nations bound to the Empire.

Huang Zhen suffered an irritating itch where his drenched shirt-sleeves clung to his armpits, further aggravating a rapidly spreading sweat rash, painting engine room ventilators and skylights on the boat deck. Blistering heat from the funnel towering above the nine seamen, added to the searing intensity of the overhead sun beating down on the ship, drained the strength of those who laboured without head protection, unable under the strict eye of supervision to seek respite in what little shade offered or take a drink. Foolishly, a futile but desperate effort to cool off, Huang removed his shirt. Barely had a minute passed before he came under the notice of the twelve to four quartermaster on the port wing of the bridge, his state of undress immediately reported to the officer of the watch.

From the serang came a withering rebuke to replace his shirt; he thought later possibly making himself decent saved him from third degree burns from a Red Sea sun, but did little to temper his anger at an irked quartermaster taking offence.

The Chinese Seamen's Children

Painting high ventilator cowls dangerous enough work using conventional ladders, even more so perched on rickety bamboo poles and rope yarn lashed cross members purloined by the serang in Hong Kong; a request for another hand to steady the flimsy contrivance finding deaf ears. Broken bones on this occasion would not add to sunburn, luckily for Huang and his fellow seamen the ship sailed a flat calm sea, her wake stretching wide, true and unbroken to the horizon.

"Deeper in the cowl! Reach deeper with your brush!" the serang berated, incensed at his call to the bridge by the second officer, an order Huang dress appropriately or face punishment.

With his long bristle paintbrush affixed to a broom handle by a clamp and two butterfly screws, he suffered a forced blast of engine room heat; choking fumes constricted his breathing and his eyes streamed water. Why not a job on the focastle head, the chance of catching a breeze painting goalposts and sampson posts, swinging in a chair and not a soul to bother you?

"Stop daydreaming, foolish boy! You should know better than to take your shirt off where an officer can see you!"

Begrudgingly, he accepted the criticism. "Any deeper and I will be sitting in the donkeyman's lap." His leader with no equal onboard in seamanship worked under constant duress from the white bosun and officers, even the two midshipmen with the need to shave once a month. He learned early in his seagoing life officers and engineers, with rare exceptions, had imbedded in their psyche intolerance and contempt for race, demeaning of those in their service.

Huang did not feel inferior, why should he? Even if a child of the slums of Singapore his confidence and bearing made him the equal of any colonialist habitually dressed in copious layers of clothing to shield their dough white bodies from a merciless sun. Instinctively he gave white people a wide berth, amused at their propensity to play sport in the hottest part of the day, collapse saturated in sweat to boast of their prowess under rattan fans while pouring gin down their throats.

Sometimes a sense of inadequacy surfaced when looking through the steel bars of tall fences at stucco mansions set in the midst of lush tropical foliage and sweeping lawns. Why this affluence when he a Chinese of Singaporean birth lived in a humble single room dwelling with his parents?

Though good fortune did look upon him because his father knew a man who knew a clerk in shipping circles who could arrange for a boy to go sea, catering, deck or engine room, the choice his at fourteen. Alfred Holt's Blue Funnel Line, magnificent ships working cargo alongside Singapore wharves, barges at anchor in the roads, exuding the omnipotent power of a nation ruling the seas, an easy decision.

Born of a sickly mother in 1920, her tenuous health not improved by the family's only means of eking an existence, a father who crafted metal ornaments and jewellery. Their home differed little from others in the area, a dwelling of rusted iron, tar paper and pine casing. A single room filled with smoke and toxic fumes rising from a small coke fired furnace in one corner, a cut down oil drum for washing clothes in the other. Three rattan mats on the earthen floor, a table, four stools, hooks affixed to the walls for hanging clothes.

An image of his father indelibly imprinted in his young mind, a figure permanently stooped over a furnace, wheezing as he worked his bellows, a man old before his time, smelting scrap lead, tin and brass. Silhouetted in a hellish red glow pouring paperweight and pendant moulds, unwittingly hastening his demise. When the acrid haze cleared at the end of a long day, the odours of their dinner of boiled rice and fish filled the room.

Of all his memories the most cherished, the love and affection of two special people whose lives were a daily struggle of existence, but who never once failed in their doting parentage. Their guidance, a hand always ready to caress a shoulder, not the smarting smoke, holes in the roof and an earthen floor. Also a father's wish, like so many of his race, to one day return to China. Something else he remembered of his father, a man who forged in his son's pliant mind the English language paved the pathway from poverty. Not a smattering of words, a full grasp of the language, the reason he demanded English only be spoken in the home.

The Chinese Seamen's Children

Sadly his father's wish to return to China failed to become a reality, the prematurely old man stricken with lung cancer, on his deathbed gripping his son's hand and a whispered plea to scatter his ashes in the land of his birth. More tragedy followed for the boy, his grief-stricken mother wasting away, her will to live gone. Now burdened with two urns and because of his tender years easy prey on the hard streets of his birth.

Unable to protect his home from the opportunist eyes of predators and their prowling minions, shadowy figures who traded in human misery and the bodies of the young, he joined his first ship as deck boy, the *Eurypylus*. One small boy among thirty-eight seamen crammed in an open focastle. Probably as many greasers, firemen, stewards accommodated aft, wedged above and below the steering flat, but so awestruck with the throbbing pulse of the ship beneath his feet, he never bothered to count.

From an early age Huang as a progeny of the lowest rungs of society became aware of the privilege and opulence taken for granted by those with pale skins and clipped accents. This no more apparent than onboard the *Eurypylus,* and without exception all the Alfred Holt ships that followed in achieving endorsed sea time to sign articles of agreement as AB.

Excruciatingly thin, an acerbic face heavily furrowed and scarred by life, the serang of the *Menelaus* ruled the focastle supreme. Huang held the man in veneration and the old serang's humbling by his superiors, his submissive acceptance of his inferior status, filled him with bitter gall.

In the latter part of the last century Lau Yi as a young man joined an American clipper in Kowloon, sailed to San Francisco where he shipped out for fifteen years from Alaska to New York.

Passing on daily orders from the first officer to Lau, the bosun commented. "Serang Lau, the chief officer and I on our rounds have noticed the poor quality of the priming coats applied on the foredeck. We are recommending more red lead be added to the boiled oil," he said patronisingly. "My personal thinking is much greater effort should be applied when mixing red lead and boiled oil. This instruction to be stamped rigidly in the minds of those charged with the task, also that the chief officer and I will be scrutinising future endeavours with an eagle eye."

Unwaveringly, Lau could have held the other man's eyes; head bowed and hands intertwined, he turned away.

Parting words from the bosun cut even deeper. "Performing your role as the company expects, you would have noticed the priming of the windlass and forward winches on the outbound passage has distinctly faded. On another equally important work related subject the master, chief officer and I are gravely concerned that even though the preparation work is acceptable to our exacting and exceptionally high standards, you have failed in some areas to ensure more stringent wire brushing of bare metal."

Lau's audience of seven seamen painting bulwarks on the starboard side feigned ignorance of the conversation; his face passive, he said submissively: "Sir, I shall make certain the incompetence does not occur again, and thank you for bringing it to my attention."

"Yes, you will. Now, jump to it."

Huang seethed, grinding his paintbrush into the prepared metal, willing Lau to cut the pompous petty officer down, tread on him like he would a slug. Both he and Lau shared a common allegiance, members of the militant Liverpool Chinese Seamen's Union, a union with an agenda for equality. Not so a parallel union purporting to represent Chinese seamen, the Chinese Seamen's Union, no more than a submissive arm of the Kuomintang government, demanding of its members unconditional subservience to their British employers.

Lau increasingly assigned Huang to the bosun's store to learn wire and rope splicing; locking splices, Liverpool splices, cut splices, short and long splices and aerial splices. With time to spare Lau would sit on a coil of rope and talk of sail, bucko Yankee mates and bully masters, merciless drivers of men, brutal taskmasters and sadists. Of sea-hardened men who fought with knives and belaying pins over women worth no more than a few pesos in the guano and nitrate ports

The Chinese Seamen's Children

of the west coast of South America.

Observing the fascination on Huang's face starting to interfere with his work, he would quickly change the subject and question anyone who met his eye the formulas for condemning stranded wire, safety weight and breaking strains of wire and cordage.

Work ended for the day Lau would gather those interested around him to teach seamanship on No. 6 hatch, macramé, ocean plaits, Turk's heads, grommets, bell ropes, Yokohama fenders, pilot ladders, sennits and every conceivable knot from sling shortening to barrel hitches. No matter how tired or the weather he never wanted for men wishing to learn their profession. No lesson would ever pass without a tale of life under sail and fearsome mates who without hesitation would batter a man to the deck for daring to challenge an order, speak, or even look him in the eye. Huang would glance at Lau's knuckles, bone hard and gnarled and know for certain this man could give as good as he received, and did.

Overhauling gear the task of entering letters, numerals and survey dates in the gear registry book exceeded the mental capacity of a Chinese seaman, usually a quartermaster seconded from bridge duties or a midshipman to check and record the information stamped on shackle lugs and block bindings. Lau accepted this secondary role with his usual passiveness, a fatalistic acceptance of his position; he and his fellow Chinese seamen were no more than a physical means to maintain the ship under strict and constant officer supervision.

Communication by officers and engineers, petty officers, pursers and chief stewards rarely arose above brusque orders, whistles or pointed fingers. Huang quickly came to learn of his lowly level in the shipboard strata, resented by white seamen his presence aboard a British flagged vessel, his status no better than a coolie labouring in a rice paddy, a means of shipowners to cut wages and conditions and destroy the influence of virulent white unions.

According to some the Chinese grasp of the intricacies of seamanship, at the best minimal, made them unable to work unsupervised, barely capable of comprehending the bare basics of working on deck.

Bumbling and inept when confronted with simple decisions such as rejecting a loose mousing or a cross-threaded grease nipple, their knowledge of knots mostly limited to bending a heaving line to a mooring line.

Well discussed and universally agreed theory among disgruntled white seamen unemployed in waterfront pubs, one white seaman equated to five Chinese, deck or below. This racially based ratio also applied for shipowners though for different reasons, primarily Chinese seamen were a fraction of the cost of a British equivalent.

Huang found it difficult to accept his position based on race, a frustrated anger when his fellow Chinese meekly accepted the contempt of officers as their lot in life. Lau also stirred resentment when a second year midshipman gave him orders in tones a dog's master might give to bring his unruly animal to heel. His mentor rarely spoke of it, sailing as uncertified third officer, the second officer lost when swept over the side doubling Cape Horn. Lau failed to find time to sit for his certificate, but sailing as an officer under sail in Huang's mind the zenith of his profession.

It filled him with a sense of pride that a man of Lau's ability took an interest in him. Constantly testing him, questioning him on finer points of seamanship, scorning him for his lack of knowledge or skill. Then would follow a lesson in rope work after a tirade his level of knowledge little better than the lowest carter of human dung to fertilise rice paddies, nothing more than an object of ridicule.

"Seamen must draw from the past, from the birth of their profession in canvas and cordage, the miracle of transferring wind through shrouds to the hull of a vessel under sail," Lau would expound. "Where men rightly called seamen sailed their ships at the whim of wind, tide and current. Your profession, like a dormant bud at the first warm ray of spring, grew and grew until it filled man with a unique craft called seamanship. Skills now relegated to a few old fossils at great loss to the industry by those who followed in steam and motor."

The Chinese Seamen's Children

Throughout the ship an air of levity prevailed, the *Menelaus* abeam of Ushant homeward bound. Also effected, the bosun's pudgy face glowed, even remarking to Lau he hoped the voyage report on maintenance would reflect well on the serang and the majority of his men, though not to be too overly confident as some of his members came under notice as lazy and exceptionally incompetent.

Escaping German naval attention in home waters, a four month voyage would soon end, profitable and successful, officers, engineers and senior catering with home on their minds. Huang, not entirely unaffected by the high spirits, showed a more tempered outlook than his fellow Chinese married in Liverpool with children, in some cases many children. Expectation of fires burning in home hearths and loved ones overcame fears of U-boats, dive bombers and mines. Also the *Menelaus* would be at least a month alongside discharging and loading for Far East ports.

Barely containing his excitement, the bosun cornered Lau overseeing four of his men replacing triatic stay halyards. "Serang, we lads will be receiving a visit from management when we berth, exemplary reports for the master and officers no doubt. She does look a picture. There will be well earned kudos for our esteemed officers."

Lau never replied, distracted, turning his back on the bosun as he watched with narrowed eyes an ordinary seaman bend new signal halyard from a hessian wrapped coil to the old with sail twine, test it with a tug and await Lau's order.

"Never bothered to ask, suppose never saw any need. There family in Liverpool for you like the others?" the bosun said, showing no displeasure at the snub.

"No," he said, with a sharp nod giving his approval to overhaul the signal halyard.

"Dingle's crawling with Chinese. Could rightly say without fear of contradiction the place is overflowing with them. So many the rats moved out, so say them living there."

Lau sighed. "Liverpool is as much our home as those born there, and with little or no recognition serving the Empire, Mr Hewitt. It is not our war but still we are called upon to make the supreme sacrifice."

"Watch what you're saying there, fellow. It is your bloody war." Momentarily the jollity faded. "Don't you ever forget who gave you bloody Chinese a decent life worth living."

For his effrontery an apology should be forthcoming, distracted and pleased the ordinary seaman's whipping survived its journey through the single sheave halyard block seized to the triatic stay thus saving the young man a lambasting.

Almost in step and in single file the forward gang marched to No. 1 hatch. The third officer and midshipman awaited them, both snug and warm in greatcoats, beading rain glistening on their white peak caps. Berthing orders passed down the chain of command, first order to lift the gear, remove tarpaulins and rig tents.

Lau received instructions to close ranks and await orders. One shrill blast of a whistle demanded complete silence, orders relayed to the serang in a clear and sharp tone: "Lift No. 1 gear, derricks amidships and secured. Two winch drivers and six men standing by guys. Two men to each winch running off and flaking runners. One man at each winch to run topping lifts on barrel ends. Hatches will be stripped on berthing and the gear set for discharge."

Lau relayed the orders in sequence, indicated men jumping to their tasks without hesitation, Huang the port winch. With No. 1 gear lifted orders came in quick succession, remove battens, locking bars, lashings, tarpaulins and rig the tent. Work completed Lau's gang reformed their line at No. 2 hatch to await further orders

No. 3 hatch followed the same procedures, orders, whistles, sometimes multiple whistles if the third officer in his opinion witnessed slacking and ineptness, or a deliberate slow reaction to an explicit directive. Competency of the third officer on the foredeck would not go unnoticed on the bridge, a good report pending.

Joined headlines lowered to the line boat, rapid orders in quick

The Chinese Seamen's Children

succession as the ship slowly came alongside and the forward backspring took the weight of the ship now dead in the water. Huang did not need to be ordered with a whistle, which to his mind questioned his ability as a seaman. He knew how to run a bight, when to surge on a headline by anticipating the bow swinging or a tug nudging alongside. Also as a competent seaman he did not stand in bights and knew instinctively when to backup a fellow seaman.

Beliefs never far from his mind shared dangers at sea might lessen if not eliminate attitudes of racial superiority. Of even greater importance that the huge influx of Chinese seamen serving the Empire at sea in war, the majority who made Liverpool their home, would automatically gain British citizenship.

There were two other thoughts much more important at this time in his mind close to paying off the *Menelaus*, a hope one day he would have the privilege of sailing again with Lau, the other a girl who worked in a corner shop. She lived only a few streets from his boardinghouse and whom he had been too shy to strike up a conversation when buying a chocolate bar before joining the *Menelaus*.

Elsie, he heard someone in the shop call her, others Miss Smith.

5

MRS HOGAN, A WELL known identity in the streets of Dingle, mummified with advanced age, purported to know everyone's business and what she didn't she fabricated with an acerbic tongue, always to the damning detriment of her victims morals and character. Some thought possibly her accrued years as old as the street of shabby tenements she prowled.

Her pinched and bitter face supported a sharp bridged nose from which peered out upon a world she took umbrage piercing black eyes, cold and calculating, reptilian some said. Being of short stature her detractors with equal spite gossiped made her the ideal boardinghouse keeper for those whom she supplied lodgings, Chinese seamen. Some of her more malicious critics shielded their mouths and whispered her skin once olive but now with the texture of dried leather and black eyes originated from old Spanish blood, a sailor washed ashore from a fleeing Spanish Armada ship wrecked along the Scottish west coast.

Mrs Hogan's boardinghouse prior to the war stood as two tenements, one her home with twelve boarders, the other rented to a family. In her crafty mind with Liverpool streets swarming with Chinese looking for lodgings, she planned to cram as many men of Oriental origin as possible into her newly expanded establishment.

The Chinese Seamen's Children

Evicting the family a double brick party wall came down under an assault of heavy hammers wielded by burly labourers, supporting lintels erected and newly opened spaces partitioned for sleeping quarters. With calcimine coated plaster her two properties became a boardinghouse accommodating forty Chinese not particularly fussy if one could reach out a finger and touch a sleeping neighbour.

Once a small living room it now served as a dining room with two narrow tables and side benches, at a squeeze able to appease the hunger of twenty men of slight build. Those tardy in arriving for dinner would wait patiently in a two shoulder width hallway to sample Mrs Hogan's fare which some with good cause associated with what sustained starving sailors sentenced to penury in sailing ships.

Mrs Hogan retorted with a stock answer for her detractors, war and her patriotic sacrifice for the cause of victory. Furthermore, she rasped with vitriol, her cook Choo Tian, as old and as wizened as she and paid a pittance and forced to sleep in his kitchen, should receive only the highest regard for how he managed under wartime austerity to place upon Mrs Hogan's table fare fit for Chinese emperors.

Rumour had it Choo survived being thrown over the side of his ship in the wintry waters of the Mersey, accused of poisoning the crew with meat so rotten even the maggots died. Ashore for a long time his cooking skills deteriorated even more as his eyesight and memory grew poorer with advancing age.

Huang boarded at Mrs Hogan's, usually no more than a few weeks, surviving her fare for two years with rarely an upset stomach. He paid off the *Menelaus* the day after arrival, four and a half months pay at £4/13/9 a month less deductions. This amount did not make him a seaman with deep pockets, able to swagger through the waterfront streets of Liverpool tossing pennies to urchins begging to carry his seabag. As customary he would have to be frugal with his money, pay his board of 17/6 a week in advance. Some items of clothing needed replacement, pictures and dances and money left over to supplement what Mrs Hogan sparingly put on the table.

Mrs Hogan's front door made unwieldy by a half-inch board affixed with screws to its bottom panel, repaired where a peeved boarder kicked the door in when locked out on a night raining horizontal sleet one minute after Mrs Hogan's imposed 9:00 pm curfew. Chue Song, a brawny fireman with Alfred Holt, whose only footwear consisted of his stokehold boots, kicked the door with all the strength he could muster in his freezing body only to spend the remainder of the night in police cells, a chagrined Mrs Hogan seeking sympathy from her neighbours for the foreign ruffians the war effort forced her to suffer under her roof.

Normally ten others shared his room, comparatively roomy because of its smaller size compared to the other two partitioned bedrooms, making it an impossible to jam another mattresses in a space once a pantry. Windowless and malodorous with rising damp, no furniture only hooks on the walls for hanging clothes. On the bare board floor ten mattresses sparingly filled with kapok, kapok pillow, bottom sheet and one blanket. Mrs Hogan subscribed to a theory of physics that ten bodies or more would generate enough warmth to eliminate the need for internal heating and more blankets.

Employed by Mrs Hogan a cleaning lady, a withered stick of a woman, lived in constant fear of ravishment by a slant-eyed heathen. Huang sympathised with the distraught woman, attempting unsuccessfully to dispel her obsession of a lascivious Chinese seaman intent on defiling her pitifully thin body. Her phobia making her life a misery, he thought she must be desperate to work for Mrs Hogan on wages less than Alfred Holt paid a catering boy, not far from the truth with a bedridden husband.

Always a source of bemusement for Huang a common misconception; if one of Mrs Hogan's boarders did take advantage of the cleaning lady's body there would be small chance of her positively identifying her assailant. She, like Mrs Hogan, convinced all Chinese originated from the same mould. Amazing when Chinese of different height, width, weight, complexion, aged sixteen to seventy and even older for those who falsified their papers, Caucasians could not tell

The Chinese Seamen's Children

one Chinese from another.

Huang smiled at Mrs Hogan bent over her roll top desk checking her guest register, squinting in the poor light filtering from a small window off the dining room, a mixture of vanity and meanness to wear spectacles. Against his name in black ink two weeks board paid in advance plus a one pound refundable bond for breakages or further damage to her front door; with politeness, he requested his receipt.

Looking up, her black eyes mere pinpoints scrutinised the young man; late teens she thought. Then who could tell the true age of a Chinaman, though she had to admit his fine features strikingly handsome. Make flirty hearts flutter, of course only with certain young Liverpool girls of questionable morals, those types known to openly consort with foreigners. Scrubbers, she thought, hoisting their skirts to service the hordes of little yellow devils in the city.

Also the boy towered over his stunted fellows, his thick black hair having a penchant for falling over his forehead. Possibly Chinese blood mixed with Mongolian, even worse, contamination from the northern regions of Japan. Puzzling though because his eyes were not the usual puffy slits Mrs Hogan associated with such people. What did it matter anyway how the blood of inferior breeds infused at conception, there being no difference she could accurately discern between Asian breeds?

"Thank you, Mrs Hogan."

"You've stayed here before, boy, you I remember. Our God made it so difficult for us to tell you apart. Left to me all of you would be made tattoo your horrible names on your foreheads." She tried to make light of her damning statement with a rasp mimicking a chuckle, the mirth causing two thick folds of loose flesh at the base of her throat to quiver.

"Yes, I suppose when after so many catastrophic failures the Supreme Being eventually created the perfect human form with beauty and intelligence, compassion and empathy. As such it would have been be difficult for the Creator to break the mould He used to populate the great land of China. Correct, Mrs Hogan?"

She really would have to expend money and have her hearing checked. Did she detect sarcasm in his voice? How come a Chinese could speak such good English? Amazing, Chinese so stupid and kowtowing. Of course the money these little bandy-legged men earned, huge sums from their benevolent employers, and then for a pittance fed the best of scarce food and luxuriously accommodated ashore, their remuneration rightfully returned to the land that gave them succour and not the opium dens of Asia.

For Huang much more enjoyable matters occupied his mind than discussing racial profiling with a bigot; buying a chocolate bar in a corner shop.

Elsie Smith maintained a slim figure by watching what she ate, especially sweets to keep her face clear of pimples. Barely a few inches over five feet tall in her high heels, Huang correctly guessed her age a year or two younger than his twenty. Not pretty in the sense of drawing immediate attention to herself, her rosy cheeks were free of adolescent outbreaks, her eyes sparkling blue and her teeth straight and white. Her most alluring feature, a gift of nature even the baggy sweaters she wore in winter failed to conceal, her full bosom.

Favouring blouses one size too small, she sometimes dared to leave two buttons undone. Not flirtatious by any means though consciously aware from a young age where boys eyes lingered. Early blossoming had lessened teasing about her plainness and frizzy red hair from girls at school slower to develop, envious of what swelled her school tunics while conscious of their own flat chests.

Cautiously she welcomed the attention of boys, bumbling and awkward adolescents her own age. Hot and sweaty encounters on the living room couch with her parents' bedroom door ajar, the ceiling light on. She experienced urges to be daring; she allowed a hand to knead her breasts through her blouse, stopping the more adventurous bunching the hem of her dress, edging as if by accident up her thighs,

The Chinese Seamen's Children

ignoring pleas to open her tightly clamped legs. She knew of girls who allowed boys bold liberties beyond this, girls now shamed and paying a dreadful price for their folly.

She remembered the young Chinese boy, tall and very good looking, who spoke perfect English. With a sneak peek at him, she dug a metal scoop in a jar of humbugs and transferred the contents to a brown paper bag. She would serve him next, wishing the shop empty so she could talk to him, about what she would think when the time came. Taking the proffered sixpence for the humbugs, she rang up the amount in the cash register and handed the customer his change.

"Yes?"

Only one other customer. "Please, I am in no hurry," he said nervously. "Serve the lady first, I don't mind."

Her gushing smile hid a dusting of near invisible freckles on her cheeks. Elderly and unsure on her feet, cane shopping basket in one hand, ration book in the other, the woman seemed unsure whether or not she should allow the precious newly issued book out of her possession. Elsie solved her dilemma with a murmur of mutual displeasure at the imposition, took her ration book and served her: two ounces of butter, four ounces of bacon, one egg, two ounces of cheese. With a sympathetic smile for the enforced austerity, she turned her attention to Huang.

Try as he might he could not avert his eyes from the imagined soft white mounds pressing against the light cotton fabric of her blouse, her cardigan undone. Swallowing forcefully, he said with all the confidence he could muster: "Elsie?"

"How do you know my name?" she teased.

"When I came here months ago I remember someone in the shop calling you Elsie. Elsie is a nice name. Though I can call you Miss Smith if you prefer."

"Did you hear Miss Smith also, eavesdropping on people's conversations?" Smiling her best smile, she rotated her shoulders in a circular motion she had practised in her mirror. Mischievous thoughts of what would her father reading his newspaper by the parlour fire coaxed into life with another precious lump of coal think of her flirting? "People of impeccable manners who come in the shop call me Miss Smith. Have you been spying on me?" She took delight in the red tinge spreading on his face.

"Of course not!" he stammered. "I heard people call you Elsie and Miss Smith. My name is Huang Zhen and I live down the street in Mrs Hogan's boardinghouse. You can if you wish call me Zhen which is my given name."

"By what I see coming out of Mrs Hogan's you could well be a spy," she giggled.

"Miss Smith, all those men without exception are doing their duty for the United Kingdom."

"Father says for our family's safety we should avoid passing Mrs Hogan's boardinghouse, we live not far. I remember you, you were in the shop a few months ago."

"So you don't think all Chinese look the same?"

"Do all Chinese look the same?"

Catching a glimmer of amusement in her eyes gave him hope his next words would achieve a favourable outcome. "Would you go to the pictures with me?" There, he had said it and without a stammer.

"*Gone with the Wind*?"

"What is *Gone with the Wind*?"

"Clark Gable."

"Would you like to see it with me?"

"Are you are asking me to go to the pictures with you?"

"Yes, yes, I am."

Irritating and tinny the bell over the door tingled and she made a fuss rearranging hard boiled lolly jars on the counter; she smiled at the small boy with a note in his hand.

"Miss Smith?"

With a quick glance at him, she beckoned the boy closer. "Elsie. Yes, I will."

"You said you live close to Mrs Hogan's?"

Choosing to ignore him, she read the note. "Meet me here at the shop, 7:00 pm."

"Won't the shop be closed?"

With a yapping fox terrier on a lead, a matronly woman entered the shop, the agitated animal darting between her stockinged legs and entangling her, forcing her to clutch a display unit to stop falling; Elsie clucked sympathetically, a scowl at Huang who could only stare at her bemused.

"Oh, isn't that Clark Gable a dish?" she said dreamily, clinging to Huang's arm.

"Which could be said about Miss Leigh." Holding her hand, her warmth and closeness dispelled the damp chill of the night air.

"Exactly what I would expect a boy to say."

"I simply made a compliment about his leading lady."

"Girls have to be careful when boys are free with their compliments. Who knows what boys have on their minds, though it is fairly easy to guess."

"So as a boy my compliment could be seen as a forerunner to more intimate endeavours, but not you as a girl with similar thoughts about Clark Gable?"

"Clark Gable could seduce me, I wouldn't mind."

"Do you let boys seduce you?"

"Might, but if I did it would be no business of yours." She pinched his arm, an impish smile playing with the corners of her mouth. "There are many times when I get offers from boys for more than a kiss."

"Offers of what?"

"What brazen boys always want from girls, but I soon give them their comeuppance, I do."

At her front door an awkward silence fell between them. "Zhen, I would like to but I can't invite you in," she said, a tremor in her voice. "My father ..."

Of course, her father. To nurture any relationship with this girl he would have to overcome more difficult barriers than saying goodnight on her doorstep protected by the late hour and darkness. She lifted on her toes and raised her head, offering him her closed lips. Her mouth tasted of peppermint, his lips gently pressed against hers.

Attempting to put his tongue in her mouth she drew back as if shocked, then shut her eyes and returned his kiss. As if by accident he pressed against her, lightly at first, then harder, a hand easing down her rib cage to feel the first rise of her right breast. Again she pulled away, breathless, but as quickly closed the gap between them. Through their clothing she could feel him, a wave of heat pulsing at a place she tried unsuccessfully to forget existed.

With his hands following the soft curvature of her bottom she knew instinctively what would follow if she allowed him to touch her in a more intimate place; a light appeared in the curtained glass panel adjacent the front door. At anytime the door might open and her father appear and catch her with her dress bunched around her thighs and in the lie of going to the pictures with a girlfriend.

Something else, what would Zhen think of her if she allowed him a wickedly naughty liberty, to touch her through her underwear? No more than a trollop for the taking, free with her favours with any boy, uncaring where her shameful and immoral path would eventually lead her.

Heavy footfalls sounded in the hallway and both of them separated, making frenzied adjustments to their clothing; an internal door opened and shut.

Regaining her breath forcefully, open mouthed and her face flushed, she said without meeting his eyes: "Zhen, I have to go in now."

"Can I take you dancing Saturday night?"

Staring at her feet, she nodded.

"Outside the hall?"

Reaching out to touch his face, her voice broke: "Zhen, it's not me! Not me!"

The Chinese Seamen's Children

Through sharing stories at sea he knew of the prejudices confronting British women married to Chinese seamen, as well as their children, in predominantly working class Liverpool. No doubts lingered in his irate mind how Mr Smith would react to his daughter being seen in public with him. Many Chinese seamen married local women and reared families long before the war induced influx of their brethren, family men with strong allegiances to their adopted country, men who considered themselves British.

Hardworking, dedicated, competent, many drawn through loyalties and necessity to two unions which gave Chinese seamen a voice. One union with more demanding vocal cords raised serious concerns for shipowners who expected unfettered fidelity if not cap-in-hand subjugation from their Chinese crews. With reasons predominantly financial and trading routes, British shipowners instructed their boards to implement policies of replacing white uncertified crews with Chinese and subcontinent ratings.

British maritime unions fought a losing battle to retain their members aboard British flagged ships, the foreign remanning so clinically final the dispirited footsteps of British seamen forced down gangways might well have been an industrial flash flood.

Notwithstanding maximum financial returns employing low paid Chinese, Chinese seamen traditionally posed little discipline problems for their superiors. Bare subsistence wages guaranteed only a few could be drunkards, even able save enough money to jump ship and cause problems with local officials.

Huang could hardly conceal his disappointment when he visited the shop to see Elsie. Mr Gresham, old and in poor health and years beyond retirement age, said she ailed, probably flu prevalent in Liverpool. Not to despair, she managed to write a note, her single sheet of writing paper faintly scented with lavender. In her neat script, she informed of a cold and apologised she could not go to the dance and she would be back at work in a few days.

Four days passed before he saw her behind the counter, pale and drawn. "Elsie, is it wise to be back at work?" he said concernedly.

Eyes red and swollen, her cheeks inflamed, she sniffed and drew a lace handkerchief from the sleeve of her cardigan. "I'm all right," she croaked. "Poor Mr Gresham is all alone in the shop and he needs me more than ever with the new rationing. Doesn't cope very well and gets into a dither."

Both could hear Mr Gresham in the back storeroom unpacking his small allocation of tinned fruit, and when his impatient muttering ceased Huang blurted out: "I want your permission to meet your parents."

Her head sunk even lower in the thick woollen scarf wrapped around her neck. "No! Please, Zhen, if Father knew I went to the pictures with you he would be terribly angry."

"Because I am Chinese, yes I know. It need not be, Elsie. Meeting me he might change his attitude, who knows? All I want is to be able to walk down the street with you. Stand at your front door with you in my arms and not be afraid it will be open."

"My father does not speak kindly of people who are foreign, nor does he treat them with respect. I think he may be frightened, why he condemns so angrily, especially the Chinese. Please, Zhen, we can still see each other."

"With you continually having to lie?"

"Father would never know, he wouldn't, Zhen," she pleaded, wringing the small handkerchief in her hands.

"Of course if my race achieved an impeccable British standard he might slap me on the back with a hearty well done lad, you do the Empire proud on your ships."

"Father is very strict. Please, Zhen, we can still see each other," she pleaded, tears welling in her eyes.

Mr Gresham hobbled from the storeroom, frowned at Huang and said to Elsie: "There is cardboard needing to be cutup and tied with string. Finish serving the young man and see to it, please."

The Chinese Seamen's Children

Memories of Elsie in his arms lingered as he lay on his thin mattress listening to the snores of his companions, wondering if he would ever taste peppermint on her soft lips again, feel her tongue in his mouth. Plain girls like Elsie with so many pretty ones who openly flirted at the pictures and dances were not worth worrying about, even worthy of a second glance from a seaman ashore with money in his pocket. Wrong, the self inflicted pain of an improbable relationship.

Somehow he would find a way to convince her he should meet her parents. Convince her father he served the nation at sea, offering his life like his fellow countrymen for the United Kingdom.

Slim though his chances of success when he thought about it, a lowly Asian seaman on call for benevolent British shipowners who out of the kindness of their hearts employed him. Treated with contempt by a superior elite enthused in their achievements of nautical science. A British way of life protected by impregnable barricades and multiple layers of racial and class segregation.

Tomorrow he would go to the shop at closing and walk Elsie home.

By the determination in his face, his stony silence, she knew. Gripping her hand, he started walking in the direction of her home. She looked at him with alarm, a small cry escaping her as he tightened his grasp. "Elsie, it is something we have to do. Something we cannot escape."

Stumbling, she tried to match his hurried footsteps, slipping on cracked paving slicked with the first spatters of rain. "Zhen, we don't have to. We can still go the pictures and dances. Father doesn't leave the house much these days. Did I tell you of his tuberculosis?"

"No, no you didn't," he said despondently. Stopping abruptly, he took hold of her other hand; drawing her close he could feel her heart beating against his chest. "Elsie, I'm sorry. I have no right to force you to do something against your wishes. Make you afraid and cry."

Attempting a brave smile, with hope in her voice, she said: "There will come a time when we can go to my parents and say this is Zhen and I am going to the pictures and dances with him and so what. It will, Zhen. I know it will."

Deflated, he nodded miserably.

Huang befriended a donkeyman home after eighteen months running from the Persian Gulf to Australia, his ship now in dry dock in Glasgow. Donkeyman Keong Chong signed articles with Anglo-Saxon Petroleum for the past fifteen years, Liverpool his home for the same period after marrying a girl from Birkenhead. Their family grew to five, three healthy and robust boys the eldest ten, eight and five.

Keong and Kate knew only too well the animosity in the streets of Dingle, the parks, shops, pubs, places where people congregated. Kate felt the brunt, ignored in shops or deliberately served last when first to enter. Also painfully aware of the malicious gossip she sought sexual liaisons to make ends meet due to her husband's low wages.

On a Friday evening the Keongs invited Huang and Elsie to dinner, a plain meal shared with their three well mannered and polite sons. Huang and Elsie sat hand-in-hand as Kate served in white bowls a stew of beef and potatoes, Keong placing on the table a basket of thickly sliced homemade bread spread with precious butter.

Reluctant to closet themselves in two small and dingy bedrooms the family spent most of their time in the combined dining and living room, Kate to free herself from a kitchen slightly larger than a pantry. When the children were going through the crawling and toddling stages and in danger of falling down a steep flight of narrow stairs that accessed their upstairs home, Keong had unsuccessfully tried to rent the bottom floor of the tenement.

Their only comfort a three cushioned sofa salvaged from the street to listen to an old wireless on the mantelpiece of a gas fire the family could not afford the extra money needed for the metre.

The Chinese Seamen's Children

Kate's stew received the tributes it deserved. "Kate, you are truly British," Huang said. "No rice, noodles or dumplings, wonderful." His plate no different than the others at the table, wiped clean with bread, he added: "In times of austerity you have performed a miracle."

Elsie agreed enthusiastically. "Rationing creates so many difficulties, Kate, you have created a marvel with what is available in the shops. Thank you for sharing with us."

Keong's opinion differed on deprivation. "Shipping companies paid us wages comparable to British for doing the same job we would be able to sustain a decent lifestyle, even able to put money in the gas heater without breaking the bank. Not affluent, but able to replace a pair of school shoes Kate has to save three months for. Also if we were paid the war risk bonus."

"We have a fight on our hands negotiating with the companies for its inclusion in our wages, as we do wage parity," Huang said, drawn even closer to Keong with his membership of the Liverpool Chinese Seamen's Union.

Keong's fists clenched on the table Kate and Elsie cleared. "How do you think I feel working next to a first trip seventh engineer at sea with the knowledge he is paid a war risk bonus that I am not worthy of? We constantly bombard Anglo-Saxon Petroleum for payment of the war risk bonus to Chinese nationals. What makes me so bitter is the payment does not come from the coffers of the shipowners, but the government. Also are we not British signing on a British ship under British Board of Trade articles of agreement? When a prime target like a tanker is blown up by mine, enemy fire or torpedo and turns the sea into an inferno, I die the same death as the seventh engineer."

"United and strong we will win our claim one day," Huang said, watching the movement of Elsie's bottom in her mauve satin dress at the sink with Kate, the kettle on the boil to wash the dishes. "We have right on our side as well as a union run by members for the members. Not like the Chinese Seamen's Union, a union in name only and no more than the political voice of the government of China, the Kuomintang."

Keong agreed, "Unfortunately for its members, a union much beloved by British shipowners."

Kate's mother, a widow living with her elder sister in Birkenhead, took ill and not wanting to expose their family to colds and flu in the night air, Keong asked Huang and Elsie would it be convenient if both could mind the children for a few hours, an enticement dinner.

Unable to remember ever being in love he supposed spending much of his formative years at sea afforded little chance of meeting a girl or the time to nurture a relationship beyond a casual acquaintance. Beside his growing emotional attachment to Elsie something equally as prominent filled his thoughts; her father. This eventual meeting would not be pleasant. He could walk away, Elsie lived under his roof.

Kate culinary skills again came to the fore with chunky pieces of cod deep fried in a light batter, seven pieces of fish in a flat wicker basket. Another basket steamed with a pile of thick cut chips again deep fried in dripping, instructions to her hungry children one piece of fish each, the chips divided equally. She rolled her eyes at Huang and Elsie. "I shouldn't complain, our boys have exceptional manners."

Bathed and dressed in pyjamas handed down and threadbare, the boys ate their meal quickly and in silence, when finished asking permission of their father to be excused from the table. Time for bed, a precious half hour of light to read.

Their goodbyes said, Elsie whispered conspiringly: "Told father a friend asked me to mind their children until late."

"Wonder what his reaction would be if he knew the unacceptable company you keep?"

"Zhen, please don't make something of this. We have a responsibility to Kate and Chong and we should not argue."

The Chinese Seamen's Children

"Elsie, I feel like a coward not grabbing your hand and rushing down the street to confront your father."

"Also I might be accused of being a bit naughty."

"Naughty?"

"Said I might be very, very late, but not to worry. Big girls can look after themselves."

Almost on time the light in the boys' bedroom turned off. For his sons a resourceful Keong created a bedroom with exceptional carpentry skills, salvaging around the waterfront packing cases and pallets which he machine planed in a friend's backyard workshop. Tightly grained pine, brass screws and wooden dowels created a set of two tiered bunks, a third bunk at right angles. Varnish and wax polish and the bunks could have come from the bench of a master furniture maker.

Sitting on the sofa he took her in his arms and asked her a question on his mind. "My daring girl, what did your father say to you being out very, very late?"

"Even said to him I did, might have to stay overnight," she said with a squirm.

"No! Your father wouldn't allow that. Incensed, he would drag you home through the streets by your hair."

"Said only really, really late and raining. Anyway, couldn't, there's no room here."

"Elsie Smith, I love you?"

So large the tears he could almost see his face reflected in her eyes, then with almost impossible slowness rolling down her cheeks.

"Soon will come a time when I knock on your father's door and in a loud and confident voice declare my name is Huang Zhen and I love your daughter, Mr Smith."

Unchecked tears now streamed down her wretched face. "Oh, Zhen, I love you."

So still and quiet, the steady and metallic tick of a clock on the mantelpiece above the stove sounded loud and invasive. With barely a movement the boys slept soundly, blankets snug around their chins. Darkness all around except for a small candle burning in a jam jar on the table; it saved electricity and could at a stretch of the imagination be a heater, joked Kate.

Why the sofa ended its long life dumped on a Dingle pavement, free for anyone desperate enough for a decrepit piece of furniture, became obvious when first sat on. Keong replaced missing slats and strengthened weaken joints, but failed dismally as an upholsterer. Framing timber chaffed the fleshy backs of legs, but for Huang and Elsie nothing mattered except being close.

"Did you really say to your father you might sleep over?"

"Hmm, but I don't think he would really let me," she said with a giggle, making herself comfortable against his chest. "Father being unwell the night air makes his cough worse. If not I suppose he would be searching the streets for me."

"Because he loves and cares for you as a devoted parent should."

"Father doesn't show his affection outwardly, but I think he does in his own way."

At last he found a degree of comfort, his hip sinking between two prominent lumps of stuffing, shredded old shirts and dresses of Keong and Kate. Gently he caressed the swell of her breast through the thick wool of her jumper, first one and then the other, breathing her natural scent into his lungs as he kissed her. "My beautiful, beautiful girl."

Parting his lips with the tip of her tongue, she whispered: "… my love must be blind."

"What I see is what I see and my girl is beautiful." Lifting her jumper from around her hips, he eased it up her body to feel the incredible warmth she generated through her blouse.

Feeling her body tense he thought to protest as he released the buttons of her blouse. Instead she eased off his chest to allow his hand more freedom; his hand moved to the small of her back, higher to where two metal hooks fastened her bra. Fumbling, his fingers were like marline spikes trying to release tiny hooks the more delicate touch of a female found simple. At last he succeeded, the twin straps hanging free, his hand now fully cupping one bare breast.

Passing through her lower body a warm tingling sensation, a wetness she dared not think about as she felt him move against her, a hardness that caused her breath to catch. Involuntary she returned his pressure, the enormity of him she could feel through her dress the reason she knew for her secreting, why her breath laboured and why she held him to her.

From an instinct wreathed in old reservations until this moment dormant within her female core, a continuance of the species from the very first inception of humanity, she knew what her man wanted. What would happen if she allowed her emotions to overcome her better sense? She mentioned some girlish misconceptions to her mother the first time she bled, receiving dire warnings of allowing aroused men their way would result in a lifetime of regret and shame.

On the threshold of life a curious girl received no motherly advice to explain the function of her period, though later she would discover through friends middle age would end her monthly discomfort. At school she learned rude names for reproductive organs causing fits of giggling and, and this really made her think, pregnancy, illegitimacy and disgrace. Even more forbidding, iron bars and stone walls, grim institutions for unmarried mothers.

Gently stroking the firm flesh of her belly, his fingertips slipping under the waistband of her dress. She should say no, the utterance of denial far beyond what remained of her rational reasoning. Instead she drew a breath and pulled in her stomach to allow his hand to slip inside her underwear. Fully stretched on the sofa, her dress bunched around her waist, he eased the garment over her hips, knees, at last freeing them over her feet.

Stop him now; all it needed from her lips a firm no and he would understand. His trousers were around his hips, his straining organ pressed hard against her and she didn't care. The exquisite sensation of his lips suckling her nipples, trying to take all of one breast in his mouth while a finger parted the wet and fleshy lips of her sheaf. Then a sharp intake of breath as he parted her legs and she felt his weight press her into the sofa.

All reason gone, she instinctively arched her body as he slowly entered her. Her love thrusting deep inside her body wrought a sensation she never imagined possible, so wet and what consumed her so hard, overwhelmed by a contraction of muscles that made her chest heave as she fought for breath.

For him it would be over almost before it began, slowing and attempting to think other thoughts that might prolong the sensation of his possession, of being one body with the girl he loved. Impossible, impossible, and when he felt her buck beneath him, heard her muted cries, the first rush of semen burst from him, then a suppressed roar caught in the base of his throat as he ejaculated.

How long he remained inside her he did not know except he wanted more of what tugged at his still hard erection as her own spasms lingered. Did his weight make her uncomfortable pressed into old rags packed on board struts? Also maybe one of the boys would get up for a drink of water, or the need to go downstairs to the lavatory.

Slowly he withdrew to her meek protest, rolled on his hip and found his feet. Both were composed and sitting at the table with cups of tea when Keong and Kate arrived home at 10:30 pm.

Lying on her back in bed and staring at the ceiling, sleep seemed far off. Both hands moved down her belly to rest on her pubic mound, the tender flesh beneath sore and incredibly wet. She thought of what happened a few hours ago on the couch, feeling Huang inside her, thrilled at her own body's exquisite reaction to the throbbing heat of the man who possessed her.

The Chinese Seamen's Children

Vaguely remembering something discussed with friends in hushed voices, she tried to recall her last period. It might be due in a week, maybe more. She did not know for certain and thought no more of it, closing her eyes as a contented sleep overcame her.

6

AT HER TEARFUL INSISTANCE, reluctantly retreating from what he thought proper for their relationship free from guilt of association, Huang abandoned a plan to meet with her parents.

Walking the streets of Liverpool, the tired lovers would rest on park benches, uncaring even when cold and slicked with rain. Always an eye on the passing time, Elsie expected to be home at a given hour. Any notice passerby's took of the obviously infatuated couple mattered not, wrapped in a cocoon of their own making. So strong their bond it even shuttered out the ever presence of war, sombre men and women in uniform.

When saying goodnight he would speak softly in her hair words of endearment, of joining their lives. Elsie, tearful, her small body clinging to his, wishes with all her heart to be able to wake in the morning with her love beside her.

With no opportunity to be alone since the Keongs, the remembrance of that night a flood of raw emotions, though for Elsie a concern she did not mention to Huang; her period, though again as in the past she had never counted the days with any degree of accuracy, or found the need to.

Their nocturnal meetings commenced at the shop, a halfway point for both, their first embrace and kiss in the protective darkness in the

The Chinese Seamen's Children

front door alcove. Her parents queried her more than usual nightly outings, especially with the weather so inclement, both putting the glow in her eyes and her flushed face as the exuberance of the young. Parental advice for their girl to rug up warm and be sure not to catch cold, also a fatherly warning of an eye on the grandfather clock in the hallway.

Her love would be late tonight attending a union meeting at 4:00 pm which might extend into early evening if important business warranted an extension of time.

On the stage of the small church hall Hsien Wu sat perfectly erect on his straight-backed wooden chair behind a table stacked with bound folders. Perched on top of his head a black felt hat no one had ever seen him without, missing though the string-like upper lip hair that would have made him the ideal artist's portrayal of a Chinese family elder. Cast in clay, a stoic figure, olive skin, the hair visible beneath his hat black without a single thread of grey, waited patiently for the conversational noise to abate.

Hsien imprinted an indelible impression upon those he dealt with in his role as secretary of the Liverpool Chinese Seamen's Union, shipowners, politicians, union officials, rank and file members, as honest and forthright, articulate and strong willed with a profound sense of empathy for those whom he represented. No one dared accuse him of corruption, though the temptations existed for envelopes to pass over his cluttered desk, offers to exchange his austere lifestyle for a more affluent area of working class Liverpool.

Working all his seagoing life as a steward for Alfred Holt, he understudied the meticulous bookkeeping of Blue Funnel Line chief stewards and pursers, storing in his keen mind their unchallenged competence passed on from generations of maritime actuaries for a planned future. Not of affluence or homely comforts, assured security, but to serve others. Inequality to his fellow Chinese guided his chosen path through life, a crusading resentment rarely visible in his deadpan face but always simmering within. Deeply embedded within the man a strength and determination on accruing knowledge to combat the glib tongued gurus in the employ of shipowners, who devoid of any trace of empathy and the stroke of a pen decreed minimum wages and conditions for Chinese seamen signed on British ships. Even bitter astringent, this pittance never enough to satisfy the greed of their employers.

Speaking at meetings Hsien had what some might adjudge to be an impediment; slow, annoyingly slow, reacting to questions from the floor, seemingly his acute mind mulling over the implications an incorrect reply might portray misdirection and false hope. When he did speak his words rolled from his tongue without ambiguity, the reason why when he addressed meetings questions from the floor were few, proposing solutions to issues in his elocution from the podium. This sometimes frustrated him that officials and their recommendations simply led the membership without fully involving them in the formulation of union policy.

To his membership he did not portray the archetypical British union official, table thumping and extreme militancy, loud, brash, instilling in the membership forceful and clenched-fisted leadership against a ruthless and merciless industrial foe. Soft spoken, good sense and advice uttered from an ordered mind without embellishment, above all truthful with the facts carefully calculated.

Dismissed as an annoying and pedantic nuisance by shipowners, nevertheless Hsien received guarded respect, dealt with in extreme caution. His members saw him as hope for the future; he might have been likened to a luxuriant flower in full bloom shedding a seed in each individual member no more would the Chinese be a race to exploit, throw crumbs to in payment for gruelling, menial work. Chinese, men of dignity and pride, skilled seamen serving in the British merchant marine.

Enemies were numerous in the Chinese community, extremists and advocates of the Chinese Seamen's Union. The Chinese Seamen's

The Chinese Seamen's Children

Union, financed and influenced by the Chinese government, inevitably agreed with British shipowners conditions granted at the turn of the century should be the datum for current negotiations, of course the nation at war and for austerity reasons there being no argument for change.

Huang and Keong found seats at the front of the meeting, as many as eighty seamen sitting on hard wooden chairs. Numbers present were disappointing with more and more seamen entering the United Kingdom and registering for work, but to Hsien's thinking even one seaman with the cause in his heart represented a step forward in the battle to win conditions equal to British seamen.

Hsien's eyes passed over the gathered men; mostly the same faces, a few new. Many would have problems of disputed payments, illegal loggings, harassment, bodily harm, refusing lawful commands resulting in termination of employment. With almost paternal consideration would try his best to successfully resolve their problems with the limited resources at his disposal. Success he could count on one hand, the failures major issues of wage parity and war risk bonus, a frustration that grew with each day of war and the increasing losses of seamen in the line of duty. What made it even worse pitted against him at every turn the indifference to the deaths of his nationals at the negotiating table.

Nominations for chairman were called for, Hsien recording the minutes. For this meeting a mere formality elected unopposed, Liang Tao; an AB actively employed at sea he held the position of honorary assistant secretary.

Fluent and intimidating, Liang's fierce and heavily scarred face reflected his unwillingness to retreat in the path of adversity. Some years back he clung to life by a few weak heartbeats, beaten senseless on a Jakarta wharf hours before sailing by a drunken quartermaster concealed in the shadow of drums and crates with a length of dunnage, intent on settling a score against Chinese in general.

Left for dead some opportunist dockers opted for a chance to better their miserable lives and robbed him of his clothes, watch and money, then dragged his body behind a shed and kicked him in the head for good measure.

Liang's ship sailed, in his absence logged and reported to authorities for desertion. Suffering appalling injuries, he somehow found the strength to crawl to a shack perched on stilts on the banks of a black mud backwater, beg for clothing and water to bathe his wounds. Dressed in a hessian sack, he appeared at the agent's office who immediately called police to arrest him as a deserter.

From that day on without justice and a long fight to have his papers re-endorsed to sail on British ships he stood his ground with white racists. From that day on he never took a backward step, his presence treated with caution on any ship he joined. He, like Hsien, became prominent members of the British Communist Party. Now seated beside his secretary, he called the meeting to order and called for the reading of a report on current negotiations with British shipowners.

"Comrades, your union is engaged in difficult and at times aggressive negotiations with shipowners in an effort to force them to pay the war risk bonus currently paid to British nationals. We contend that a British ship with a complement of seventy or eighty or more, a mix of British nationals and Chinese, is not paying the war risk bonus to the Chinese as should be the case. Two questions aside from discrimination based on race immediately come to mind are shipowners pocketing this quite substantial amount paid by the government, or are shipowners in a patriotic stance of nationalist fervour advising the government to withhold payment to the Chinese?"

Disquiet passed through the meeting, some lively conversation at the back of the hall which the chairman silenced with a sharp command: "Order! Show proper respect for your secretary with your complete attention. At the appropriate time questions will be called for from the floor."

Hsien continued: "It is indeed an unfortunate situation we find ourselves burdened with, though affording great comfort to shipowners, two unions representing Chinese seamen in the United Kingdom. One a true union, the other a union in name only, a pandering arm of the Kuomintang government. The Chinese Seamen's Union advocates as acceptable our continuing foreign status on ships articles of agreement, the pivotal point why Chinese seamen suffer inferior wages and non-payment of the war risk bonus.

"It accepts for its members conditions established in the early years of this century without question, without condemnation. What infuriates members of the Liverpool Chinese Seamen's Union is the war risk bonus is a payment additional to wages of British seamen paid by the British government, not from the profits of shipowners who enjoy war indemnities for their losses while ignoring the families of survivors.

"Legitimately a question is raised with monotonous regularity, at war is not the risk of death at sea the same for Chinese seamen as for British seamen? Are we by some divine intervention immune? Are we not at war beside our British comrades, supporting with our lives the freedom of the British Empire? Are we not a vital link in the chain to rid the world of fascism? This brutal and violent regime, this scourge upon the world, whose rise to power came about with the incarceration and slaughter of unionists, racial minorities and Communists. Comrades, I want you to pause and think next time you encounter racial abuse aboard your ship.

"Our numbers are strong. Remove Chinese manning from British shipping and their ships would lay idle alongside wharves throughout the world. Within a month the United Kingdom would be in the grip of starvation! Her hungry armies forced to lay down their weapons, her malnourished workers unable to work at their machines. Think long and hard of this nation who believe because of their benevolent colonialism a debt is owed by those who live under their yoke. We have no indebtedness to any power in the world. Chinese are dying for the British Empire, the number increasing as the enemy saturates the Atlantic with their surface ships and submarines."

Pausing to retrieve a flask of water beneath his chair, he took a few sips before replacing it, straightened and acknowledged a raised hand in the front row.

Though Liang rigidly applied the laws of debate and meeting protocol he sometimes allowed the occasional lapse, especially for a militant member and an old comrade.

"We also have to consider in our deliberations with shipowners our status in the United Kingdom. Japan has occupied large tracts of China and may soon have the Kuomintang seeking surrender terms. Where does that leave us with no homeland?" Hsu Kang said; a heavily blotched skin hid the scars of his many encounters with officialdom.

"Our status is important, yes, and even though we despise the Kuomintang it is the only body the British government will deal with. Our problems will be compounded if continued Japanese aggression forces the Kuomintang to lay down its arms," Hsien replied.

"Comrade Chairman, I know what our status will be. We'll be stateless with no support from any government." Hsu looked around the meeting with a wry smile on his craggy face. "Comrades, the only positives in that outcome would be the loss of Kuomintang support for the Chinese Seamen's Union."

"Let us fervently hope then that the Kuomintang continues to sleep in the same bed as the Chinese Seamen's Union," Hsien said, he too with a smile on his face.

"Generalissimo Chiang Kai-shek retreats in rout from the Japanese! If we had a Communist government the invader would by now be drenching the Yellow Sea with their blood."

Hsien agreed. "Japan has its expansive eye on the western rim of the Pacific where the colonial powers govern vast territories. Colonies with abundant reserves of minerals, rubber, oil and manpower. As such we may take cold comfort these inviting targets for a natural resource starved nation might relieve China of the brunt of further suffering under the brutal heel of Japanese imperialism."

"Why doesn't the British Empire support China in its fight against Japan?" Hsu persisted. "Surely it must be obvious the aggressive parallels of Japan and Germany."

"Quite simple, the British Empire expanded its border and

The Chinese Seamen's Children

influence with China with acquisition of the New Territories in 1898. The United Kingdom had nothing to gain administrating a sprawling and ancient land mass widespread with famine and pestilence, disease and illiteracy. Of course still able to siphon inconceivable amounts of wealth generated by hundreds of millions of people through Hong Kong without the need to spread its tentacles of colonial governance throughout the hinterland as it did in India."

Not a single man disagreed with their secretary's assessment.

Another member of the Communist Party sitting close to Huang and Keong rose to his feet. "The United Kingdom turns its back on China, ignoring the burning, pillaging and devastation caused by the Japanese Imperial Army. With arrogant pomposity of those burdened with a self-righteous born-to-rule mentality, continue to spew lies the corrupt government of Chiang Kai-shek prevails.

"Fabrications there are the forces of freedom and democracy thriving in China, with the might of arms repelling the Japanese with stirring victories. We are told Mao Zedong is a Communist tyrant who will enslave his country if he overthrows the Kuomintang, the government recognized by the colonial powers as the legitimate rulers of China. Our union should march in the streets with banners proclaiming Mao Zedong as the people's leader of China."

By allowing the meeting to run freely, the chairman received a scowl from the secretary to draw the discussion to a close, but not before Huang found his feet, his right hand raised.

"Comrade Chairman, we are fifteen percent of the British merchant marine, yet we receive only fifty percent of wages paid to white ratings and no war risk bonus. Over a designated number of years we have learned the skills of seamanship to be accredited by the British Board of Trade for endorsement to sail as qualified seamen both on deck and below. We are the equal of British seaman.

"On our ships we are led by our own competent leaders only to witness them suffer humiliation and disrespect being ordered by British bosuns, quartermasters and officers. I cannot accept competence of seamanship based upon race, nor agree with the premise

Chinese seamen are unable to work without white supervision. That we are simpletons who stumble incompetently on deck, directed by abuse, shouting and whistles.

"Continually it is raised at meetings wage inequality and how our union seeking parity has been rejected time and time again. We have the Chinese Seamen's Union supporting shipowners, who might even agree if placed on the table as a patriotic war effort a cut in wages, and of course continue to not pay the war risk bonus. What I am saying here now is we need unity, not two unions. To succeed with our claims we need the Chinese Seamen's Union to unite with the Liverpool Chinese Seamen's Union, a single front aimed directly at the heart of the shipowners." Huang resumed his seat to mumbled agreement throughout the hall.

Hsien remembered the young man from previous meetings, making a mental note to use him in the future. "What you say is true, comrade, the shipowner is overjoyed to negotiate with a union which is no more than a public servant obeying his government master. We continue to talk of wage parity and war risk bonus with shipowners. Of conditions which have not changed significantly since the turn of the century, in some cases even retreated where our men continue to live in open focastles and subsist on substandard food. Our union continues to press our case of the skills of Chinese seamen and how important to the economy of the British Empire the Chinese are."

At the rear of the meeting a hand raised caught the attention of the chairman.

"What is the union's response to the murder in the United States by the master of a British ship who shot dead the delegate?" the man said, his voice pensive; he lowered his hand and continued: "Delegate standing on the master's rug wanted to know when the steward would issue fresh food, the ship alongside already two weeks and the steward issuing spoiled meat and mouldy rice."

Hsien knew of the incident only too well. "Police arrested the master on a charge of murder and locked him up. Then the judge he faced the following day ruled no case to answer and released

The Chinese Seamen's Children

him immediately," he said, then questioned the shocked meeting. "Comrades, do you think the judge dismissed the charge of murder against the captain because the man in the dock happened to have same skin, the victim no more than a lowly Chinese?"

Anger like a wave breaking on a rocky shore passed through the hall.

"White judge! White court! White system!" Hsien said, his voice reverberating throughout the hall. "Unfortunately for our comrade the United States has a poor record of racial equality, proof in their cities of endemic black poverty. Beggars, emasculated in a land that enslaved their forefathers. As for the Chinese who built their roads and railways, mined their gold and then cooked their food and washed their clothes, we are even poorer and degraded."

Reading the financial report and taking two more questions from the floor, there being no further business the chairman closed the meeting.

On the street Huang and Keong before going their different ways, Keong asked a favour of his friend; could he and Kate again call on him and Elsie to mind the children? Would it be an imposition? With Keong due to return to his ship in two days, it would be a rare treat for both to visit friends alone for a meal and a few drinks.

Social and racial barriers separating the lovers might well have been prison walls, their only closeness holding hands and a lingering kiss before she disappeared behind the closed door of her home.

7

ELSIE'S HEART BEAT WITH excitement at the prospect of their being alone, though she reminded herself not really alone with three boys sleeping in the next room. Of course there had been no reservations that one and only night; in her bed at night, unable to sleep with thoughts of Huang, memories filled her mind of a sofa with barely enough room for one let alone two.

Girlish hopes filled her mind, if only her father would accept Huang and recognise their love for each other, remembering at dinner his remonstration of the increasing number of foreign seamen in the streets of Liverpool. Many of them in company of girls of highly suspect morals, uncaring of public values and blatantly flaunting themselves.

Chinese in particular with slits for eyes perfect for concealing their true intentions for the opposite gender, Liverpool streets not safe for decent people to walk. Common knowledge, including those concealing their shame of illegitimate children with sham marriages, strumpets of all ages readily available to appease the animal needs of foreign seamen.

Elsie stared at her untouched food and prayed her father would not question why her face burned red.

The Chinese Seamen's Children

Huang made himself comfortable on the eldest boy's bed at right angles to the double tiered bunks, racking his mind to think up a story demanded by all three. "There sails out of Liverpool a shrewd old bosun named Lau Yi, wiser than all who in ignorance decry his proud nationality. Lau Yi could have stood a watch on any ship's bridge, the bosun's profession forged under drum taut sail and straining cordage. Who with great courage navigated seas where steamers rarely ventured, sailing greyhounds of the sea contemptuous of the raging gales in the loneliest reaches of the world's oceans.

"Lau Yi, strong, iron willed, a survivor of ships that habitually starved their crews, drove and worked them like beasts of burden. Accommodated in open focastles, bitterly cold and forever wet. He rose above the deprivation while those of lesser fortitude succumbed. Grew stronger and stronger, his mind filled with knowledge of the sea he adopted and conquered."

Eyes grew heavy, the two youngest boys almost asleep; he tucked their quilts around their chins, his mind on the young girl on the sofa in the other room. Without him realising she had quietly entered the room to sit beside him.

"Lau Yi would tell of stories doubling Cape Horn in storms men like Joseph Conrad and R. H. Dana described as monstrous beyond belief. Storms that reduced strong and brave men into a stupor of petrified fear. Swells two miles long and 200 feet high called greybeards, even larger seas which carried greybeards on their crests called rogues." Flickering, the eldest boy's eyes finally closed. "So much for my enthralling tales of monstrous seas and valiant seamen who kept the weather leeches taut running down the Howling Sixties and the Screaming Seventies.

"Cape Horn, the tormented graveyard of thousands of ships, their eternal resting place marked only by the ferment of two mighty oceans forever at war through Strait Le Maire and Drake Passage. Unimpeded by land mass or mountain range jutting their high peaks from the sea in an entire circumference of the world. Two awesome and unforgiving oceans, the crazed sculptors of the fractured coasts of Chile and Terra del Fuego. Ships driven as far south as seventy degrees, entombed for eternity in ice. So said Lau Yi, conqueror of Cape Horn." Snuggled down in their quilts, the boys slept soundly.

Elsie might also have nodded off, her head resting against his shoulder, hair across one eye. No, a hand reached for his, brushing aside her hair and a smile. On the sofa she unbuttoned her blouse, raising her bottom to remove her dress; her underwear she left for her Huang, his to free from her body and position her for their act of love.

Bathed in faint candlelight from the kitchen table he looked down at her on the sofa, naked and ready for his touch, offering her firm and rounded breasts, her lightly downed sheaf dipping in two distinctive folds between her slightly parted legs.

Accepting his weight, she gripped his shoulders, his intense hardness probing between her legs. She lifted her bottom to help him, not needed as the thick secreting head found the moist folds of her sensitive flesh and in one forceful thrust entered her.

Teetering almost instantly on the point of orgasm all thoughts of her late period flew from her mind as she tore at his back and sobbed. Then at that very moment she knew for certain how a man and a woman created life, the sensation of a man's seed throbbing spasm after spasm inside her, the guttural sounds of its release.

With nuisance rain more a mist, a chilly darkness closed in with more heavy clouds massing over the city from the Irish Sea. Huang drew his padded jacket tighter around his chest as he waited outside Mr Gresham's shop. Elsie waved from inside, through the window most of her body obscured by faded cardboard advertisements for New Zealand butter and cheese. Serving two customers, one argued the correctness of the government decreeing those who did not consume their rationed apportionments would be prosecuted, most certainly making it known to her member of parliament her full support.

Mr Gresham without customers closed the shop at 5:30 pm, time

The Chinese Seamen's Children

for tea and a muffin in the small café around the corner. Then for his girl a quick dash home for dinner on the table precisely at 7:00 pm. Precious minutes ticked by with the front door still open, Huang's attention drawn to the bent figure of a small man shuffling as quickly as his emaciated legs would carry him down the street.

Oddly a sense of relief filled him; caused by a mistaken identity, but he did not think so, his calmness growing stronger the closer the man approached. Closer now he could hear his wheezing, the painful struggle for each laboured breath. This first meeting should have been behind closed doors, not in a cold and rain-slicked street.

Scorn flared in the man's hate filled eyes, yet unable to form words, exhausted from his exertions, the mere act of walking a short distance down the street. Huang experienced an inner peace that surprised him, only a slight tensing of muscles. Elsie glanced up the street as she closed the shop door and froze.

Cured of tuberculosis, the man still suffered the ravages of the disease. From his heaving chest rasped words dripping in venom: "Me the last to know! Everyone knew before I did! Laughing their heads off behind my back!" Forcefully sucking air into his tortured lungs, he swiped his phlegm flecked lips with the back of his hand. Swallowing forcefully caused his pinched face to twitch in a spasm of pain. "Chinaman, I spit on you!"

Huang reached out for Elsie whose fear caused her legs to buckle. "Mr Smith, Elsie and I love each other," he said, still composed. "Mr Smith, I want your permission to escort Elsie."

Mr Smith laboriously extracted a large handkerchief from his coat pocket and hacked into it. "Escort her, that what you Chinamen call pulling down her underpants in back lanes? You can do better than escort her, you can use her as you see fit and when you tire of her pass her on to your Chinese mates because that's all she'll be good for. Chinamen!"

Stricken, she tried to conceal most of her body behind Huang.

"Filthy Chinese scum! Go back to China and die!"

"Mr Smith! You are an evil old man and not fit to be a father!"

"Chinese pig! Chinese pig!" he mocked, his head bobbing with each breath sucked through his gaping mouth. "Come on, hit me. Come on, Chinaman, knock me down in the street and let us of British stock see how brave and strong you yellow bastards are!"

So easy to take hold of the little man's scrawny neck and squeeze the life from him. Hold him aloft at arm's length and allow it to jerk its stick legs as its eyes bulged from its purple face. With the odds stacked heavily in favour of the younger man Mr Smith took up a ludicrous fighting stance, stretching to his full five feet six inches and puffing out his sunken chest. Ducking and weaving, a pathetic mime of a boxer sparing with an imaginary opponent, his fists little larger than those of a child.

Suddenly his anger left him, filled with sympathy for a father distressed for his daughter. No way did he want to hurt this man who gave life to the girl he loved. A desperate need to reach out to him, tell him of his love and that he should be proud of his daughter, of her gentle and caring nature. Of her shyness and affection, her bubbling laugh.

Aggression sapped his weak body of its last reserves of strength. "She's too ugly to get herself a white man. Chinaman, you're welcome to her."

Somehow she found the courage to look around the body protecting her and croaked: "I'm pregnant!"

Both men stared at her, stunned, Mr Smith first to react with a grotesque distortion of his mouth which fully exposed his saliva slicked gums. "No child of my blood comes from fornicating with a Chinaman in a back lane! Find your belongings in the gutter, slut! Never dare step one foot in my home again!" Mr Smith's legs might have been those of a newborn foal's first struggle to remain upright, staggering erratically up the street.

"I am with kiddie," she whimpered pitifully.

Because he had ignored, even given it a thought, the high probabilities of conception making love to this girl, he had created a new life and destroyed another. So easy to seek advice about contraception,

The Chinese Seamen's Children

but he hadn't, and for this he felt a huge burden of guilt. This small girl now in his arms, her grief captured in his chest, carrying his child. Homeless even though she lived only a few houses up the street.

Trauma crushing down on them this moment exposed on the street, their ordeal would expand even more in the morning when he registered for work. Searching through the turmoil of his mind a single semblance of rational thought emerged. "Elsie, your mother. We need speak with your mother."

Partially losing the use of her legs, he half carried her along the street; at the front door of her home he reached in the pocket of her cardigan and found a key. The door opened into a narrow hallway and staircase, only a few of its lower treads visible in the semidarkness; a faint glimmer of light shone through a fanlight at the rear of a hallway.

Upstairs drawers forcefully being opened and shut, something heavy falling on the floor. Elsie slumped on the bottom tread of the staircase; rocking, her arms wrapped around her shoulders, there were no more tears to cry.

"It's going to be all right," he said, though with little confidence in his voice. "Where would your mother be?"

From the darkness above came the scraping of something dragged to the landing and he looked up and saw a figure outlined against light filtering from an open bedroom door. Then with frenzied rasps for breath a suitcase slid on its flat down the stairs, barely enough time to drag Elsie clear before it struck the newel post and split open; he saw the sleeve of a pink nightgown, a purple flower embroidered on the cuff, a tiny touch of femininity that caused a sinking despondency in his chest.

Cheap and flimsy, a small suitcase held a young girl's life. Lives torn apart by racism, its poisoned tentacles not only affecting a young man and girl, but a mother hiding behind a locked bedroom door. Cowering from a man no more than a sick and hollow shell, but because of his skin a superior being without flaw.

"Not all is lost, we have friends," he said, dropping to his knees to repack the suitcase. "Elsie, no matter what happens we have our love and we have our lives. That's all we need for a beginning, our beginning." With all his being, he wished his words true, in his canvas wallet two pounds.

8

CHAIRMAN BARRETT DUMBRILL SAT perfectly erect at the head of the Alfred Holt boardroom table, fully assured of his peak position in the Blue Funnel Line structure of management. Also at the table, euphoric at their selection to sit in the exulted boardroom, senior seagoing staff on leave or in command of ships in port.

Masters and engineers, between them 300 years of dedicated service to the company, all having attained the highest qualifications in the United Kingdom, and hence in their chosen fields no nautical equal in the world.

Chairman Dumbrill's austere features softened a little as his steel grey eyes passed around the table, first making contact with Captain Thomas Draper, thirty-five years a faithful servant of Alfred Holt. Beside him, Captain Harrison Nicholls, old now with a well deserved retirement deferred, fifty faultless years service at sea. Captain Whitely Saxby, Captain Xavier Hickman, their stern faces and posture reflective of the pride felt their invitation to sit at the boardroom table.

In this esteemed company men of supreme engineering skill, maritime engineers without peer. Chief Engineers Wade Niles, Oswald Killen, Lachlan Hayden and Irvine Tolhurst. Innovative pioneers in modern shipping with a steadfast eye on their steam reciprocating engines, turbines, triple expansion engines, steam on the up-stroke diesel on the down-stroke engines and diesel motors. Coal and oil fired boilers, refrigeration plants and cargo winches.

Pure engineering melodies to the ears, the steadily beating power plant of an Alfred Holt ship rarely failed, reason for the maritime world to envy unsurpassed engineers. This meeting and the summonsing of senior officers and engineers with only one subject on the agendum, Chinese crews.

Of major concern Chinese manning problems rife throughout the fleet, a probable cause the increasing number of their war causalities. Management explored alternative foreign manning options, subcontinent, Arab and South Shields Senegalese. Seemingly the darker the shade of skin the more adaptable and submissive, without question obeying orders from their superiors. Agreed by all sitting around the boardroom table not always the case with Chinese, especially those with membership of the Liverpool Chinese Seamen's Union.

Among members of the Chinese Seamen's Union a noticeable docility prevailed, unconditional acceptance of their subservient role. Not so dealing with the Liverpool Chinese Seamen's Union, a membership of hard core belligerent cadres with allegiance to the Communist movement in China hell-bent on confrontation, the complete opposite.

Not known to retreat or surrender easily, this highly vocal and militant union consistently hammered on the door of British shipping, submitting outrageous demands, wages and conditions guaranteed to send even the most efficient operative bankrupt. Many among Alfred Holt's management and senior seagoing staff held the view, an opinion becoming more widespread as the war continued badly for the Empire, the Chinese continually exhibited disgruntled and unpatriotic behaviour patterns threatening the supreme commitment expected of the nation's shipping industry.

Many of the more virulent agitators with paid membership of the Liverpool Chinese Seamen's Union had without notice and right of appeal received dismissal notices, in some extreme cases instant dismissal and their names blacklisted. Even with a large common

The Chinese Seamen's Children

pool of Chinese seamen to draw from, at times manning difficulties arose due to a shortage of men; apart from war casualties, one reason being the greater numbers required for an Asian manning scale.

Where did the Chinese disappear to when not on their ships? Did the Chinese slink to the safety of the countryside to avoid wartime duties? Some thought so, this train of thought responsible for unfavourable public conception the Chinese unwilling to place themselves in harm's way, whereas officers, engineers, petty officers, senior catering and white ratings literally charged up gangways to be the first to offer themselves for service. Even more harmful assertions, the most painful to accept in the Chinese community, cowardice.

Chairman Dumbrill knew Captain Saxby well, their association going back many years, probably more years than he would like to remember when his lumbar regions twinged with arthritis. Captain Saxby, a faithful servant and stern disciplinarian, feared for his hedged brow known to turn erring young midshipmen's legs to jelly.

Selecting a master, the chairman posed a question. "Captain Saxby, in your valued opinion apart from the obvious recalcitrant hostility rampant among members of the Liverpool Chinese Seamen's Union, what do you attribute to the unrest we are currently experiencing with our Asian manning?"

Captain Saxby's jowls quivered before launching into a long diatribe, his piercing eyes narrowed to mere slits as he stretched to this full height and firmly planted both spread hands on the table. "Quite obvious the Communist element is strong and thriving in one particular union, the Liverpool Chinese Seamen's Union. Dominated by a recalcitrant leadership with a destructive policy of continued confrontation entrenched in Communist indoctrination originating from China, and of course Stalinist Russia. To a man opposed to British colonialism. God forbid if not for the governance and bounteousness of the United Kingdom the entire yellow race on the face of the earth would be extinct to famine and pestilence.

"Due to the current emergency the frontline agitators are stirring their seditious vitriol this is the prime opportunity to gouge from their employers higher wages, war risk bonus and working conditions. If only these loudmouthed ingrates, and those who slavishly follow in their wake, would truthfully acknowledge their conditions of employment, especially those provided by Alfred Holt, are second to none. Accommodation specifically designed for Chinese, excellent food and working conditions. High remuneration, plentiful rest periods and the privilege of serving on the finest built and maintained ships in the world.

"Oh no, all their union can do is condemn and scheme, meet in secret enclaves to receive orders from their Communist masters in China. Of course the leadership is using the non-payment of the war risk bonus as a rallying call as well as wage parity with British ratings. Chinese seamen are discriminated against by our owner's reluctance to pay them the war risk bonus from government coffers, so decry their rabid leadership. What is the war risk bonus? I will tell you what it is, British tax! From the sparse pockets of the taxpayers of the United Kingdom!

"Let the Chinese government pay the war risk bonus from their own funds! I have said over and over again, a virulent element of Chinese have no allegiance to the United Kingdom and would suck this nation dry of every penny in this our direst of times. I am a known advocate of a cut in wages for our Chinese crews, the money paid to the Exchequer as their contribution to the war effort, a sacrifice I am told by loyal Chinese would be acceptable to the Chinese Seamen's Union." Expanding his chest in his well worn but comfortable navy blue suit tailor-made in Hong Kong twenty-five years ago, he accepted with puffed cheeks and extended lips the accolades of his fellow officers.

Not all around the table agreed with Captain Saxby, but kept their silence.

During this lapse the chairman's mind wavered, remembering this morning in a rare burst of sunshine the immaculate Blue Funnel Line ships anchored in the grey and choppy waters of the Mersey. Funnels tall and blue, the top one third glistening black. Ageing ships, new

The Chinese Seamen's Children

ships, a credit to the dedication of their masters, officers and engineers. Ships the marine community bowed their heads to, flawless workhorses of the sea the envy of shipowners worldwide. Fast and efficient ships, the lifeblood of a great nation and its Empire.

Even when the sun disappeared and leaden skies descended, light rain failed to dispel the majesty of the Alfred Holt ships in all their home port splendour. How rapidly must beat the hearts of the people of Liverpool and Birkenhead, on their bustling waterfronts honoured to witness such a spectacle, the splendid image carrying them through their day with the knowledge their nation with such maritime might would prevail against all odds.

Captain Xavier Hickman, twenty-eight years service, his business suit of better quality and cut than Captain Saxby's, spoke, choosing his words carefully: "I fully concur with Captain Saxby and it is obvious even to the more tolerant observer our problems lie with the Liverpool Chinese Seamen's Union, not the legitimate Chinese Seamen's Union. Recently I had the unpleasant experience of having to break up sometimes bloody skirmishes between the bombastic Liverpool Chinese Seamen's Union and the peaceful Chinese Seamen's Union. Their ranting thick-headed thugs convinced wrongly their members innocent victims of prejudice. Total nonsense, I also had to put a stop to the circulation of seditious literature advocating the overthrow of the government of China. Not pretty stuff, I can tell you firsthand."

Chief Engineer Tolhurst agreed wholeheartedly. "Pay the lot off in Shanghai, the Japanese would know how to deal with them, I say. Ceaseless talk of more wages in their greedy, greasy palms. Payment of the British war risk bonus, accommodation and food befitting royalty. Be it I had my way I would have the troublemakers accommodated in the scavengers or being of a deck persuasion, the chain locker. Think about these selfish Chinese for a moment, if not for our ships the beggars would be hauling rickshaws for a handful of pennies a month."

Captain Draper voiced his thoughts: "On the *Polydorus* we might have more than seventy Chinese on articles, but to my mind, as it is my officers and engineers, we could get rid of forty of them if replaced with British nationals."

Nods and hear-hears passed around the table, the heresy quickly quashed with a sobering remark dealing with rapacious white deck and engine room crews, though of smaller number, presented pernicious problems on a similar scale.

"Chinese, as we are aware, cannot work without strict supervision, unless an officer drawn from other duties is present and directing operations," Captain Draper added, speaking on a favourite issue. "In some cases you have to stop squaring up or stripping to explain such rudimentary tasks as attaching slab hooks correctly through ringbolts, or to stand free of bights, when and how to stopper a line. So much valuable time is wasted, irreplaceable company time."

Captain Hickman sat quietly, absorbed in his own deliberations. Some points he could agree on, not on others. In private he emphasised with the Chinese on matters of wage inequality and war risk bonus which needed addressing in their favour. One reason being he held an opinion through long observation Chinese seamen were as efficient and skilled as their British counterparts. Under dire threat in the South China Sea, he faced the fury of a typhoon north of Luzon, his ship on it beam ends. All hands turning out at midnight to re-lash a deck cargo of large diameter concrete pipes and heavy machinery at No. 1 and No. 2 hatches, the ship rolling thirty-five degrees and burying her foredeck in a solid wall of water. Exposing his beam to come about and run before the storm risked a catastrophic movement of cargo, possibly the loss of his ship, all he could do maintain her current heading into the seas and call upon that mystic guardian of seamen created in myth and invincibility, for a lull. It came, the men ready, spare runners, backsprings and breast wires from the lower peak store hauled taut with steam on deck, bottle screws, multiple parts of wire frapped with gantlines. Then came a lesser degree of roll, a brief respite to take up more tension, hands bloodied and raw, minds set only on saving the ship.

Their reprieve only lasted a few hours, close to the change of

The Chinese Seamen's Children

watch and hove to, driving rain and hail failing to flatten mountainous seas, when the jumbo purchase lower block snapped its heavy wire strop shackled to the deck. Normally on passage the topping and hauling parts would have been rove two blocks and protected by a canvas sheaf, but with heavy lifts in two ports only a few days apart, for ease of breaking out, the purchase remained extended almost to the deck. In total darkness the multi-roved purchase whipped with a demonic intent of destruction from side to side with every violent roll of the ship. With each pitch that buried the focastle head in a wall of seething water the purchase would slam into the foremast, the block now a mangled mass of twisted metal, buckled sheaves and stranded wire. Captain Hickman and his officers on the bridge could only look on helplessly as the serang and six carefully chosen ABs stood by at the break of the focastle head, waiting for a lull in the nightmare of darkness, sea, wind and rain.

As sometimes happen with violent storms at sea, when all seems lost, a single moment in time gives seamen the slightest of edges in a one-sided battle, the ship sunk almost to its crosstree in a trough, for a few seconds stable in the calm. Unnerving, a frightening phenomenon known to becalm sailing ships in raging gales, buried in seas higher than their masts. Taking their given moment the men never hesitated, as one falling on the block and capturing it between the winches, six turns of a gantline, lashed to any deck fitting close by.

With the men safely off the deck and only the watch and the first officer on the bridge, Captain Hickman thought of what happened during the night. Some romantics would say those ABs inherited the gene of cord and canvas suspended aloft by chain and wire. No, he thought, those men simply performed their job as any seaman would, no race, no creed, just simple seamen going about their work in their environment sometimes placid sometimes deadly.

Chairman Dumbrill asked a question around the table. "There is a list of ports where Chinese are literally deserting in droves. San Diego, San Francisco, Los Angeles, Seattle, Vancouver. Knowing these North American ports, is there a reason why these ports are favoured more than others?"

Chief Engineer Killen voiced a popular theory. "Well, you could say that the promise of a workers paradise in the United States, of course myth, an inducement for seeking employment in Chinese restaurants and laundries. Then there is United States neutrality protecting their cowardly yellow skins."

Some chuckles and a few deep throated guffaws sounded around the table.

"No, I am serious. Construction of the vast system of United States railways and roads built by teeming hordes of Chinese navvies now history, the opportunities for gainful employment exist only in their smelly restaurants and laundries. Of course the neutrality of the country the carrot dangled on the stick for most."

Captain Hickman could no longer remain silent. "One reason I hear repeated frequently, the Japanese have invaded their homeland and because we do not accept Chinese serving on British ships as nationals most with ample cause consider themselves stateless. Many have news of their families killed by the Japanese so I would assume the United States with its vastness and ease of assimilation fair game to jump ship and make a new life. Also there is among mainstream Chinese thinking the United Kingdom should have militarily intervened when the Japanese invaded China and that the United States is more sympathetic to the fate of their country."

"How could the Chinese harbour such absurd beliefs in the current world situation? With the United Kingdom, their bread and butter, fighting for its own and its Empire's survival against a powerful and forbidding scourge?" Chairman Dumbrill said, aghast. Quickly regaining his composure he added: "Have we a solution to the desertions, in a time of war an inexcusable situation bordering on cowardice, which is affecting our sailing schedules in Canadian and United States ports?"

"Suggestions from my officers the banning of shore leave is plausible," Captain Saxby said.

"Wouldn't that be drastic for the entire ship?"

The Chinese Seamen's Children

"I speak only of the Chinese. Chinese are the problem, not our loyal officers and engineers."

"Our empire has an inherent right to loyalty from the Chinese and the coloured races. Good Lord, haven't we held their hands long enough, given them our lives and sweat, the fruits of our science and investments, especially the Chinese since 1886?" Damning words from Chief Engineer Haden which most around the table needed no prompting to agree.

9

KATE STOOD BEHIND ELSIE'S chair and looked forlornly around her home, without a second thought willing to share. She gently kneaded her fingers in her shoulders, a reassuring smile at Huang who sat opposite at the table with a cup of tea.

"Kate, we thank you so much," he said, then with resignation: "My total worth amounts to two pounds, a statement I am not proud of."

"Somehow we'll make do. Always have no matter the challenge. Reckon without much hullabaloo I can convince Mr Herbert the rag-and-bone man to swap our old tatty sofa for a decent bed and mattress, maybe a few shillings extra for his trouble."

Adding a teaspoon of fresh dry tea to the pot made earlier in the morning steeped a strong brew. "Kate, I have to ship out. There will be money so Elsie can pay her way."

"Huang, we'll manage, don't worry. Anyway, Elsie will be company for me. Might be a year before I see Chong again, possibly more. Of course she'll continue to work at the shop for a little time yet. By what I hear she's indispensible to old Mr Gresham."

Later when alone she would have a long talk with Elsie, her pregnancy, of being the partner of a Chinese seaman. Constant negative reactions from people, at times ignored in the street, whispers behind

The Chinese Seamen's Children

her back, all those jealous of a Chinese husband who did not associate in public houses and beat his wife.

Future plans; home in four months, arrange a wedding, find a home and carry his bride over the threshold. The next day he joined the 1926 built *Idomeneus* sailing in thirty-six hours for Singapore, Fremantle, Melbourne, Sydney and Brisbane, back loading chilled beef in Brisbane and Sydney for the United Kingdom.

The Machon class *Idomeneus,* 7748 gross registered tons, pioneered a revolutionary system of maintaining peak quality meat over long sea passages. Imported frozen beef to the British palate tasted inferior, whereas chilled beef preserved a high quality taste and texture. Loading in various ports and a five week 12,000 mile voyage from the southern hemisphere freezing meat provided the only option to avoid spoilage.

Alfred Holt engineers disagreed, devising a simple solution, their ships able to preserve chilled meat for extended periods by adding carbon dioxide to the air mixture in the refrigeration spaces. Prime Australian and New Zealand meat delivered chilled guaranteed a first quality product to the discerning British housewife queuing with her ration book.

With only No. 1 hatch to square up, the *Idomeneus's* sailing board 4:00 pm, Huang felt despair, unable to overcome the depression which held him in a vice-like grip. The loss of Elsie for at least four months, longer if routine disputes on Australian wharves escalated. His girl would have changed by the time he got home. Not their home, in the care of Kate until he gave their baby his name; the thought of a baby growing inside her caused his despair to escalate. His girl needed him by her side to protect her, tend to her if she became sick. Distracted he stumbled, causing the man on the end of a king beam floated on the yard derrick to lose his grip on the rope tail of the beam hooks, causing it to tilt.

"Bumbling dolt!" third officer Alistair Morecombe bleated, the single gold bar on his greatcoat the only bright spot on a cold and miserable day. Turning his attention on the serang, he snapped: "Wake that moron up, will you! It gets its idiot head knocked off it will cost the company good money to soogee its shit for brains off the deck."

Giving a good dressing down to a moron on deck might take his mind away from something troubling him; the scabbed lesions of unbridled passion would heal, he just hoped the trophies of conquest nothing more than surface wounds with nothing more unpleasant in store for him over the next few days. Slack Birkenhead bitch, good piece of crumpet though not worth the pain of a self-inflicted cure.

How many times his rampant and potent weapon had rammed her large snatch he could not remember, but a lot shredded skin and jism got lost in that slack hole. Then again listening to her shrieks of joy raised his ego no end, her multiple orgasms broadcast blocks away. Stud extraordinaire, fact proven.

Huang received a scowl of displeasure from Mai Qiang to which he replied with a sullen shrug, turning his back on the third officer. His first meeting with the serang on boarding to be shown his bunk and steel locker in the certified accommodation for Chinese seamen. Mai, prominent in the Chinese Seamen's Union, sectionalised the ship to favour members of his union. Other traits about the serang he took an immediate dislike; the man would not look him in the eye and refused to take his offered hand.

Fiercely proud of his Liverpool Chinese Seamen's Union membership, Huang immediately filled with misgivings. Stepping forward as a delegate of his union the ship's representative body effectively would split, also assuredly the master would not negotiate with the Liverpool Chinese Seamen's Union with a compliant Mai to acquiesce to his and the company's demands.

Division throughout the ship immediately became obvious, especially during meals where groups of three or four sat alone, ignoring intruders who offered conversation or advice over some matter. Asking the serang for the names of the delegates for an answer he received a frosty glare. "I choose the delegates, their names are of no interest to you."

There and then he made a promise to himself never to ask this man to represent him.

Orders to plumb the amidships derrick for landing beams in the coamings were relayed from the third officer to the serang, passed on with short bursts of staccato Chinese to the fifteen men forward gang. Seamen with years of seagoing experience no more than a voiceless and pliable extension of the officer's undisputed competence and seamanship. Variations at times did arise with a white bosun overseeing a Chinese serang, allowing busy officers to concentrate on their own important arrival and departure duties.

Floating and landing hatch beams, the yard and amidships derricks sharing the plumb in union purchase, alternatively paying off and taking up the slack, no more than basic seamanship warranting a competent seaman to direct the winch drivers. No, not on the *Idomeneus*. Chinese could not work unsupervised.

Huang made up a gang of six men on the starboard side, each man instructed to hold firmly with feet planted apart the manila tail of the beam hooks to guide the beam into its slot in the coamings. Thinking of Elsie, his foot came into contact with a ringbolt in the deck and again he stumbled, causing the beam to swing erratically, a cry of alarm from the man behind him. Reacting instantly, a shout from the third officer brought the landing to a halt, the beam a few inches above the coamings.

"Stand out this instant!"

Countless times over the years he had performed this simple task, backing up the man closest the beam and when ordered let go the tail and take up a position opposite to land it between the coamings. With his hands spread in a gesture of futility, Huang frowned at the furious serang whose darting finger ordered him to stand aside.

Suspended aloft by runners and silent winches, the beam now floated motionless over the coamings as the men waited for the drama to unfold. Haung looked away from the serang, straightening and flexing his shoulders as the third officer advanced on him and thrust his face in his.

"Seaman, your name?"

"Huang Zhen."

Fumbling angrily in his pocket, he withdrew a small notebook and pencil. "Spell it."

"What have I done?"

"Have I given you permission to speak? I have not! Spell your name!"

Confused but calm, he spelled his name and repeated: "What have I done?"

"Address me as sir!"

"What have I done, sir?"

"How about we start with a threat to life and limb?" he said tight-lipped. "Incompetency? Recommendation the master checks your papers thoroughly? By what I have witnessed on deck serious reservations are raised. Who knows among you lot, you might have done your time on the door of a Shanghai brothel."

"I am an AB."

"Sir!"

"Sir, I am an AB."

Scribbling an additional entry in his notebook, he squirmed as a crusty scab on his penis chaffed loose and the weeping lesion stuck to his underwear. "Endangering others on deck with gross incompetence, contempt of an officer. Present yourself to the master at a time of his choosing, dealing with shit like you probably 0900 hours."

"Sir, I am sorry if I offend you. I don't understand this."

"Sorry you might and should be, but it makes no difference to my report. As for understanding the implications of working safely, of course you don't because you're an imbecile. Step lively you lot and land that beam! Quick about it, you hear me!"

Why did this man, a pained expression on his insipid face, who continually scratched his genitals, a bully protected by his skin and uniform, take umbrage at a small and insignificant incident like tripping on a ringbolt? To defuse an obvious issue of personalities he could request the serang to speak with the bosun and chief officer, but he wouldn't. Among his fellow shipmates there would be friends, later seek them out and build alliances to combat those who accepted the status quo.

Huang might have been facing a judge in a court of law, an arbiter with a reputation of merciless dispersal of justice to the lower labouring classes, a penchant for the lash and noose. Captain Willard Firth's unforgiving demeanour betrayed his middleclass Manchester birth to a coal merchant father and seamstress mother. Young Firth, drawn and fascinated by the sea, fortunate in having parents who believed hard work and the rigors of the maritime environment forged character, resolutely guided their only son to sign indentures with Alfred Holt.

Gifted with an exceptional intellect Midshipman Firth rose steadily through the ranks, achieving the ultimate goal with honours, his master's certificate and finally command. Each step along the pathway of achievement further imbued in Captain Firth's psyche he belonged to an elite race destined to rule, his credentials British blood and the indomitable spirit that carved an empire in every corner of the world. Huang Zhen and his fellow Chinese to his mind of no more importance than the tools affixed to the shadow board in the bosun's store, in fact he would put greater value on the expensive tools contained therein.

Captain Firth ignored Huang standing before his desk, instead addressing the third officer relieved from his eight to twelve watch duties to be present at the hearing. "Mr Morecombe, has the man requested the presence of the serang?" he said throatily, a fold of flesh at the base of his throat reminding Huang of a turkey. It caused him to smile which switched the master's attention immediately to him. "Huang Zhen, are you proficient in the English language to understanding the gravity of these proceedings?"

"I speak English well." Reacting to a fierce contraction of wiry eyebrows and a slit of bloodless lips, he added: "Sir …"

"Repeating, do you understand the seriousness of the charges against you?"

"Sir, I am unaware of any wrongdoing that would warrant charges against me," he said, balancing on the balls of his feet. Pretentious prig, dripping in gold braid, a big head made even larger with a hat weighed down with gold leaf and insignia. Are you trying to intimidate me? Well, you are not succeeding. You and your kind will never humble me.

Open on his desk the official log book, beside it a typed sheet of paper. "I have spoken at length with Mr Morecombe and a witness to the incidences on deck and have deliberated. My first conclusion is your disrespect to an officer in pursuance of his duties is noted for future reference."

"Who is witness against me?" he said, no enlightenment needed.

"Dialogue will be entered into and I will issue a warning your contempt of authority is officially noted," Captain Firth said, filigrees of tiny purple veins on both cheeks pulsing with blood.

Noted for the omission of a few sirs, his name. Huang stared at the man ensconced in his symbols of power and rank, an open log book. Clogging his nose the smell of the trappings of authority, the nutty lingering trace of furniture polish applied by a Chinese servant, a pathetic creature who would scurry from sight with his polishing rag in fear his presence might offend.

Judgement passed, formal sentence pending.

"Huang Zhen, you are logged two days pay and an entry with date and time of offences entered in the log. Now to another matter, Mr Morecombe holds grave reservations of your competence and claim to the rank of AB."

Humiliation would now follow the loss of two days' pay, a damning notation against his name. Without exception a sense of achievement always filled him when his discharge book received an official stamp of endorsement of character and ability, his seamanship learned from

The Chinese Seamen's Children

men entitled to call themselves seamen. Men who doubled Cape Horn under sail, men of the calibre of Lau Yi. Not like Mai supporting the third officer against his own kind, but then what could he expect from a Kuomintang man?

"My final judgement on your competence will be withheld until more facts from various sources are forthcoming. Instructions have been issued to Mr Morecombe, midshipmen and petty officers to personally monitor your work on deck and to report to me periodically." Captain Firth handed him the typed paper; his copy of the log entry. "If your behaviour is exemplary for the remainder of the voyage I have an option which I will weigh heavily whether to rescind the logging, the entry of course remaining. Dismissed."

Before he folded it and placed it in his top pocket he noticed the typing smudged and black, a scrawled signature and the ship's official stamp; whoever typed the entry should clean the keys of the ship's typewriter.

10

MAI KEPT HIS DISTANCE, his suspicions of the young AB's loyalties no longer in doubt with credible information proving his first impression correct. Mai eyes and ears missed nothing, Huang one of a few but still threatening number of Liverpool Chinese Seamen's Union members spreading their discontent onboard.

Openly observed by Mai's spies, Huang attempted to form a militant group of Liverpool Chinese Seamen's Union members, the overwhelming number of Chinese Seamen's Union members more than enough to quell any usurping of the ships union affairs.

With the *Idomeneus* passing through the Strait of Gibraltar and on course for Port Said, Huang's only success in promoting his union befriending AB Yang Hui, a few years older than himself and equally committed to the progressive Liverpool Chinese Seamen's Union. Thoughts were he might be able to muster ten allies, though when he called a meeting and only Yang attended a full retreat ensured and he found himself ostracised.

Yang, Shanghai born, home ported in Liverpool, refused to accept Merseyside as home. Fiercely adamant he would not forsake his roots until routed Japanese blood congealed the points of liberation army bayonets. Unknowing of his family's fate filled him with constant grief, and reading the atrocities committed by the Japanese army he

The Chinese Seamen's Children

held little hope for them. Yang, like many Chinese, held the United Kingdom responsible for the loss of vast tracts of his homeland, for abandoning China and seeking appeasement with Japan. Filled with a passion bordering on the fanatical, he never tired debating his fellow countrymen, those that would listen and not scoff, China's only hope for the future free from foreign exploitation and dominance, famine and poverty, rested in the hands of the liberation forces of Mao Zedong and the overthrow of the Kuomintang.

Both men would sit on the lee side of No. 5 hatch, always alone, those passing by ignoring them, head down and eyes averted, hurrying their step. Isolation only drew the two young men closer.

"Those among us with progressive ideals live with hope one union for all Chinese seamen," Yang said, sewing a seabag on his knees, a scrap of old bottom tarpaulin saved from being cut into a save-all. "Deliberately we are driven apart by politics, a subservient Chinese government, and of course in the wings the avarice of shipowners."

"Counter arguments are made by the Chinese Seamen's Union which makes sense to their members, why the membership should accept low wages and make no demand to have the war risk bonus paid," Huang said.

Yang waxed a length of doubled sail twine, focused intently on where to insert his needle. "So I have heard."

"Achieving the war risk bonus and wage parity we price ourselves out of work, cheaper to sign on Senegalese, Arab and Lascar crews."

"Labouring mindlessly for swill and pennies, yes a sound argument."

"Same of which could be said of Chinese, and I understand the resentment of British nationals to Chinese. For instance Blue Star Line, a British company with a long and successful history, manned with full British crews, so it's not difficult to reason why there is animosity when the magnificent ships of Blue Funnel Line sail up the Mersey with large Chinese crews hard at work under the shade of the red duster. British flagged ships for British nationals! Hell and damnation with low paid Chinese, let them man their own ships."

"Then why are there Chinese in their thousands signing articles in Liverpool? Where are all those white ABs and firemen?"

"When your nation has half the world's shipping under its flag it is difficult to maintain full crewing levels. Alfred Holt can say in all honesty its major revenues are generated from trade with the Far East, Australia and New Zealand, why Asian crews are preferred."

"Does Alfred Holt employ Australian and New Zealand crews with this benevolent Asian policy?"

Huang smiled. "Can you imagine an entire ship of militant Australian and New Zealand unionists wearing out the carpet in the master's cabin? Baiting and hounding officers for the sport of it?"

Yang agreed. "Wouldn't that be a sight to behold."

"Pure havoc. The Australians and their union have a formidable reputation with shipowners, not to mention those who make our lives a misery."

Huang cornered the serang when he came to knock them off for lunch, a ten man gang painting deckheads. Mai used no vocal commands, his simple brooding presence and the ringing of eight bells on the bridge all the men needed to know the time of the day. Only then could tools and paintbrushes become idle without fear of reprisal.

"Serang Mai, why are we not one union fighting for the war risk bonus and wage parity?"

Mai crouched as if preparing to fend off a frontal attack, his eyes mere slits. "So you still scheme," he growled, then allowed himself the briefest of smiles that held no trace of mirth. "Have you forgotten so soon your dismal failure to garner support to inflict your demands upon the ship?"

"Not the ship, management in Liverpool. Except for maintaining unity there is nothing we can do on a shipboard level, but we can on a combined front and not founder with mistrust of each other."

"Tread with extreme caution, many eyes are upon you, not only the officers."

"Of course, what I encountered squaring up in Liverpool. Let me tell you, Serang Mai, my eye is on you, too."

"War risk bonus is an entitlement for British nationals, paid by their government in recognition of their service at sea in war to their country, as such not applicable to Chinese."

Huang stared at him in amazement. "How can you and the Chinese Seamen's Union hold such absurd views we have no right to the war risk bonus?"

"Legions of Lascars, Senegalese and Arabs standby on United Kingdom wharves for that day when the greed of the Liverpool Chinese Seamen's Union make hard working and loyal Chinese seamen financially unviable. Our replacements marching up gangways with joyous laughter for good pay and conditions, our conditions, now under threat because of scheming, snivelling agitators like you. Keep your seditious Communist spiel to yourself and the handful of others you have corrupted! It has no place here! Nor you!"

"Which will be reported to the master?"

"My responsibility is to the ship. Curb your tongue!"

"Responsibility? Taking orders from white bosuns who get theirs from white officers? That, too, one day will change. I wonder if a white master advised Admiral Zheng He and his Grand Fleet in the thirteenth century. Did our forefathers need white overseers in the building of a wall? What is superior about the colour of a man's skin?"

Mai's lips curled with repugnance. "Courageous Kuomintang sacrifice their lives fighting the Japanese while the Communists gather their disloyal forces and retreat to plot the overthrow of the glorious government of our people."

"Spoken like a true Kuomintang. It is not Mao Zedong who is the traitor! It is Mao Zedong and his liberation forces who will deliver us from the Japanese. Not the sacred white skins you grovel to, Chinese led by a leader of the people."

"Your tongue will hang you!"

Coming from the mouth of a man a mere puppet he expected no

more, though a powerful entity on the ship with his own sphere of influence. "Do what you will, what you consider correct procedure in dealing with a threat to your position. Serang Mai, I am guilty of the unforgivable sin of tripping over a ringbolt and offending the sea-wise eyes of a third officer who is now standing judgement of my right to call myself an AB. Assisted by you of course, which to me is more offensive because you are what I am, Chinese."

Mai's forehead beaded with sweat, his eyes sweeping the deck as if seeking an avenue of escape.

"Because you would not support me, a third officer is judging my ability to tie my bootlaces," his tirade continued. "Serang Mai, I am going to prove to him I am a seaman. I did a cook a favour making him a canvas bag and when asked he gave me a hank of butcher's twine."

Sprawled on his back in the windlass bed the previous week, scaling rust and red lead priming, he heard laughter. Craning his neck he saw from his cramped position the third officer and two midshipmen examining a bell rope; the work of the senior midshipman, a bell rope to replace the old attached to the focastle head bell.

Words of praise flowed freely from the third officer for the creator's seamanship, passing the bell rope between them for inspection. Huang of a mind the clumsy fingers of deck boy could do better, an idea forming in his mind.

Created with nimble fingers, meticulously woven with butcher's twine around a filler of three strand manila rope, his bell rope would pass the critical eye of any man in sail. In fact the bell rope originated from the days of sail, twenty-one-strand interlacing chain sennit with a pronounced grip formed with a Danish rose knot. Along its twelve-inch length pineapple shroud and triple manrope knots. Gloss white paint, prominent fancy work highlighted in Alfred Holt funnel colours, it could well have been the work of a sailor sitting in the shadow of a set main course. This bell rope fit for a knot board, even greater praise, acknowledgment by a supreme seaman, Lau Yi.

Subject to his observation of competency by the third officer, he thought it only fitting the bell rope be presented to him, the officer not relieved on the bridge until 12:30 pm. "Serang Mai, I am curious, how do you rate me as a seaman?"

"That is not for me to decide."

"Yes it is, serang and the most competent seaman on the ship. Correct?"

"Correct," he said, relaxed now certain no physical harm threatened him.

"Serang Mai, it has been my good fortune to sail with men who can rightly call themselves seamen," he scoffed. "So being I would have thought there would have been among the officers, quartermasters and bosun, including yourself, those who knew how to make a bell rope and impart that knowledge to a midshipman. My mistake."

Huang climbed the ladder to the port bridge wing, further access barred by the burly form of the twelve to four quartermaster.

Not carrying a tea tray or bridge box immediately put the quartermaster on guard, also the paint spattered trousers and shirt. "What business you got on the bridge?" he challenged, by instinct kneading his beefy hands. "What you got there?"

"No business of yours. I am here to see the third officer."

"You'll see the end of my boot up your arse if you don't get off the bridge!"

Exchanges of voices caught the interest of the relieving second officer still belching pleasurably from his lunch, also the third officer hungrily looking forward to his; both men stepped through the wheelhouse door.

"Perkins, there a problem?" the third officer inquired.

"Nothing my size twelve boot can't fix, begging your pardon, sir," he said, lowering his voice in deference to the officer he addressed. "Says he wants to see you, Mr Morecombe, sir. Excusing the vulgarity, sir, told him get his arse off your bridge."

Recommended by the second officer a fresh bread roll dipped in spicy mulligatawny soup had caused the third officer's taste buds to salivate; swallowing, he advanced on Huang still standing on the top rung of the ladder. "Huang! You better have a good reason for being on the bridge, if not you will be explaining your disregard of standing orders to the master."

Blocked from the bridge wing it became increasingly difficult to conceal his growing anger. Even more so shut from his mind the contempt in their faces, their simpering voices. How pretentious these men were strutting in their white shirts and black ties, pressed trousers, peak caps and gold braid. Who but indifferent seamen at sea to bear witness to their maritime achievements, an audience of toiling men covered in grease and smelling of wire rope oil?

Gripped in his hand he now realised a mistake, the act of making it no more than a naive means to vindicate himself in the eyes of an officer not worthy of the effort. Retreat now before the situation brought others of higher rank into the confrontation, his obsession to prove his seamanship overcoming good sense. Then good sense failed him and he pushed past the quartermaster who caught by surprise fell hard against the dodger. "I have done nothing but make a bell rope which I offer to you."

For a moment he thought the third officer intended to strike him, a clenched fist and a livid scowl darkening his face. "How dare you address an officer in such an insolent tone!" Instead the hand darted out and grabbed the bell rope. Holding it at arm's length, he sneered: "My opinion has not changed about your competency, and with this obvious mass manufactured fake I will be adding to my compilation of your suspect abilities your disgraceful contempt for an officer's intelligence. Where did you buy this, Huang? I would hazard an educated guess in some grotty ships chandler in Hong Kong, Singapore perhaps?"

"Someone who calls himself a seaman made it."

"Rubbish! This came from a Chinese sweat shop, turned out in the hundreds by tiny Chinese fingers. Also I take umbrage you have wasted good ship's paint to enhance the fraud. Personally I will see the cost of the paint is deducted from your wages."

All about him his world crumbled as a vice-like hand gripped his shoulder, the quartermaster almost begging either of the officers to give him instructions to throw the young Chinese upstart off the bridge.

With the barest negative movement of his head to the quartermaster the third officer walked to the wing of the bridge; for a moment he paused as if having second thoughts, then tossed the bell rope over the side. "Huang, the master can have the dubious pleasure of your company in the morning," he said. "Advice you would be foolish to forget in the future, never step foot on this bridge again, and never insult my intelligence with some grubby imitation made in a back alley in Hong Kong. Escort him off the bridge, Perkins! My nose tells me you may even need to wash down."

On the master's desk the report stated Huang Zhen's unauthorised presence on the bridge constituted a hazard to safe navigation of the vessel. Attached also a statement of opinion Huang Zhen attempted with a manufactured maritime artefact to influence Third Officer Morecombe's report of said person's competence to sail as AB.

Captain Firth needed no further convincing, having earlier spoken with Mai. Undoubtedly the man before him, for the second time in the voyage, a virulent cadre sent to the ship by the Liverpool Chinese Seamen's Union to set in train disunity and malcontent, the eventual demise of the prevailing Chinese Seamen's Union influence crucial to discipline.

Swift judgement contained a small degree of mercy, Huang Zhen's discharge book stamped *endorsement not required* and dismissal on arrival in Singapore.

11

DEVESTATED AND FILLED WITH remorse even the unwavering support of Yang failed to ease, Huang held grave fears for his future. Through stupidity and naivety he had failed the girl who carried their child. Elsie wholly dependent on him, without a family and he destitute in a foreign port 8000 miles from home. What were his chances of shipping out on a British ship, any ship for that matter, seriously impeded with a damning entry in his discharge book of *endorsement not required*?

Counting down the days to Singapore he suffered in misery, except for Yang ostracised by his own, at times threatened by those with loyalties to the Chinese Seamen's Union. Mai's smug smile reflected his exultation, evidence a young Chinese militant advocating mass exodus from the Chinese Seamen's Union proven to be nothing more than show and bluster, a nonentity without substance.

Destroying his credibility of offering alternative leadership, his arrogant act of forcing his way on the bridge and demanding an audience with the officer of the watch busy with important navigational duties. No more than a shameful act of egotism, contempt and absolute disrespect for authority. Also using an obviously contrived bell rope to enhance his claim to be a seaman, the officer with every right to toss the offensive article over the side, a common item easily

The Chinese Seamen's Children

purchased in Asian waterfront gift shops for a few shillings.

Originating from the serang and his supporters warnings of stern reprisals against certain individuals with suspect loyalties, the master with a report on his desk of irrefutable evidence of a plot by members of the Liverpool Chinese Seamen's Union in the first Australian port to request Seamen's Union of Australia intervention to hold the ship indefinitely in support of a new and outrageous log of claims.

Wild rumours circulated, the most daunting all Chinese crew members would be dismissed without notice and declared illegal aliens, jailed and replaced by a Lascar crew already booked in hotels in Fremantle. Clear proof one of the ringleaders dismissed on arrival in Singapore and his discharge book stamped *endorsement not required*. Be that a warning taken with the utmost seriousness, dissenters faced certain and severe punishment.

Isolated and suffering depression, he might have been a distant observer to the innuendo and malicious gossip plaguing the ship, only one man courageous enough to sit with him on No.5 hatch. On deck he went through the motions, following orders without thinking as the *Idomeneus* tied up in Singapore, hope in his heart maybe the master would have a change of heart and rescind his decision.

Throughout the ship a feverish expectation of arrival caused smiles and laughter, for the officers and engineers, senior ratings and men with family in Singapore, a jaunty spring in their step. Orders were relayed in a less belittling tone of voice. Three days alongside part discharging, then sailing to Australia with her first port Fremantle.

Huang stared over the stern, the last quarter line made fast and the slack taken up on the breast bight of wire, waiting with dread for an officer or midshipman with orders to present himself before the master.

Smiling, the senior midshipman seemed amused by the anguish in the young AB's face, out of sight of an officer wearing his hat at a jaunty angle, a chuckle as he relayed the master's orders. Shore authorities and government formalities of arrival completed within the hour Huang Zhen would respectfully present himself to the master on the bridge. Also he would have his personal belongings by the gangway for inspection by an officer preparatory to his escort off the ship, his services officially terminated.

On the chartroom table his meagre pay less loggings and deductions, his discharge book stamped *endorsement not required.* Eyes fastened on the black ink, fascinated yet crushed in mind and spirit. Before entering the wheelhouse he looked around the harbour and lost count of the ships flying the red duster, but what chances did he have of joining any of them with what stared at him in official ink?

Captain Firth intoned sentence, not bothering to look at the seaman with his head on his chest. Much more pleasant things on his mind than dealing with and eradicating a bothersome individual threatening the company, thoughts of dinner tonight with the agent in Raffles. Magnificent fare, service unsurpassed, a credit to colonial training of the native staff. Especially a quaint custom he liked, the freshly roasted peanuts served with one's drink, an almost apologetic invitation to cast the shells on the polished floor to give Raffles its unique appeal.

For Huang his torment reached a new high the moment he stepped off the bottom platform of the gangway onto the wharf, above some of his fellow seamen with nearby duties looking down; whether their expressionless faces hid sympathy or triumph he did not know. Another barb of depression, humiliation when the senior midshipman emptied his seabag on deck and with the point of his highly polished shoe sorted through the meagre contents. Satisfied of no pilfering of company property, he bowed with broad sweep of his hand. "Sir, we officers bid you goodbye and good riddance."

Furthering their business interests in a hub of Asia, a large number of British shipping companies maintained a high profile in Singapore with old and established shipping agents acting in their stead. Starting immediately he would put his name down in every office in Singapore. At the wharf gates, ignored by a disinterested watchman studying a newspaper, he turned for one last look at the *Idomeneus*. Two sets of gear swung over the wharf, one set outboard to discharge into two

The Chinese Seamen's Children

doubled up barges. To the critical eye of those knowledgeable in matters of the sea, a fine looking ship maintained to the highest order.

From a distance no hint of dissention, struggle for supremacy, racial profiling. The *Idomeneus* seemed to be at peace secured alongside, even with her hatches open and under assault by dockers. Chatting stewards gathered at the top platform of the gangway, pushing and shoving playfully, money in their pockets and a few hours ashore. Some most certainly would have to be back onboard at 3:00 pm to run the master's tray and serve afternoon tea in the saloon for the officers.

Engaged in cheerful banter, two engineers saturated in sweat, dressed in suits and ties in the sweltering heat and humidity, hurried down the gangway. Not a care in the world, Singapore to explore, eager for the fleshy delights of sweet Chinese girls theirs for the picking.

At last he turned away from the *Idomeneus*, a lump in his throat so heavy it made it difficult to breathe. Passing through the wharf gates he entered a familiar world of hawkers burdened with yokes from which dangled their wares, old women tending blackened and steaming pots of noodles and rice on cracked pavements or bare earth. People rushing as if their lives depended on their reaching their destination. Shopkeepers cajoling and shouting their bargains competed with barking dogs, aggressive dogs with bared fangs, a pack of mangy mongrels waiting their turn to mount a hairless bitch offering her rump to all takers.

Once his home, he felt no affinity for this foreign place. Body sapping heat, a continual crush of humanity in a daily ritual to survive. On his mind his destination, Raffles Place, a thriving centre of commerce created by Singapore's founders. Shipping agents, then a search for accommodation.

It took two hours to put his name down with the various shipping agents, harried clerks prisoners behind their desks. Windowless, stifling, musty pigeon-holes, noisy overhead fans stirring oppressive air to further exacerbate their discomfort. Some gave the last entry in his discharge book a cursory glance, a few of the more curious a quizzical uplift of eyebrows before adding his name in a ledger, those he felt certain erasing his name the moment the door closed behind him.

With the little money he had he could afford a doss-house accessed by a lane six feet wide, a rat and cockroach infested cesspit with loose stone paving sunk in a quagmire of raw sewerage. So decrepit he even wondered if the proprietor rigged a sleeping rope for latecomers when the greasy mats on the earthen floor could squeeze in no more bodies.

For a few cents he squatted in the gutter and ate noodles and steamed rice, boiled fish and vegetables; the cook old and toothless, her wizened face and flapping gums proof of not ageing gracefully, forced to scrounge an existence from those desperate enough to eat her food. Grateful thoughts her servings a little more than she gave others, and for a man who could afford only one meal a day he showed his gratitude with an arm around her shrunken shoulders.

Sharing his small portion of gutter with others more adaptable to survival, he ignored hundreds of well-fed rats with no fear of humanity fighting vicious running battles for territory, giving or asking no quarter, ripping each other's throats out as the strong overcame the weak. Garbage dumped in the laneways and streets from restaurants and markets rotted quickly in the heat, casting a pall of putrescence that seeped into every sweating pore.

To survive he would need to blank out the hopeless poverty of Singapore, incongruous to the well-fed soldiers, airmen and sailors in the street, an infectious confidence in their step, the invincible guardians of Fortress Singapore. Business in Singapore proceeded as normal, but an undercurrent of unease gave many a sense of paranoia, causing the occasional glance over a shoulder, conversations outdoors held in hushed tones. With the white population of Singapore firmly believing the British Empire's Fortress Singapore

The Chinese Seamen's Children

impregnable, identifying possible spies became a sport. Especially Japanese couples posing as besotted honeymooners, photographing their blushing partners with fortifications, harbour and naval installations in the background.

Among the native population grew optimism bordering on jubilation colonial ascendancy would soon end, the armies of the Emperor of Japan crushing the British Empire cowering in their fiefdom of Hong Kong, a spent force who bleated like sheep prepared for slaughter. Soon the Japanese navy would steam into the Singapore roads and aim their guns at Raffles Place.

Politics dominating everyday life Singapore mattered nothing to Huang who found a cool and green reprieve in a park after his daily trudge to the shipping agents, time to write a letter home. Tears formed in his eyes as he wrote: *Think of me and I will be your strength and guidance along the separate pathways life has forced upon us. Forever in my heart I am with you and our child that grows inside you.*

Another week's paid accommodation reduced his funds alarmingly even though he continued to ration himself to one meal a day. Drinking from public fountains where Europeans gathered and walking saved money, his confidence waning as his daily treks to the shipping agents proved unsuccessful. Two weeks ashore and now living with a growing desperation, five dollars in his wallet.

Concluding his daily ritual, usually around midday, he trudged wearily to his small park. In its serenity and bathed in soft green light he thought it would have been comforting to be able to write another letter to Elsie, and he would with the last of his money. Native to Malayan rain forests, an especially large tree with a huge spreading crown shaded the park bench on which he sat. Protection from the searing sun and oppressive humidity, and under the bows and lush foliage of the giant tembusa, home to a family of squabbling macaques, fate took an unexpected turn for a seaman on the verge of destitution.

Sitting beside him on the park bench a man in his mid-thirties offered fatherly encouragement to a small child of about four with a leg brace who played clumsily with a ball. Overcome with delight, he would clap his hands with gusto when she managed to toss the ball in the air, drag her misshapen leg and with widespread fingers fumble, but finally catch it. She missed more often than she caught and close to tears looked at Huang expectantly. "Catch?" she lisped.

She threw the ball erratically and would have missed her target if not for Huang throwing out his arm to catch it. Squealing with glee, she clapped like her father. "Catch to me."

Missing the ball by a few feet, she toppling over on the grass; struggling to her feet she picked up the ball, an appeal in her eyes. "Catch again?"

Huang held out his cupped hands.

"Victoria, let the man be, don't bother people," her father chastised.

"No, no, it's all right. I don't mind."

"Victoria doesn't usually take to strangers, she is very shy. She likes you."

Dragging her leg she limped to Huang's side and smiled; a few months back she had fallen and lost two front teeth.

"Amazing, you must have a special charm for children. Are you the Pied Piper of Hamelin, perhaps?"

"No, not the Pied Piper. About children, I'm not certain if children like me or not. There is in Liverpool a girl who one day will be my wife. She is having our child."

"Liverpool, are you a seaman?"

"My ship sailed without me."

"Would I be prying if I asked why?"

"Over and over I keep trying to convince myself because I am Chinese in a white man's world. I suppose that is the easiest way to blame others for your stupidity."

"You do not look and most certainly do not speak stupid."

The Chinese Seamen's Children

"Stupidity is proof of my dismissal from the *Idomeneus*. Self deluding myself that my race and my seamanship, my total worth, the equal of my deemed white superiors."

"Would you think the reason being the British fear Chinese?"

"Not the Chinese as a nation. Hardworking and dedicated Chinese seamen are the ones feared. British seamen consider British registered ships their own, and I suppose rightly so. Chinese seamen are no more than low wage factor for frugal actuaries to tally in their ledgers, a cheap and plentiful commodity crammed in open focastles. If the ship had Singapore, Shanghai or Hong Kong painted on the stern it might make a difference to what British seamen think of us, I don't know. Probably not, their biasness is generation bred and does not like a good wine improve with age."

Retreating with three ungainly steps, the girl demanded Huang catch her ball. It passed wide of him; retrieving it he gently tossed it back only for it to bounce lightly off her chest.

"Being guilty of stupidity, I am also guilty of stepping out of my customary role as a bumbling Chinese seaman to become arrogant and conceited. With hindsight, I could have handled the situation that led to my dismissal far better than I did, attempting to prove my ability when no one gave a damn anyway."

Beckoning the child, he raised a topic on most minds and never far from any conversation. "Do you think Germany will prevail in the war?"

Huang tensed, a sudden thought the man might be a Japanese spy, the city buzzing with rumours spies lurked everywhere. What would a spy want with him? "The United Kingdom will lose the war if Russia remains true to the pact signed with Germany and the United States stays neutral. Both are vital to the United Kingdom's survival."

"From historical fact the British are a resilient race with a strong leader who knows not the meaning of the word surrender. My opinion is Russia's pact with Germany is to grant the sprawling republics time to mobilize their armies and put the nation on a sound war footing. As for the United States, their industrialists are making millions from the war without shedding a drop of blood. Their neutrality could continue for a long time."

"Are you a spy?"

Slapping both thighs he roared laughing. "No! No!" Startled, the child let out a cry and buried her head in his lap. "Then I suppose a father and child playing ball would be a perfect cover for a spy. No, what would there be to spy in a park?"

"That's all you hear in the streets, Japanese spies. Japan, a barbarous nation that has much to answer for with not one country in the world courageous enough to stand up to them except Mao Zedong and the Revolutionary Army."

"Mao Zedong's cure might be worse than the disease," the man said, lovingly sifting his fingers through his daughter's long silken hair.

"Japan has China on her knees and I have no doubt her eyes fixed firmly on the outposts of the British Empire, Singapore, Malaya, New Zealand and Australia."

"No matter what the peril to herself the United Kingdom will fight to the end to save her Empire."

"I disagree. Forced to sue for peace on German terms, the United Kingdom would abandon its possessions to salvage from the ruins whatever it could."

"Possibly Asia overwhelmed by Japanese forces, but Britain would never abandon Australia and New Zealand."

"Facts that can't be ignored or buried in newspaper lies, the Empire is fighting a war it is losing. Australians and New Zealanders fight side-by-side with their British kin, their generals with orders to save the United Kingdom. These nations will fight and die to save the United Kingdom first, their own fate secondary."

Assured her father's raucous outburst over, she staggered back a few steps and held her ball up. She looked at Huang with a silent plea and when she saw him cup his hands she did a little hop on her good leg and threw the ball which flew over her head.

"Have you registered with the shipping companies for work?"

"All of them, yes."

The Chinese Seamen's Children

"Jardine Matheson?"

"Jardine Matheson the first."

"Reputable old firm and respected throughout Asia. My business is only small but I have bunkering contacts with various British shipping companies, especially tankers. Why I mentioned Jardine Matheson."

Turning his head to look at the man, he did not trust himself to speak.

"There is an Anglo-Saxon Petroleum tanker in Keppel Dock, sadly not a tribute to growing old gracefully, but essential to the United Kingdom's survival, hers as well I must add."

"What is her name?" Hope surged.

"*Turbo*. Would you believe she came down the slipway in 1912?"

"Crew?"

"British officers and engineers of course, Chinese of which she is currently many men short. Seems the deserters prefer Singapore to chancing the Pacific with reports there are two German raiders on the loose. When she docked her orders were to load in Trinidad for the United Kingdom. This meant if she survived the raiders she had to extend her luck avoiding the submarines packs in the Atlantic, adding impetus to the exodus."

"Have you any influence with Jardine Matheson?"

"Normally I speak most days to a senior executive, my daughter's uncle," he said with a broad smile.

"Are there positions on deck?"

"Ah, I would chance a guess in all departments."

"My discharge book is stamped *endorsement not required* which for a seaman is akin to a death sentence."

"Coupled together a death sentence and the *Turbo* might well be apt. If you could see the old ship now lying alongside a fitting out berth with her innards ripped out you might prefer the former. My brother is my source of information and he carries great influence in shipping circles. I am sure he will recommend you on my advice. No, not me, his favourite niece Victoria who with the innocence of a child is able to judge people outside the predetermined parameters of accepted behaviour we adults burden ourselves with."

Unable to suppress the excitement in his voice, he offered his hand. "Huang Zhen, AB."

"Zeong An. I will speak with my brother this afternoon and I am reasonably sure he will inform the master of the *Turbo* he has at least one replacement. I would say an opportune time to meet the master might be after commencement of work in the morning, around 9:00 am. My brother says the poor old *Turbo* finds herself under invasion each morning by thousands of highly animated boilermakers and fitters, but I would believe a few hundred. Even that figure is proof she has not aged well."

"I don't care if she is a rust bucket. I just want to get home."

"Which you eventually will with crude oil a premium in the northern hemisphere."

"Depending on a master being desperate enough to ignore the last entry in my discharge book." Anxiety tempered his elation.

"Why is this so? You say *endorsement not required*, to my mind with little knowledge of maritime law it doesn't seem such a damning statement."

"Some contend a discharge of *endorsement not required* a lesser punishment to *bad*, but I would differ. An entry stamped *bad* is an explicit reference to your character and ability. *Endorsement not required* means an offence has been committed of such gravity the master is not prepared to make an official statement, leaving others with an interest in your discharge book to imagine all sorts of acts of dissent against authority, physical and verbal."

"Hmm, not as innocuous as I thought, but with so many men short and a high reluctance to join tankers in wartime, your troublesome problem of endorsement will not be of great concern to the master. I will tell my brother you will present yourself at 9:00 am."

Hardly daring to believe his turn of fortune uneasiness niggled at the back of his mind how the master would interpret his last endorsement.

"My brother said her previous orders mentioned the Caribbean,

The Chinese Seamen's Children

now as her docking nears its completion there is talk of a loading port in Texas, making what crew she still retains quite happy and making plans for new and more prosperous futures in the United States. Also willing to forget about the raiders. I think my brother said her crew might be more than sixty."

Long past her afternoon nap, the girl crept into her father's lap and snuggled into his chest; she gave Huang a tiny smile as her heavy eyelids fluttered.

Raging through him emotions about to reduce him to tears, he searched for the words to thank this stranger, a simple family man and his disabled daughter playing ball in a park. From the depths of despondency his life had changed course in a few minutes of conversation, through a brief encounter the chance of a job and going home replacing hopelessness. Journeying through life, he thought, could be likened to a not important river interrupted at times by turbulent tributaries contributing highs and lows, anguish and elation, achievements and failures, but in the end all joining as a single entity, pointing in a single direction.

Zeong gently rocked his daughter close to sleep in his arms. "My Victoria is named after a British queen, a memorable woman in British history. I suppose I am more British in my mind and bearing than I would like to admit in the Chinese community. Do you know what I named my eldest son?"

"What did you name your son?"

"Winston, another memorable person in British history. You mentioned the importance of Russia and the United States to the United Kingdom's survival, yes, but their great leader steadfast at the helm will play a determining and crucial role in how the British people unite in extreme austerity and fear." Rising from the bench made cumbersome with the now sleeping girl in his arms, he added: "Goodbye and good luck, Huang Zhen. I will not forget to pass your name to my brother."

The *Turbo's* extended life only came about with the advent of war, no other reason for a ship whose warped and pitted steel plates should have bubbled and burned under the breakers torch years ago. That she survived twenty-eight years carrying corrosive and volatile cargoes, added to being submerged in the extreme environment of the sea, gave tribute to her British builders, J. Liang. Smothered in welding cables, electrical leads, air and gas hoses, seemingly what held the old ship alongside the fitting out wharf, could easily be mistaken for the entanglement of coloured streamers the day she left her builder's yard.

Compounding the discomfort of burning and banging, two gangs forward of the bridge grit blasted the foredeck, another gang a deafening and painful cacophony on the focastle head using a pneumatic contraption similar to a lawn mower with a dozen lethal chipping heads. Listing ten degrees to starboard, engulfed in a roiling cloud of black grit, choked with the acrid stench of burned paintwork, the three island ship resigned herself to her fate. Not a single clear space existed abaft the bridge, stacked with bundles of pipes of all diameters, flanges, valves, bags of bolts, sheet steel. Dogmen landed drums, bales of asbestos lagging, staging planks, trestles and portable fans.

Observed by the unfamiliar the ordeal subjected the *Turbo* in dock seemed improbable this worn and tired old vessel would survive the onslaught. Buckled hull plates holed, pustules of rust inches thick in her tanks, steelwork not replaced further weakened by hammering and intense heat. Further anxiety for her master protecting their only means of survival, his lifeboats covered with dockyard tarpaulins, explicit instructions to the bosun their davits, chocks and sheaves be heavily greased and the falls free running prior to sailing. Leaving the dock a full boat muster and drill with every man no matter what his duties at his station, all boats away when the ship finished swinging compasses.

That good order would emerge from chaos seemed incomprehensible, pandemonium on deck, in the tanks, pumproom, engine room, accommodation, hundreds of workers like ants rushing with seemingly no defined purpose in mind, but in reality a well organised colony proceeding with the daily work schedule.

Huang hoisted his seabag over his shoulder and climbed the dockyard gangway aft, accessing the engineers, senior catering, petty officers accommodation and galley perched over the engine room. Under his feet the feel of the *Turbo's* deck sent a thrill of exhilaration through him, but failed to lessen the niggling of nerves in the pit of his stomach.

With deft steps he managed to find a clear passageway to the centre castle and climbed the steep starboard ladder to the officers accommodation, then another ladder equally steep to the master's cabin. Barely wide enough for two people to pass, an athwartships alleyway divided the accommodation; owner's and the master's cabins. One door open, within white painted steel bulkheads, iron bunk, green painted concrete deck, desk, cabinet and settee. Two small portholes bare of curtains and heavily speckled with grit filtered a murky light.

Accommodation deemed luxurious for the senior officer, he didn't have to deliberate in great depth what he would find forward, one of the first things he saw from the fitting out berth awning spars on the focastle head.

Captain John Hill looked up from the untidy pile of manila folders and clipped papers on his desk, a look of expectation on his tired, unshaven face. "By any chance have you brought coffee or some other stimulating beverage?"

"No, I am not a steward. AB."

"Oh yeah, someone in this madhouse made mention of an AB, but I forget. No one bar a cantankerous marine superintendent can blame me for that! You have a British discharge book?"

Stepping through the doorway he handed the master his discharge book, averting his eyes as he opened it and thumbed through the pages.

Stabbing his finger on the last entry, he glanced up. "Of course there is a reasonable explanation for this last endorsement?"

Cool, calm, breathe easy. "Rightly or wrongly another in a position of authority adjudged my character, and all I can say in my defence is my immaturity will never be repeated. Of that I vow that, sir."

"Did you assault with a deadly weapon an officer or engineer, one of your fellow shipmates?"

"No. I made a bell rope."

"Bell rope?" Captain Hill rested back in his chair and folded his hands behind his head. "Amazing, please explain your side of this bell rope."

Clenching his hands to stop them shaking, his head lowered, he did in a voice he fought hard to keep from breaking.

"Under normal circumstances you would be wasting my time, but as you can see things are not what one would hope for in a world of disorder. Any prior bell rope character references?"

"No." Believing in God, he would have prayed.

"Then again I've never put much credence in references anyway, the bad ones you light the fire with, the good ones you use to dupe people in accepting you of pure and noble character. Old *Turbo's* many men short, and if I remember among all the chaos of yesterday some mention of someone's sterling character might have been made whose name I forget and truthfully couldn't care bloody less."

Looking up, he met the master's eyes.

Still with hands folded behind his head he resisted the temptation to put his feet on the desk, kick the mountain of paperwork on the deck and dream of calm and balmy seas. "When all this craziness is a bad memory and we can feel the old girl pounding away beneath us, I want a bell rope from you. Last time I looked our focastle head bell had a tatty rope yarn befitting her current status. Fail to impress me and I will know your story came direct from the focastle and I will never turn my back on you."

Gratitude filled him for the man sitting behind his cluttered desk with all the burdens of the docking bearing down on him. "Thank you, thank you."

"His voice a beacon among chaos, you'll find the bosun giving them hell in either the port or starboard wing tanks scaling rust where

The Chinese Seamen's Children

I pray to any listening deity there is not too much overzealousness, some spirited sailor putting his hammer through the old lady's hull. Later I will arrange your signing on, and be assured my memory is excellent."

Like so many seamen he had a false image of tankers, broad beamed ships pushing massive bow waves, so low in the water when loaded even flat seas engulfed their freeboard, their cluttered decks constantly awash. Their Persian Gulf ports brought to mind Arabian magic, the Caribbean tropical paradise, the United States industrial efficiency.

Reality emptied his mind of past misconceptions in an instance and assaulted it with a barrage of terminology that might well have been a foreign language, a stunning reversal of everything learned from a boy squaring up hatches and derricks. Almost fully recycled, this old tanker represented an entirely new world.

Descending a vertical ladder, he entered a subterranean world of artificial light eerily etching in dark and grotesque shadow ribs and web frames. Hot and fetid, a poisonous atmosphere no matter how thoroughly tank washed and vented, overpowering and nauseating even to the desensitised.

Spread between the ribs and web frames of the port wing tank seven men with scrapers and chipping hammers, wire brushes, bags of rags, buckets and scoops, laboured without respite. Their faces were protected with what may have been old bed sheets fashioned into crude full head and neck coverings, slits for eyes and mouths, all exposed skin except hands protected.

Growing panic relayed frantic signals to his legs and arms to not let go the ladder and step from the last rung, to flee this manmade hell; he sucked a toxic mixture of gas and metal particles rising from thick slabs of shattered rust into his lungs and joined his fellow seamen.

Demanded from the bosun bare metal wire brushed to a mirror

finish. Inspected by Tsui Shi, his eyes able to spot a blemish in paintwork at twenty feet, his acid tongue for slacking and bad work cutting to the bone.

Even the tiniest of pustules missed because of poor light sent the bow-legged, barrel-chested man into a fit of rage, threats of sacking and in extreme cases castration with his deck knife. Deafening noise dulled senses and eardrums in the first few minutes, above their heads, magnified a thousandfold in their steel confinement, pneumatic hammering.

Ingested oil residues mixed with a haze of rust and lead paints, even with their rudimentary face protection, settled like concrete in their lungs and stomachs, causing vomiting and a constant battle for breath. Tsui considered time off to vomit slacking, warranting a threat the unfortunate victim faced replacement by a pansy steward and rewarded for malingering with pumproom bilges. Some wondered if their lives could get any worse.

Each tank when close to being passed for painting, the confined space a forest of rickety bamboo poles lashed with rope yarn, Tsui's final scrutiny became an obsession not a square inch of prepared metal would escape his attention, an extreme fixation of demanding to see a seaman's face reflected in polished steel.

Fans sucking air from the tank failed dismally in their intended role, a thick blanket of deadly lead paint fumes settling among the bottom web frames. Rare for a man condemned by Tsui to the lower levels of the scaffolding not to have his lungs fail and his brain close down all functions, causing a disgruntled bosun to have him ingloriously hauled out of the tank by a set of sheerlegs. Fighting for his life did not excuse the barely conscious victim from work, a deck hose on standby with a full head of polluted Singapore harbour water a tried and proven method of revival.

Huang should have felt injustice, the safety of his life in jeopardy, a gruelling twelve-hour day in appalling conditions. Hours after knocking off hacking up the contents of his lungs, chest pains and excruciating headaches. Even calls of nature sent the bosun into a

The Chinese Seamen's Children

tantrum, a waste of precious time, a bucket in a corner hauled out the tank only when overflowing.

One force alone motivated him, gratitude for Captain Hill and home. Borrowing paper and a stamp he wrote a letter to Elsie of the voyage ahead sitting on his bunk in an open focastle he would share when fully manned with thirty-five other seamen.

Tsui, a brooding dynamo of a man, fascinated Huang, his seamanship without question as well as the obvious respect shown him by the officers. Stretched to his full height he barely reached Huang's shoulders. Lack of stature reflected no indication of the power and strength he packed into a frame of solid muscle, his fierce and intimidating scowl all the man needed to enforce his will and crush dissent. Huang admired him, a leader of men with allegiance to the Liverpool Chinese Seamen's Union.

Slow weeks passed with work progressing to the satisfaction of a still apprehensive Captain Hill and his officers, especially Tsui. Even so on deck, in the spaces and tanks, disorder never seemed to abate, continuous burning and welding resulting in freshly primed pipes, flanges, valves, ventilators, sheet steel, ribs and framing, the evidence teetering stacks of the gouged and decayed innards of the old ship under assault. Reduced to scrap metal, the dockyard workers seemingly reluctant to remove it as proof of their expertise, above all, proof of their herculean labours.

Dockyard management presented the fraught master an estimate for completion of work, four weeks.

Even with intolerable living conditions the officers, engineers and crew continued to live onboard. Not one single area on deck escaped the grit blasters and chipping machines, the aftermath of their onslaught a team of boilermakers with sheet steel patching gaping holes.

Huang kept his misgivings to himself about the substandard accommodation, tiers of iron bunks bolted to buckled ribs forming the flare of the bow, not a single adornment to give the open focastle a touch of humanity. Even with the docking not a true reflection, the accommodation could hardly be classified fit for seamen of any race. Port and starboard heads, two washbasins, six buckets, a seawater tap and a steam pipe. Admittedly the food passable, the money assuredly, £5/15/0 a month.

On the odd occasion speaking without a barrage of brusque orders and insults, Tsui ushered Huang aside after he crawled from a centre tank dry retching and forcing air into his lungs. "Are you a man who keeps his word?" he inquired in his throaty growl.

Fighting for breath, he managed a few garbled words: "What do you mean?"

"Our captain is a fair man, a man who has earned our respect. Captain Hill informs me you have a suspect reputation and he made a request of you."

Pincers gripping the base of his throat, he forced out three words: "Captain Hill did."

"Whatever your needs, ask. Captain Hill graciously gave you time, I do not. 0800 in the morning or slink down the gangway a liar."

Then he remembered, the windlass steam casings renewed, the windlass primed and painted a high gloss black; its first paint in years. Even though racked with pain he managed a smile, an old windlass with a new lease of life, someone even taking the time to polish the bell.

Replacing a tatty rope yarn a bell rope made by a seaman!

Shifted from the fitting out wharf to the floating dock for the applications of primers, topside, boot-topping and anti-fouling, dockyard management assured the master the ship working around the clock would be ready for sailing in five days.

During the early hours of the morning before entering the floating dock, now with a full complement, almost miraculously jagged and twisted piles of scrap steel vanished, welding and electrical leads, hoses and countless forty-four-gallon drums of rubbish. On turning

The Chinese Seamen's Children

to the crew with high pressure fire hoses washed three feet high drifts of rust and paint chippings, grit and rubbish into the harbour. After washing down eager hands breathing fresh air into their ravaged lungs followed with soogee wads and buckets, straw brooms and holystones.

Order finally restored and the sailing board hung by the gangway there remained only one job, the final layer of icing on the cake, the work purposely left for last; pots of paint, bosun's chairs, paint-brushes affixed to long bamboo poles, the *Turbo*'s funnel glowing in high gloss enamel. No more though than a bell rope of intricately knotted twine, coated also with company funnel paint, shackled to the focastle head bell, a fitting tribute to the craft of seamanship.

Even the most reluctant of detractors would admit the scope of the work and money spent worth it, the *Turbo* close to that one and only moment of perfection in a ship's life, the day she sails festooned with streamers from her builder's yard.

Floating free of her blocks, her boats swung out for boat drill, a tug standing off to secure at the break of the accommodation to swing compasses, a change of orders came from the breathless agent in a frantic dash to the dock. The *Turbo* would proceed to load in the Dutch East Indies for Melbourne, Australia, then in ballast to the Panama Canal for orders to load either in the Gulf of Mexico or the Caribbean for the United Kingdom.

Slow, barely raising nine knots with a feather fluttering at her funnel, her main engine guaranteed to fail every few days, drifting for long periods loaded to her marks with crude oil, the *Turbo* berthed in Williamstown. Sailing three days later in ballast with stores to last three months, evidence her chief steward, acting on advice from Captain Hill, little confidence of a fast Pacific passage. The *Turbo* wallowed her way on a general north-easterly course to Balboa, passed through the Panama Canal and received orders to proceed to Trinidad to load for a yet to be determined port in the United Kingdom, Atlantic convey arrangements to be announced.

Huang nervously calculated the months, his girl would be close, convincing himself every day he would make it by her side, a seaman homeward bound.

12

HUANG PAID OFF THE *Turbo* in Tilbury and caught the train from London to Liverpool, the last day of July doing little to instil confidence of a warm northern hemisphere summer, the city under barrage balloons supporting a dismal grey sky banked with scudding storm clouds. Even so the depressing weather failed to dampen the euphoria of homecoming, familiar voices overshadowing tense memories alone in the North Atlantic. Hours that seemed like days, days that felt like weeks, the *Turbo* breaking down with frightening regularity. Dead in the water wallowing helplessly in a low swell, an easy target for U-boats.

Nervous lookouts scouring the heaving seas and broken horizon, their heart rate lessening when 750 miles southwest of home waters the presence of HMS *Vanessa* among other convoy escorts instilled hope of survival and a joyous return home. The *Turbo*'s old and worn main engine gave an additional beat, more a weary thump, as the destroyer at full speed swept around her stern, ahead a fleet of ships low on the horizon, a westbound convoy about to lose its naval escort.

Failing to dampen his homecoming euphoria he wondered if the sun ever managed to break through and bathe the streets of Liverpool in its life-giving warmth, the collar of his watchcoat turned up around his ears to ward off the chill. According to alarmist authorities a godsend, the city on high alert the Luftwaffe planned to unleash its destructive forces on the city's docks and industrial areas.

Walking from the station through bustling streets, his heart beating rapidly with expectancy as he turned around a familiar corner, hurrying now as he neared the Keongs' home. How would his girl heavy in pregnancy look?

Knocking on the door, clouds of steam gushed from his mouth, listening to small footsteps in the hallway, the turning of a lock and the creaking of hinges. Her nose and upper lip almost touching, a child's pale face peered through an opening no wider than her head; a girl of nine with pigtails tied in red ribbons, one of a family of eight in the downstairs tenement.

She cocked her head and squinted suspiciously. "Are you with them, mister?"

Did she mean the Chinese family upstairs? "Yes."

Accepting his simple verification with more authority than her years engendered, she fully opened the door. At the head of the stairs a suppressed cry, in the gloom the ponderous shape of a woman taking one ungainly step after the other as she tried to hurry down the stairs.

"No, Elsie! I'm coming up!" he cried in alarm, his eyes fastened on the swelling that filled her maternity smock. Taking the stairs two at a time, his protective arms reached for her.

Blubbering, her lips searched frantically for his. "So certain I would never see you again …"

Standing at the bottom of the stairs the girl watched them with hooded eyes, her head near resting on her shoulder; she further screwed her face up until the upper lip blocked her nostrils and poked out her tongue.

"No more tears, Elsie. I am home."

"Only to go away again!"

The Chinese Seamen's Children

Where to hold first, where to kiss, where to touch, rubbing his nose in her wet cheek as he drew in the sweet scent of her. His Elsie in his arms! "My written words could never have told you the anguish I suffered separated from the girl I love. Never out of my mind, never for one moment. Your pain my pain, my girl frightened and away from her home because of me." Gently he extracted her from his arms, and then as if touching her might bring pain, traced his fingertips over her belly.

Kate, arms akimbo, smiled. "Eventually you sailors do find your way home," she said cheerily, trying to make light of the intensity. "Zhen, I kept trying to convince her seamen always do, that knowledge from a great deal of experience, I might add."

With a protective arm around her waist, he helped her up four steps to the landing. "Kate, has there been any difficulties with the pregnancy?"

"We have seen grumpy old Dr Jones three times and he reckons your Elsie's a natural mother-to-be. Another few weeks he'll be proved right."

"Kate, Kate, thank you so much. Words cannot express my gratitude to you and Chong. Is he home?" As if in his hands he held a priceless object of fragile art, he eased her down on the bed next to the kitchen table, settling beside her and nestling her in his arms.

"Last letter I got from Abadan said hopefully he might be home in a few months for an overdue docking and repairs."

"Tankers are tramps as you well know, unlike Alfred Holt in the liner trade. How have you and the boys managed with another in your home?"

"Our boys love her, we all do."

"Kate, what of her parents?"

"Rarely does a day pass when it doesn't bring tears. She tries to hide them, but she never can." She looked around the room with a sigh. "Haven't we enough troubles in this world not to add our own to make our lives more miserable?"

Elsie might have been asleep in the protective warmth of his arms.

Kate whispered: "She doesn't go out now. Upturned noses and sniggers from those she once called friends. I tell her to ignore them, hold your head up high you have nothing to be ashamed of. Your man loves you and your child, that's what matters, nothing else."

"Kate, we can never repay your kindness."

"Zhen, we are family, a big family really. More and more of us, but forget that, there is a list of things she will need when her time comes. Packed in a small suitcase and left at the head of the stairs. She is close, very close."

So quiet the creaking of a loose floorboard as he made Elsie her tea caused him to pause in mid-step, afraid of disturbing Kate and her boys sleeping close by. Elsie occupied the entire single bed; he slept on the floor, wakened when she craved a milky tea with sugar.

Sitting ponderously at the table with her tea she cried out with excitement, lumbering up from her chair to grab his hand and press it against her side; a moment later another hard kick. "Our little boy is welcoming home his dad," she said, a lilt in her voice that gave him a sense of pleasure the months of despair she had endured were buried in the past.

"Does he—or she—do that all the time?"

"Oh yes, all the time. Kate is certain I will go early. Not a she, Zhen, our baby is a darling little boy just like his big dad."

"How could you know that?"

"Mothers-to-be know these things, like a kind of instinct. Anyway Kate said she has three sons and I am carrying the same. Enormous, a lot of noise and much kicking of his mum's tummy. It's a boy, a boy for his proud dad. Might even get to play for Liverpool the way he kicks."

"Now wouldn't that stir the some hackles in the local pubs."

"What do you mean?"

"Our son wouldn't quite exactly fit the mould."

"What a thing to say about our son," she said indignantly.

"Not being derogatory, far from it. Our baby will be both you and me, he or she can't escape that. Whatever precious bundle we hold in our arms we can be assured our little one will be special, who one day will make a mark on the world. If a girl she will inherit the beauty and charm of her mother. My contribution I think we'll leave in abeyance."

She pouted. "Ugly mother."

"My girl is beautiful, and if you didn't resemble a beached whale and with room on that bed I would prove how desirable you are."

"By making love to me?"

"Devouring you. It has been so long."

"For me, too. Wanting you beside me, holding me."

"Making love?"

"Oh yes. Kate says we'll have to wait after the birth for me to heal."

"Did she say how long?"

"Months."

"Months!"

She blushed. "Kate said there are other ways."

"What would we ever do without our Kate?"

Hidden, the sun speared a narrow footprint of intense light through scudding clouds, bathing the young couple sitting on the park bench in a false sense of warmth. Both were rugged up snug, a woollen scarf wrapped around Elsie's neck and a thick beanie pulled tight over her ears.

When asked for advice on marriage procedures, Kate shyly admitted she and Keong had never bothered to legitimise their union.

"Legitimise, that sounds awful, Kate."

"Fancy bit piece of paper does not a marriage make, though most of the Chinese we know are legally married. Elsie being under twenty-one would probably need parental consent."

Raising the subject of parental consent, Elsie withdrew into herself, stared at her huge belly and started crying.

"Kate says parental consent for a girl underage is law," he said desperately.

"Then we wait until I am of age."

"Three years!"

"Kate says when the baby is born all we need do is register with the government. That's all we need to do, nothing else."

"Elsie, I want to marry you. No argument. No excuses."

Sniffing loudly, she wiped her nose with the small lace handkerchief she habitually tucked up the sleeve of her baggy cardigan. "Father will never give his blessing."

"Maybe being pregnant might circumvent the law, the requirement of consent. Elsie, we need to find out."

"How?"

"Kate doesn't know she will know someone who can advise us."

Of indisputable bureaucratic importance behind his oak and polished brass counter, the superintendent registrar at the general register office did well to conceal his contempt for the overawed bit of young skirt clinging to the young Chinaman's arm. Her advanced pregnancy and company obvious proof of her preference in regards to sexual liaisons. Regarding the Chinaman, no doubt in his mind a seaman among a growing number besmirching his office, would of course claim paternal responsibility and use the slattern as a means to advance his claim for British citizenship.

Huang took an instant dislike to the man, his thin grey hair swept back over his high forehead, a sour set to his pasty face.

"Both parties will require the appropriate documentation, the girl's birth certificate proof the party has attained the age of eighteen years. Underage a consent form must be attached, completed and signed by both parents." Obvious working class, underage, poorly educated, an easy mark for the hordes of Chinese plaguing Merseyside streets for prostitutes and others of easy virtue.

"Elsie is eighteen," Huang said with relief, slumping against the counter and grinning at Elsie.

"Nonetheless, proof of age is required," the superintendent register said in a flat monotone, fully convinced the union no more than a sham marriage to circumvent immigration laws, its by-product the unfortunate conception of issue. "My office will require proof of names from passports or documents of identity, birth certificates, addresses of permanent abodes, occupation and nationality. Finally, you both must have lived in the district seven days."

Alien card. Document of identity. Discharge book. Mrs Hogan's Liverpool address. Looking at Elsie he knew immediately the meaning of her crestfallen face. "Birth certificate is home, right?"

Blowing her nose noisily, she crossed her legs, the need to relieve her bladder causing discomfort. Waddling to a long wooden side bench set against the wall, she sat down fighting back tears.

"We will have what you need in the morning. Can we be married then?"

"Documentation in original form and not tampered with, no legal reason why not. I am of the mind you are not a British citizen, seaman perhaps?" he said scathingly as he reached under the desk for the forms.

"Chinese parents born in Singapore. Yes, seaman."

"Which of course necessitates the British government issuing you an alien card?"

"My documentation is in order."

Devious young buck would have plentiful advice from his fellow scheming Chinese. Following the same nefarious path to gain United Kingdom citizenship, arranged marriages using hussies freely available on the streets. Would it further his cause when his use to the United Kingdom no longer existed, the war successfully concluded? He sincerely hoped not, others of a similar train of thought extreme and politically courageous measures would need to be taken to correct any future imbalances due to the excessively large numbers of foreign seamen essential for the war effort. First and foremost those manipulative individuals and their cohabiting strumpets who debased the sacredness of marriage.

Choosing to go alone, he knocked nervously on the door with the hope the man whose bent fingers partly drew back the glass panel curtain might fulfil a wish dreamed by his daughter and offer him her hand and his blessing.

Arthritic fingers fumbled with locks and catches before the shrunken frame of a man dressed in a tightly knotted dressing gown appeared in the doorway. "Don't want any," he rasped, clearing his throat of phlegm. "See them next door! Be off with you now!"

"Mr Smith, I wish with your permission to speak for your daughter. My name is Huang Zhen and Elsie and I are to be married. I need her birth certificate."

Mr Smith reached in the top pocket of his bathrobe for his spectacles, put them on and drew back with a snarl. Chinaman! All of them foreign devils looked the same though this one had a certain familiarity. Elsie! Stuffed with kiddie, all the neighbourhood laughing in his face! Seething with rage and about to slam the door shut, a frail woman appeared beside him, pushing him aside to look up into Huang's face.

"How is our dear Elsie?" she said in a quavering voice. "I do pray she is all right?"

"Your daughter misses you, Mrs Smith," he said, resisting the temptation to reach out and touch her. "Elsie and I are to be married, she needs her birth certificate."

Then the woman turned to her husband with firm resolve in her face and courage in her voice. "Archibald Smith, you are an ungodly man to denounce your daughter, our flesh and blood. Give him what

The Chinese Seamen's Children

he wants and grant our Elsie a chance to hold her head up without shame."

Consumed with rage, he wheezed air into his lungs, expelling it in whistle-like gasps between his teeth. "Get inside with you, woman! Top drawer of the bureau is rubbish I intended flushing down the lavatory! Damn all Chinamen!"

Attached to Elsie's birth certificate with a bobby pin a colourful card caught Huang's eye; a helmeted knight in chainmail armour standing fully erect, both hands resting on the hilt of a broad sword planted between his parted legs. Elsie's Church of England baptismal certificate.

Huang and Elsie exchanged vows two days later, their reception a bottle of raspberry cordial and a shared cream bun in the park, their honeymoon him sleeping on the floor with his seabag a pillow that grew more comfortable with each day.

Finding a home confronted the young couple with almost insurmountable problems, the choices few and most on offer within their small rental range rejected outright until desperation lowered their standards. Crumbling masonry and corroded iron lacework, evidence of years of landlord neglect, ignored in the excitement of entering their first home even if only four small rooms in a street of identical tenements.

No one had bothered to clean up after the last tenants departed with what seemed obvious haste, newspapers on the floor littered with dried food scraps; a distinct acidic odour of urine, certainly a cat or cats. Blackened pots and encrusted plates tossed in a porcelain sink badly stained with rust did little to raise Huang's enthusiasm of a home suitable for his wife and child. More troubling, aside from the stench of animals, a sickly sweet presence of gas.

Above their heads watermarked plaster sagged, speckled with mould, posing a serious health risk, failed plumbing. Something else both found difficult to refrain from, test with a fingertip walls smeared with a residue of fat and rising damp. To do so would definitely influence their decision to sign the lease agreement, so desperate their need for a home.

Boasted by the landlord as substantial and valuable, a double bed with an additional mattress, the old not dumped in the streets as it should have been but used as a base for its second-hand replacement. Crudely repaired a kitchen table with mismatched legs, four rickety chairs, a chest of drawers missing the bottom drawer and sofa with prominent springs about to burst through the worn upholstery. Quality furnishing added 2/6 a week to the rent, damage justifying professional repairs or replacement at full cost to the tenant. Elsie agreed with her husband, the furnishings came from the yard of Mr Herbert.

Then again, easing his bride across the threshold, he thought with an open window, carbolic and paint, it would be liveable. Also close to Kate and four other women married to Chinese seamen. Under the weight of Elsie's extra pounds, the sofa creaked, a worn spring threatening to burst through the badly stained fabric.

Unable to avoid the subject any longer, he took hold of both her hands and asked her about the Chinese families.

She remained silent for a long time before replying. "Kate is the only one I know."

"Have you tried to make friends? There are a lot of women with Chinese husbands."

"Some awful people are saying our Liverpool boys are fighting the war while the cowardly Chinese stay at home to have their will with the wives and sweethearts left behind."

"Those lies are not new. So easy to ridicule and ignore Chinese, British and allied seamen are dying at sea. That the Chinese are fighting a scourge that will one day turn upon the United Kingdom with the same vengeance as Germany."

"Zhen, it hurts. Kate tells me some of these women are working three jobs to make ends meet, those with larger families to provide for. Good women."

The Chinese Seamen's Children

"Mothers and wives the innocent victims of malicious lies bred in the infantile minds of bigots! No woman should face condemnation and abuse because she chose to share her life with a man adjudged by racial purists as inferior."

Resting her chin on her chest, she never replied.

"Hardworking women and innocent children suffering a life of denunciation. Aren't we all human beings? Right this moment are we not fighting for the same cause? Do people make you walk in the gutter when passing in the street?"

"No!"

"Well, let's hope your good fortune holds. When you are wheeling our baby you will not be forced to genuflect so as to allow unimpeded passage to the high and mighty, the racially pure."

"Kate said it is jealously."

"She may be right. By what I hear most Chinese husbands don't spend their time in the pub with their mates. Or fit the role of the wife basher when the meal is not on the table the moment the master staggers through the door."

"Their boys find it difficult at school with bullies."

"Of course their boys do. Chong and Kate's courteous and respective kids are different only on the outside, not inside where it counts. Wrong of me, so wrong to expose you to this bigotry."

"... you don't love me?" she said, her voice almost a whisper.

"Our marriage, not my love in question," he said abruptly.

Then as if a knife blade twisted inside her belly she threw herself back and screamed.

Almost immediately another contraction gripped her, and at that moment her water broke. Frantically he tried to remember Kate's advice, a drill she made him commit to memory. Somewhere a small packed suitcase, confused in his mind a kind offer from a neighbour to drive them to the hospital depending on rationed petrol, but not to worry he would have some put aside. Above all do not panic.

When Edward Huang entered the world, his cries were drowned out by the deafening roar of aircraft engines overhead. The date on the calendar in their home marked the day August 28th and Liverpool from this day onwards would not only grieve its war and sea dead, it would now mourn the smouldering soul of a city called home.

13

ON THE NEXT THREE nights the Luftwaffe bombed Merseyside. Liverpool, Birkenhead, Prenton, Wallasey and Walton, streets where only hours before children's shrill voices rang and people gossiped, reduced to rubble, partitioning walls free standing like pastel painted buttes, teetering brick facades defying gravity.

Raging, uncontrollable fires completed the devastation. With nothing left to burn now smouldering ruins, the tombs of men, women and children. Feelers of white smoke rising eerily in silent streets. Baffling phenomenon confused already numbed minds, a single dwelling of no particular structural integrity saved from obliteration while all around lay in ruins.

Sound planning logic lay behind the enemy's strategy to target Liverpool; docks, railways, heavy industrial. Against all reasoning the blitz gained limited but highly visible success. With each bomb and incendiary that shrieked out of the sky Merseyside unerringly grew in strength, its people from all tiers of society linking their lives to overcome adversity.

People rallied with a grim determination, going about their daily routines ignoring rubble blocked streets, blackened and twisted steel, teetering brick walls, toys and dolls with missing heads, shreds of clothing like tiny flags fluttering from ruptured water pipes and reinforcing.

Huang felt the pulse of the people in the streets and it stirred him, made him feel accepted and part of this rare breed of people. Not another race or creed, the feeling with every breath, every heartbeat, this old city would with each bomb dropped from the sky grow in strength.

Like wildfire a truly British spirit of defiance spread throughout the nation. If the fascist hordes with their pagan banners and rituals, jackboots and raised arms salutes, stepped on hallowed British soil, the Luftwaffe blotting out the sun, the Kriegsmarine supreme in the Channel, the British to the last man, woman and child, would be waiting.

Roads would not be clogged with endless streams of pitiable refugees, children in hand, chattels tied in bundles. No one would flee for the word surrender, their great and omnipotent leader berated over and over, no definition existed in the English language. With the determination of a people spawned from great historic warriors the enemy would writhe eternally in hell, their graves the cold waters from whence their ungodly forces emerged.

Huang and Elsie's home survived the blitz, as did the Keongs', Mr Gresham's shop and Elsie's parents. Urgency drove him now with a wife and child to support, even overcoming the fear of leaving them alone with Liverpool a target for German bombers; he would have to ship out. Buoyed by a good discharge from the *Turbo* he held high hopes the precious entry would temper close scrutiny in the office of Alfred Holt.

Ninety percent of war materiel entered the United Kingdom through Merseyside, and even with a new influx of Chinese from Hong Kong, Shanghai and Singapore, the prospects of work remained good. Still he felt nervous when he registered, surprised when the clerk made no comment on the entries in his discharge book. Name and alien card number recorded, he wondered what the disinterested man would note if he knew of his joining the Communist Party of the United Kingdom the day before.

The Chinese Seamen's Children

Next day on presenting himself to the same clerk, he received instructions to present himself to the shipping superintendent to join the *Asphalion*.

14

September 1941

HUANG, SIGNED OFF AFTER four months on the *Rhexenor*, reflected with Elsie the horrendous toll inflicted by the Luftwaffe on Merseyside. The May Blitz, still a weeping wound that refused to heal, took the lives of 1700, adding to the horror on the third day of the same month the explosion of the *Malakand* in Huskisson Dock. Though the docks and industrial complexes were the primary targets, bombing of neighbourhoods where the working class of industry dwelled offered alternatives equally as good. Subjecting Merseyside to sleepless nights huddled in damp and cold shelters, returning next morning to homes that no longer existed, distressed and whimpering dogs searching for lost owners buried under rubble.

Edward on wobbly legs managed his first step, his active mind and gentle disposition bringing the utmost joy to his parents. Allowed to test his newfound mobility in the park so if he fell, which he did with regularity, he would not hurt himself on the grass. Spread on a colourful check blanket fish and chips wrapped in newspaper became a family treat, steaming hot and soaked in malt vinegar.

Throughout the park nothing seemed to have changed. People still laughed, sang and argued, greeted with passion and hugged each other. Imbued with an unconquerable gene some said and most agreed, With so many homes destroyed their modest abode might

The Chinese Seamen's Children

well have been a palace among streets of rubble, now with a definite homely touch with Elsie's inspirational touches. She hung her newly painted walls with soft animals secured with drawing pins, hers and Edward's fairytale land, certain the toys talked to Edward at night.

Edward's cot and the toys came from Mr Herbert's before its obliteration, now no more than a large smouldering crater, the junkyard and its decrepit dwelling erased from the face of the earth. Luck held for its inebriated owner carried comatose into the pub's cellar when the sirens sounded.

She dreaded the long separations, nights the worst with her longings a leaden weight in her chest. Kate's support never faltered, always close at hand. She would ease the despair of loneliness with positive words such as her man would be home on a certain date and to mark it on the calendar. On that day she should prepare herself as only a woman could. Take her man into her bed and in offering herself take the initiative. Always hers to give love, the joining of bodies a never-ending joy. To languish in love again and again.

Both she and Kate never spoke of the dangers their menfolk faced at sea, as if ignoring it the danger would cease to exist. Even so it became more difficult to shut from her mind when women in the neighbourhood married to men at sea openly cried in the street.

Using her imagination to escape the loneliness she dreamed of the future, sometimes her mind so detached from reality she bumped into people in the street. Visions of a home with a white picket fence and a riot of colour in spring when her dormant bulbs burst into new life. Roses bloomed in wild profusion, her lawn often mistaken for a lush carpet. Her Zhen played a leading role in the fantasy, leaving early for work and home in the afternoon, his job of no importance except he came home each day. Edward with a small yard to play in, cleanse his lungs with air not contaminated by leaking gas mains and smoke rising from the ruins of Liverpool.

She could almost taste the chunky braised steak, simmering on the stove, boiled potatoes and minted green peas grown in her garden, dinner for her family. Reliving her dream one afternoon an elderly woman stopped her in the street and asked if she could take a peep at the baby snuggled in its pram.

Wrinkled and puckered, her leathery face creased even more with distaste as she drew back the blue bunny rug from the sleeping child's face; cherubic red lips formed tiny bubbles that burst with each breath. "Foreign blood there, girl?"

"My husband is Chinese."

Black pouches of pooled blood cushioned her beady eyes; she peered closer, curling her thin lips over bare gums. "Those foreign devils breed like rabbits."

She cried that time.

Edward attracted attention, a pretty child, the mixture of blood only slightly discernible around the eyes, more notably his black, spiky hair; the little boy's smile a delight to behold, his chuckle a melody to the ears.

Huang husband noticed changes in his wife, blossoming motherhood. Bearing a child had given her a fuller figure, a satiny skin with hardly a blemish. Even her hair normally frizzy and hard to manage grew luxuriant, framing her heart shaped face in a lustre of curls.

Commenting she countered he should have been born Irish, full of the blarney, but she cherished his flattering words and later with Edward in his cot for an afternoon nap their lovemaking would seem even more fulfilling.

Hsien Wu and Liang Tao, Liang recently paid off the *Sarpedon*, called a meeting of the executive of the Liverpool Chinese Seamen's Union in the cramped union rooms once a storeroom and workshop in an old warehouse in Dingle, an invitation extended to Huang to attend as a rank and file delegate; Hsien's signature seconded Huang's Communist Party membership.

Sitting with the high profile executive of the union he felt an honour, a privilege not offered to many, but listening to their deliberations aggravated him with its repetition.

"Wage parity with British seamen is no further advanced than prior the war, a contagion we naively thought would add to our bargaining power. Our claim for the war risk bonus is stymied continuously, ignored by politicians in the Labour camp who avoid our overtures it is not in their power to have the payment passed on."

Old and tired arguments raised again and again, Huang thought, the gulf between Chinese and British growing even wider with wage increases paid with little resistance from the shipowners.

"Union officials meet in meaningful discussions with government and shipowners and plead do not we share the same dangers as British nationals? Can you refute that our work is not equal to that of British nationals? For our wasted breath we receive no answers and our members grow more agitated on their ships and threaten industrial action of which I fully concur. More spent words to politicians and government we are not aliens in your country, we are serving the British Empire of which we are a part. Are not Singapore and Hong Kong stained in the same red ink as South Africa, Australia, Canada and India?"

Hsien requested Huang to remain behind after the meeting. From a pot of green tea he poured two small porcelain cups.

"Are you married, Zhen?"

Nodding, he winced; the tea, boiling hot, burned the tip of his tongue.

"It pains me greatly to say this but your wife would have been more fortunate if she had remained unmarried," he said, not taking his eyes off him.

"Why would you say such a thing, Wu?"

"Please, do not take offence at my words. Your wife has made an excellent choice of partner, I refer to something insidious." Hsien paused, carefully choosing his next words. "Do you realise with your vows your wife has now your status in the land of her birth? She is an alien?"

"My wife is British. Our son is British."

"Granted, but the British government thinks otherwise."

"No government can take away a person's birthright!"

"Governments in extreme emergencies can and do enact whatever it foresees is in the best interests of the nation at war. Entering into the sanctity of marriage the wife and all issue produced of that union are now legally the status of the husband, the same conditions of residency given Chinese seamen in Liverpool."

"My wife has no alien card. She can never be issued an alien card because she is British!"

"Your wife would have received her card in the mail a few weeks after the wedding."

"Elsie would have told me …" his words trailed off as he racked his mind; had she told him and he had forgot? Impossible!

"By a freak chance she may have slipped under someone's blotter in the bureaucracy, but she is a registered alien, Zhen. That is the law of the British government at war."

"Elsie and Edward aliens in their own land, that's insane. What can happen to her and Edward?"

"Liverpool women who marry Chinese forfeit their birthright of British citizenship, as simple as that. What can happen to her and your son? You can well ask what does the future hold for all of us. Who knows what a victorious United Kingdom will do when our services are no longer required in a national emergency, when a large surplus of seamen has to be culled by any expedient means."

"How can the British Government do this? Even war cannot excuse those freely elected enacting laws we would expect from the enemy, a regime enforcing their will with brutal suppression of freedom."

Hsien agreed. "For want of a better description we are a naval force of seamen at war directly under the control of the Ministry of War, a military arm of government not only administrating the war but with directives to oversee the peace when victory is achieved. When the bands fall silent, the banners and flags are furled and stored away, the government will have a large number of foreign seamen to deal with. Consider your armies at peace and those not required for occupation returning from war. Hundreds of thousands of demobbed men and women with two major hopes, home and reunion with loved ones, the second a promise by a grateful government of jobs.

"Chinese seamen who have made their lives in the United Kingdom and served at sea in war share the same hopes. Newspapers with no sensational headlines to print will editorialise post-war promised prosperity is not be the blessing we fought and died for. Machines of war will be geared for peace, production a mere fraction of war output. There will be no boom many talk of after the war, it will be a dog fight for jobs, a government swamped with the unemployed demanding answers what did the nation fight for?

"Zhen, there will be no favouritism for Chinese seamen domiciled in Liverpool after the war. Also there will be a need for a lesser number of Chinese on British ships, similar for Arabs, Indians and Senegalese. Still financially viable to cram into open focastles, but written in the blackest of ink in the articles of agreement homeports Asia. Then eventually in the economic cycle there will come a time when even we are deemed too expensive and British boardrooms will look elsewhere."

"So until the war ends we are hailed heroes, our sacrificial contribution to the nation lauded by government?"

"Aptly put, yes. Come war's end Chinese seamen and their families will be deported to China and the war weary British flocking to their pubs to toast victory and the saviour of freedom and democracy, Prime Minister Winston Churchill."

"My wife and son are not aliens!"

"Victory to be achieved in war, a population is forced to surrender every basic right of humanity without a single murmur of dissent, an act of total submission that in times of peace would have had enraged mobs hammering down the doors of parliament. To wage and win war the deliberations of the governments of the United Kingdom and Germany differ little where human rights are concerned, even though one is democratic and the other fascist. Then again I am being harsh on the British government when Germany's ascension to Nazism came only by the murder of union officials, Communists and those certified racially impure and sub-human. While there is a national need for our services and our sacrifice we will be welcomed by the flag waving populace, invited to stand as equals beside war heroes with chests bedecked in medals. Like all sane men I crave for peace, and though it is a contradiction in terms, I am not looking forward to it."

Huang's mounting anger flared in his eyes.

"Some solace can be taken in what will happen in the United Kingdom, with the exception of the Communist world, will be little different from other nations . Our leaders no different from those who have gained power through propaganda, mass hysteria, the point of a gun, lies, coup, and in the name God."

Huang had no words to refute Hsien's bleak analogy.

Hsien continued, not about the fate of his fellow Chinese, but the war. "Peace may be a long way off, the conflict escalating until the carnage reaches a point where even the most insensitive of minds will begin to wonder the wisdom of sending humankind into an orgy of killing. It may even resort to the unthinkable where those who hold humanity in their grasp will agree to the premise the last man standing in his trench, or if there are none the last worker fuelling the mayhem, be declared the winner.

"World leaders and their financial supporters can then return to accruing peaceful wealth. In the name of freedom and democracy creating a litany of lies a workers paradise can only be achieved with the crushing of the union movement, in effect the worker's only voice. Oh yes, those who control and manipulate will spread their sweet syrup, trust us because we have only your interest to heart in our corporate mission. Ignore the bleating repetitive voices of unions promoting confrontation, dissent, strike, sabotage and slow work.

"Cynical, yes. Biased, yes, but unfortunately that is how I envisage the world with sincere hopes time will prove me wrong. Zhen, we are mere pawns on a world stage. We will fight, we will make our voices heard, but in the clear light of day it will be government policy

The Chinese Seamen's Children

that will defeat us. Policy enacted by those who fear us."

Huang's mind spun out of control, a desire to crush underfoot a world of defined boundaries ruled by the colour of a man's skin.

"Excuse my defeatism, who really knows what the future holds. How the spoils will be divided and how benevolent the government of the United Kingdom will be to those who survive the raiders and battleships, torpedoes and mines, at mast level the Luftwaffe."

Elsie felt a huge relief with the onset of her period; there would be time for more children when the world returned to normalcy. Often her thoughts wandered, of falling pregnant when she and Huang made love. Their bodies had created a child that first time, but now she seemed safeguarded from a natural course of events which should have been otherwise with the frequency of their lovemaking.

Edward with a brother or sister would be nice, but not yet. With the war over and the world at peace and her husband safe.

Huang, unusually quiet on his return from the union meeting, kissed Edward on the forehead asleep in his cot, then without a word stretched full length on the bed and stared at the ceiling. Concerned, she lay beside him and rested her arm across his chest.

"Zhen, have I said something to annoy you?"

Turning on his side, he faced her. "What do you mean?"

"You came in the door and looked right through me."

"Elsie, I have done a terrible wrong to you and Edward."

She tensed. "Zhen, the love we share is not wrong."

"Not our love, our marriage."

"No!" She struggled to sit up; he restrained her, his face only inches from hers.

"Elsie, I would marry you a thousand times over!" he beseeched, his grasp on her shoulder causing her to cry out in pain. "Understand this, because of marriage you and Edward have lost your birthright!"

"Zhen, I know."

"What do you know?"

"Some weeks after you sailed a letter from the government arrived in the post," she said softly, a sharp intake of breath as he increased pressure on her shoulder.

"Why didn't you tell me?"

"Because you would be angry and have words with the authorities and be deported."

Releasing her, he sat on the edge of the bed and held his head in his hands. "We die every day at sea under the red duster. For what, to support a system rotten to the core. Chinese sweat and muscle nothing but a submissive commodity for accountants to gloat over, our wages so low the shipowners can double, even triple, our numbers compared to British manning. Now our families are forced to suffer as we do. Read history and it is there for all to witness, nothing has changed for a hardworking race, muscle and sinew to be used and then discarded. Ask me to choose between Churchill and Hitler? I do not know."

15

December 1978

ALLOCATED TO PORT KEMBLA from the Melbourne pickup and three months on the Broken Hill Proprietary Limited's 38,000 ton *Iron Kestrel*, Alex experienced a feeling of accomplishment as he felt the gangway swing with a large rebound into the side of the ship stepping on the wharf. South Wharf, Melbourne, home with articles closed the previous midnight.

Time passed quickly, two coastal trips from Newcastle and Port Kembla to Kwinana with steel, back loading pig iron and pellets for Port Kembla. While on the *Iron Kestrel* he made a decision even his shipmates argued the height of folly, a transfer from Melbourne to the bastion of industrial anarchy and Iron-boats, Port Kembla.

One simple reason, long leaves accrued on Iron-boats the motivation. Three months articles on the *Iron Kestrel* earned almost ten weeks leave.

With a seabag of working gear and tote bag waiting for a taxi, he looked up at his home for the last three months, her coils of wire and plastic wrapped automotive steel already cluttering the wharf, no regrets at paying off even though for an Iron-boat a good job. Support from a union conscious crew, a strong willed bosun who ran the job fairly and competently within the restrictive constraints of BHP's rigid and at time virulent industrial policies.

Past remembrance of the steelmaker's intractable industrial officers in Newcastle and Port Kembla left a lasting disagreeable taste. As a delegate having to deal with university graduated industrial officers indoctrinated in BHP dogma of biblical proportions, memories steeped in frustration and futility.

Some industrial officers not yet fully programmed, immaculate in grey dustcoats and dazzling white hard hats, admitted most of the difficulties dealing with the maritime division of the company could be accredited to being bundled in the mass of complicated and multiple steelworks awards. Two opposing mentalities were continually at odds, the BHP board charged to maximise shareholders dividends and the unions submerged in worker sweat which made huge profits possible for the idle few.

Both sides with a concrete bunker mentality also proved a drawback, allowing no room for manoeuvring, easing the rules and softening the rigidity of BHP and union policy. BHP appealed to pandering governments, industrial courts and a favourable media, it carried an unacceptable burden on its broad shoulders dealing with seven maritime unions. Standing dominant at the top of this pile of dissent, the most rabid and volatile, the Communist dominated Seamen's Union of Australia, a fanatical organisation with a psychopathic hatred for the company and the modest returns on investment it paid its shareholders.

BHP's first officers would have been more comfortable turning to a docile crew of Lascars or Filipinos, their reference guide written in large print in the BHP interpreted seamen's award book, a tome according to the Seamen's Union of Australia carried snugly in the back pocket of every BHP first officer. Both the master and the chief officer through long experience knew that to give a chink of light to this contumacious union could be likened to switching on the floodlights of a sporting field. Always hovering in the background like vultures, ready to pounce and devour at the first sign of weakness or breach of the award. On any flimsy industrial or political pretext, holding a ship to ransom while their hierarchy of commissars decided how better to attack the bottom line of the company's accounts.

The Chinese Seamen's Children

Life at the top of the maritime division of BHP could be multifarious, from lowly apprentice through the ranks of deck officers to master, junior engineers to chief engineers, even to the supreme, marine superintendent. Demanded from the pinnacle of management full and unconditional adherence to all seven seagoing awards. Non-compliance by managerial staff meant severe reprimand, for unforgivable transgressions, disloyalty on the top of a long list, dismissal.

Command demanded a rigid fortitude when dealing with seamen and engine room delegates, firemen in rank smelling flannels and stokehold boots. Alcohol saturated breaths, dripping oil and grease on the carpet, in the coarsest terms and vulgarity expounding their worldly views of current political events. Of world shattering importance which necessitated sticking up the vessel for twenty-four hours so their members could march chanting in the streets with hammer and sickle banners held aloft.

In these disagreeable circumstances utmost calm became an asset, essential a profound knowledge of the navigation act and the lawful procedures mandatory to log the crew on tidal movements or every four hours according to the posting of the sailing board. Stand firm and fearless in protecting company resources from union demands, the ability to successfully arbitrate disputes in the company's best interest. Resolve requisitions conjured in the devious minds of union schemers, demands for the issue of a glass of fruit juice each day when company vessels crossed the Tropic of Capricorn, lobster salads, smoked salmon, instant coffee, crumpets, chocolate biscuits, bread rolls, and six movies a trip instead of four. Tropical days when the temperature caused a delegate to wipe his brow of a light sheen of sweat.

Fortunately on the *Iron Kestrel* the only disputation a few grumbles, the three months almost enjoyable, though a trip to Hong Kong and the Philippines, the ship's normal run, would have been acceptable.

Among three months mail a letter with a British stamp postmarked Liverpool caught his attention. Edward asked would he give some thought of taking one of his ridiculously long leaves in the United Kingdom, possibly around May when the weather might be suitable for an Aussie who boasted of endless summers. Alex reread the letter, an idea forming in his mind; Dampier, Port Hedland, Hay Point, Newcastle, Port Kembla, Japan, ideal for accruing long leaves on the iron ore and coal run.

When he thought about it his deep sea experience over the years only amounted to sailing in two oceans. The *Iranda* bulk sugar Townsville to Auckland, chartered for seven trips. Nauru and Christmas Island. The *Iron Wyndham* steel for Hong Kong and Manila. Memorable under the command of one of BHP's most detested masters, an ex-AB super militant held in high regard by union officials. Even when studying for his ticket his militant façade held firm, an intrepid delegate, Sydney branch officials even considering him among a select few to represent the union at a Moscow trade union conference. Moving up the ranks, or as his victims and those forced to suffer his obnoxious presence cynically observed, crawling and sliming his way to the top, finally four gold bars adorned his intimidating breadth of shoulders and the true man emerged.

Elected delegate he forgot when a day passed without an order to stand before the master's desk and listen to his harangue of the union, the union sabotaging the financial bottom line of the company in overseas voyaging knocking off one minute early. He thought he might be the casualty of a trip too many in the tropics, a manic obsession for bilges on the lightship leg of the voyage to Yampi Sound to load iron ore. Adorned in his immaculately pressed khakis, attached four gold bars to remind those soaked in vomit inducting bilge sludge of his illustrious rank, he pressed his overly large nose mere inches from cleaned strum boxes and hessian wrapped cover plates, condemning them for whatever reason filled his hate generated brain.

Sailing with Newcastle and Port Kembla seamen he supposed hardened him to the ceaseless struggle to maintain conditions

The Chinese Seamen's Children

achieved at great cost with loggings, sackings and suspensions. More importantly, to become active and vocal at stop work meetings formulating policies to keep the union on course and combat substandard third world shipping threatening Australian jobs. At rowdy shipboard and stop work meetings there might have been a lack of finesse, but when it came to tying up a ship in extreme weather situations no better seamen existed, or squaring up hatches and tween decks with hundreds of iron ore impregnated hatch boards no more difficult than the pampered who dropped a MacGregor hatch lid with the tap of a hammer.

Tempting, a visit to the United Kingdom.

Laurie Moorland dithered like a mother hen fussing her constantly scattering chicks, Alex's next-door neighbour and his meticulous collector of mail. She worried about him, his comings and goings at odd hours, his long absences, even though she knew he sailed on those ships in the bay. Being a nesting type, she lamented a home needed a woman's touch, not deadlocked doors and shuttered windows.

Neighbours did not describe the Moorlands aptly, more close and sharing friends, honest and trusting country folk. Laurie at least twice a week honed her baking skills with fruit pies, scones and lamingtons, without fail a knock on his back door and a plate covered with a tea towel.

Her sister moved to Auckland after marrying a New Zealander, rearing two girls only to having the youngest recently move to Australia, working as a barmaid in the Bonbeach Hotel. Laurie opined, of course not interfering because Alex might have a romantic interest in those exotic places he disappeared to for long periods, but with his monastic-like existence and the stark absence of a feminine influence in the home, he might like to meet Roxanne.

Try as he could his persuasive powers failed, pleading an excessive number of eligible young women in Sydney, Newcastle and Port

Kembla begged for his company, all to no avail.

"Look at you, facing the fate of permanent bachelorhood," she admonished. On his kitchen table cooled an apple pie, a tub of thick homemade custard.

Trapped, he replied lamely: "Honestly, Laurie, I do have an interest in Port Kembla at the moment. Not serious, but worthy of further exploration at a later date."

"Port Kembla is New South Wales! Look at you, you live alone and correct me if I am wrong, but do I see framed photographs of past and present smiling girlfriends on your walls? No, I do not." This damning accusation ended all argument. "Vance has invited friends for a barbeque lunch on Sunday and I am inviting our Roxanne." With finality, she added brusquely: "Be there with no excuses. Not one to boast, but I believe our Miss Roxanne Holmquist causes quite a stir in the Bonbeach Hotel."

"What if I have other plans?"

"Did you hear what I said? She is quite the attraction in the public bar."

How it happened he had no recollection, possibly Laurie may have cast a spell on him, but after the barbeque he asked Roxanne next door for a drink, offering his hand to help her negotiate the Moorlands uneven backyard in her ridiculously high heeled shoes. Also he continued to hold her hand as he led her around the high privet hedge separating his home from the Moorlands. Both barely spoke more than a few words during the barbeque, Alex more amused at the frequent glowers from Laurie, though admitting Roxanne an imposing young woman. Tall with a willowy figure, her lavender perfume causing a flutter in his belly.

Hot summers in mind his father had created an outdoor area of brick paving furnished with wrought aluminium table and chairs, shaded beneath an immense olive tree with foliage so dense even the fiercest summer sun failed to penetrate. From a liquor cabinet he chose a bottle of Jim Beam, the refrigerator two cans of cola and a bucket of ice.

"Enjoying Australia?"

So brief were her denim shorts he could see where her legs joined, a low-cut white nylon top minimum containment for her full breasts, prominent nipples dark peaks jutting against the light fabric. She shrugged and rattled the ice in her drink which might have been annoyance; peeved because he found it difficult to stop staring at her legs, breasts that could with a sudden movement remove the erotica of secrecy?

So what? Warm beers he had lost count of in the sun next door his excuse for blatant male chauvinism. Topping his drink with a jigger of bourbon and three ice cubes, he had a blurry remembrance of Laurie's gushing endorsement of her niece, mid-twenties, unattached, attractive and an outgoing personality. Even the smallest movement caused her shorts to bunch, exposing a teasing glimpse of white panties; her inner thighs might have been satin, her long legs honey. Stop dreaming and enjoy the view.

"Half Aussie, right?" Total sophistication, he thought, guaranteed to win the heart of a fair maiden. Downing a stiff slug of his drink, he winced at its strength. "How do you compare Australia to New Zealand?"

"Australia's okay except for the superior-than-thou attitude of Australians to New Zealanders. Born in New Zealand I consider myself a Kiwi. Australia could learn a lot from New Zealand, but it won't. Australians couldn't care less."

Moving in the chair, her shorts dug even deeper; she raised her bottom and unsuccessfully tugged down the legs.

"Can agree with that, and I found the Kiwi attitude to us returned with the same venom. Our union long ago won washing machines and TVs, everything the Kiwis bogged down in a strike fought to achieve, and when we offered their union in Auckland to use us as an example for the cause we got told to mind our own business. Lost count of the pubs I've been in and challenged to aim up because of being Australian."

"Australians bring it on themselves," she said defensively, finishing her drink and holding out her glass.

"Suppose some of us do. Like we put down poor old Tasmanians we believe are burdened with two heads. We humans suffer a common superiority complex." Relaxed and at ease he refilled her glass, lulled by the olive tree's soothing ambience. Its slender lower branches and delicate leaves brushed his unruly brown hair overdue for a haircut, the filtered warmth of a northerly breeze on his bare arms and legs in shorts and t-shirt.

Again he caught a glimpse of white underwear. Averting his eyes, a stupid thought filled his head; if he licked her face his tongue would come away tasting of coconut ice, no, on deeper reflection, salt. Definitely salt, a beautiful young woman naked on the beach, in later years when resorting to jars of creams, or worse treatment of skin cancers, regretting her naivety of the power of the sun.

"You did say where you live, I forget."

"Chelsea," she said, then with a snigger: "With a couple of right faggots."

"Girl faggots or boy faggots?"

She frowned, with her free hand adjusting her top which threatened to fully expose her left breast; she took a deep swallow of her drink. "One of each."

"What's the girl like?"

"Bloody rough first comes to mind. Sneaked in the bathroom once with me stepping out the shower, can tell you she never tried it again."

"There anyone in Chelsea?"

"Back home came close to falling in a trap when silly young, a farmer in Tauranga. Bloody creep, the bastard didn't want a wife, he wanted a young and supple body to get his rocks off at night and work the farm from sunup to sunset."

"Roxanne, reckon you would look quite fetching behind a plough."

"See that you're asking the personal questions, what about you?"

The Chinese Seamen's Children

"Few years back had this heavy crush on a girl from Sunbury. Backed off when things started to look serious. Said something about we should expand our horizons, some bullshit like that to dump me."

"Tomorrow if you feel like competing with the Bonbeach hayseeds, I finish at 7:00 pm."

"Thanks, that competition I can deal with." Changing position on the chair exposed more of her panties as her legs unconsciously opened. "Roxanne, I should offer to drive you home …"

Watching him unsteadily refill his glass she thought better of another drink. "Sensible. Aunty Laurie offered."

"Did you notice the leer on her face when we disappeared around the hedge?"

Changing her mind on the drink, she clamped her legs shut. "Matchmakers abound in my family."

Edward included two phone numbers in his letter, his in the chance he might be home and his mother's. Edward's international direct dialling number it rang for a long time, then dropped out. Dialling the alternative number it rang even longer; eventually a woman answered a little breathlessly.

"Mrs Huang?"

"Yes."

"Mrs Huang, Edward gave me your number. My name is Alex Nielsen and I am ringing from Australia." He heard a gasp on the other end of the line, a fumbling of the phone.

"Edward's in America. Oh dear me, is it important that you are ringing from so far away?"

"No, not that important. Do you know when he will be home?"

"Alex Nielsen, yes! Edward spoke of you and hoped one day you might come to England, is that correct?"

"Thinking seriously of it."

"Edward spoke so highly of you and your help in Australia."

"Mrs Huang, we became good mates in the short time we knew each other. Please, when you hear from him let him know I rang and that I am interested in coming to England."

"My Edward will be so happy to know that."

Staring at the far wall and a framed print of the *Titanic* sailing into a bright yellow sunset, her last, he hung up. When certain of Edward's movements, their leaves coinciding, he would make the journey to the United Kingdom, a colonial son returning to the bosom of the mother country, or as some said, home.

16

BLEAK AND STANDING ALONE the Bonbeach Hotel gave the impression of foundry bricks laid with mechanical precision, a two storey rectangular building devoid of adornment, even a veranda to protect patrons from the prevailing south-westerly gales with origins in the Southern Ocean. Facing the Melbourne-Frankston railway line if not for a dimly illuminated circular brewery sign the building could easily be mistaken for a prison.

Massive square pillars in the public bar supported a pressed metal ceiling, its original paintwork debatable, now caked a deep mustard colour with nicotine. Sporting fanatics in a fervour of football driven hysteria plastered walls with newspaper clippings of their leaping heroes in full flight, tackling, handballing, booting goals. Another wall of dartboards, hooky boards, grubby white cardboard sheets of names and accrued points smeared with fingerprints, racing and football tipping competitions.

Four regulars attached to barstools crowded around the service area so the barmaid with her beer gun would not have to apply any exertion refilling their seven ounce glasses. Alex wondered if any of them lived in conventional homes, or resided under the railway bridge that crossed a creek close by.

Roxanne in a tight fitting white silk blouse and an equally snug black mini-skirt came around the bar, Alex noticing no smile or acknowledgment exchanged as the publican's wife relieved her a few minutes before 7:00 pm. Wearily, she flopped on a barstool.

"What would you like?"

Opening a large leather handbag in her lap she searched for and finally found a red lipstick and applied it to her mouth, a swipe with the tip of her tongue and a few noisy puckers. "Certainly wouldn't recommend the beer, been pulling flat all day. Idiot cellarman forgot to clean the pipes again. I'm hungry."

Gourmet dining Monday night in Bonbeach, for that matter anywhere along the Mornington Peninsula? There should be a menu on the bar, a blackboard of the chef's daily specials, some indication the hotel served counter meals. Nothing except an empty pie warmer on a shelf behind the bar.

"Only place I can think of is the Greek fish and chip shop at the Chelsea lights," he said, remembering the dingy cafe with a warped screen door and a Greek family within, cast in perpetual gloom and a mist of grease, hopeful the last train after midnight would funnel down the concourse a desperate customer.

Recapping her lipstick, she grimaced. "Opposite the lights I catch the bus to work and can smell it across the road, no thank you!"

"Can't think of anywhere else."

"Each week we put money on the table to share expenses and usually there's something left in the fridge and pantry come Monday. That's of course if Sheila isn't breaking up with a girlfriend and on an eating binge."

Peroxide and busty with the assistance of a padded bra, the publican's wife tried hard to compete in a one-sided contest against her younger competitor, her forty-odd years the telling blow and why she haunted beauty parlours while keeping a vigilant eye where her husband's eyes strayed. Against her advice he chanced a seven ounce beer, nothing for Roxanne who screwed her mouth up; the beer's head died the moment the glass landed on the bar, so flat it formed a jelly-like dome defying gravity.

The Chinese Seamen's Children

"Might be vinegar, but there's a bottle of French wine in this stupid concrete pipe thing Mark built in the living room. Reckons he got it from a bloke for doing him a favour, yeah I bet. Seems he has a gift for people giving him things, reckon he's an easy mark in the Melbourne poof bars."

"French wine, sounds nice."

Sliding from her stool, she headed for the door.

Ignoring his beer, he followed, reaching for her hand.

Roxanne's shared three bedroom home on the beach side of the Nepean highway in Chelsea had fallen victim to its advancing age and environment. Salt laden air from the bay, rain and sleet in winter and searing hot summers, peeled paint from timber, corroded guttering and iron veranda posts. Even in a state of decay and sinking in sand, the home represented prime real estate, west of the railway tracks with absolute beachfront of stunted tea-tree, gnarled banksia and coarse marram grass.

Early in the century the wealthy of Melbourne ventured from the city to the Mornington Peninsula, building substantial homes among the spindly scrub which surrendered to miles of broad beaches of yellow sand. Land east of the railway line, mostly sand dunes infested with banksia and tea-tree scrub, deemed suitable for the less moneyed class desperate for a seaside address. High rents made it essential for low income earners to share.

Eerie and scary for young children, he thought, the no-through street in darkness, the only sound after an unseen train passed the soft lapping of waves on the beach close by. Shining at the far end of the street a single streetlight created a pale footprint of illumination, shrouded in a halo of sea mist. Parking his Ford Cortina he locked it, overcoming an urge to look over his shoulder.

Wire mesh fences overgrown with agapanthus and fishtail fern, more sinister in the darkness the large bulk of Cyprus hedges grown wild. Unseen at night, an opening overgrown with tea-tree accessed the beach, bare feet over the years polishing old railway sleepers buried in sand and bound with pig face.

Passing beneath an arch of borer riddled banksias she led him along an uneven brick path to the porch; a hallway light glowed in reds, blues and greens, the stained glass front door. Loose floorboards covered by a threadbare carpet runner creaked underfoot, the hallway opening into a living room divided from the kitchen and dining area by an arch almost the height of the high ceiling. Original linoleum covered the floor, in high traffic areas worn through to the floorboards to expose newspaper underlay.

Mismatched lounge chairs, a sofa, television, pine shelving sandwiched between concrete blocks, magazines, cassette player and radio. Mark's wine cellar, six terracotta sewer pipes, held a lone bottle of wine.

Roxanne introduced an overweight young girl with her hair cut short back and sides and severe acne, dressed in black trousers and a white business shirt buttoned to the neck, as Sheila; a box of chocolates and potato crisps rested in her lap, her mouth full and barely able to mutter a greeting.

Sprawled in a lounge chair with his right leg pumping with a nervous affliction, the young man rolled his narrow shoulders to a silent tune from his Walkman headphones. Alex thought he might well haunt gay bars, effeminate, a plump and wet lower lip and a waxen face. A handshake and a silently mouthed Mark left his hand cold and clammy.

"See what you can find in the kitchen cupboards. Excuse me, I am off to the shower."

Their staple diet came from tins and colourful boxes of sugary cereals. Braised steak and onions and a packet of bowtie noodles offered possibilities, as did a half loaf of bread. Emptying the braised steak and onions in a saucepan he lighted the gas and turned the jet on low. Another larger saucepan he filled with water from the sink, the gas jet on high; five minutes for the water to boil, another ten for

The Chinese Seamen's Children

the noodles to soften. Cutting four slices of bread, he found butter and grated parmesan cheese in the refrigerator, side and dinner plates in the cupboard above the sink.

Highly satisfied with himself, his meal cooking, he sat on a kitchen chair and gazed at the bathroom, whispers of steam curling under the door. She would be rinsing her body of soap, reaching for a towel to dry herself. Other more intimate thoughts started to form, then the door opened and his vision of her became a tightly cinched white bathrobe and a towel wrapped around her head.

"Smells good."

"Probably marginally better than the Chelsea Greek's, but then that's not much of a commendation. Do you want to dress first or eat now?"

Steaming noodles swamped in braised steak and onions, sprinkled with parmesan cheese; first shaking and then nodding her head, she pounced hungrily. "What an awful hostess. Invite you home for a meal and you have to cook it yourself. Sorry."

"No cooking involved, believe me." Watching her as she delicately wiped her mouth with two fingers, licking her lips, he knew how this night would end. Warm and soap scented, the silken skin of a desirable woman, a stirring within him as old as time.

Tonight would be his and tomorrow others could beg for a smile, a glance, a flutter of incredibly long eyelashes. Ogle her fluid motion in a short skirt, the teasing of a low-cut blouse. No way could he compete with BMWs or yachts, expensive restaurants and Armani suits, or could he? Did he want to? Yes, he did.

"Alex, would you agree with me a successful meal should be accompanied by French wine? Wine probably earned by an unnatural physical act I shudder to think about? Our present company not conducive to stimulating conversation, we can sit on my bed and toast the world. I'll uncork the wine with a word of advice, keep your bum to the wall when you pass Mark."

Mark looked up with a wistful expression on his foppish face; oh yes, he could more than vie with any sloppy bitch visibly squirming on heat if only given the chance. Poking his tongue at Roxanne, he pouted at Alex.

Through the open bedroom window a fresh sea breeze gently toyed with the curtains. "Even with a big house and only three people privacy is a premium." Handing him a glass of wine, she sat on the bed and patted a place beside her.

Sinking deep in the soft bedding he drew into his lungs the scent of the woman whose body it warmed. Taking her glass he lifted off the bed in one fluid motion to place both on the dresser; wine would come later. Undressing quickly, he turned to face her.

Creasing her lips a triumphant smile also as old as time, her bathrobe discarded, on her back with one leg crooked. Without taking her eyes off him and two slightly parted fingers between her legs she revealed a teasing peek of where a delicate razor had removed her pubic down.

Settling beside her, he marvelled at her concave belly, her silken skin a pale coffee colour in the flattering light of a tiffany lamp on the dresser. Causing his breath to catch, her prominent sex clearly defined, swollen and protected by two darker creases of even softer flesh. So easy to take quickly and satisfy what throbbed for release inside him, an act of physical love wasted. This wondrous female creation like a vintage wine should be savoured slowly, his last rational thought as he knelt between her legs.

Closing her eyes she opened her legs to welcome his mouth, groaning and raking his shoulders with talon-like fingernails as she felt his teeth nipping her protective folds, his tongue trying to force a passage inside her. She bucked and writhed in orgasm, drawing blood on his shoulders.

Spreading her thighs even wider with his knees, a cry of anticipation as she felt an incredible hardness probing and slipping inside her, her frantic hands now on his buttocks the impetus to drive him fully inside her.

"Don't stop! Don't stop!" she cried hoarsely, racked by another orgasm, bucking under him, trying to draw more and more of him

The Chinese Seamen's Children

inside her, frantically jamming a pillow under her to change his angle of thrust.

Then he lost control, now only concerned with his own release, the exquisite sensation of feeling the rippling muscles inside her contract and draw every last drop of him into her body.

Light streaming through the window woke him, tangled in top and bottom sheets; Roxanne lay on her side, the pronounced curvature of one hip and her rounded bottom an invitation. Eyes transfixed on her sleeping form his body reacted, first touching one smooth and firm cushion, then the other, letting his fingers trace between an incredibly warm divide.

Wild and uninhibited, his to wholly devour. Bodies slicked with sweat, suckling as if to draw the other into their own body; this New Zealand girl who sounded her S's and C's with an inflection, his and his alone.

Stirring, she murmured something in her sleep, rolling over on her back with a groan. Bruises marred the otherwise flawless flesh high on each of her inner thighs, her neck covered in red weals. More bruises on tender flesh normally protected by silken hair.

Amazing, his last rational thought as he rolled on top of her, his endurance, a small cry and a wince of pain from her as he forced through her swollen cleft to enter her.

17

April 1942

SINGAPORE SURRENDERED TO THE Imperial Japanese Army, resourceful generals and battle hardened veterans of the China campaign, disciplined men of diminutive size peddling bicycles and living off the jungle in a relentless drive down the Malayan Peninsula. The Emperor of Japan, his victorious battleships anchored in Hong Kong, claimed the colony as a war prize, British citizens interned. In Shanghai British subjects faced the same ignoble fate. Though catastrophic for the British War Cabinet and Prime Minister Churchill whose fortress Singapore he boasted impregnable, it represented a reprieve for Chinese seamen. Deportations to these ports of blacklisted militants, though small in number, were suspended for the duration of the war.

Huang paid off the *Orestes* early in January, completing a 107-day round voyage to Australia. He, like other members of the Liverpool Chinese Seamen's Union, declined to re-sign articles, also to make himself available for employment. Two days later members of the Chinese Seamen's Union with an about-face supported the action In the port of Liverpool all shipping manned by Chinese became strikebound.

Shipowners and the government realised quickly a serious dispute existed, the years of exploitation and outright dismissal of Chinese

The Chinese Seamen's Children

claims at last coming to a head. It caught the shipping industry and government by surprise, no more so than the unforeseen support for the strike by the Chinese Seamen's Union. Abandoning their past differences with the more progressive union, the Chinese Seamen's Union united to engage on a single front their common adversaries.

Ships engaged in liner trade, tramps and tankers arriving with regularity in the Mersey, Chinese crews paid off, almost to a man declining to sign their names on newly reopened articles of agreement. The Liverpool Chinese Seamen's union placed high on its long list of grievances equal pay with British nationals, recognition of their role in wartime and payment of the war risk bonus.

Shanghai, Hong Kong and Singapore occupied by Japan, the United Kingdom found itself in a quandary with its first parry to crush the strike; it had no acceptable country to deport officials of both unions and a long list of identified militants. With this highly effective method of eliminating dissent closed the government floundered how to end the strike, the unions offering a plausible solution; sit down at the negotiating table, talk, listen and learn. Openly discuss deprivation, racial and physical abuse, war risk bonus, wage inequality and living conditions little changed from the last century.

Hsien conscripted Huang for a significant role, boarding ships and convincing non-members of the union and those wavering only complete solidarity would win the struggle for equality. Armed with a copy of an extremely important letter, also a warning to reconnoitre carefully around the waterfront and when boarding ships, his face becoming known as a militant and ships' officers briefed to be observant for non-crew members within the vicinity of the gangway. One organiser did manage to reach the top gangway platform only to be met with the fists and boots of two briefed watchmen, hospitalised and held as an alleged enemy agent.

Some thought went into perfecting a stereotype disguise, a meek figure scurrying along the wharf with short pronounced steps, a woven cane shopping basket on his shoulder, weaving and genuflecting to whoever stood in his way; a not overly bright steward.

His bizarre subterfuge guaranteed of success with the assurance all Chinese looked alike.

Elsie held grave concerns about her husband's involvement in the strike, the growing intensity when he talked of bringing the British shipowner to heel, winning for his fellow seamen justice and recognition. Made even worse when their meagre money ran out, only a few coppers in her purse to buy food.

Somehow he managed to scrounge money from where he did not say, probably a union source. She could cope, even when Edward cried with a gnawing in his belly, giving up her own small portion of white bread soaked in milk, but not the long periods of silence between them.

Striking and ending Chinese exploitation consumed the man she loved, this she knew and in her own simple way accepted she had to share him. Also the important role the union placed upon him, but not the changes it wrought upon his person. She tried to enter his closeted world, offer what she could to lighten his burden, all to no avail. Concerns for her husband escalated, some prominent strike leaders already under arrest and facing lengthy jail terms, word on the street ringleaders might even remain incarcerated until the end of the war.

Head bent low over the kitchen table, his hair almost brushing the surface, he poured his heart out on cheap writing tablets. After hours in poor light, cramped and cold, he would screw up page after page, glare with frustration at the walls upon which hung a menagerie of soft toys. Elsie would come behind him and rub his shoulders, bend and kiss the top of his head. Edward asleep both would lead the other to bed and fully clothed slip under the blankets. Only the clothing needed to free those parts of their bodies both sought removed, their lovemaking akin to a stolen and guilty moment.

Later, troubled and unable to sleep, she would try to decipher what he wrote, making sense of his scrawling handwriting made even more difficult with the crumpled sheets. Garbled words written in haste of suppression of initiative by an officer elite at sea, themselves no more than tools manipulated by those higher up the strata. Class segregation of the working class, a proven doctrine of control and discipline.

Long sentences without punctuation of the stirring masses of China under the banner of Mao Zedong. Mao Zedong and his millions of followers marching a hundred abreast across China purging the country of a foreign pestilence. Enemies driven into a sea stained with blood, China emerging from suffocating darkness into a new dawn of greatness. China the world would bow their heads in reverence.

Huang travelled a tortuous path, uncaring of the ramifications of his extreme beliefs. Something even more portentous entering his life, his deeper association with a group of shadowy men members of the British Communist Party.

When Huang boarded ships, the letter he carried in his pocket never failed to win a positive response; support from the Chinese ambassador to the Court of St James, Wellington Koo, addressed to Lord Leathers, Minister of War Transport.

Wellington Koo admonished Lord Leathers for allowing by his non-intervention the flagrant racial and physical abuse of Chinese seamen serving on British-flagged ships. In addition the ambassador, who in the past served his county as president, a founding member of the League of Nations, wrote of his outrage of a past incidence when a British master shot dead a Chinese seaman in New York to be found by the judiciary to have no case to answer.

Wellington Koo called upon Lord Leathers to publicly acknowledge the vital role of Chinese seamen in the defence of the Empire, and of no less importance, recognition of Chinese war dead at sea.

Union activity at its height and the support of Wellington Koo a confidence among mainstream membership burgeoned that their claims would have a favourable acceptance at a proposed meeting of the unions, government and shipowners, but the union executive held reservations.

Standing room only a special meeting called to brief the membership of this heartening turn of events were shocked when Liang vacated the chair and made a statement: "Comrades, we have been off wages since early January and our members and their families are suffering great hardships. What little money we collect to support our membership is so scant it can only briefly sustain a meagre few. For this sacrifice we have gained no ground and are told the government and shipowners are agreeing to talk but I am of the opinion we have turned down a blind alleyway, ahead an unassailable concrete wall."

Concurrence in a wave of voices passed through the hall.

"Reason? Shipowners and the British government will only negotiate with the Kuomintang. Our ambassador has broken with tradition and the Kuomintang and spoken out in support of us. Informed the Ministry of War Transport it is not acceptable the inhuman treatment of Chinese seamen, wage discrimination and attacked and vilified because of race. His message is clear to the Kuomintang, British government and shipowners, when we return to our ships we will have equality. No one will spit upon us again. Our members never again bow for not jumping with profuse apologies to obey an order. We are seamen. We are Chinese seamen!" Liang resumed the chair.

Hsien held his hands up to conclude the standing ovation. "Lord Leathers says he is quite willing to negotiate with the unions but only if the unions adopt a Kuomintang recommendation all strike action cease immediately and we return to our ships without resolution of our claims. This is counsel from the government of China! Government that purports to represent the people of China and their nationals overseas. We will stand submissively to attention with the benevolent and wise Kuomintang in support and beg forgiveness for our transgressions, for our wilful and seditious sabotaging of the United Kingdom in her direst hour. Good sirs, we are not deserving of the war risk bonus, also because we are Chinese we should be accommodated thirty to forty in open focastles."

Again the meeting rose to its feet, a roar from 200 men inside

The Chinese Seamen's Children

and those milling outside on the pavement unable to get through the doors.

Huang, pushed to the front of the meeting from a group pressed against the wall, received a beckon from Liang to come to the official table. Clearing his throat, he stood with his feet set wide apart. "Unity within the hierarchy of the Kuomintang government is divided, important officials advocating the unions fight this strike to the end," he said, his voice loud and precise. "To stand solid and demand what is our right, not as in the past retreat defeated, cowering from authority and intimidation. Our sacrifices at sea will be acknowledged and the rights for the grieving families of those lost at sea treated with sympathy and dignity. We Chinese the same status of nationality as the British seamen we die with.

"That British women married to Chinese seamen in the service of British shipowners, our children, have their birthright made sacred and inviolable. We will take to task those who with righteous impunity blacklist us for having the audacity to stand up and be identified in the struggle for our rights at sea. Timidly accept deportation when the need of our services is no longer required to fight their war. No man subjected to bashings or the threat of sacking or worse, shot dead! Let it be from this day on! Touch one, touch all!"

Jubilation filled his entire being as he threw back his head and combed his fingers through his hair in acknowledgment of the cheers from his fellow seamen. When this strike ended there would emerge militant delegates, union men able to quash aggression and bullying, bigotry and racial slander, enforce a voice recognisable by shipowners and authority as supported by the strength of numbers.

Regardless of his own needs lead with greater commitment, assume the responsibilities of delegate and fulfil the role as a leader of men.

With only a proposed future meeting of government, shipowners and unions, a stalemate existed, the government warning the unions a state of national emergency would be declared and the strike leaders charged with sedition and affording comfort to the enemy. So damaging to the war effort the government would not hesitate to seek the supreme penalty for those proven guilty.

Both unions convened yet another meeting, same agenda, same frustrations. Complaints abounded about the frequency of meetings, replied to by officials members needed to be kept informed of developments, a day-to-day event. Some good news did give heart, the unions informing their disgruntled members every ship berthed or at anchor in Merseyside that only one man out of 600 had chosen to sign articles.

Behind the closed doors of the church hall the meeting of the executive, delegates and twenty-five selected rank and file members, convened in a charged atmosphere, interrupted time and time again with frustrations and demands the executive approach the British trade union movement for support. Possibly this directive might have been the blind alleyway Liang referred to in the past, the British union movement fearing low waged foreigners a threat to British industrial awards.

Huang sat with Keong at the back of the meeting, Keong home after six months running out of Abadan. His ship torpedoed in the engine room the gallant old tanker showed a great reluctance to sink, the U-boat forced to surface to finish her off with gunfire. Only a shift of wind saved Keong's lifeboat from a sea of blazing oil, repatriated to Malta to join a tanker a survivor of a similar encounter with an Italian destroyer, thirty of her crew lost. After loading in Abadan, the ship received orders to discharge in United Kingdom ports.

Earlier he opened his heart to his friend about his fears for his family. "Elsie and Edward will be targeted, of that I am certain," he said, his voice quavering with emotion. "As soon as Churchill declares victory orders will be issued to deport aliens, Chinese at the top of the list. There will be a new order in Asia with the European powers returning to resume their colonial suppression. China will be

The Chinese Seamen's Children

in turmoil if not civil war, though deemed suitable for the deportation of Liverpool Chinese and their families. Also an unstable Singapore filled with resentment for those who abandoned them to the Japanese. Historically the British are specialists at relocating people, just look at their transportation of convicts accused of stealing a crust of bread to their Australian penal colonies.

"Those permitted to remain in the United Kingdom will be the docile, the mute, the genuflecting, offered jobs at whatever British shipowners decree is sufficient to sustain a coolie, of course not taking into consideration his family. Choice is yours, a few of pounds a month or go wade in a rice paddy, for all we care pull a rickshaw. Paid even lower wages more Chinese will be crammed in the focastle, upwards of seventy or more." Emotion turned to despair. "For myself I don't care! It is Elsie and Edward who are the innocent victims!"

Keong sympathised. "My friend, I know, I know. At this juncture it is more rumour than fact the government will deport Chinese seamen and their families, wartime thinking and fear mongering by vested interests."

If only he were able take comfort from his friend's reassuring words.

"Look at it from the perspective of a politician seeking re-election, for instance our Liverpool politicians," Keong continued. "Picture in your mind wailing British women struggling ahead of their bowed head husbands, clutching terrified children, forced by police batons and snarling dogs to climb gangways. Can you in the clear light of reasoning envisage the government of Winston Churchill guilty of that? Adolph Hitler, of course, the British government, no."

Wielded forcefully a blunt instrument sounded on the door, followed by a short pause then another staccato applied by a heavy and impatient hand. Portentously, a pall of silence fell over the meeting, all eyes turned to the door and the elected doorman struggling to his feet to answer it.

Hsien and Liang knew in their sinking hearts what those authoritative knocks meant, both men speaking in private of possible police intervention, though with optimism dismissing the threat at this stage. Muttering under his breath to be patient, the doorman reeled backwards in stunned shock as the door burst open and six uniformed constables and a sergeant forced their way through. Parked outside, engines idling, waited a fleet of paddy wagons and reinforcements.

Filling the entire doorway with bone and muscle, a brutal countenance not improved with a nose broken in his youth, the sergeant led the charge with his booming voice and barrel chest expanded. "Listen to me well, you are hereby ordered this instance not to resist! Remain orderly in your seats and you will not be guilty of a breach of the law resulting in arrest! This meeting is terminated and I command those not responsible for this illegal gathering to immediately vacate these premises peacefully and with haste!"

Sergeant Bell's fierce face glowered, thick rubbery lips protruding with disappointment, the patriotic task of rounding up a few timid Chinamen too simple, not one broken head to add to an extensive lifetime tally in the service of His Majesty. Orders to bring in Hsien Wu and Liang Tao for questioning on information received from some seaman peeved of being on strike a meeting of cadres were planning to sabotage installations vital to the war effort.

Forming a tight wedge, six men at the back of the meeting, denizens of the back streets of Shanghai with second and more ominous professions, enraged at having their union meeting broken up by the hated symbols of enforcement, prepared for battle. Their battle plan simple, a full frontal attack, but disciplined British bulk and abhorrence of all things Chinese, assisted by lignum vitae batons wielded with the intent to maim, swung the battle in the police's favour. In under a minute all six lay unconscious on the floor, a dozen others less aggressive given a lick of wood seasoned to the hardness of iron to make victory sweeter.

Huang and Keong kept their backs to the wall, edging cautiously closer to Hsien and Liang, their intent to take the brunt of the assault upon themselves. Their self-sacrificing action proved unwarranted

The Chinese Seamen's Children

as the melee ended as quickly as it had commenced. With the skill and ease of those with the law on their side and no need to vindicate their brutality, the major combatants lay manacled on the floor, the unconscious dragged by the hair to the waiting paddy wagons. Sergeant Bell, gloating with the ease of the victory, thrust his face into Hsien's. Hsien recoiled, the man's fetid breath reeking of a garlic paste he spread on his breakfast toast to maintain regular bowel movements.

"Mr Chinaman, you and your mate are coming with me for questioning on matters that will be revealed by my superintendent and government officials who want answers to some serious matters of national security. Understand?"

"No, I do not understand. Are we are under arrest?" Hsien said.

"Wax in your ears, Mr Chinaman? Clear them out and listen to plain and simple English, questioning is what I said," Sergeant Bell snarled, his slow brain perplexed; did he mention arrest?

"What you and your fellow officers have inflicted against this union is illegal and against civil liberties. Assault without provocation with deadly weapons will be made public and every man's number taken for further action."

Sergeant Bell looked about quickly to see if he had anyone of importance within earshot. "Oh is that so, Mr Chinaman. Foreigners like you lot got no rights. Gutless Chinaman quaking in their boots too afraid to go to sea. What I hear we might have the pair of you on a boat back to China by early next week."

Hsien and Liang avoided arrest, their interrogation no more than a rebuke from senior police their volatile membership should show a more lawful response to police investigating serious allegations of sabotage. Besieged by war, the enemy could strike at the heart of the United Kingdom anywhere and anytime.

Completing the rout an eviction notice landed on Hsien's desk next day. Overwhelmed with patriotic fervour, the owner of the building with compassion for the homeless on the razed streets of Merseyside, offered his newly vacated premises at competitive rents, even though some said the remuneration sought no more than gouging from the vulnerable.

April saw a softening of attitude to the strike with shipowners and government finally agreeing to a meeting in London with Mr Dao of the Chinese consulate as mediator. With a sense of relief mixed with pathos, the striking seamen had reached the end of a frustrating and arduous road with little fight left in them.

Mr Dao, a wise choice according to the unions, having witnessed firsthand the solidarity of the unions and made known to his government there would be no retreat or lessening of demands.

On the negotiating table a settlement document aptly titled the London Agreement. New wage scales for both liner trade and tramp ships, £6/13/9. Tankers £7/15/0. Four months of strike and years of struggle gained the Chinese unions a raise in wages of two pounds a month, still far below what British seamen earned. Also on the table, its adoption sought with passionate intent by the Chinese negotiators, recognition of the Chinese role in the war.

Representatives of the Ministry of War Transport who played a leading role in negotiations, remained silent on the issue of payment of the war risk bonus. When prompted about the omission Lord Leathers somewhat reluctantly pushed a paper across the table.

Mr Dao picked it up; he read its contents quickly, only a few paragraphs. He looked down the table where the representatives of the Liverpool Chinese Seamen's Union and the Chinese Seamen's Union sat, especially at Hsien and Liang having glumly accepted the paltry wage settlement.

Unable to conceal a satisfied smile on his face, he indicated it be handed to Hsien; the paper read all ratings of foreign nationality would without precedent be entitled to a monthly payment of ten pounds, the payment included in wages as war risk bonus.

18

May 1945

REJOICING SPREAD THROUGHOUT THE United Kingdom with the deafening metallic cacophony of church bells. The bells heralded the defeated armies of the German Third Reich, the laying down of their arms in unconditional surrender.

Peace at last for a wasted Europe. May 8th 1945 ended years of blood and brutal occupation, persecution and the slaughter of untold millions. These figures would double and treble as the world with disbelief watched on their theatre screens the liberation of death camps, films of gloating SS troops forcing entire villages to dig mass graves, then on their knees expose the whites of their necks to make the task of their blond-haired handsome young executioners less arduous. Crematorium ovens now cold, their iron doors swung open to expose twisted piles of fire bleached bones. Grainy and flickering scenes of mountains of clothing, baggage, bales of human hair, the most heart wrenching, rag dolls of children who clung to their parents' hands when showerheads in ablutions blocks turned on.

Liverpool again showed its grit overcoming the destruction of war, building anew, the streets alive with good humour to embrace a new world promised after the years of suffering and sorrow. From the Houses of Parliament grandiose rhetoric flowed to every corner of the land, promising a future with no boundaries. Rejoicing people could now without fear of subjugation plan their destinies, rear their families, pray without prejudice and orate in the streets with freedom of association.

On the bottom of the sea lay fifteen million tons of allied shipping, almost twelve million tons of this horrendous toll British flagged, fifty-four percent of the nation's fleet. Gaunt skeletal remains of steel and flesh, a graveyard for 30,000 seamen and their 2828 ships, a casualty ratio of seamen far greater than any other branch of the services.

Absorbing the physiological as well as the financial impact of such massive destruction the boardrooms of British shipping companies planned a future of larger and more efficient ships. Weeks slashed from time spent in port with specialised ships, heavier gear, cranes, faster fuel efficient vessels able to move the post-war manufacturing might of the United Kingdom to its world and Empire markets. Ships returning home crammed to the coamings with the bounties harvested on the prairies of Canada and the plains of Australia, the fertile fields of New Zealand. Free trade and generous freight rates for those loyal nations coloured in Empire red.

Accolade upon accolade heaped upon a weary old warhorse who guided his nation to victory with his towering strength and unwavering conviction the English speaking peoples of the world would prevail, Prime Minister Winston Churchill. Not forgotten in the adulation engulfing the nation, the strength and symbolism of an unconquerable British spirit, the beloved royal family, standing as an example of strength and will at its head, King George the VI and Queen Elizabeth.

Germany crushed and reduced to rubble, occupied and surrounded by new European boundaries, smouldered and awaited its political future. Armies of the Soviet Union, in violation of their non-aggression treaty with Japan, deployed forty divisions from Europe to Siberia, poised to invade the Japanese home islands.

United States armed forces under the command of General MacArthur with the liberation of the Philippines, prepared to strike at the southern islands of Japan. The United States with a million

The Chinese Seamen's Children

men faced the daunting prospect of fighting an army of three million fanatical Japanese, anticipated waves of suicide forces on the beaches and hinterland, in the cities and villages. Predictions of a death toll even those immune and insensitive to mass extermination found difficult to accept.

Japan foundered in its death throes, its once all-conquering armies stretched thinly throughout the Pacific, its merchant fleet destroyed. Japanese naval ships dormant in port without fuel. Manufacturing destroyed by carpet bombing and incendiaries. Peace feelers through the Soviet Union for an armistice came with the proviso Japan would lay down its arms but no mention of withdrawal from occupied countries. The emperor would remain on his throne.

Rejected outright by the allies, the United Kingdom prepared to send its armies, navy and air force to the Pacific theatre, Churchill unwilling to allow the Americans all the glory of victory over Japan.

8:00 am on a clear day on the 6th of August, 1945, people queuing for trains and buses to go to work, others still eating breakfast, some frustrated with slow moving traffic in their cars, families with children feeding pigeons in parks, a new age dawned.

Some people for no particular reason, possibly to stretch their necks, looked up and saw a slow moving silver speck in the sky, a lone B-29 bomber. Those who observed experienced a sense of relief, expecting wave upon wave of planes and carpet bombing. Only one bomb fell from the sky and Hiroshima ceased to exist.

Returning to base, the tail gunner of the B-29, a grandstand view, wondered in God's name what his captain had unleashed, gazing stunned into the maws of hell. In that few seconds of history 80,000 people vaporised, another 100,000 doomed to die of hideous burns and wounds and radiation. When the benumbed remnants of humanity stared at the utter annihilation of their city none would have known that the nightmare far from ended had just begun. The aftermath would condemn their children and their children and their children to suffer slower deaths, mutations and a trauma that would engulf Japan in grief for generation after generation.

On the 9th of August a second atomic device erased the city of Nagasaki, and Emperor Hirohito ordered his Imperial Council to surrender Japan and his throne to the enemy. August 15th witnessed the instruments of surrender signed onboard the USS *Missouri* in Tokyo Bay and Prime Minister Churchill's Grand Idea closed it final chapter. Tallying the dead, mutilated, maimed, missing, insane and displaced in the second world contagion would cause historians and researcher to recoil with repulsion and disbelief.

Men and women returned home from war, hollow-eyed, young but old before their time. War weary heroes marched heads held high in the streets, flags flying, cheering and wondrous relief, tears and mourning for the large gaps among their numbers.

Stirring tributes for the gallant merchant service flowed from the benches of the parliaments, commoners and lords in fine voice revering the men who went down to the sea in ships, unsung saviours of the British Empire. On the first day of peace Alfred Holt's board of directors in a nationalistic gesture to relieve the government of a further drain on its greatly reduced reserves ceased immediate payment of the war risk bonus for their Chinese crews. Worst followed for the Chinese seamen when the same board announced an increase in dividends to shareholders and the cutting of their wages by fifty percent.

Informed of the removal of the war risk bonus and wage cut, the Chinese crew of an Alfred Holt ship in Melbourne sought help from the Seamen's Union of Australia. Only too willing to advocate on behalf of the Chinese against a despised enemy, the union took great delight in the request, seeking support from a brother waterfront union equally held in dread by shipowners.

Threatened in bludgeoning terms there should be an immediate re evaluation of the board's Chinese wage decision, Alfred Holt through their Australian agents received further chilling information; the Waterside Workers Federation in a gesture of worldwide working class solidarity had great sympathy in the cause of justice, a stance which could lead to their ships rotting alongside Australian wharves.

Regrettably Australian union influence did not extend into

international waters, British shipowners with the first deep sea roll shedding their conciliatory facade and compiling lists of the names in the blackest of ink those who had had the temerity to challenge a sound management decision.

Registered deep in the back pages of a shipping register, the chances of Huang joining a ship before Christmas or even early in the New Year seemed improbable. What money sustained the Huang household, as it did many Chinese families, came from illicit labour digging sewer trenches with a picks and shovels in rain, sleet and biting cold. For the Chinese navvies their gruelling labours might extend sixty hours or more a week, the pay five pounds paid on Saturday evening from the unscrupulous contractor well aware of the government edict banning Chinese seamen from working ashore.

Peace lengthened the registers of seamen seeking work, replacing war losses with new builds a slow process. Also a new breed of shipping entrepreneurs of Mediterranean origin now competed on traditional British trade routes with cheaply bought war built ships now declared surplus.

Many began to query claimed post-war prosperity, the political slogan of a land fit for heroes. Clement Attlee, the new Labour prime minister with a landslide majority of 145 seats in the House of Commons, relegating his ousted opponent, a chagrined wartime icon, to retreat to the Opposition benches and question loyalty.

Labour's massive mandate came with a hefty price tag for a nation with a severely depleted treasury; a national health scheme, social reform and full employment. Whereas the Conservatives, bathing in the glory of victory, swamped the country with the triumphs of a single man, cigar in one hand, cane in the other. History recorded rare men and women who emerged in times of great crisis, who with their unwavering indomitable will and tenaciousness raised the fighting spirit of their nations to unimaginable heights. Winston Churchill such a man.

Winston Churchill rebounded with more important worldly matters on his mind to be bothered with nationalised medicine, social reform and the myth of full employment, the re-establishment of world status for his beloved Empire. Reclaiming lost influence in the subcontinent and economic supremacy in Asia, armed support for a crumbling government favourable to the United Kingdom in China. Stand shoulder-to-shoulder with force of arms and naval power Dutch and French allies proudly hoisting their flags once again in their reclaimed colonies. India, its economic ties to the Empire as vital as its teeming hundreds of millions, also held concerns for the great man, an undercurrent of independence driven by a man of diminutive stature, some said close to divinity, called Ghandi. On the world stage the Soviet Union as a burgeoning world power deeply troubled him, with impunity carving up Eastern Europe and installing puppet governments of similar autocracy and brutality.

British shipowners on a boardroom level became aware soon after the declaration of peace the challenges that lay ahead, fierce competition with surplus war built tonnage now being disposed of for the price of scrap metal. Only shipowners who pared costs to the bone, even deeper to the marrow, slashing costs such as wages and conditions would survive, the adoption of such policies an immediate priority.

War built ships in the United States and Canada proved to the world the engineering genius and production skills of a severely depleted workforce had more than achieved the almost impossible tasks demanded of them by war. Testament to the women who stepped into the breach with welding and cutting torches. Of 15,200 tons 531 Victory class ships and 2710 Liberty class ships of 10,100 tons entered the water in an explosion of keel blocks and smoking grease. Not to be outdone by dry cargo ships, 500 T2 tankers of 15,850 tons.

Greek shipowners, mercenary businessmen devoid of scruples when it came to profit making ventures, streetwise and lacking any trace of empathy for seamen who sailed their fleets, haggled with

The Chinese Seamen's Children

dogged tenacity for mothballed Victories, Liberties and T2 tankers. Who ill-fed poorly paid and accommodated crews, operated substandard ships and drove their competitors from the sea with freight rates commensurate to their employment and maintenance policies.

Among the new brethren of shipowners shedding wartime restraints, there emerged even more enterprising owners who insured their ships triple their book value, seamen suspicious of their employers criminal set of mind on high alert if a new master boarded with only the clothes on his back.

Alfred Holt and other old and reputable British shipowners competed in a world order devoid of the old rules where ethics and gentlemanly agreements decreed the means of conducting business. British shipowners showed their true spirit of survival by instructing their marine and engineering superintendents to investigate modern propulsion system and maintenance programs to ensure longevity of their investments. Accountants poured through ledgers and balance sheets, their pecuniary agenda crews' remuneration.

Implementing the first step in restructuring and competing proved simple, halving Chinese wages and drawing up new crew agreements. Chinese crews would have the option of signing the new agreements or not, their right under British maritime law. Sign articles or stand aside and allow the man in line behind holding up his discharge book to step forward.

While the nation in a state of delirium celebrated victory and paid homage to their merchant navy the government faced a dilemma, 20,000 Chinese seamen. These seamen, recruited over the war years in addition to a large pre-war core of men, were now deemed surplus to needs. An insupportable situation existed demanding a solution by those who foresaw the Chinese as a threat to post-war jobs.

Government policy carried out by zealous officials of the Home Office to correct the large imbalance in Liverpool became a subject raised repeatedly at union meetings. Those with jobs kept a low profile ashore, the destitute a miserable existence on the streets sustained by charitable handouts.

Voiced with monotonous regularity how could shipowners vindicate cutting Chinese wages from a peak of £17/17/0 a month to £7/17/0 a month, then raise by two pounds the wages of British nationals? Why this blatant discrimination against already low paid Chinese? These unanswered questions gnawed at the minds of those standing in queues in freezing conditions outside shipping offices. Sometimes a faint glimmer of hope dented their hopelessness, a rumour circulating the waterfront the government would in the coming months be offering Chinese seamen citizenship.

Cruelly, this rumour extinguished with grim reality two weeks before Christmas with the rounding up of 200 men in Liverpool and Birkenhead, boarded on trains to Tilbury where a ship sailing for Hong Kong secured tugs alongside.

Both unions protested to the Chinese consulate and the Home Office that these 200 men had committed no crimes warranting deportation, all of them seamen registered for employment. Credited to a government official a vague statement hinting without being quoted as a reference source, the men might have incriminating notations against their names in the registers of shipping companies, hence the reason for repatriation to their Asian home ports.

Chinese crews of ships alongside and at anchor lived in constant dread; a simple mistake, a dropped plate, even a glance in the wrong direction, the miscreant faced instant dismissal and deportation to the country of their birth. Though never initiated the boardroom deliberated on further wage cuts, expected recriminations in this climate of anxiety, negligible.

Mounting a strong case against the deportations, the unions claimed the government acted unlawfully because the men had committed no indictable offences, had no criminal records and had the means of achieving gainful employment. Their most significant rebuttal, raised at every union meeting, Chinese war service.

Chinese seamen, like all seamen in war, carried no immediate visible evidence of their service. There were no uniforms for ABs and firemen, greasers and trimmers, motormen and catering. Chinese

The Chinese Seamen's Children

seamen who walked the streets were survivors against great odds, men who packed their meagre belongings in battered suitcases or canvas bags. Some wore patched clothing scrubbed on the deck with a block of sandsoap, and when the wind blew cold their watchcoats or flannels their only means of warmth.

Acting with what seemed confusion the Home Office informed both unions defending their members and consulate officials that those with their names on deportations lists would be given a date to voluntary leave the country. How seamen on lengthy shipping registers with little prospect of work, no money, could give a specific date to leave the country officials failed to explain or ignored the question entirely.

Neither did the government bother to clarify its reason why large numbers of Shanghai men appeared specifically targeted for deportation, rounded up with near frenetic haste, their mass deportations on the first available ships. Without hesitation the unions had the answer; militancy, against the Shanghai names a profusion of black marks.

Of greater importance than his own future for Huang, the lifting of a depressing burden; a government change of policy due to the success of the ongoing deportations, reprieve for Elsie and Edward with their British citizenship restored.

Christmas found the United Kingdom slowly but surely lifting itself out of the dark mire of war with optimism. Even though the Christmas-New Year season brought the joy of family, of giving and sharing, past suffering and grieving still lingered.

During the weeks leading to Christmas the Home Office worked without respite in their poorly heated offices arranging deportations of a large number of seamen to Shanghai, Hong Kong and Singapore. Methodical and ruthlessly efficient, the processing devoid of empathy or pity for the traumatised, also the crushing of yet another rumour the government planned legislation in the New Year granting citizenship to war service Chinese seamen.

Home Office lists of proposed deportees filled thick files. Advocates for the Chinese brandished reports from the chief constables of Liverpool and Birkenhead supporting what most knew; with rare exceptions the Chinese were peaceful and law abiding citizens.

Searching in desperation for reasons why the deportations continued unabated, the Liverpool Chinese Seamen's Union attacked the government on the issue a critical shortage of housing stock existed in Merseyside. Outraged, the government howled unfair and derogatory.

Reasons for the deportations demanding answers many could be found; slowness of shipping companies replacing war losses, dockyards retooling from naval construction to merchant, company reluctance to engage marked individuals and high national unemployment. Obvious even to an unbiased eye in the streets of Liverpool, large groups of Chinese seamen which in itself gave credibility to another problem; idle and desperate men posed a threat to law and order.

Publicly the government sympathised with the sacrifices endured by Chinese seamen, defending their deportation policy as an assessment of a local phenomenon, a surplus of unemployable foreign seamen.

Truth and lies abounded; Chinese recruited from crippling Asian poverty and trained to exacting British maritime standards, rewarding their benefactors with greedy demands for higher and higher wages and bonuses, compensation far in excess of their pound, shilling and pence value. Did not these ungrateful Orientals sup at the trough of plenty, feed and grow fat on the largess of British shipping companies? Fact, in war these Asian seamen offered their services for remuneration, fully cognisant of the risks involved while performing menial tasks on British ships. Debt repaid if ever liability existed, paid in full with wages twenty times in excess these recruited Asians could ever hope to earn in their countries of origin.

The Chinese Seamen's Children

On Christmas Eve the Liverpool Chinese Seamen's Union called an extraordinary meeting of the executive and selected rank and file, alarmed at the increase in the numbers of members scheduled for deportation. Constituting the union rooms, effectively Hsien's one bedroom home in Birkenhead barely large enough to accommodate a full meeting of the executive, seven men.

Huang, allowed two unpaid hours off from work, attended the meeting alone, Keong with good fortune mixed with relief and melancholy he would miss Christmas, signing on an Anglo-Saxon Petroleum tanker sailing for the Persian Gulf. He held no illusions, even though his marital status now protected him from deportation due to yet another twist in government policy, his name featured prominently on a list of undesirables noted to receive high priority assessment. Even so he remained hopeful that being Christmas Eve the government's minions who conducted the ethnic cleansing might show some seasonal goodwill to all men.

Hsien grimly passed around the kitchen table a memo originating in the Home Office. "Deportations in the last few weeks leading up to Christmas makes one feel the government has adopted its defeated enemy's means of disposing those superfluous to their needs." Pausing, he waited for his words to take effect. "Empowered as a union official I am not presently in danger of the current government initiative. Anyway, I don't think anyone in the Home Office would know how to deal with an irritating old Chinese Communist. Also I have been in the country even longer than those who are signing our lives away. Depressingly, the memo you are now reading is confidential information unemployed married seamen, seamen recently granted unofficial temporary British residency, are to be reassessed immediately." With a glance at Huang, he concluded: "I say immediately, it is already fact."

Huang's voice caught. "Comrade Hsien, surely not Christmas Eve?"

"My informant said there is a ship with steerage berths for 550 in Southampton sailing Christmas Day."

"No! The government could not be so heartless!"

"Already their officers and the police are acting upon the directive."

"There wouldn't be time for them to assess married men!"

"Government assessment is three simple questions answered without hesitation in your doorway," Hsien said resignedly. "Name your ship, its master, and what time are you turning to in the morning."

"Have we asked the consulate the legal standing of Chinese married to British nationals?" Huang said.

"Yes, the deportations are illegal. No grounds exist to deport but the government continues to expel hundreds each week. Government has taken the high ground in finding work for returning military personnel, munitions workers, men and women who built tanks and aircraft. Rhetoric be assured aliens will not compete for your job."

"We are seamen who pose no threat to shore jobs! No one wants to dig sewer trenches."

"Unfortunately we have a visual impairment against us, reminding people with ruddy faces and blue eyes Chinese compete with them for British jobs, also fuelling the lie we Chinese will work for pennies."

Huang noticed him at previous meetings, mostly silent but when he spoke members listened to every articulate word he uttered; his words came deep and meaningful. "So quickly is forgotten the *Bellerophon* transporting the British Expeditionary Forces to France to repel the Nazi blitzkrieg. That she played a major role in the Norwegian campaign and the evacuation of allied forces when the Germans overran France. Forgotten the *Teucer* and *Diomed* served as military transports for the invasion of Sicily. Oh yes, and rarely mentioned in company when war exploits are boasted, the crew of the *Talthybius* standing firm and fighting when the Japanese bombed Singapore.

"Then of course the courageous heroics of the unarmed *Menelaus* refusing to stop on command from a German commerce raider. Radioing her raider signal under gunfire and torpedo attack, outrunning her pursuer. Alfred Holt ships manned by men who did not condemn each other because of their skin, who fought and died for the cause of freedom."

Huang felt a flush of pride for his old ship and wondered if Serang Lau Yi had been there, on the poop shaking his fist at the raider *Michel* wallowing in their wake.

Hsien put the final damper on the meeting. "One of our executive members who has lived in Liverpool for seventeen years, father of four children, has been caught in the net. Nose-to-nose with the authorities he produced evidence of his marital status, children's birth certificates, his position high on Anglo-Saxon Petroleum's register and expecting a ship within days. His defence fell on deaf ears, a notation against his name proof of his undesirability, sufficient evidence for his detainment and forced boarding of a ship sailing from Tilbury. Damned an undesirable alien possibly because an irked officer complained the way he said sir! Seventeen years he gave this country! Wife and four children!"

Fortunately for another high profile union executive, Liang joined the *Glaucus* which sailed the week previous.

Using her imaginative initiatives, Elsie transformed their home into a haven of festive gaiety. She had given up trying to calm Edward, in a constant state of feverish excitement, unable to stand still for more than a few seconds. From the ceiling she hung a net of balloons attached to the light fitting which Huang thought an electrical hazard, but at the almost begging insistence of his wife and son yielded.

Somewhat of a Christmas tree he named it, a small artificial tree many years discarded from its original owners but worth two shillings in the second-hand shop with equally cheap stars and baubles for an extra sixpence. Draped in silver tinsel the tree sprung to life, a delight for Elsie and Edward who dreamed of the presents it would conceal beneath its near bare branches.

Happiness, a family Christmas, though with a trace of sadness for Elsie; Mrs Smith defied her husband's wrath to meet regularly with her daughter and her beloved grandson. Reconciliation with her mother somewhat eased the pain of separation when Huang sailed, still living in hope one day her father would come with her mother to the park to play with Edward.

On their meagre income the family went on a Christmas shopping spree. Wartime austerity though still a fact of life might well have been no more than a bad memory in shop windows decorated with elves and reindeer, Santa Claus and the Nativity. Tinsel hung with abandon, anything that did not move wrapped in bales of multicoloured crepe paper and swamped in cotton wool.

Planned for Christmas dinner a baked meat loaf, a recipe of her mother's, glazed with honey. Baked potatoes, pumpkin, parsnip and onions. Plum pudding, the recipe exchanged while sitting rugged up in woollens on a park bench, an exhilarating mother and daughter bonding, both with an eye on an adventurous Edward. Added to the dough four sixpences, plus two from her mother; another recipe she found leafing through an old magazine, fruit mince pies.

Stretching the budget to its limit allowed the purchase of a bottle of cheap port and two bottles of lemonade.

On Christmas Eve with a hum in her voice she prepared for the next day's feast, first her meat loaf; one precious egg added to minced beef, grated onions and carrots, parsley and mixed herbs, stale bread crusts rubbed to a coarse meal, beef cubes, salt and pepper and a dash of Zhen's port.

With her husband home and up to his neck in mud and clay and worked until he could barely stagger home, her happiness and contentment abounded. Also from the breadwinner an admission, even though he dreaded the thought of water filled trenches in the dark of early morning and groaning his body out an eternity later, he too experienced the warmth and joy of home and family. Thoughts when slowly walking home with every muscle knotted what awaited, kisses and hugs, a wondrous sensation missing in a seaman's life at sea. Arms outstretched and a kiss, his wife eager to tell him of an exciting day, a son of a train set he thought he might find under the

The Chinese Seamen's Children

Christmas tree on Christmas morning.

Occupying pride of place in the window of a toy shop a train set drew the family noses to the cold pane, its price far out of the reach of their budget. Four days' wages, a father attempting to convince his son of other toys far cheaper in the window he should consider. Again and again the family returned to the toyshop to hypnotically gaze in the window, a father finally wilting when he looked into a young son's eyes brimmed with tears, then delight when he said he would ask Santa Claus. Work boots to replace those no more than uppers held together with sail twine would have to wait until the New Year.

Hearing the knock on the door, she decided to put the glazed meat loaf in the ice box after she answered it; she glanced at the clock on the mantelpiece above the stove: 6:40 pm. With a hop in her step she skipped to the door, a happy thought it might be her mother with a gift for Edward, even better an answer to her prayers, her father. Opening the door, she felt her bladder constrict as she clutched her throat with both hands and screamed.

Rain soaked the two burly men in heavy overcoats needed no introduction, their expressionless faces imparting no festive cheer or greeting.

Staggering back from the doorway, she found herself unable to speak or breathe so tightly she gripped her throat. She knew as did all the wives of Chinese seamen in Merseyside. Edward looked up from the floor playing with his wooden truck, making rumbling noises, puzzled by his mother collapsed in the arms of his father.

Huang whispered in her hair: "Elsie, it's a mistake." When he left with the men soon after he would repeat the same words, the last she would ever hear him utter.

19

May 1979

ROXANNE DREW BACK THE heavy drapes and brilliant sunlight streamed through the large bay window, silhouetting her lithe body. Across the rooftops of the houses below a broad expanse of blue sea flecked with sparkling shards unbroken to a faint image of a mountain range shrouded in haze forty miles west.

What he saw from his bed roused him more than the magnificent view, the vision of womanhood at a peak in life where she commanded the terms of yielding to the partners of her choice. Ridged down her spine tiny knuckles of bone, anchoring her ribcage from which her breasts sprung. Perfectly proportioned hips flared from a narrow waist, thighs supporting two perfectly rounded globes as soft as velvet.

Incredibly wet and sticky, how she felt, a not unpleasant sensation, but not of fulfilment. Twice during the night he had taken his release, too quick for her to reach a climax. Turning from the window she smiled as if reading his thoughts, tracing a finger from between her legs to her naval as she padded on thick carpet back to bed.

Sleeping over for the first time, he felt the still warm impression she left in the bed on his right, the sweet and yeasty smell of her body everywhere. It felt right, felt good, and he thought Laurie Moorland would be pleased.

About this beautiful girl he juggled feelings of mixed emotions.

The Chinese Seamen's Children

Fond? No, fond could best describe feelings for a friend, not a woman who shared the intimacy of her body. Love, shouldn't that emotion hit a man between the eyes like a sledgehammer? Did a knot in his belly when he saw her naked or when he possessed her signify love?

Taking hold of him, she said petulantly: "Why do you come so quickly?"

Succeeding with her ministrations, he thought of his long swing on the *Iron Shortland*, paying off in Newcastle the day before. "Roxanne, four months running Port Hedland to Japan a very good reason. Please be patient with me."

"Japanese girls nice?" she cooed.

"Japanese girls nice, wouldn't know. Saw a couple down the hatches driving frontend loaders. Seen from a great height and covered in iron ore, hardhat, goggles and facemasks, who would know."

"Suppose you'd be angry if I told you I ran into an old flame from New Zealand?"

Turning his head to look at her, he frowned; why did he feel a sudden twinge of jealousy? There were no commitments of fidelity between them, both free agents.

"Do I need to know that?"

Yawning, she squeezed harder, causing an even more pleasing and positive reaction.

"Roxanne?"

"Questions, questions," she said petulantly, releasing him and flinging herself on her back. "You were gone forever and as you are aware after having taken your pleasure, I am a woman."

"Sleeping alone for four months, is that an unacceptable denial? Did he satisfy you?"

"You have no right to ask me that."

"No, I haven't. Sorry."

Raising himself on one elbow, he sifted his fingertips through the light brown ringlets that nestled between her legs; he wondered why she had changed her preference. Did a lover request the sensation of a cushion of silken down upon which to grind his lust? Jealous, yes!

Roxanne lived her own life by her own rules as he did which gave neither the right of possession or reason to pry. All that mattered now an aroused female body moved on top of him, guiding his arousal inside her.

Thwarting his upward thrust, she instead slowly sank down on him, a s cry of pure pleasure. Gyrating her body, she threw her head back, mouth wide open, past frustrations dispelled in the ecstatic sensation of what drove inside her, every muscle and nerve gripping and alive where a pulsing heat and hardness filled her. This time her evasive release did not disappoint her, her climax causing her to cry out again and again as each fiery spasm coursed through her body.

Four months of mail lay strewn on the kitchen table; direct debited bills, bank statements, company pay slips, flyers, charitable organisations, two letters from his parents. Affixed with a British stamp and in familiar scrawled handwriting, Edward would be home and paying off around the end of April from the *Argentina Star* and would Alex have leave around that time?

Brewing a pot of coffee, a retreat outdoors seemed a good idea, pulling on a thick hand knitted woollen jumper from his mother to ward off a chilly south-westerly wind from the bay. Autumn in Frankston, cold and miserable, a portent of approaching winter. Spring in England might not be a bad idea. Anyway, a trip to the United Kingdom did at times pass through his mind remembering his conversation with Edward's mother. Renewing his friendship with Edward, a journey farther afield than any he had ever taken as sea.

On his second cup of coffee, he reread Edward's letter; he would ring him when their times coincided, not fully certain a thought that engrossed him did not originate in the soft yielding folds of a beautiful young woman. Asking Roxanne if she would come with him to Liverpool.

The Chinese Seamen's Children

"Edward, how are you, mate?"

On the other end of the line a faint metallic crackling lasted for a few seconds, then a loud whoop. "That's got to be an Aussie accent! You got my letter! Next question, are you going to use some of that grossly obscene money and leave you blokes on the Aussie coast take home in wheelbarrows and come visit me?"

"Could well be, Edward. How's it been with you?"

"Unfortunately I seem to be getting more home time which could be indicative of the sorry state of our shipping flagging out in record numbers. Then again I'm avoiding tramps for the liner trade with some prompting from home."

"Our resistance against flag-of-convenience is still working, shipowners still wary of the union and our reaction to little brown guys in sandals with their gear wrapped in banana leaves creeping up gangways at midnight. Though what the future holds who knows. Prompting from home?"

"Could say a warm and cuddly incentive to go offshore with the planned North Sea development. Big money, good leave and home regular."

"Same here in Bass Strait on the rigs and tenders. Though I like something big around me, like 165,000 tons of iron ore."

"Enough of that, are you coming?"

"Edward, there's something else, a girl I seem to have a thing for, asking her to come with me. Bringing her with me might lead me to rethink where I'm heading. Would that make things awkward?"

"She your typical Aussie, tall and bronzed and a beauty to behold?"

"All of that."

"I share digs. No problem, plenty of room."

"How long are you off?"

"Did a long spell on the last job, about ten weeks. Alex, the welcome's there, for your girl as well."

"Before I go through departures, I'll give you a ring and to hell with time zones."

She stared at him, her lips almost a perfect circle. When she closed her mouth, she furrowed her brow. "England, a long way away, right?"

"England is. Over 12,000 miles by sea, shorter though by plane."

"Not that. How long in time?"

"Probably about a day via Singapore and the Middle East." She should be consumed with excitement, leaping into his arms and showering him with kisses; instead she stared at him with a derisory expression on her face.

"Cooped up in a plane for a whole day?"

"Not all day. There's not an aircraft in the world designed to fly to England in one go." He tried to make light of it, piqued by her humdrum reaction to his offer. "You flew from New Zealand."

"Oh come on, barely enough time to have a few of them small bottles of booze before we landed. Anyway, I get leg cramps."

"Roxanne, I would like you to come."

Suppressing a slight tremor, she clasped her hands in an attitude of prayer. "Some of my girlfriends went to London, couldn't get back home quick enough. Out of the question, there's my job."

"Pulling flat beer for country bumpkins in the public bar of the Bonbeach Hotel? Christ, there's got to be more to life than the public bar of the Bonbeach Hotel?"

"So much you know about me and my future aspirations." Coming into his arms, she offered him the invitation of her lips and tongue. "Not that I'm complaining, but you were so obsessed getting into my black lace panties your conversation never rose above my navel. I'm leaving the hotel, been offered a job in the Southern Cross Hotel."

"Some flash pub."

"Better known as the who's who of Melbourne, and I wouldn't dare call the Southern Cross a pub," she said, pleased at what she felt growing against her. "More money, fewer hours, the opportunities of serving celebrities."

Swollen headed local television minnows prowling for a sweet and easy titbit. Did his nomadic lifestyle condemn him to a life of casual relationships, the occasional ego trip of sidetracking from the stream of seemingly unobtainable women one not so particular in her choice of partner? Maybe he should stop dressing in dungarees and t-shirts, shorts and sandals. Get his hair cut regularly and shave more often.

With long separation words of endearment should come easy, and some did at the height of lovemaking, usually quickly forgotten. Could he say the words *I love you, there is more to our relationship than physical*? Try as hard as he could, the words would not come. Soon their bodies would be joined, the act of love sweat and incredible wetness culminating in breathless exhaustion. What the hell did he want from life and Roxanne Holmquist? Think himself lucky with a passing conquest, breast the bar and brag to his mates. No, the bitterness of rejection his to suffer alone.

Using the services of a local travel agent he booked a six week return ticket with British Airways, scheduled to fly from Melbourne to Sydney Wednesday to join his international flight; Singapore, Muscat, London.

Roxanne started work at the Southern Cross Hotel the same day.

Calf muscles knotted like wet rope, cartilage tauter than a strung bow, worst of all his stomach felt like a ball of undigested lard reacting to what substituted food. It did not make flying more enjoyable having the middle seat in a window row, reduced to begging an obese Scotchman to vacate his seat, impossible to pass with his fold down tray piled with dossiers and folders, an added hazard of tripping over his brief case on the floor.

Overcoming the urge to hold the small pillow he found on his seat over his mouth, he suffered the window seat passenger who reeked of body odour; he might have begrudgingly accepted the sour smell which seemed to intermittently waft and disappear in the sterile atmosphere if not for a nasal condition afflicting the man, continually snorting mucus and swallowing.

Some eight hours into the flight and the aircraft on its approach to Singapore he thought bearable, only the slightest annoyance of leg muscles and the occasional twinge between the shoulder blades. Also wearing off quickly his first amazed impression of the cavernous interior of the Boeing 747, wonderment how it could ever lift off the ground. Then any kudos for British Airways quashed with painful realisation of minimum legroom, narrow seats and a corporate policy to cram as many obnoxious human beings with disgusting habits in the cabin as possible.

Singapore could be likened to a steam bath, herded off the aircraft in darkness and down a steep gangway to board terminal buses spewing diesel fumes as black soot. Two hours later a repeat performance, silent prayers the Scotchman now reposed in a hotel in Singapore dashed when he asked him to vacate his seat so he could take his own. Ingesting poisonous emissions from the bus had inflamed the window seat passenger's condition, his eyes red sinkholes and now using his fresh pillow case as a handkerchief to stem the flow of mucus.

Muscat from the air banking over the turquoise waters of the Gulf of Oman could well have been the terrain of the moon. Painful to the eyes in searing sunlight, a jagged mountain range of barren rock dominated a landscape of sand and rubble. Decreasing time zones confused the mind, bodily functions monitoring normalcy in chaos attributable to what the airline served on small plastic trays.

Muscat mercifully supplied an air bridge, a reprieve from what shimmered in waves of pure malevolence from stained and cracked concrete. Alex ordered a coffee from an old Arab, his weathered face and permanent sneer indicative of his abhorrence serving infidels; he might well have dwelled in the desert, or more fittingly a driver of camels visible on the northern perimeter of the airport.

Coffee, or the inch of black mud in the bottom of a tiny cup, would have supported the spoon proffered to add sugar. Milk plopped in green curdled lumps from a jug, the Arab with a fiendish glare waiting for a signal to stop. Alex smelled the jug, pushed his coffee out of reach and almost vomited. Another dashed hope and acceptance of

The Chinese Seamen's Children

his fate, the Scotchman speeding on his way to make an oil deal, the window seat passenger rushed to hospital.

Endurance now at its lowest ebb for its tortured human cargo, the aircraft tracked its course over the Persian Gulf, the Mediterranean and France. Through the window a murky day dawned as the aircraft banked and made a course correction over Kent, and if thoroughly sapped passengers racked their minds to nominate the day he or she would have had to think hard to reply. Announced in clipped and professional terms from its third captain since leaving Australia, fog causing earlier delays at Heathrow had lifted and their arrival on schedule.

Even though unable to escape his seating companions, forced to stand sandwiched between them in the aisle with his carryon bag held tightly against his chest, the sense of relief he experienced teetering on his feet with release imminent filled him with exhilaration. Self admiration for mustering the good manners to nod to the smartly attired male steward as he disembarked, even as he passed disinterested airline staff studying clipboards and talking into radios on the air bridge. Dulled thoughts filled his mind as to where on the planet he now stood, and that it took a tramp steamer six weeks to travel the same distance this aircraft flew in twenty-four hours.

Claimed baggage, passport stamped and nothing to declare, he found himself in a fast moving stream of people entering the main concourse of the terminal, a thought he could well be staring down the tube of a kaleidoscope. Clothing cheap and expensive, business suits, outrageous miniskirts, flowing Middle Eastern and African robes sweeping a maze of corridors of humanity on the move, spreading underfoot wads of discarded chewing gum. Kaftans, burqa, sarongs, sandals, bare feet. Pakistanis, Indians, Arabs, Turks, Chinese, Japanese, nuns and clerics.

Sullen and sallow faced eastern Europeans, Americans brash and complaining, Africans so black their chubby faces shone purple, questioning the truth of famine in their homeland. Some in a state of stress, searching for relatives or uniformed limousine drivers holding up cardboard signs. Bewildered, their dulled brains unable to decipher a mind boggling confusion of information, arrows pointing in every direction other than the one offering escape from this madness.

Trapped, the timid and unsure cowered in trepidation of stone-faced immigration, police, quarantine, Customs. Airline staff with voices more intimidating than parade ground sergeants, imbued with deft dexterity likened to sheepdog trials, corralling stupefied passengers into tight knit groups, bamboozling by intoning the minute print on the backs of their tickets. Nowhere to escape, the permeating miasma of unwashed bodies, sweat exuding from caked pores, curries and garlic. In a food court two tables strewn with fouled baby diapers discarded by a group of burqa clad mothers, tables used by others to eat and drink their flat pints.

Officialdom ruled supreme and those not complying were removed with swift and merciless, almost surgical efficiency, from the system. Either given over to patrolling police who could call upon savage dogs and batons for support, or informed because their names did not appear on fly lists their fortunes lay elsewhere.

Even for the most seasoned of travellers the ceaseless assault on the ears, the hum of thousands of voices, dialects and inflections competing against each, clinical public announcements and warnings, complete surrender offered salvation from insanity. Above this panic attack inducting din, shoving, tripping, barging, queue jumping, assault with baggage trolleys, crying and tantrum throwing children, Alex heard a single shout. Above a sea of turbans and keffiyeh, dreadlocks, bizarre headdress and wilted coiffure a hand waved.

Edward forced a passage through five Saudis leading a group of women attired in flowing black burqa, mobile black tents. "Alex!"

Since last seeing him a few added pounds around the middle gave him a more mature and robust look, his face beaming as he embraced Alex, uncaring he blocked the progress of the Saudi entourage.

Alex ignored their reproachful glares. "Edward, your last ship must have been a good feeder. How are you?"

"Might have been the cheap but suspect South American beef the chief steward stuffed down our gullets. Hey, you look great yourself which is of course testament to those gourmet chefs on the Aussie coast. Pity your girl couldn't come, women love London and its shopping. I've booked a room here before we head home tomorrow."

"Roxanne is a story of love's labour's lost, or something like that. Or thwarted. The *Argentina Star*, good job?"

"Workhouse, but a happy mob and overall not a bad job. How long our manning will remain is a question, more and more of our ships being scrapped and flagged out. Follow close to me, mate, don't want to lose you among the Empire's children returning home."

Passing a bank of open doors Alex slipped his jacket on, Edward jabbing a finger at an Underground sign ahead, his voice loud enough to carry over the noise. "Good, you'll need your coat even though it is spring. Booked into the Merchant Navy Hotel in Lancaster Gate, smack in the middle of London with a tube station close by. Can change your Aussie dollars in the hotel at a better rate than the Heathrow usurers."

Like many Australians he experienced an odd feeling of déjà vu looking for the first time at the vista of historic masonry, pediments and columns. Formative years in an Australian classroom indelibly imprinted in his pliable young mind an almost reverence to the grandeur of the United Kingdom. Opulence in all its intimidating splendour, rows of magnificent white painted mansions built with the immense wealth drawn from the far reaches of the Empire. Amid these aged symbols of a nation at the height of its world influence rose the Merchant Navy Hotel, its massive oaken doors protected by a columned portico, a Victorian relic demanding of those who stood humbled on the pavement seeking entry, a feeling of inadequacy and a reminder of their lowly station in life.

Floor to ceiling windows and pediments, each window served by its own balcony of pilasters and corbels, gave the second floor a regal elegance. Two upper floors above this magnificent symmetry, though slightly less ornate, still retained the eloquence of an era of horse drawn carriages, to the discerning eye craftsmanship without equal.

Among the other mansions it shared the street with the hotel differed little except for one profound statement, a large red duster hanging in limp folds on its gaff over the entrance portico. At the reception desk Alex presented his passport and last discharge as proof of eligibility, a temporary repose for seamen of all nationalities passing through London.

Large and with an exceptionally high ceiling the room gave the impression of bareness; two small wardrobes, two narrow single beds and a third unmade in a corner, ready for use with pillows and neatly folded linen. Alex shivered, the room cold, the heating turned off. Edward threw himself on a bed, kicked his shoes off and propped his feet on the bed end. "Look beat there, mate, but you're not being let off the hook even though you look like you've just gone twelve rounds with the crowd of the *Baron Maclay*."

Sinking down on the opposite bed, he feared if he put his head on the pillow he would drop into instant sleep.

"Staying here with your girl if she'd had the good sense to come would have caused a bit of a stir there being a strict moral code for right of entry. Heard it said by some frustrated seamen about as severe as a Vatican edict banning the priesthood from matrimony. Shore bosun who runs the place is the gaffer from hell. Able to strike fear in the hearts of first trip deck boys with a single glance, a zealot who demands proof of conjugal legality from those who pass through the front door with a tempting female on the arm."

"London, in this day and age?" he said, fighting the urge to lie down, draw back the snow white, starched top sheet and surrender to glorious slumber.

"No premarital hanky-panky allowed in this astute establishment under the despotic eye of our shore bosun."

"Bosun?"

"Second officer with British India stationed permanently on the

The Chinese Seamen's Children

China coast, not reluctant to putting a mirror polished shoe up a coolie's rear end." Edward looked at his watch. "Bar will be opened and I would not recommend using the dining room for lunch as she feeds like a British tramp, quantity and quality. Come on, mate, try a British beer, that'll buck you up."

"British beer doesn't come with good references, also warm."

"Get served a warm beer in a British pub send it back. Some brews can pour a bit flat. Now having made that statement, there are some beers the complete opposite, all head. Might take ten minutes to work its way to the top of the glass, but well worth the wait."

"Black beers?"

"Black beers, lagers, ales, porter or whatever. Reckon you could get addicted to Newcastle Brown Ale, got a whack to it which sends the Geordies into fighting mode. Put some matchsticks under those eyes and come meet Mr Samuel Morris-Dowling."

Mr Samuel Morris-Dowling would have been mortified of his pseudo demotion through the lower ranks to bosun, to his ordered mind, the white ones, usually a loud mouthed self-opinionated nuisance in the complexity of shipboard management. After long and searching observation he considered bosuns, the white ones, a single degree higher up the scale of intellectual capacity than ABs, even so still not warranting little more accreditation in the tiers of responsibility than that of a messenger boy.

TS *Vindicatrix* trained, nurtured by the elite of the British merchant marine to a class of officer unsurpassed in the world, reflected his life's achievement, an upright bearing and a barely noticeable tilt of his nose which gave the impression of being aware of a slight and distasteful odour in the air.

Slowly rising through the ranks of British India, including his indentures, accounted for fifteen years of dedicated service, achieving two precious gold bars on his shoulders before a non-life threatening medical condition precluded him from further service at sea. Not wanting to abandon his officer class when a position arose for a manager of a London hotel dedicated to merchant navy personnel he placed his impeccable credentials on the table.

Opened from 11:00 am to 2:00 pm, Edward guided Alex to a set of four comfortable leather chairs set around a glass topped table. First impressions of the bar disappointed, not how he imagined a British pub with low whitewashed ceilings, rough hewn oaken beams and open fires. Then the Merchant Navy Hotel described as a pub would be a misnomer bordering on sacrilege to its historic pedigree. It also earned its high respect with a sophisticated ambience of carpet underfoot, soft leather furnishings, wood panelling, good decorum, polished brass, and the nutty smell of wax polish. No ashtray ever overflowed and no one dared discard a wad of gum or food wrapper.

Something of a surprise, the bar well patronised at such an early hour, Edward's conspiratorial voice imparting the information the numbers represented a pre-lunch phenomenon of tea and coffee among officers and their spouses and nothing to do with legendary drinking regardless the hour prevalent amongst the lower ranks. Edward glanced around the bar, indicating a ramrod erect figure moving among the tables. "Sorry to disappoint you, but with the high number of masters and chief engineers among us we might not be included in late morning salutations."

"What do you mean?"

"Positively identified as an AB at the front desk thus very low on the greeting scale. Then again Mr Morris-Dowling might be feeling some empathy for the labouring classes with a Tory by-election win last week, who knows?"

"How do I address him?"

"Sammy, he likes Sammy." Edward sauntered to the bar.

Alex thought differently.

"Have to warn you Mr Morris-Dowling has an especially low esteem for you Aussies, though we Chinese come in much lower

The Chinese Seamen's Children

socially than you lot whom he reckons are coarse, self-opinionated, brainwashed unionised bottom feeders," he said, returning with two pints of beer.

"Well, I'm definitely not calling him Sammy. That beer's flat."

"No, it's not flat, that's how it pours. London Pride."

Not as cold as he would have liked, but the malty taste more than pleased the palate. Taking a deep swallow, he nodded appreciatively.

Mr Samuel Morris-Dowling approached on carefully proportioned steps, about to grace their table with his presence; he looked taller because of his erect posture, hands firmly clasped behind his back. From his superior position he looked down his nose at the two seamen drinking pints, noting the time in a mental clock.

"Top of the morning to you, Mr Morris-Dowling." Edward said, indicating Alex. "My mate from Australia, Alex Nielsen. Aussie AB and Seamen's Union of Australia organiser."

Tensioning of nerve ends affecting spinal bone and cartilage caused him to stiffen even more. "We have not been the recipients of late of many Australians passing through our establishment." Looking for an escape avenue he found it with Captain Hartwell and his wife a few tables away; the gracious master would not be too irked with a brief interruption to his reading of *The Times*. "Good day and the management of the Merchant Navy Hotel extend our sincere wishes whatever your business is in the United Kingdom it is successful and our accommodations according to your exacting standards receive approval."

Taking his leave with obvious relief, he hailed Captain Hartwell.

"Look around you, Alex, and tell me what you see?"

"Guests who seem at ease and relaxed. No tables overflowing with pints, only tea and coffee. Not much talking, reading newspapers and magazines. By what I see not exactly enjoying themselves, but maybe with a few pints their faces might thaw."

"Right about the booze, well down here at least, what some of them snorted earlier in their rooms wouldn't have a clue. Something else, how are these serious seafarer and their legally wedded partners dressed?"

"Suits and ties for the men, the women a bit formal. Then again you Poms are a little reserved in your dress. Me, like you, dungarees and open neck shirt. Don't understand, Edward."

"Simple, we are outnumbered by the upper echelon of our maritime industry, granted the privilege, albeit only for a limited time, to mingling in stratified air. Notice anyone, unshaven and scruffy present company excluded, you could positively identify from the focastle or beneath the steering flat?"

"Some of our blokes on the coast live in suits and ties."

"Without fear of contradiction everyone here is either on the bridge, below in pressed white overalls, chief steward or purser."

"Being a first class hotel, why not? What would you pay for a hotel in the middle of London?"

"Much more that we're paying plus VAT. Four, five times possibly. No, our blokes prefer the Ritz or the Regency."

"Ritz and Regency sounds a bit high class. Why would seamen favour those places when there is a hotel in London that specifically caters for them? We are in the middle of London, right?"

"Near enough. Yeah, it is pretty odd that. Maybe it's the company."

Smothered in soft leather his eyes grew heavy again, a rapid blinking and a stifled yawn. Mr Morris-Dowling concluded his morning rounds, a patronising enjoy-your-day to a master's wife as she prepared for an afternoon's shopping in London, she and her husband flying to Cape Town in the morning to join his ship.

"Edward, I don't think I can keep my eyes open much longer."

"Which you will because the worst thing you can do is surrender to your body clock. Lunch at Dirty Dick's, then a walk under the river to Greenwich to climb the foremast of the *Cutty Sark*. Nearby is a meridian and a couple of clocks of special interest to seamen."

Forming an image in his mind of the *Cutty Sark* and the Harrison brothers clocks, he willed his eyes to remain open."Can we really climb the foremast of the *Cutty Sark*?"

"Not recommended. Last time I saw her kinked wire and bulldog grips in her rigging didn't look very shipshape, or the Irish pennants. Some hopeful soul's placed an oil drum by the gangway with a sign to throw in your loose change for maintenance. Keep those eyes open, mate, know the feeling only too well. Tomorrow we'll be getting the tube to Upminster where I have parked the car with a mate of mine, then home to Liverpool. You want to see what happens in London if you're lucky to find a park and overstay your welcome. There's this big London council mobile crane that lifts you on the back of a truck and wherever you end up God only knows. Probably in the jaws of a crusher in a scrap metal yard."

Swamped in a huge yawn, Edward had some consoling words. "Don't worry, mate, I'll take pity on you and let you have an early night. Promise."

Edward drove his fire engine red MG sports car in early morning heavy traffic with a vengeance, attacking with grim determination a raised circular median cast in the shadow of an enormous green sign with white circles in its centre and a choice of multiple destinations.

"What the hell is that?"

"Romford roundabout. Where the meek cringe and the strong prevail." His head moved in two directions in a split second before flooring the accelerator and entering the heavily trafficked device.

Alex clung to the dash with both hands as the small car ground its rapidly spinning wheels in tar, keeping in the left lane and passing three options before exiting at the fourth. "Jesus, are these madhouses prevalent here?" Releasing a bone crushing grip, he expelled the air compressed in his lungs.

"Invented by us, though that particular one is overly large and normally congested, also confusing for the first time with so many exits. Something else, we do drive on the left. Many of the lorries, or trucks as you call them in Aussie, are left-hand drive off the ferries from Europe and do have drivers. Something else, use of hazard lights on the motorways, warning of traffic ahead slowing, congestion, accident, fog, rain, or breakdown. For no apparent reason traffic can in an instance almost stop, then just as quickly speed up. Odd."

"How far is Liverpool?"

Edward pointed to the glove box. "Roadmap's in there. About 200 miles."

Unfolding the roadmap in his lap its complexity gave the impression of a tightly woven web of blue motorways, green, red and yellow intersecting lines depicting lesser highways and roads. Populated areas shaded in sepia, some splattered blots highlighting major cities with barely an open field between them. Nothing in Australia compared with the density, a rough approximation Australian country towns separated by a distance of sixty miles, the endurance limit of a team of horses hauling a coach.

"There any place in the United Kingdom where you can't see another house?"

"Most certainly. So what do you think of the old girl?"

"True by what I have been taught and read over the years. Flying in over Heathrow, green, everywhere green. Where not green a patchwork quilt of amazing colours. Edward, this may sound crazy to you, but I feel I have been here before. In my pliable school years I lived in a country dominated by a smooth tongued knight of the realm more British than the British, a prime minister named Robert Menzies. Australia is permanently entrenched in worship of the British monarchy thanks to him, a pompous windbag who in 1966 even wanted to name our new decimal currency a royal. Now being able to feel it, breathe it, experience it, one word comes to mind, magnificent."

"Comparable to Australia?"

"Stealing a tourist brochure blurb, an emerald isle opposed to a hot and dry continent at the bottom of the world. No contest, Edward."

"Australia's got a lot going for it though and speaking of such, Otis married a Pakistani and has a fish and chip shop in Cottingham."

"Close?"

"On the east coast near Hull. Doing well so I hear."

The Chinese Seamen's Children

Memories flooded back to Wallaroo and the *Baron Maclay*. "Some trivia, your cook got away on the Australian coast."

"Good for him. Have to say he tried to do his best though the food, or the lack of it, never improved. Yeah, he'd had enough when we got back to Australia. I think he knocked over the blokes making the gangway net fast on the wharf."

"Ex-gaffer, how did he go when he sobered up?"

"Rough, extremely rough. With no more gear to flog on the ship and no subs the partygoers surrendered to the inevitable. Strange to say after that first encounter on the Wallaroo wharf most of them turned out okay. As for the job she ran with no problems, the old man you could take with a dose of salts, the mate bearable when you got to know him and where his interests lay."

"Booze does some strange things to seamen."

20

"AFTER MY MOTHER YOU'LL get a real crush on Katherine," Edward said, turning into a narrow one-way street, without exception small front gardens ablaze with flower boxes in full bloom. Three bedrooms, two bathrooms, kitchen, lounge-dining and full glass sunroom, one of fourteen identical units, exuded an air of affluence made even more apparent by the expensive cars parked in the street. "We're not that far from the waterfront, Dingle where Mother lives."

"Alone?"

"She does."

"Your father?"

Before replying he extracted Alex's bags from the boot. "My father's story is a tale of betrayal. Mother's also, disowned and abandoned by my grandfather. Sounds like high drama from a flowery Victorian novel, I exaggerate not. My grandmother, who is in a nursing home, with a lot of guts stood by my mother. Then my grandfather died and fate would have it we went to live with her, me about six."

Searching for a key on his key ring, he inserted it in the lock and pushed open the door, ushering Alex inside. Standing with his back to a large multi-paned window framed by floor to ceiling drapes, he held out his arms. "What do you reckon? Not bad for an AB?"

Subtle luxury symbolised by thick beige carpet, matching drapes and pelmets, indirect lighting and pale pastel colours. Sterility the motive a thoughtfully designed kitchen both functional and modern in white laminates, the kitchen separated from the lounge-dining room by a kidney shaped servery. Clusters of tiny spotlights highlighted cut glass decanters of spirits, wine and beer glasses in a clear glass cabinet suspended from the ceiling above the servery on slender stainless steel rods. No prompting needed to know who chose one of the expensive prints on the walls, beautifully framed in antique oak the *Cutty Sark* by John Allcot.

"Katherine and I share down the middle, me of course missing in action for more than half the year while she keeps the rich and infamous from going to jail."

"Good lawyer?"

"Here we call them solicitors, mate, but I guess the same breed. She most certainly is good at her job, junior partner or whatever solicitors call themselves in the ranks. Rabid, straight for the jugular."

"Serious?"

"Serious, yes. Married in haste and divorced just as quick, another solicitor which I suppose is reason enough to reassess an earlier decision. Making it more permanent comes up regularly, but we haven't got around to it yet. Really I must consider my options going to sea to ponder other floating alternatives." Something else on his mind, he changed the subject. "Enough of sweet Katherine for the moment, there is my mother who should be making her way home from the nursing home shortly, makes the effort to visit grandmother three times a week, bakes little treats and catches the bus."

Overflowing on the pavement an Indian hardware store had on display what seemed most of its goods for sale, even five wheelbarrows chained together stacked with tools. "That used to be Mr Gresham's corner store where you could buy a pint of milk and a scoop of humbugs, a pound of flour and a half dozen eggs. Mother worked there when she met my father, she lives just down the street."

"Again, I feel a kinship here. Then sailing on the Aussie coast with half the crowds made up of you Poms, why not?"

"Liverpool is the embodiment of working class, though with unemployment and people through hopelessness dropping out of the workforce that perception is rapidly changing. How about a prime minister who has high on her wish list the smashing of the unions and the selloff of national assets? Forced retirements and disillusionment are undermining the union movement already struggling to maintain their influence. Not to mention a pro-government media no more than an arm of the rightwing establishment espousing lies all is well in workers paradise."

"Akin to your Margaret Thatcher, we have Prime Minister Malcolm Fraser, a hardboiled conservative with a pack of baying country hicks supporting his hatred of the union movement. Then again even staunch unionists can sometimes wonder why we foolishly in the name of militancy hand the enemy the ammunition to attack us. Contracts for the building of four small bulk carriers of around 16,500 ton deadweight for the Australian National Line, a worldwide tender amazingly won against Asian competition by the State Dockyard in Newcastle supported by a federal government subsidy. Winning this order assured the New South Wales government owned dockyard would survive, and with worker support even make a profit on a four ship build.

"Before granting federal money the prime minister requested a no-strike clause be inserted in the contacts, no great deal with dispute settling procedures in place. Painters and dockers and ironworkers, boilermakers and blacksmiths, fitters and riggers, plumbers and shipwrights readied for battle, mortified the basic right of workers to withhold their labour would be jeopardised. Unanimously the unions said an emphatic no and the federal government withdrew the subsidy, the four ship contract subsequently awarded to a Japanese shipyard. Now the State Dockyard's future, never certain competing against Asian yards, teeters on the perilous, the blame squarely placed on the

The Chinese Seamen's Children

unions. Millions of dollars of money lost throughout the Newcastle area geared for ships construction, wages, small subsidiaries, goods and services. Even a plea from management if the unions would only encourage their members to give an hour and a half a day of actual productive work the dockyard might survive."

Removing a dozen small apple pies from the oven, she put half aside for the nursing home and two in bowls topped with whipped cream for her son and his guest. Passing years had been kind, a face relatively free of wrinkles, ageing noticeable mostly in her hair peppered with grey.

"From Australia you have travelled a long, long way, Alex," she said, pouring three cups of tea, placing a small milk jug and sugar bowl on a matching ceramic tray. "Ships in the Mersey continually leave for Australia and the Far East. As I know only too well those ships do not return for many months."

Thick cream melted, warm shortcrust pastry crumbled in the mouth, steaming chunky clove spiced apple exquisite to the taste.

"Edward says you also are a seaman." Not satisfied with the amount of cream topping her son's apple pie, she spooned two additional blobs from her cream bowl.

"How I met Edward in Australia, Mrs Huang." Cream trickled down his chin; about to have more cream spooned on his apple pie, he passed a hand across his bowl.

"Edward told me how you met." Her chest rose and fell slowly, a distant look clouding her eyes, her attention focused on a framed photograph on the mantelpiece above the gas fire; a family portrait of two serious faced adults staring into the camera lens, the man nursing an infant. "I still worry for my son at sea, the long waits before a treasured letter tells me he is safe on the other side of the world, then home and gone again. For wives and mothers a lifetime of waiting and loneliness."

Reaching across the table both their hands intertwined. Smiling, more years shed from her face. "Then again I suppose mothers never stop worrying about their children, the rewards of a homecoming cherished moments. My wishes are he would give up the sea and settle down. Edward and dear Katherine make such a lovely couple."

"Giving you a stack of grandkids to run riot, you would soon wish I remained single and carefree."

"Always with excuses to avoid making a commitment. Katherine is a wonderful woman, her lot in life to be smitten by a seaman who comes and goes to places one only knows by the stamp on an envelope."

"My neighbour has similar misgivings," Alex said.

"So you are not married, Alex?"

"No, not married."

"Well, you should be, Edward as well. What is it with you seamen? I keep saying over and over to Edward, you are not getting any younger, settle down. Time you married the girl you love, and love you do. I know it, one only has to see you together."

"What would we do without mothers?" Edward rose from the table and stretched; a Toby jug, a jovial red cheeked English squire in a tricorn hat, sat on the crystal cabinet. Folding two ten pound notes, he placed them in the jug, then turned and lifted his mother to her feet. Their tender embrace caused Alex to turn away as if a voyeur to a mother and son special moment.

Close to the waterfront the pub differed little from its grimy counterparts in Australia, raised and competing voices, a smoky bar filled with dockers, seamen, lorry drivers, factory and foundry workers in grease stained overalls. Underfoot littered with discarded food, cigarette packets, wrappers, butts and whatever else emptied out of the pockets of those competing for space at the bar.

Edward pointed Alex in the direction of an outdoor area through

The Chinese Seamen's Children

a glass door with long tables and side benches, a comment it seemed their fellow working class preferred smoke in their lungs to biting air off the Mersey. Raising his pint, he made contact with Alex's. "Going to say it again, it's great to see you, mate. Even better on my turf, though I do have a soft spot for Aussie."

"Thanks for having me. Your mother makes a wonderful apple pie."

"She does at that. So caring and gentle, a needless worrier though."

"Edward, you said something about betrayal and your father, your mother living alone."

"Edward Huang, son of a Liverpool Chinese seaman. One of many, which makes us the children of Chinese seamen," he said, his voice trailing away and his eyes almost closed. "Sorry, but I get bound up inside when I think of what my mother went through. Me, far too young to understand the true extend of what happened to my father. Wrenched from his family on Christmas Eve and deported, a man who offered his life for his country of adoption. Lived with the nightmare every seaman did, of their ships victims of war, tankers blowing up, ships loaded with iron ore sunk in less than a minute, munitions ships razing entire waterfronts like the *Malakand* in Huskisson Dock in 1941. My father after the war only wanted to live in peace and share the bounty of a prosperous and free community with his family. His reward, his existence erased from the face of the planet."

"How?"

"Taken by men whom I once imagined wore ankle length leather coats similar to another repressive regime, but these men were British obeying orders from the British government. Decreed by the government a situation existed of an over abundance of Chinese in the United Kingdom, and with the war won no further use could be found for them. Though of course maintaining a pool of seamen calculated by their shipping cohorts to fully man post-war British vessels with even lower waged crews. Not forgetting a stack on the beach to keep those on articles permanently giving their utmost."

"Issued a British discharge book, wouldn't he find it easy to join a ship anywhere in the world? Scandinavians are renowned for it, even with their own pickups in major ports."

"Those who rebelled against the system of racial intolerance, discriminate wages and conditions, who confronted their perpetrators, were blacklisted. My father being prominent in his union would without a doubt have had his name noted. About joining a homeward bound ship, I have given that a lot of thought. Returning home to condemn, take the fight to the core and change the system. Hell-bent on winning recognition for Chinese seamen who served the Empire in war. It didn't happen, not even a letter. My father simply vanished."

"Inquiries to the government proved fruitless?"

"Sheer concrete walls would have been is no greater obstacle when searching through mountainous files of fact and fiction, cover-ups and illegalities. Can't even find out the name of the ship used for deportation, its destination though I assume it would have been Singapore."

"There has to be records."

"Of course there are records. Mountains of them plus maddening bureaucratic obstinacy. My father for all intents and purposes vanished and no one in government gives a damn, then and now."

"Probably I'm harping on this, but how hard would it be for a seaman to join something out of Singapore? Even an old tramp would eventually end up in a British or European port sometime or other."

"Most assuredly, but visualise Singapore after liberation from the Japanese. P&O and British India ships steaming line astern from the United Kingdom crammed with bureaucrats, business as usual for the victorious Empire. Streets lined with joyous natives bowing in reverence to the courageous Empire having spilled its precious blood for their freedom. How the British government would like to envisage it, but their return met acrimony in most quarters, particularly the Malayan Communist Party who did not hand in their British weapons after the war and wanted their own brand of freedom.

"1946 for Singapore and the Malayan peninsula did not dawn well for its liberated population, food shortages and strikes, the British raj back in full force with manic intent to strip the wealth of Malaya in the form of oil, rubber and tin. Communists waged guerrilla warfare in the swamps and jungles, Australia with its blood ties to the Empire called upon with others to send troops and planes to support the United Kingdom. Of course this act of suppression never received recognition as a declared state of war, why declare it when it would nullify insurance payments to the British owners of the mines and plantations for damages to their investments.

"Given an official title, the Malayan Emergency, the conflict did bear some resemblance with the Boer War in that large numbers of Malayans and Chinese ended up in barbed wire concentration camps. Probably not as inhumane as the British treatment of Boer women and children to guarantee a satisfactory outcome to that war, but still a well practised incarceration of a population to achieve a planned military objective."

"Do you think your father might have been involved?"

"Membership of the British Communist Party, I think he may. After what happened to him I don't think my father would have had much love for the British restoring their colonial will in Singapore. Also he would have held strong opinions about the Dutch and French resuming business as usual."

Alex returned from the bar with fresh pints; placing them on the table he gave Edward's shoulder an affectionate rub.

"Makes me so angry when I read the colonial powers in Indochina armed Japanese prisoners-of-war, savage, sadistic brutes who for amusement bayoneted and decapitated their enemy, not to mention women with babies in their arms. Guarding Communist guerrillas in concentrations camps, our past allies against the Japanese. Courageous fighters who refused to accept defeat, who remained to fight the enemy while the almighty colonial powers ran with their tails between their legs."

"Such a large number of Chinese seamen effected, wouldn't there have been an outcry from local politicians? Unions? Church leaders?"

"Hardly a whimper. Only when the injustices against their fathers became known through reminiscing mothers did the children of Chinese seamen, now older and worldlier, begin the harassment of officialdom. More enlightened on worldly affairs a new generation sought and demanded answers. Lobbyists with the ferocity of piranhas would have been the most logical for success, but that is in hindsight. Mountains of paperwork leading nowhere. Shipping records, yes, also hundreds of thousands of documents of service personnel returning to the workforce. Industrial documents of winding down from peak war production, retooling and restructuring for peace. There somewhere hidden among all that, my father's fate."

"Surely there should have been some commitment of help, outrage from members of parliament in working class constituencies. By what I have read the British merchant navy at war's end had a godlike status."

"Until bellies didn't go to bed at night hungry, the need to supply and sustain a nation at war ended. With few exceptions the working class felt threatened by the Chinese taking their jobs, even more so in a climate where boardrooms were savagely cutting job numbers and conditions to compete in a world with new players. As well it would take a courageous politician to support thousands of unemployed Chinese seamen choking the corners of Merseyside with placards around their necks these hardworking and uncomplaining workers willing to work for recognition and food only."

"Not hearing from him must have caused your mother even greater pain."

"Yes, yes, yes, not a word. One letter to give my mother hope that in her despairing world a light still burned. Being only young my memories are blurred, but I do remember the long silences, of finding my mother alone and crying. Mother's anguish, the heartbreak and above all the despair of a woman alone with a child who could not understand the simple word, why? How could people do this to those who had shared the horror of the blitz and the threat of defeat? I wonder how she survived the torment that must have consumed her. Also wonder how she can forgive, which she does, bigots who

The Chinese Seamen's Children

condemned a girl for falling in love with a young Chinese seaman.

"Alone with no one to turn to except a guardian angel also married to a Chinese seaman, who to this day is still by her side. Mother's only family support came from behind the back of my grandfather, a timid old lady living in dread of a little man with a head full of racial intolerance. Making no excuses, this sounds dreadful, but it came as a blessing for the family when he died, because Mother returned to her home." Edward took a sip of his beer, a shake of his head. "Far, far too many like my mother, the same story over and over. At school we got our fair share of bullying, chants and taunts. I retaliated with my fists which I suppose hardened me for a life at sea. Sad to say after some serious confrontations on the school ground I became quite adept in head butting which quickly put an end to most arguments."

An easy silence fell between them, each for a moment in time intent with their own thoughts; Edward broke the impasse. "Some hold the opinion the treatment meted to Liverpool Chinese on a par with Nazi Germany, not an adulated government soaring in the ecstasy of victory. Chinese seamen sailed the ships that made victory possible. Did not a prime minister who could walk on water say the very same thing? For Chinese seamen the final ridicule came with the abolishment of the war risk bonus the day war ended, conveniently dismissing the fact the world's oceans teemed with live mines and unexploded ordnance and would do so for decades. Which I suppose is similar to the *Titanic* where the surviving seamen manning the oars went off wages the instant she slid bow first to the bottom."

"Something else about the war I find incomprehensible, about a prime minister you say able to walk on water, how could the British people have rejected him when he rallied them when all seemed lost? Having read Churchill's history and the awful blunders he made, plus those he took the blame for, he strode upon the world stage in a particular time in history when most needed. Referring to history we can only imagine how the British people felt in 1940 with an unstoppable juggernaut unleashed from Germany overwhelming Europe. Screaming rants of a strutting and victorious Hitler, Europe conquered and the United Kingdom about to fall."

"Churchill did stir a fighting spirit in the hearts of his people, that fact indisputable. He also proclaimed some stirring sentiments about the British merchant marine and allied seamen, of a huge debt owed these men and their supreme sacrifices would not go unheralded. Sadly for us his grand rhetoric an instant memory loss the day war ended."

"Pity the British maritime unions did not give the Chinese more support."

"Thinking back the British unions had their own problems, but yes there could have been some fraternal offerings of solidarity. There being one exception, though not in this country."

"Where?"

"Do I really need to tell you? Chinese crews of British ships in Australian waters turned to the Seamen's Union of Australia for support. Racial abuse, bashings, poor food, living conditions, wages and the final insult, removal of the war risk bonus still being paid to white crews. Throwing open their arms your union welcomed their Chinese comrades and arranged mass meetings for them. Aussie union rooms were always open to the Chinese, never once in their struggles turned away." Edward again sank into silence, then with a tremor in his voice said: "One day I will find out what happened to my father. Of that I vow!"

Alex expected a simple dinner with Edward and Katherine, informed the hostess's best friend Jennifer would make a foursome. Then another deep and instant sleep! Katherine Perry typified the classic English beauty; incredibly fair skin, a hint of rosiness in her cheeks, hazel eyes and fashionably cut blonde hair.

Exploring Liverpool in the afternoon, a pub and two pints, brought on another sapping bout of fatigue, dispelled the moment Katherine burst through the front door and her radiant presence took command,

The Chinese Seamen's Children

a kiss for Edward and a greeting hug for Alex.

"Seeing there's a shortage of Australians in Liverpool I couldn't pass up the opportunity to share you with a good friend of mine who will be sociably late due to work."

"Got to give it to you Aussies you can certainly weave your hormonal magic. My mates can't get a foot in the door let alone have one of her highly selective friends exposed to their company," Edward said in the background, selecting a bottle of Californian Merlot from an extensive wine rack. "You'll like Jennifer even though she is in an industry frequently likened to the feral practice of law, real estate. Wouldn't exactly call her the merry divorcee, a very serious girl. Lives near the park with her mother and has the sweetest little daughter, a real darling is Chloe."

Katherine poked her tongue at him, checking Edward's prepared dinner cooking in the wall oven; potatoes, onions, pumpkin and a small leg of New Zealand lamb. Edward and Katherine lived together for two years, Edward an idiosyncrasy in her wide circle of professional friends. When their physical relationship reached another plane, an emotional level of attraction more profound than a fleeting romance, she gave this simple but strong willed man her full and unconditional love. Marriage at a young age failed because even though she and her husband shared similar interests a feeling of totality with another being failed to bloom.

Long absences filled her with loneliness, the tears of separation proof if she ever needed it of her love for this seaman. On occasions her mind toyed with a truly feminine solution to have her man home on a more permanent basis, a potent weapon to wield, an incentive for him to seek work on coasters, tugs or the prospects of offshore work in the developing North Sea oilfields, she threatened to go off the pill.

Jennifer Rice's work-related lateness ended as Katherine set out the plates in preparation of serving; Alex never heard the doorbell ring, instead saw a woman handing Edward her coat. She seemed to float towards him, holding out her hand. "Jennifer Rice, I have heard so much about you, Alex."

Taking her hand he averted his eyes momentarily to avoid staring. "Jennifer, you're in real estate." His mind failed him of a more sophisticated response; tall as he, slim and lithe in her movements, a woman at a pivotal point in life where she would never be more beautiful or desirable. Though with her it would not be a downhill race against time, a truly exceptional beauty who would retain her gift for life.

She brushed dark brown hair from her brow, her hair in thick tresses falling around her shoulders; no, not an errant lock of hair, he thought, a deliberate deception to project an image of feminine frailty concealing her business acumen, a potent weapon wielded in a male dominated profession to give her the edge needed to succeed. Her loose fitting slacks and satin blouse while not intentionally drawing attention, failed to disguise her narrow waist and the flare of her hips, the fullness of her breasts. Like Katherine her skin that of a woman born in high northern latitudes, eyes brown, her nose slightly upturned above the palest of pale pink lips.

"Residential development mainly, the relevant financing with foreign investment banks. Seems everyone wants to buy a bit of the United Kingdom, especially the Middle East. Enough of that though, my little girl and I are very interested in Australia." Australia because of a possible business interest featured high on a list of countries she promised Chloe one day both would visit.

"So far from home you wouldn't feel homesick as your people have been filling the empty spaces since Captain Cook raised the flag in Botany Bay and shot one of the inquisitive locals who had been hanging around for 40,000 years. Also we have nearly all your village and city names on our maps to make the homesick British more comfortable."

Katherine's table bathed in the soft light of two lavender scented candles, reflected diamond-like the glasses of Merlot by each diner, sparkling silver and serviette rings. "To our guest, Alex Nielsen," Katherine toasted. "Welcome to Liverpool." Edward, Katherine and Jennifer raised their glasses.

Whipped cream and pitted cherries in syrup followed the roast

The Chinese Seamen's Children

lamb, the dishes dispatched to the dishwasher; more scented candles lit in various parts of the room added a final touch to a splendid meal as well as another bottle of Merlot.

"My mind is really set on Australia," Jennifer said, offering her glass for Edward to top up. "Vast and fascinating, especially the red outback country. Possibly you know the answer, why do so many of our people go there and never come back? Besides golden beaches and beautiful tanned bodies and endless blue skies and sunshine, it must have something else going for it we are not being told."

"Some do come back, and very disgruntled. Australians have a word for them."

"What sort of word?"

"Whinging Poms."

"How awful," she said with the slightest trace of a smile.

"From time to time we all like a grouch, but some of your folk make an art form of finding fault. On a shipboard level if your delegates happen to be British both are usually pretty voracious individuals not to be trifled with. Talk about a terrier with a bone. Some of our best union officials are British."

"Got some more facts about Australia, Jennifer." Edward almost simpered. "Reason why so many Brits are in Australia is the country has a phobia bordering on hysteria of being invaded by my kind, endless yellow hordes streaming out of China. Still the case, Alex?"

"Australia's got our fair share of reds-under-the-beds fanatics. Frightened of China, I don't think so."

Jennifer sipped her wine; her eyes held his, then looked away. "Is Australia racial, Alex?"

"Yes, we have not been spared that particular gene so widespread throughout the world. We may have even perfected it how we treat the Aborigines, as well as over the short period of white settlement, or invasion according to the Aborigines, honed our racial superiority to include most other races on the planet."

Katherine made up a container of cherries and cream for Jennifer to take home for Chloe and her mother, a signal for her to rise with a stretch and a roll of her shoulders. Alex scrambled to his feet. "Edward said you don't live far. I can walk you home, it's dark. Or did you drive?"

"No, I needed the exercise."

"Walking home at night is tempting fate, Jennifer," Katherine said.

She lowered her eyes. "Thank you, it's kind of you."

Alex's pea jacket with its high collar turned up failed to keep out the icy wind. "Spring?"

Jennifer in her light knee length coat seemed not to feel the cold. "Sometimes four seasons in a day."

Walking with a purpose he wondered if it may have been because she wanted to lessen the time spent in his company. Ahead an intense darkness loomed, widely spaced streetlights distinct footprints on deserted pavements adding a sinister aura to a background mass of trees and shrubbery.

"Edward is impressed with your little girl, Chloe, right?" he said, breaking the growing silence; he thought possibly only a few sentences had passed between them.

"Chloe, yes, and she's not so little. Most certainly not in mind anyway. Absolutely dotes on Edward. Brings her t-shirts from all over the world as well as dolls. Katherine and he should have children, he would make a good father."

"Never been married." Why did he say that? Who cared about his marital status? Did he want to make a statement of his availability? Expelling an exasperated breath, he wished he could retract the words. Confused, he muttered: "Even asked a girl to come with me and she rejected an all expense paid trip. Suppose that says it all how eligible I am."

"Probably she had a good reason."

"Me."

She glanced quickly at him, then looked away. "Marriage is the bonding of two lives never to be taken lightly. Impetuously I ignored my own philosophy on the matter and married far too young. Marriage should not be considered until the late thirties, my Chloe the only

The Chinese Seamen's Children

fond memory of a doomed relationship."

"My age I suppose I should be putting the cat out at night, bringing in the bins and looking with dread at the list of chores clipped to the fridge."

"How you envisage marriage?"

"From a seaman's point of view I have listened to a fair share of marital disasters in ships' bars. Again from the seaman's perspective if a marriage can survive long separations, midnight departures and arrivals, it must be one special and enduring relationship."

"Too many times I see Katherine dropping dishes and shuffling about aimlessly, moody, tears for no apparent reason after Edward has sailed. Recommending this so called bonding of two lives I might be wishing her a life of loneliness."

"Discarding the disasters I have also heard heartening stories of wonderful seagoing marriages, love and total commitment."

"Thankfully for our sanity there are exceptions. Well, there it is."

Her home might have been on the same construction plan as Edward and Katherine's; across the street fenced in brick and wrought iron a park, a rustic ambience incongruous in a large industrial and port city.

She moved closer, a smile on her face as if she concealed a saucy bit of gossip; rocking on the balls of her feet she placed her lips on his, then as quickly withdrew. "Thank you for walking me home safe and sound and my apologies for the cold. Alex, you look thoroughly worn out."

"Totally wrecked." His lips tingled with the teasing touch of hers. "Jennifer, Katherine says you are very busy, but maybe you could find time to have dinner or a few drinks during the week?"

Slow to reply, she shook her head. "Manchester for a few days, then at least two more in London. How long are you going to be in Liverpool?"

"Six weeks."

"Katharine and I keep in touch. Good night, Alex."

21

ELIZABETH HAWORTH, BARELY FIVE foot tall, a near permanent smile etched on her chubby face, a voice pure Merseyside, her Chinese bloodline apparent with her diminutive size and almond shaped eyes, gave Edward a huge hug. Achieving this affectionate gesture something of an effort as her tiny arms barely reached halfway around his ribcage. "Edward used to pull my pigtail at school. Not a gentle tug either!"

Lifting her off the pavement, he swung her full circle. "Temptation to tie it in a granny knot pretty hard to resist, which I did sometimes. Liz, why did your mother plait your hair in a pigtail, an obvious cultural statement which did not always go down well at school?"

"My mum never saw it like that. Anyway, other girls had plaits and pigtails."

"Yeah, white kids not named Wong."

"My mother said anyone who gave me a hard time to give them what ho."

"Every kid in school teased you for being a dwarf! You couldn't blow out a candle in a gale! As for me, causing a ruckus in the schoolyard brought some unwanted attention from our educators of which I found out the hard way."

Elizabeth covered her mouth and giggled. "Reckon you might

The Chinese Seamen's Children

have worn out the carpet in Mr Holbrook's office for fighting. Lots of kids would have been glad if Mr Holbrook expelled you as he threatened."

"Yeah, did spend a lot of time in his office, as well as in the hallway as a subtle method of pre-sentencing mental torture. The threat of expulsion kind of worked in my favour with the bullies lined up for a go at us Chinese kids. Most thought twice of being head-butted or kicked in the groin by a kid on death row."

Grasping Edward's hands admiration filled her voice. "Edward never gave up in any fight, always the other kids. No matter how big and mean those bullies we called Edward who never failed us."

Extracting his hands, he plucked two plump grapes from a bunch in an open case on a barrow piled high with fruit and vegetables in front of the greengrocer's. "Liz, better take a pound or else your Alf will definitely head-butt me. Keeping okay?"

"Usual crabby self, of course which he blames on having to get up early to go to the markets. Think he's hinting it should be me who gets up cold mornings, really do. Got little choice though if we are to survive against the big stores."

"Hard grind. Liz, this is a mate of mine from Aussie, Alex Nielsen. Also you're forgiven if you don't understand him, it's a colonial thing."

Throwing a mock punch at him almost caused her to fall over, followed by an outburst of giggling. "Get away with you! I've heard Australians before and I reckon every seaman in Liverpool's been to Australia. Alex, how come you know this reprobate?"

"Met on a wharf in South Australia where he should have used his expertise in head-butting. Memorable first encounter."

"Edward used to especially look after me, being so small I suppose. About my pigtail, after fourth grade I resolved, not my mother, to let it grow to my feet. I suppose that made me as antagonistic as those who wanted to cut it off. Right, Edward?"

"Antagonistic?" Edward couldn't help himself, he laughed until tears threatened. "If the weakest bully in school wanted he could have lifted you off the ground with his little finger. Liz, it's true, we kids thought a passing circus dropped you off at the school gate."

"Just small for my age is all."

"Haven't grown none since. Reckon you might even be shrinking."

"Edward, when I think about it us kids owed you big time, always being there. Sticks and stones may break my bones but names will never hurt me, that's not true. Chanting and taunting cut deep, deeper than the physical bullying because sometimes you might be lucky to land a blow."

"Liz's father went earlier than my father. From what I hear a man well known for his militancy in the Liverpool Chinese Seamen's Union, no doubt blacklisted."

She nodded ardently. "Dad came from Shanghai and Shanghai men earned a reputation for militancy. Edward's right, he would have had some militant form against his name."

From within the shop a call came of customers needing service and to stop wasting time talking to a couple of nobodies in the street; with a wink she ignored her husband's plea.

"When the war ended celebrations for the Chinese seamen with families and homes in Liverpool didn't last long," she said, placing two bunches of grapes in a paper bag and giving them to Edward with a negative wave of her hand when he reached in his pocket. "With deportation being a cruel enough punishment for innocent men, even worse faced them with the impending collapse of the government in China, also the escalating momentum of liberation movements throughout Asia. My father would have been involved I know, but like Edward's dad, we never heard from him."

"Making no excuses for my repetitiveness I keep bringing this up, why?" Alex said, mystified. "Taking the time to write a simple letter? Something else, the deportees would have had access to the crew, and if Chinese or other foreign nationals, without a doubt living under the same threat, support would be taken for granted. What form of assistance I don't know, but at least there would be those of their own kind to give optimism in a seemingly hopeless situation."

"Similar thoughts crossed my mind, yes. Mother has never spoken of any communication, and as I grew up the questions I asked from a curious young mind brought only evasion. She suffered her torment in silence, but could never disguise it in her face."

Alex grappled with a myriad of conflicting thoughts; what would he have done in a similar situation, his fate blanketed in secrecy? First he would have written a letter to appease the mental suffering of his family. Joined a ship, any ship, no matter flag, pay or conditions. "Do you know of any seamen who came back?"

"Rumours abounded all the time, but I think if any did it would be without fanfare and most certainly drawing the least attention to themselves," Edward said, sampling another grape and offering the bag to Alex. "Definitely none of them would have made a big noise of it, and equally certain their intention would be to get as far away from Liverpool as possible."

She agreed.

Edward gave her a one arm hug, about to leave when Alex asked another question. "Is there any organisation supporting the wives and children of the Chinese seamen?"

"There are people who never give up, who still write to government officials and newspapers, search musty archives, petition politicians for answers," Elizabeth said, adding with resignation: "Support for each other is taken for granted, but with time memories have healed. Awful memories of our mothers forced to work two or three jobs to make ends meet are not. Or mothers spat at, scorned and branded immoral."

"So history will record Liverpool's Chinese seamen who served at sea in war did so only to be deported like criminals, and if not for a change of government policy, their wives and children also. Chinese seamen wanting nothing more than recognition and equality, two simple things in life so easily granted," Edward said, a thumb up to a weed of a man in a shiny leather apron arguing with an elderly customer his cabbages too small to be sold in halves. "Chinese children hold some important positions in Liverpool, present company excluded of course. Of course we have Liz here married to Alf who looks like a good feed would kill him as well as in urgent need of customer management skills."

Alex watched with fascination the antics of the man inside the shop, losing self-control as he grabbed a machete and chopped the cabbage in two, thrusting one half in the startled woman's face as he tossed the other over his shoulder. "Edward, don't put yourself down, you've risen to the dizzy heights, long way from home, too."

"Gaffer of the *Baron Maclay*, yeah I forgot about my meteoric rise to the top of the pile. Come on, I need a drink. God bless you, Liz, you better go inside and cool down that husband of yours. The old girl too, she might need an ambulance."

On the way to the pub Edward raised a question on his mind. "What do you think of Jennifer?"

"Until I met her and Katherine I really thought Australia had the patent on beautiful woman. I have now had a change of mind."

"Hmm, there is this uneasy feeling Katherine's up to no good."

"What do you mean no good? Katherine's dinner, the company, walking Jennifer home. All perfect."

"Katherine's plotting something. Signs are everywhere."

"Edward, like all seamen you have an overactive imagination."

"Not so sure about that," he said doubtfully. "Katherine I know too well."

"Know her? Think again, Edward, you're only with your girl half the year if lucky."

"Maybe you're right, maybe you're right."

Edward could barely sit still, the door closing behind Katherine and the sound of her car starting. Alex spread marmalade on his piece of toast, amused at his obvious agitated state of mind.

The Chinese Seamen's Children

"Told you so, Katherine's up to her neck in a plot. Of course she's got a willing partner in this little scheme. Seems Jennifer will be finished her business in Manchester earlier than expected, cancel London and be home Thursday evening. Ample time to pack a bag, give her mother instructions no chocolate or red coloured drinks for Chloe. Get ready for a grand trip, a journey most British plan and experience only a few times in their lifetime. Enchantment, a weekend in Blackpool, mate."

Walking Jennifer home she had kissed him, not a passionate kiss, a thank-you kiss. She then declined an invitation for dinner because of work, the truth. "If this is intrigue, Edward, I like it."

"Katherine rang her and said would she like to come with us to Blackpool for the weekend, conveniently forgetting her business commitments. Jennifer complained of being up to her pretty neck in work, Manchester and London, but she didn't sound too convincing according to Katherine. So straight for the carotid artery goes my Katherine and I'm thinking it might be the bronze Aussie image knocking them dead, mate. Jennifer has done a bit of shuffling here and there and relegated others down the chain to take up the slack so freeing her for the weekend. How about that?"

Thinking of Jennifer's kiss, a tease of a woman's soft lips, he never heard Edwards's excited chatter in the background, his mind wholly engrossed on that fleeting intimacy.

Katherine's 1979 Ford Granada's boot with her suitcase of immense proportions barely allowed room for Alex and Edward's two small bags, space for Jennifer, a comment about the duration of their excursion, weekend or a month? Also under mention, the vehicle obvious proof of her lucrative and rabid profession.

"Strange I never hear any slurred criticisms from the inebriate sprawled beside me when I pick him up from the pub." She blew him a kiss, half turned and rolled her eyes at Alex.

Looking up into an early morning grey and heavily overcast sky, large rain drops spattered on the window; working his shoulders, he wished he had worn his jacket and not taken Edward's advice Blackpool and sunshine were inseparable. Katherine might have read his mind.

"From one who knows it is not advisable to take notice of the weather going away for a weekend. If you did you would never leave home."

"She's right, but we can certainly guarantee your survival, Alex," Edward said, gloating at Katherine. "Assured by the British Board of Tourism your absolute safety Blackpool has no ravenous man-eating sharks waiting to snack on unsuspecting weekenders. Now you blokes can't say the same thing about those golden sands drenched in eternal sunshine you're all the time bragging about. Mention must be made about ever present danger, bluebottles, jellyfish, sea snakes, saltwater crocs, stone fish, Portuguese man-o-wars, not forgetting an exceptionally large and active shark population cruising the rips and gutters for an easy snack?"

"Edward, are your beaches pebbles and gravel? Or is that a fallacy exaggerated by Aussies more used to golden and sugar white sand tickling their toes?"

"Straight from the mouths of your tourist blokes coaxing innocent Poms to Australia as shark bait. Not correct, some of our beaches, which are not advertised in Australia for some unknown reason, could compete with yours and win. Sand, we got plenty of sand."

"Wallaroo beach, what about those beach belles?"

"God, bloody rough is not the word!"

"None of your mob would have won any beauty contests."

Jennifer waited by the front gate, a bag by her side and a girl of about nine wearing thick framed spectacles with both arms wrapped around her waist; an older woman on the porch, evident by the facial similarities Jennifer's mother.

Dressed casually in deference to the threatening weather, shorts and a floral cotton blouse, she draped a light woollen cardigan around her shoulders secured in front with a half knot. Slipping in beside Alex, her bare leg brushed his, a quick rub and apology, a husky greeting to all as she made herself comfortable with a few squirms and bumps.

The Sands Hotel with its Elizabethan façade offered a change within for its eager holidaying clientele, a more modern theme. Possibly a psychological design factor to ward off the chill and drabness of British winters, a contemporary welcome to those who travelled from all over the United Kingdom to sample the excitement of Blackpool on the Irish Sea.

"Bring the bikini, Jen?" Edward inquired with a snide grin, rubbing his hands furiously and stamping his feet.

Ignoring him she gave Alex a demure smile. "Certainly, this is Blackpool I'll have you know, but it would seem to our shivering Australian guest he thinks the Polar Regions."

Taken aback by their light heartedness to the weather, he felt certain a drop of icy rain dripped on his nose entering the hotel.

"Blackpool will soon get you into holiday mode, mate. Famous for it, never fails. There's the choice of piers with superb rides and entertainment. For those in their dotage bingo, the pubs, and of course not forgetting the beach, a joy to behold." Edward arranged their bags around the front desk to check in, three rooms.

Alex could smell a slight musty odour, Edward assuring him coming summer would quickly dispel, and that a more disagreeable odour would permeate the hallway, holidaymakers sweat. How would an Australian tourist compare Blackpool against the Gold Coast of Queensland, he thought? Gold Coast glitz and glamour, towering high-rise, endless beaches of surf and sand, hot summers and mild winters. First impression of Blackpool, an icy raindrop on the tip his nose. Any judgemental comparisons would be unfair as one locale lauded itself in the tourist brochures as golden sands and semitropical while the other shivered at latitude fifty-four degrees north.

From the window of his room he watched an elderly man in brief trunks and a large overhang of dough white belly paddling in the lifeless grey sea, definitely raining now with a light slick on the street below. Edward promised a warm pub with an open fire, lunch and heady beer. Also the company of two beautiful women.

Alex's fish and chips so the blackboard menu stated came in the size of a whale of a fish; haddock in tempura batter sitting atop a pile of steaming hot, thickly sliced chips. Advice came from all quarters, lashings of salt and malt vinegar.

Stunned, he could only stare at the meal, no sympathy from Jennifer beside him in the booth, her meal half the size of his, a ham and cheese salad. "Well, you did order a whale of a fish."

"No human could possibly consume it," he said despairingly. "Jennifer, help me. What you have in front of you wouldn't feed a baby."

"Obviously a whale of a fish should have warned you something abnormally large." Pushing her side plate across the table, she plucked a single chip from his plate. "I'll have a few more of those, thank you."

Over the meal a warm camaraderie developed, a comfortable association; feelings Edward and Katherine shared for each other no more obvious in their constant touching, their eyes, small courtesies that came naturally such as opening doors, pulling out chairs, helping with coats.

Jennifer's hand would at times as if by accident brush his arm, lingering, a smile only for him as if sharing a secret. Edward and Katherine planned the evening, on their minds now an afternoon nap and hope for an improvement in the weather.

"Alex, would it bore you if I shopped for a blouse?" She reached for his hand as Edward and Katherine waved goodbye, joining the thinning lunchtime crowd and heading in the direction of the hotel.

The Chinese Seamen's Children

"Go ahead and buy your blouse, I wouldn't be bored."

"Truthfully, don't really need a blouse, but I love to shop which should not come as a surprise to a man who has in the past probably suffered long waits."

"First time."

"Really?"

"True, and if my memory isn't failing the last time I went shopping with a woman my mother bought me a pair of short pants."

She squeezed his hand, her smile for him only. Not really, but the thought made him feel every man in the street envied him. "Blackpool and England what you expected?"

"Driving through the countryside yes, Blackpool not yet quite certain. Though what I saw briefly in London, excluding the centuries of history, depressed me. Wads of chewing gum ground into footpaths, in fact entire footpaths black with gum, litter ankle deep on the tracks in the tube."

"Many of us take our environment lightly, or more truthfully ignore it. London is not my favourite city, too large and impersonal. Time being in your favour you could visit York, book into a hotel built into the ancient walls of the city. Stroll narrow, winding streets in early evening, the unassuming lights of small boutiques, craft shops, cafes and bakeries reflecting on cobblestones. So much to see and your time far too short. Don't be quick to judge us."

"Australia has its fair share of insensitive people who don't give a damn for their environment. We might be big and rugged, dry and dusty, but our environment is fragile. We despoil our pristine waterways and slap politicians on the back for their inspiring vision legislating raw sewerage outfalls a few miles offshore. Discard our rubbish on rail tracks, roads, waterways, dump cars and tyres in the bush. Cut down old growth forests and sell them to Japan for chopsticks as if there is no tomorrow."

Walking with a spring in her step, she swung his hand.

"Driving from London to Liverpool when we left the motorways I saw a country I imagined as a child in school. Green fields and hedgerows, church spires and pub shingles, stately mansions and thatched roofs. Jennifer, I am not disappointed."

"Time to form an opinion about British girls?"

"Miniskirts are driving me crazy, and I am sorry if my eyes do stray from time to time. My attention shouldn't because I am holding hands with someone who does not need miniskirts or outrageous hairdos to make a man's heart pound. Beatles and Rolling Stones, well, I can take or leave them which I suppose is heresy to you Liverpudlians."

"Alex, saying no to your dinner invitation I found difficult but my first thought at the time work came first. I felt awful and couldn't get it out of my mind, but then Katherine rang about a weekend in Blackpool. Worked to a frazzle, never a moment for myself, so why shouldn't I take some time for myself? So here I am being very selfish by piling work on others and enjoying my weekend. Glad I did."

In a small café Alex ordered a pot of tea and a cream lamington to share, the narrow booth causing their legs to make contact; he moved his legs, but hers followed, pressed against his.

"Katherine has told me Edward experienced a difficult upbringing. Has he mentioned his father?"

"Yes, he has."

"My mind cannot even begin to imagine how I would have felt in similar harrowing circumstances, someone you loved taken forcibly from you. Poor Mrs Huang must have suffered terribly." Reaching across the table with a fingertip she wiped a smear of cream and coconut on his upper lip. "Childhood memories are dim in respect of large numbers of Chinese in Liverpool, but I know there were and most were discriminated against and treated badly. I do recall children taunted at school, whether Chinese of British I am not certain as I suppose bullies don't discriminate except for the size of their victims. Being different would make targets of Chinese children, then again I am referring to the period I attended the same school years after Edward finished."

"Do you consider Edward different?"

The Chinese Seamen's Children

About to remove another blob of cream and coconut, this time on his chin, she drew her hand away as if scolded. "Yes, Edward is different. We are all different. He has Chinese blood whereas I have Anglo-Saxon blood. There though the irrefutable dissimilarity ends as it does for friends of mine born in Nigeria and India. Friends in South Africa both white and black."

Then she did remove the offending cream and coconut, stuck her finger in her mouth and crinkled her nose at him.

Edward offered no defence for his partiality for pub fare, dinner being no exception. Friday night Blackpool, streams of animated people invading the city for the weekend.

Soothed into a sense of warm wellbeing by an open fire in a pub and dinner with friends would end a wonderful day. Alex and Jennifer held hands, speaking with their heads close, sometimes their hair touching.

Alex's steak and kidney pie, mashed potato and green peas, overwhelmed. Even more so Edward insisting on pints of Guinness, cocktails for the girls.

Jennifer, heavy eyed, slumped and found the strength to shake her head. "Edward, you pair slept all afternoon while Alex and I walked and walked."

"Slept all afternoon? Do you know what this woman did, she brought a bloody brief with her, would you believe? Read all afternoon while I had other things on my mind. Suppose why she can afford a new car!"

Katherine glared at him, then smirked. "Did not, just brought a few papers with me. My intentions are to enjoy this weekend as we don't get many of them. Tomorrow we are off to Bowland Forest, and we just might leave you there."

"Alex, our day's been special, thank you," Jennifer said, her back pressed against the door of her room. "Hard does not make for a social whirl. Sorry for all the yawning."

Their heads slowly closed, their lips touching before she fell back with her eyes firmly shut. Inhaling slowly a hint of roses, fascinated by the slow rise and fall of her breasts, he wanted to take her in his arms. Instead she opened her eyes and smiled wearily, another brief kiss and a murmured goodnight.

Almost a repeat of the previous night Edward after losing count of his pints thought a couple of Guinness's would top the night off, groans from the three sitting with him in the booth, their dinner plates long cleared away.

Katherine scowled petulantly, finishing her brandy lime and soda, a good natured grumble of driving all day and tramping through a wet forest, not to mention her feet killing her. "This woman is headed for a bath and someone to rub her feet. For which at the end might be a reward for which I believe hints have been dropped. Edward, I think also there are a couple of people who might like to be alone."

Their corner booth in the dappled influence of an amber coach light offered a precious privacy in the smoke filled and noisy bar; he raised his near empty pint, Jennifer her gin and tonic no more than ice cubes, clinking glasses. "Thank you for partnering me to Blackpool. Also the kiss, two kisses."

"Were you disappointed with my kiss?" she said, her eyes studying him over the rim of her glass unwavering.

Muscles in his stomach tightened. "No."

Putting down her glass she reached for his hand. "Alex, you mentioned a girl in Australia. There are times I meet someone and I think is this it, my second chance? It never is. Mostly it is my doing, perceptions either real or imagined which cause me to veer away before that final step is taken."

"Based on my male ego thoughts were in the short time we knew each other there might be more than just a physical attraction. Hoped it would be, but I think inside I knew I lived with false hope. She is her own person and will do well in the world without me."

"On your return to Australia will you see her?"

"She may have moved on, I don't know. Probably she saw me as a change in lifestyle, something like that. Unkempt and scruffy, dressed out of an army disposal store. Edward's invitation to come to the United Kingdom didn't help. Jennifer, I don't really know."

"Do you regret coming here, jeopardising a possible deeper relationship?"

"Gradually I am coming to think deeper relationships are not for blokes who get their best gear from military disposal stores and marine outfitters. Blokes who get their hair cut in Whyalla, the worst barbers in the world. She proved any rapport based on separation would have failed by my being a seaman, not a trip to the United Kingdom. That alone should have made me think twice. What about your marriage, Jennifer?"

"Falling madly in love and rushing into marriage far, far too young. Then with a baby in the tummy and watching others your age climb the social scale and achieve, you start to think am I destined for a life of motherhood and homemaker."

"Which is not a bad thing."

"Of course not, but spoken like a true man."

"Another drink?"

She shook her head; in the dim and smoky light her beauty held him spellbound, her skin in this flattering light flawless, not even a tiny mole to mar the satiny perfection. Her eyes shone and her bottom lip glistened as she moistened it with her tongue. Two girls by the jukebox selected "All You Need is Love", the volume turned up full.

"Liverpool, a quite distinct sound." she said.

"John Lennon and a few others equally talented, yes."

"It's been a long day and I am tired, am I always saying that?"

Standing at her door, a brief touching of their lips, a taste of breaths, murmured goodnights. That single moment in time he knew with absolute finality he loved this woman, Jennifer Rice. She said something he barely caught, the bathroom and for him to wait.

Watching her retreating figure down the hallway, mesmerised by the flow of her dress against her buttocks, brushing the fullness of her thighs, her dress modest by what other girls and women wore, he felt a yearning bordering on the painful. On her return she again lifted on her toes and placed her lips on his. "Can I tell you something, Alex?"

Unable to speak he could only swallow forcefully.

"Katherine asked me how I felt about you, did I consider it a waste of money booking three rooms, Katherine the ever practical girl. Suppose there is a little of the puritan in me, an old fashioned ethic of not blatantly advertising one's eagerness, urges a good girl should suppress. Aghast, I said a complete stranger, Katherine! Do you consider me that sort of girl?"

Words at last rasped from his dry throat: "Are you that sort of girl?"

Gazing up into his eyes and placing a finger over his lips, she said: "Must be because I made certain of something practical in my handbag, one of the reasons my visit to the bathroom."

Light from the street filtering through the drawn drapes bathed her body silvery. Propped on an elbow he ran a hand over her breasts, tiny pink nipples, down her flat belly, tracing his fingers through exquisitely soft hair. Using his feet he straightened the top sheet and pulling at the blanket managed to kick some resemblance of covering over them.

Awake, she turned on her side and snuggled against him, teasing the hairs on his chest. "My lover, I'm so glad I finally realised the sort of girl I am and brought my diaphragm."

The Chinese Seamen's Children

"How you protect yourself?"

"Only during my fertile cycle."

"Which is now?"

"Might be, not really sure." She squirmed pleasurably. "Better to be certain than sorry, but I have a premonition what I am feeling warm and incredibly wet and tingling between my legs, I would have been nervously counting the days."

"Jennifer …"

"Shush, not yet. Not yet, Alex."

22

JENNIFER SAID THE WORDS first, nestled in his arms on her mother's comfortable velvet cushioned divan, the house silent and in darkness; Elspeth Fearon had retired upstairs to read, Chloe in her bed. "Alex, I love you."

Tracing a line down her cheek, her lips and chin, his finger paused above the top button of her blouse. "When you stopped me in Blackpool those were my words."

"Yes, I know."

Releasing the first two buttons, the finger slipped under her bra.

"Can now if you like."

"Jennifer, I love you."

"Say them again."

"Jennifer, I love you. As a sole traveller lurching through life with its complicated ifs and maybes, providence has truly guided me. Edward joining a ship in Wallaroo, having a bottle thrown at him. Edward and Katherine's dinner. Jennifer, we live in diffcrent worlds yet fate by some miracle has crossed and joined our paths."

"Mother would cringe with shame if she had an inkling of the base carnality that must have been lurking in my mind, preparing my diaphragm for a weekend with a stranger. Little use it turned out to be so close to my period. There, I didn't need to be protected from your little boys and girls after all."

"Would it have mattered?"

"Now aren't you the smug one! Well, let me tell you if it had been in the middle of the month and I succumbed to the charms of a complete stranger it would have."

"Our baby in your belly?"

"Your baby in my belly, you put it there. Alex, am I a wanton?" Her hand rested in his lap, aware of his arousal.

"Hope so."

"Normally I don't bleed heavily, first few days just a show." Then she drew away with a gasp. "What am I saying? My goodness here I am discussing a very private female function with a man like discussing how to mop the floor or turn the washing machine on."

She might well have been lecturing advanced medical science for all he knew about the menstrual cycle of women.

Surreptitiously, she gently stroked him. "Chloe is jealous of you, have you noticed?"

"That seemed obvious when she said a quite formal goodnight to you and your mother, for me a glower of complete disapproval. Then I cannot blame her, using her mother's body as a convenient vessel for my gratification. Are you aware of what you're doing to me?"

"Successfully, too. Am I making it uncomfortable for you?"

"Yes, but don't stop. Do you think Chloe might be acceptable to a bribe? Maybe the offer of a trip to Australia where she can cuddle a koala bear or pat a kangaroo?"

"Coincidentally, my firm is considering a joint venture with a Japanese consortium building a resort in I think the Rockhampton area of Queensland. Is there a Rockhampton in Queensland?"

"Tropic of Capricorn passes through Rockhampton. Few years ago I loaded salt in Port Alma which is the port. Sandflies, mosquitoes, sea snakes, sapping heat and stinking mangrove mudflats. Not a pleasant place."

"So you wouldn't recommend building a resort there?"

"Not in Port Alma, but along the coast there are probably some spectacular beachfronts the Queensland government would be prepared to give to the Japanese."

"Substantial amounts of money would be involved in purchasing the land."

"No, with some knowledge of the redneck Queensland government give. Would you come to Australia if the project went ahead?"

"Possibly, but you wouldn't even give me the time of day with all those Australian girls competing for your favours."

"Not a single one of them would stand a chance against you."

"Hmm, no doubt you say that to all the poor naive girls you seduce in your worldly travels."

"Jennifer, sweeping girls off their feet is a rarity with me."

She nipped his bottom lip.

"Jennifer, can we?"

"Can we what?" She knew exactly what he meant.

"Make love?"

"Chloe and I share a bedroom. Also, what if mother puts her book aside and comes downstairs for a warm glass of milk?"

"This is neither the time nor the place. Sorry."

"Don't say that, don't give up so easily." she said, easing off the divan and going to the laundry for a towel, unzipping her jeans when she returned.

Placing the towel under her bottom, she made herself comfortable and drew him down on top of her, guiding him; with a sigh of pleasure she felt his ease of entry, sighing and matching his movements. Immediately the first contractions began, regret that her eagerness caused a similar peak in her partner. Both hopelessly tried to prolong the exquisite pleasure, ineffective as she felt the first throb from him as he began to ejaculate and then nothing either could do would stop the flood.

The Chinese Seamen's Children

Edward arranged to meet his mother in Sefton Park; the startling news he wanted to share with Alex obvious in his excited face. "My father did write a letter from Singapore!"

Alex showed no surprise, scuffing his feet in the fine gravel which embedded the park bench on which both sat.

"Least you could do is let out a gasp or something relatively close to shock. From Singapore my father wrote a letter, a letter all these years Mother didn't want to share."

"Amazed, no, Edward."

"Somewhere in time to place a man!"

"Edward, your father would have had to make contact with his home, especially what you know of him from your mother."

"All these years she has concealed this letter. I knew my mother lived with the forlorn expectation that one day my father would walk through the door and life would return to normal. Hope in my childhood fantasies, my father would return and we would be a complete family."

"There might have been insurmountable obstacles barring him from shipping out of Singapore, but writing a simple letter, no."

"My thoughts exactly," he said despairingly. "Mixed with more gruesome ones of him being bashed and robbed and left for dead on a wharf somewhere. Reasons why he couldn't find a scrap of paper and postage stamp."

She walked determinedly down the pathway, a thin gabardine coat buttoned to her chin, a mauve headscarf keeping her head warm. Getting to their feet, Edward hugged his mother as he guided her to sit between them.

"Edward told me you are seeing young Jennifer," she said, rearranging her headscarf and grasping her son's hands. "She is a lovely girl and her mother justly proud of her achievements in her profession. Also herself a mother to a sweet daughter, very intelligent and gifted by what I hear."

Edward broached the subject of his father's letter with the subtly of a broadaxe. "Mother, Alex and I have spoken about the deportations.

Now there is the letter ..."

Across a grassy expanse, her eyes followed the progress of an old man shuffling along an adjacent pathway, his painful gait assisted by a cane he clutched in a hand of bone and sinew. She might have been talking to herself: "Every moment of every day I lived in hope my Zhen would return, but he never did. That he would walk down the street with a smile on his face, beckon us both to run to him. My Zhen ..."

"Growing older I began to understand the injustice of my father's deportation, then betrayal he never attempted to make contact. What would a stamp cost, a pittance to say I am safe and wait for me? Elsie and Edward Huang, I am coming home and no one in the world can stop me. Now I learn my father did write a letter."

Passing from her line of vision a jogger overtook the old man, causing him to lurch in fear of falling in the lumbering athlete's wake. Gathered at the base of a large tree a family of squirrels foraging held her attention, hoping two large dogs let off their owner's leashes would not harm them. Then she said: "I never told you about the letter for a very good reason."

Edward stared at his mother's hands, soft and comforting in his.

"Because your father never wrote the letter."

His head shot up. "It's his handwriting, you said that."

"My Zhen would not write such hatred to us. To himself at a table, but not to his loved ones."

"Filled with loathing for those who ordered his deportation, why wouldn't he express his anger?" Looking dejectedly at Alex, he seemed a man seeking a lifeline in a stormy sea.

"My mistake telling you about the letter, it only makes it worse." Spooked, the family of squirrels scampered into the branches of their home, the dogs leaping in a frenzy of barking at the craggy trunk as their quarry disappeared from sight.

"For my own peace of mind I needed to know my father did not abandon his family. Mother, I feel your pain because it is my pain. My father a seaman who served his country in war, the United Kingdom

The Chinese Seamen's Children

not Singapore or China, deported like a common criminal is criminal in itself and a shame on government."

"Edward, you are my Zhen. My Zhen, my true Zhen never left me and would have so much to boast about, his son. Easter when I received the letter, yes around that time because your grandfather lay sick in hospital and died a few days after Easter Monday. Like a foolish little girl I carried that precious letter with me everywhere, too afraid to open it. Then at the insistence of my friend Kate I did. It should have remained unopened."

"Singapore?"

"Singapore, yes. Over and over I read the letter, praying I would see our names. Never once a mention of our home, or his homecoming. My heart broke, so much hatred."

Tears flowed down her wan cheeks, also Edward's as he nursed her in his arms, gently rocking. Alex looked away, again an intruder.

Jennifer thought her planned weekend in Chester the advantage Alex needed, working unsuccessfully on winning the affections, even a smile, from Chloe. Chloe's continued censure seemed even more damning by the studious spectacles she wore and the disapproving scowl on her pretty but unforgiving face when in his presence. Although he understood little about children he could her resentment of a stranger competing for her mother's love.

Children of single parents in similar positions resorted to some potent weapons of retaliation; ignore the threat, throw a tantrum, or assume a sullen disposition of contempt. Jennifer understood and held her daughter especially close, placating her fears the man who spoke too fast and at times might be difficult to decipher did not pose a threat to their love and closeness. Mother liked Alex very much, an Australian seaman visiting their best friends Edward and Katherine.

With the Vauxhall Cavalier packed, a brooding Chloe in the back seat, Jennifer handed Alex the keys.

"Jennifer, would you trust your most precious possession in the hands of an Aussie? By that I mean Chloe not the car."

"Certainly. Right, Chloe?"

Chloe acknowledged begrudgingly, unwilling to speak and reveal her bubbling excitement; Alex and Jennifer glanced at each other, a shared smile. Unlike doing battle driving in Melbourne and even worse in Sydney's narrow streets, he felt at ease and comfortable, the traffic far better regulated. What soon became apparent in heavily congestion Liverpool, the prevalence of British motorists to obey the rules and drive with good road sense.

Jennifer chose a route that took them south through Runcorn to the M56, the M53 and finally the A56 to Chester. Chester, an historic tapestry woven over the centuries, gave the world without embellishment a true reflection of the United Kingdom, a window into a rich and turbulent past. From buildings raised in already ancient earth, narrow cobblestone lanes steeped in the shadows of crumbling masonry, great minds dreamed of visionary wonders and quackery. Flat-earthers held court and zealots burned at the stake those who dared to differ while the multitude toiled long and hard to make their lords and masters richer.

"The Pied Bull," she said, looking for the Northgate Street sign, finding it and directing Alex to turn left. "Extremely old, dates back to the twelfth century."

Australia in the twelfth century an undiscovered land mass roamed by nomadic Stone Age tribes with a close and spiritual affinity to the land, carers of an undiscovered continent with its blank space marked on ancient charts with a sea serpent.

"Shame we haven't the time to visit Stratford-upon-Avon. Visit the home of Shakespeare and be on the alert the huge swans don't chase you. Over the years we have grown a few inches, too."

Concentrating on his driving, he dropped down to second gear as the narrow street grew more congested. "Grown?"

"Visitors have to stoop to enter his home."

"Definitely our heads."

The Chinese Seamen's Children

"Hotel's half way down the street, and if I remember rightly the parking's at the rear, but a very narrow entry so be careful."

Width of the laneway measured for the size of coach, he barely had a couple of inches clearance of his side mirrors, long gouges and scraped paint in the brickwork evidence of past lapses of judgement.

The Pied Bull stood a magnificent example of a British hotel, its façade given added structural strength to withstand the ravages of time with multiple brick arches spanning the footpath. No more apparent the bricklayers craft than the inclusion of masonry cornerstones and lintels, embedded with iron bolts a pied bull's head shingle.

"Magnificent," Alex said, following Jennifer and Chloe from the car park to the front entrance.

"Most certainly the old masonry is," Jennifer said; both she and Chloe carried small overnight bags. "Food is excellent and the accommodation as good as a first class hotel should be, some that leave a lot to be desired. Last time I stayed the cook barged from his kitchen and challenged anyone to make a disparaging comment."

"Did anyone?"

"Oh no, most definitely not. That man had a ferocious head and a gruesome scar down his cheek, but could he cook."

"Does mine host wear a check waistcoat and bow tie?"

"Why would he do that?"

"Only an image of your typical British publican. Oak log fires burning in stone fireplaces, rough hewn ceiling beams, whitewash, coach lamps, prints of old steam trains, hunting scenes, beer pumps and dartboards."

"Somewhere in our travels we will find such a pub. Though about the fires, there may not be any because this is spring, I'll have you know. Right, Chloe?"

Chloe thawed slowly, impressed how the man who obviously infatuated her mother and all too frequently made her giggle, drove. Not prone to swearing like Mother when stopped at heavily trafficked roundabouts and junctions, and he knew well in advance when to brake, and he most definitely did not overtake out of pure frustration.

Also he changed gears much smoother than Mother and she felt safe with the engine braking the car and the faster acceleration response. This of course originated from her grandmother, no doubt the best driver in the world, all the time taking Mother to task for her tardiness. She looked up at Alex and said: "Grandmother would give you a high mark for your driving, not like some."

Jennifer choked. "Does that mean I get a fail mark?"

"Dismally Grandmother has lost all patience about your riding the clutch."

"What!"

"Though I am not too sure what riding the clutch is, Grandmother says it is extremely dangerous and if you underwent your driving test again you would fail."

Bystander to the joust between mother and daughter, he smiled with amusement.

"Well, I know what riding the clutch is and I most certainly do not!" she said indignantly though finding it hard to keep a straight face.

Jennifer and Chloe's room overlooked the street, Alex's room adjoining with a connecting door. Jennifer's room came with its own bathroom, a bath but no shower. "Us British like our baths," she said, smiling at his disappointed expression as she tested the double bed, Chloe discovering a bible in the bedside chest of drawers.

"Forget the car, Chester is to be explored and discovered on foot," Jennifer said. "This wonderful city is history, an ancient Roman town. Soaking in the past as we amble along crumbling Roman walls that once fortified and protected this city, the Rows Medieval shop fronts and visit Chester cathedral and stand in awe of its stained glass window."

"Thanks for bringing me here, both you and Chloe."

"No thanks needed, Grandmother says a break is as good as a holiday," Chloe said, her nose buried in the fine print of the bible. She glanced up from the book at her mother. "Should have brought Grandmother, she would have enjoyed the safe car ride and Chester."

The Chinese Seamen's Children

"Grandmother has her bingo on Friday and bowls on Saturday which has little chance of competing with Chester," Jennifer said, then with a thinly veiled inflection of sarcasm in her voice tempered by a smile directed at Alex: "Though she would have most certainly enjoyed the safe drive, awarding high marks for exceptional driving skills."

"Compliment accepted."

"Have you tried your bed?"

"Starched linen as stiff as a board. You British like your starch, I hate it. Room and bed are excellent."

"Yes, we do like our starch."

"Grandmother does not starch our sheets," Chloe said, losing interest in the bible and replacing it.

"No, she does not. Your grandmother is a seer without equal, all-knowing and a mind of staggering proportions."

"Grandmother is all that," Chloe said smugly, then to Alex: "On the way home will you teach me to drive?"

Chester with its stark remnants of invasion and foreign occupation profoundly affected Alex. Not only did he gaze with wonder at Roman engineering, fortified walls, forts and amphitheatre, his fellow travellers a beautiful woman and her serious daughter. Joined by their hands, absorbing Chester, imagining centurions in beaten bronze and vermillion robes marching with a clatter of weapons down streets now the foundations for modern roads.

Chester tempted taste buds, Devonshire teas, coffee and sticky date pudding. Treasures to be discovered in The Rows, lunch in the beer garden of a pub within sight of crumbling Roman ruins. Chastised by Chloe for having a streak of treacle on his chin he acknowledged as acceptance of sorts, the barriers fast fragmenting in the small hand reaching for his when a busy street crossing posed danger.

"Grandmother will teach you how to eat sticky date pudding

without making a mess," she said primly, plucking a serviette from a table dispenser and offering it to him.

Almost, he thought, and his heart went out to the serious girl in her bookish glasses, at pains to mention her mentor as the progenitor of etiquette.

The Pied Bull's chef's intimidating reputation failed to eventuate, his beef steak and caramelised mushrooms superb. Jennifer ordered lambs fry and bacon, garlic bread and a side order of chips to share. Chloe took ten minutes to study the menu, a large plastic folder of six pages which might have been a declaration of independence as she adjusted her glasses on her nose to read the fine print; every so often she glanced at the blackboard menu as if seeking additional guidance. "After careful consideration I will have the small portion Cumberland sausage and baked vegetables, thank you," she said to Alex who slipped out the booth to order at the bar. "Plenty of extra thick onion gravy, please."

Returning he juggled a pint of Guinness, gin and tonic and a lemon squash for his family who acknowledged his prowess of not spilling a drop. His family, the woman he loved and a child much older than her years.

"*Lord of the Rings* is showing at a theatre in town somewhere, saw it on a poster." he said. "Wouldn't it be an awesome picture if a director could make it in reality and not animated. Have you read the book?"

Jennifer shook her head, Chloe doing a little bounce in her seat and stabbing her hand in the air. "I know *The Hobbit*."

"You know *The Hobbit*?" he said, amazed.

"Grandmother has Mr Tolkien's book in her library and says I should read it as a prelude to *Lord of the Rings,* when I am much older of course."

"Very wise of your grandmother. Would you like to see *Lord of the Rings?*"

Hopefully glancing at her mother all she needed to break into a huge smile and a loud clap of her hands.

Chloe, near asleep on her feet, clung to her mother's skirt. "Come on, Chloe, one last effort," Alex encouraged. "Been a big day with the picture a bit of a letdown from the book, then how could anyone hope to better Tolkien?"

Getting no response, he bundled the girl into his arms, the Pied Bull illuminated in streetlights no more than a hundred yards distance; she nestled her head against his chest, wrapping her arms around his neck. Jennifer slipped her arm through his.

"Are you thinking like I am a certain girl is having a change of heart?"

"Hope so."

"Quite an accomplishment as Chloe is a very perceptive child which I do not say lightly and quite choosy whom she befriends."

Jennifer dressed a groggy Chloe in her nightgown and tucked her in bed; about to shed her own clothes the girl stirred, suddenly awake and confused. Returning to the bed, she soothed: "Now, now, dear, it's only a dream."

"… love you, Mother."

"Love you, too." She looked up to see Alex standing in the connecting doorway, smiled and brushed her lips on her daughter's forehead.

"… say goodnight to Alex."

"Alex is right here, you can say it yourself." Moving a little on the bed she made room for him to sit beside her.

"… goodnight, Alex."

"Goodnight, Chloe. Sleep tight." About to give him her trust, so close, so very, very close.

Alex and Jennifer rose from the bed, holding hands. "Finished," she said.

"Finished?"

"My period, also for a little time my excursions to the bathroom to protect myself from you."

"Oh that."

"Well, you don't have to sound so complacent about it," she said with feigned indignation. "If that is how you feel I will also say my goodnights, too. Be aware we do have two bedrooms."

Releasing her hand, he cupped her bottom and pulled her hard against him. "So you won't be using your diaphragm?"

"Yes, so you can spend your lust freely without a single thought of the poor woman under you who has a reprieve from motherhood. Give me a few minutes."

Undressing she carefully folded her clothes and placed them in the wardrobe; naked except for her bikini panties she caught sight of herself in the wardrobe mirror. Straightening her posture and shoulders back gave lift to her breasts, the body of a young woman. She thought of the man waiting in the next bedroom, the mere touch of his hard body causing her belly to fill with butterflies. Completely abandon herself and her strict self applied libidinous boundaries.

Never could she have done that with Declan, would never have thought of begging like a common slut in heat for more of what gripped her in the excruciating intensity of climax. Making love to a husband might be different, she thought, giving her body to a lover the true expression of love.

Flexing, the pink camisole she slipped over her shoulders fell in sheer folds around her waist; should she take her panties off or leave them on to savour the growing excitement of complete submission?

Their eyes held as she came around to her favoured side of the bed; resting a knee on the bedding her camisole exposed a tiny wisp of silk.

"Jennifer, you are doing it to me again," he rasped, hooking a finger in the leg of her panties.

"No more than what you are doing to me." Moving on top of him, she filled his mouth with her tongue, raising her hips to allow him to draw her panties down her thighs. While arched she freed his pyjamas, a cry of satisfaction as she felt him enter her almost fully in one thrust. "There is nothing to protect me from you now," she said in a rush of breath, matching his rhythm and feeling her peak fast approaching.

Any chance he might prolong their joining gone as he felt her tightened around him, heard the first cry of release catch in her throat to escape through gritted teeth.

"Masons of old built their walls thick and filled the cavities with cement, hope so," she murmured, warm and comfortable in his arms, sated.

"Jen, you are a wanton."

"That I truly am, and your fault entirely. Something else, I think you are close to captivating another heart."

Edward planned to fly to Singapore! "Have to help me with this, mate. Madness, but I have to do it."

Alex's mind held only one thought, his rapidly approaching departure from the United Kingdom.

"Did you hear one word I said?" he said desperately.

"Every word and I don't need a public announcement in respect of your obsession with Singapore, but you going there on a moment's notice is puzzling. Also, you look bloody awful, has Katherine commented you need a shave?"

"Alex, I need the support of a mate."

"Edward, in a week for me it's departures at Heathrow. Then two days after I land, Port Kembla where my name will go to the bottom of our compulsory roster. How can I possibly support you?"

"Flying to Australian your final flight leg is Singapore, right?

You're there on the ground, able to give a mate a hand."

"Edward, as a seaman you would have navigated your way with little fuss in some daunting places in this world, why now the need of a helping hand? My time on the ground in Singapore only a couple of hours, the time it takes to clean and refuel the plane."

"Breaking your trip is easy. No sweat."

"How?"

"British Airways do it all the time. I'm booked to fly out in five days."

"So factoring me into this Singapore escapade, what did you think my reaction would be?"

"Said to myself, let's go do it together. Hopes were to fly with you, but your flight's fully booked."

"Firstly, contacting Port Kembla shipping office is a must, the shipping master with the temperament of a dog with rabies. Suppose being half a world away he will dispense mercy and give me a week's suspension of obligations. Okay, now your plans for Singapore?"

"Attempt to find a man I only remember as a shadow. One week!"

Breaking his journey proved simple, payment of a small fee, British Airways only too eager to assist. Informing Jennifer she fought hard to hold back her emotions, a losing battle as tears welled in her eyes.

"Jennifer, do you and Chloe want me to come back?"

"When I first saw you I tried not to stare, tried not to blush like some silly awestruck teenager. Frightened you would hear my heart beating in my chest."

"No, me who gawked. My Jennifer, so sophisticated, beautiful and distant."

"My only pathetic defence against you I kept telling myself over and over he will be gone from your life in six weeks and you will never see him again. There were even long and hard thoughts about that, chastising myself for wanting to throw myself at you. Does that

The Chinese Seamen's Children

sound like your sophisticated Jennifer Rice?"

"Sounds like the Jennifer Rice I love."

"Alex, I can't bear to think of your going," she sobbed, clinging to him.

"Jennifer, there is so much I have to attend to, especially work." Tasting her tears, he gently kissed her cheeks, then as if not to bruise them, pressed his lips to hers. "Then home to my girls."

23

EDWARD FLEW TO SINGAPORE Friday, Alex's departure Sunday. Acting on advice he booked into a hotel that once might have been white masonry but now so soiled with luxuriant black mould and carbon soot the owners could have advertised it as ancient ruins. Its only redeeming feature its location not far from the main tourist haunts of Orchard Road. Accepting a bed in the hotel came with a warning from past guests, old shipmates, though ably suitable for a seaman's budget, health, safety and security came with a rating of highly suspect. Edward held no such qualms, more important matters to be dealt with: libraries, shipping companies, agents, government offices and seamen's missions.

Jennifer planned to drive to Windsor early Saturday morning and spent their last days together in a hotel, not counting on Chloe whose big doe-like eyes begged to come. Jennifer, beside herself, wanted this man to herself, not to share even with a beloved child.

Making a rational decision in Jennifer's state of mind seemed improbable to Alex, taking her his arms and making his judgement. Chloe rushed to her bedroom to pack a bag, in her creative mind certain she would meet the queen or a prince or princess strolling along the High Street shopping.

"Alex, I hoped to have a sailor all to myself for the weekend, but it seems I will have to share him. Well, some of him."

The Chinese Seamen's Children

Windsor, time worn cobblestone and masonry entrenched in ancient history, flowing from the skirts of a massive compilation of stone, Windsor Castle.

"Chloe might just be right about meeting royalty doing their shopping in Windsor," Jennifer said. Again the navigator, she directed him to turn into Datchet Road. "Heard the queen does her own shopping at times, though I would suppose surrounded by an entourage of security people."

Chloe, almost overcome with anticipation, searched for a royal personage amongst people waiting for a crosswalk single to turn green. "She wears comfortable shoes and carries her own shopping basket, and of course a headscarf if it's cold."

Windsor rested on its ancient stone foundations, raising a handmaiden of extraordinary structural beauty, the Royal Oak Hotel, what the world expected of an English pub. Overshadowed by Windsor Castle, brick with a high pitched slate roof and dormer windows, Elizabethan whitewash and black battens. Overflowing flower boxes in bloom wafted their intoxicating perfume over patrons sitting at tables on the footpath.

Theirs to explore winding streets, small boutiques and craft shops, a visit to the castle, dinner and their last hours in the Royal Oak Hotel.

Chloe at last fell asleep. It might have been fear of waking her daughter in the adjoining room, tiptoeing to the bed and slipping in beside him.

"Jen, our girl asleep?"

"Over excited, babbling on about the castle and searching the corridors for the queen and members of her family. Our girl, that's nice, Alex."

Drawing her close, his hand slipped under her camisole and traced along her spine, then down to her bottom. "Got a question for you, Jen, why do you always wear panties to bed?"

"For you to take off, that's why. Don't you like taking them off?"

Dictated by society she should wear for modesty, the silken feel of which caused a rush of blood to his head, the exquisite touch of flesh even softer. Easing the tiny undergarment down her thighs and over her knees, his breathing as forced as hers as she opened her legs to receive him.

Listening to his soft breathing beside her, she lost count of the times she had taken him inside her, her sensuous flesh raw and tender, the sheet beneath an embarrassment in the morning. Unashamedly she wanted to completely drain his body to sustain her for the long period of separation. Running her hand lightly over his shoulder, he stirred, his hand covering hers.

"Sorry, thought you were asleep."

"Sleep's far away."

"Tell me you love me."

When his words finally spilled out it mattered not he choked them, a plea, burying his head in her chest. "Please wait for me!"

Resulting from a substantial bribe stars were awarded its rating would classify the hotel a hovel. Not even an increased sweetener could add a star for fine dining, anything ingested within a certain risk to the human intestinal system. Jammed on high and secured to an exposed rafter by suspect screws, the overhead fan at any moment threatened to decapitate anyone unfortunate to be beneath when it and the warped beam finally collapsed. Their room came furnished with two highly unstable single beds primarily used for short time liaisons, two army steel lockers and a chair under the only window overlooking a lane jammed with humanity. Someone in the past had used the leg of the chair to prop the window open, why questionable when the room filled with the putrescence of dried fish and human waste. From the street the noise of commerce deafened, footpath vendors selling a hotchpotch of steaming noodles, rice, vegetables, flyblown meats and fish.

"So your mates passing through recommended this establishment? Please notice I said establishment because no way am I giving the slum owner the satisfaction of calling it a hotel." Alex said, both feet overhanging the rickety bed end.

"Came highly recommended, much favoured by frugal British shipowners for their crews in transit. It's cheap and close to everything, what more do we want? Having said that though, under no circumstances lift the bottom sheet."

"Of course you would have noticed the working girls bunked down in the foyer? Excluding the girls as an enticement, how many stars you reckon?"

"Got to admit even the mob of the *Baron Maclay* would have drawn the line with some of them. The bloke on the front desk is friendly and helpful enough, gave me the name of his Singapore library second, third or fourth cousin, Miss Soong. For that effort, maybe a minus two, three stars. Christ, the front desk man must have a reputation. Rang her and spoke about my reason for being here and when I told her how I'd got her name she went to great pains to deny any family connection with the hotel. She's agreed to have lunch where she and her fiancé eat and bring some papers which might be helpful in heading us in the right direction."

"How come I'm not surprised about her reluctance to admit family ties? First thing I'm going to do is stop that homicidal fan."

"Tried juggling that bunch of wires hanging out the base but it didn't work Odd thing, keep moving the bunk against the wall, but each morning it's back under the fan."

"It's called vibration. Do we have room service?"

"Nope, all we got is a toothless old crone who shuffles around with a backpack spraying for cockroaches. Reckons mosquitoes, but I've seen some of the cockroaches around here and boy let me tell you'll need a broom and dustpan if you happen to step on one going to the toilet."

"That's another question, where?"

"Believe me I did ask for a room with shower and toilet. Down the hallway, but wouldn't recommend using it. Tiled with a hole in the floor where it seems a national sport to drop little piles around the perimeter. Bloke with a shovel has been trying to unblock it since I got here, so would avoid it. Sold me a plastic bucket. Been pissing out the window. Also wouldn't recommend eating here, the toilet is part of the kitchen. Relax and enjoy, lucky the manager had a deluxe room left, think about the other rooms classed budget."

Oppressive, sapping heat mixed with a blue haze of diesel and petrol fumes made breathing difficult, Alex reaching for a towel the size of a washcloth to breathe through. He thought about his situation, ideal for a seaman on limited funds, money needed for better things like bars and fleshpots and buying junk for family back home. Maybe in the past, but not now an English girl had changed his life. Somewhere away from this awful heat he would write his first letter to her.

"Excluding Miss Soong, there any other pointers where you might start looking, Edward?"

"Yes, the sky pilot at the Missions to Seafarers. Old bloke's a wealth of knowledge, a chaplain in the mission when Singapore fell to the Japanese and did his internment in Changi prison. Fascinating, hasn't been home since with a memory you and I could only envy. Stored away old guestbooks he reckons should be of interest, possibly somewhere to start. Goes back to 1927 when the mission first started up, he's going to search them out. Asked him the obvious question of what would happen to a seaman dumped in Singapore without means of support after the war.

"Never hesitated, seek the help the Missions to Seafarers, an important aspect of their work as well as spiritual to assist destitute seamen. God on his side my father's next logical step would have been shipping agents to put his name on their crewing lists, a ship home to fight for his right to be a British subject. Although at that time with the war just ended some of the better known agents were yet to return to Singapore. Nonetheless, the most urgent need would be to find a ship. Miss Soong said she would do some digging around."

Alex preferred to swelter in a lather of sweat than risk the tempest of forced hot air generated by the crazed ceiling fan, accepting Edward's advice to move his bed nearer the wall. Fears also the screws holding the fan to the rafter might have further worked loose. "Has the Missions to Seafarers air conditioning?"

"Fans which stay attached to the ceilings if you're worried about losing your head."

Glued to the lumpy mattress of his bed, he could stand the heat no longer; finding his feet he lurched to the window where he sucked even more fetid air into his lungs. "Edward, I agree this dump is okay to get our heads down at night, but right now let's get out," he said, a note of desperation in his voice. "I need to breathe! I need air!"

Japanese automotive engineering had progressed immeasurably since the battered Toyota rolled off the assembly line many years past, its battered panels riddled with rust; the back windows missing their handles caused no problem, the glass in both collapsed in the door panel. Padding in the back seat had long disintegrated, bare springs and shreds of vinyl upholstery stretched over skeletal remains threatening severe injury those lax in separating lethal sprung metal coils to sit down.

Edward continued where he left off with the padre. "Drawing on the strength of the Lord the reverend saw the occupation by the Japanese as a mere pothole in the bumpy road his faith ordained him, heathen little yellow devils sent by the Almighty to test him. After the war he remained with his flock, also to tend to a burgeoning number of new arrivals, Liverpool Chinese. His guestbooks, a record of those who passed through his hallowed haven for seamen, signed with some enlightening comments according to the sky pilot."

"Read them?"

"Patience, the old bloke's got to sort them according to age first. Then again my father might have had an aversion to signing his name under God's roof. Maybe not, some words to point us in a direction. Remarked he noticed an oddity with the Liverpool Chinese, after the first few days of assistance many never returned, and he wondered about that at the time because he assumed all of them destitute. He thought maybe some because of their qualifications may have shipped out on Dutch ships resuming trade in Indochina."

"Sounds feasible. Ship out and earn money to return home."

"Then he came up with another theory, something more sinister."

Sinister caught his attention, forgetting the imminent threat to his life propelled at breakneck speed through congested Singapore streets, sitting in a pool of sweat and his lungs clogged with emissions pouring through holes in the floor. "Sinister, can't say I like the sound of that word, Edward."

"Crossing the causeway."

"Crossing a land bridge, what's ominous about that?"

"For those with an obsession to join the Communist insurgency. More a manic fixation to get even with anything British, especially the elite who owned the rubber plantations and tin mines, the visible symbol of the British raj."

"Edward, do you really think your father with a young wife and son at home in Liverpool, a seaman who probably wouldn't know which end of a gun fired, would take up arms against the British in Malaya?"

"Anything's possible."

Their ordeal in the taxi finally ended, the right side back passenger door falling off its hinges as the vehicle braked violently to a halt, the door flattened by an oncoming vehicle and fired like a missile across the street to collide with another.

Thick concrete and stucco absorbed heat and humidity, within the walls of the Missions to Seafarers a cool respite given added

The Chinese Seamen's Children

impetus by the blades of softly whirring ceiling fans spreading air evenly throughout the building. Edward spoke with a portly man in his seventies, a cheerful face webbed with tiny broken capillaries spreading from his nose, evidence he occasionally imbibed. Edward introduced him as Reverend Moynihan.

Shaking hands his grip surprised Alex, then again a man who survived Changi would have to be a man of exceptional strength. "So you two are on an undertaking of discovery, raking over the coals of a racial injustice. In doing so you must realise with dubious peace on earth there were millions and millions missing, and even more millions who simply ceased to exist.

"Heartrending the fate of those Liverpool men wrenched from their loved ones by government decree. Hour after hour their stories poured out. I listened and gave what solace I could, usually to no avail. Many of those good men, men who until this travesty of justice professed no political affiliation, turned their backs on British society to throw their lot in with the liberationists. Not that I am opposed to the grand concept of liberation, the tragedy being these men like so many victims of war were stateless and not wanted except as fuel for the radical movements."

"Reverend, your guestbooks, the ones from early 1946, might be of help to us," Edward said.

"Come," he said, leading them through a foyer into the darker interior of the building, through a series of doors to a cluttered storeroom. "Where the remnants of my past and our founding fathers gather dust, of little use to most, but one day might be of historical interest to those seeking insight into humanity cast adrift. Those books I have set aside and should be of interest. Flex your muscles those books are heavy and come with me."

Even cooler in the deeper reaches of the building, an arched alcove with potted palms and timber shuttered windows ideal for writing a letter home or reading a book or magazine, comfortably furnished with rattan chairs and side tables, overhead fans soft and lulling. Alex and Edward joined two tables and placed fifteen leather-bound guestbooks dating from 1946 to 1947 in two neat stacks. Then began the task of meticulously passing their fingers down columns of names, dates and comments, many smudged, others painstakingly printed. Names of seamen from all corners of the world, all nationalities, recorded in Reverend Moynihan's guestbooks.

Edward, rubbing his eyes, looked up from the last guestbook; he closed it shut with a thump, a dispirited expression on his face. "My mind prepared me for his name to leap out and pinpoint him in a moment of time, maybe an address or a ship he had joined. Nothing."

Before leaving Edward bought Reverend Moynihan a bottle of whisky.

Susan Soong, tall for a Chinese, bespectacled and crowned with hair as black as pitch to her waist, confronted life with a confident and reassuring air ensconced behind her highly polished teak counter befitting the National Library of Singapore. Always a ready smile, an infectious eagerness to assist those lost and confused in the vast catacombs of the library.

Lunch with an overly excited Englishman, completely outside the edicts of protocol she chastened herself, might be a waste of her short meal break if he and the friend he spoke about lost their way finding the tiny two table restaurant at the back of the covered market area.

Assailing their senses an overpowering aroma of food, smoked, dried, deep fried and steamed. Fried and boiled rice, chicken, fish, pork, glazed duck, beef, vegetables, boilers of steaming noodles and a dozen varieties of soups brimming with claws, shells and wantons. Baking heat generated through the low iron roof could well have been an oven, Alex wondering how the locals dressed in their business finery managed to look so at ease, though not the visibly distressed Europeans swamped in sweat, their clothing hanging limply from their overweight frames.

Two unshaven and tousled haired men in shorts and t-shirts

nursing Tiger beers sat at one of two tables, undoubtedly her target. She flashed her most professional smile, introduced herself and sat down, an apology for her absent fiancé having unfortunately eaten something at breakfast that did not agree with him; he also worked in the library, she added with a note of pride. All business, she pushed aside an assortment of condiments, chopsticks, spoons, forks, pots of chilli of various potencies, to make room for a thick manila folder which she opened.

"Miss Soong, thank you for your time," Edward said, indicating Alex with his beer, "This is my mate Alex Nielsen with a primary role in this endeavour is to keep me sane."

She offered her hand to both men.

"Mr Huang and Mr Nielsen, it is my pleasure to meet you both and my sincerest hope I can be of assistance to you. Singapore immediately after the war experienced difficult times, a transition from a stagnated occupied country to a free enterprise post-war economy," she said, fanning out a sheaf of clipped papers across the table. "According to government archives Singapore experienced a large influx of Chinese from the United Kingdom in 1946, but scant information that could prove useful in locating a particular person. We spoke briefly on the phone these men were mainly Liverpool Chinese who made permanent homes in Liverpool and married British nationals. For many of these displaced persons their situation would be compounded by being preyed upon by the unscrupulous taking advantage of their vulnerability. Though I would think in the circumstances of their arrival in Singapore the pickings for predators would be slim."

Handing Edward a single sheet of paper the list of names were familiar, the first few imprinting in his mind: Jardine Mathieson, C. F. Sharp, Ben Line, Alfred Holt, Straits Steamships. "Shipowners and agents who may have offered him employment or at least recorded his name on their books. Possibly the person in question may have left a contact address, a name to point you in a specific direction. Though it is thirty-four years ago and locating more extensive records might be difficult if not impossible. People grow old and memories are not always reliable."

Without the need to refer to a menu written in Chinese, a single piece of paper in a plastic sleeve, she ordered a noodle dish and vegetables, for the two men more intent on drinking beer, curried seafood and rice. "Shipping companies come and go either through mergers, takeovers or investing their assets elsewhere. Agents are a little more permanent, especially C. F. Sharp, quick to resume business after the war. With big guns still smoking this company sloshed in the footsteps of General MacArthur when he waded ashore in the Philippines. Ben Line did not come to Singapore until 1950. I have taken the liberty to check with these firms and none have crewing records that cover your period of interest. Of course records prior to the Japanese occupation were hastily crated and in some cases lost forever."

Edward grew silent.

Their meals came and Alex wondered her wisdom ordering a spicy dish sweltering under an iron roof. Folly, yes, but worth the sweat streaming down his face after spearing a still simmering chunk of crab meat that threatened to fall apart on his fork, exposing a bed of boiled rice soaked in nose tingling curry sauce. Crab meat and juice slid down his throat, a deep breath and a roll of his eyes; the meal Singaporean perfection.

Edward signalled for two Tigers and a pot of Chinese tea.

Saddened by the defeat clearly evident in his face, she said: "Leon and I eat here when we can, a lot cheaper than the commercial and tourist areas. Also you get a lot more for your money. Please understand it is not the end of your search for your father. If you consider it worthwhile to visit the library I will direct you to our government archives and historical records section. There you would be able to access unclassified government documents, newspapers and shipping company news. Never know though, your father's name might pop up."

"Only if he committed murder or robbed a bank," Edward said glumly. Swallowing his beer in three gulps he signalled the waitress

The Chinese Seamen's Children

furiously chopping herbs for her husband obscured in a cloud of smoke and flames from his woks for two more beers. Shrugging at Alex's raised eyebrows, he muttered: "Us Poms drink pints, mate."

Wielding her chopsticks with the ease of someone born to them, she mentioned the Malayan Emergency. Edward nodded a thank you to the waitress who dropped more ice in a bucket for their fresh beers.

"My father joined the Communist Party in the United Kingdom. Wonder if that information found its way into official documents which might have made him a person of official interest."

"His membership might. What do you know about the Malayan Emergency?"

"Only what I have read in our highly biased version of the conflict."

"As for me my knowledge is based on how my union reacted, opposing the Australian government sending armed forces to Malaya to suppress a liberation movement. Also government support for the Dutch in Indonesia," Alex added.

"Two different actions, but comparable liberation movements against colonial rule. Now the hypothesis in Malaya, fabricated by the United Kingdom and her Commonwealth of Nations allies, the Emergency represented an armed intervention to save Malaya from a Communist insurgency. More correctly a liberation movement commanded by an elusive guerrilla leader named Chin Peng from 1948 until its conclusion in 1960 with Chin Peng exiled."

"Beyond belief after twelve years of jungle fighting involving naval, aircraft and ground forces, the British government didn't declare war against the Communists. Edward mentioned something about insurance, is that right?" Alex said.

Resting her chopsticks in her bowl, she took a delicate sip of her tea and replied: "Insurance, yes. Call it a war and the rubber plantation owners, oil drillers and tin miners would not have been indemnified by their insurance providers, so the term Emergency is used to describe the bloodshed."

"No matter what in this world the establishment's always got an angle, endless spin to baffle and worm its way out of taking responsibility for the destruction and misery it inflicts upon the masses," Edward said, on his third Tiger.

"To defeat Chin Peng's liberation movement, the United Kingdom called upon 300,000 combatants, army, naval, air forces, drawn from the Commonwealth of Nations and Home Guard," she said. "Chin Peng might have been defeated and hounded out of the country, but his guerrilla forces inflicted 8000 casualties."

"So it could be a possibility my father crossed the causeway and joined the liberation forces, but you said 1948, right?"

Her voice gave him little to lift his confidence. "Yes, a time gap which does not synchronise your father's arrival in Singapore. In that timeframe though he would have seen a different Singapore from his early years and how he would react to these changes who would know. Singapore during those immediate post-war years would rather be forgotten by the Chinese community. Your father would have landed in a British colony where he had no right to vote because of his ethnicity, even with a large and productive Chinese population. High unemployment and low wages, food scarce and where available costly.

"Among the Chinese population there would have been open hostility to British rule, living in hopeless poverty, starving, jobless, their clothes falling off their backs and disfranchised. Their suffering made even worse by the white colonial grandees in their white linen suits sipping gin and tonics in their clubs. Cheering their teams on the polo fields, the horses better fed and quartered than the Chinese eking an existence in squalor."

Both men went quiet.

"Huang Zhen your father married a British subject and served the entire war at sea on British ships only to be deported to Singapore when the conflict ended. Please tell me from your perspective how and why this could happen."

"Firstly, the government had no grounds to deport the Liverpool Chinese, and even though illegal, continued the culling with callous efficiency at the behest of those who claimed Chinese in the community

The Chinese Seamen's Children

threats to British jobs and British way of life. These seamen committed no crimes, freely gave their services to a nation at war, and supported their communities as decent upstanding family members."

Among her files again she found a document of at least ten pages of close print. "Complex details of which I have no legal background to form an argument for or against government policy, except of course to feel outrage," she said with a serious set to her face. "There were many government pronouncements of acting in the best interests of Singapore, reams of paper vindicating racial cleansing, all of it pure bunkum. What I have here is a mere few minutes of long and boring debate to vindicate retribution against innocent people classified as a threat to the state," She flicked through the pages, copies of original documents. "The 1946 deportations of Chinese from Singapore to China. Ironic isn't it, here is the British government prepared to annihilate with its might of arms hardened by five years of world war a liberation movement to save Malaya from Communism while deporting Chinese to China on the threshold of civil war between Nationalists and Communists. Some of those Chinese might well have been your Liverpool seamen."

Hopelessness like a crushing weight bore down on his shoulders, Edward pointing to his empty beer, then holding up two fingers. "What bloody chance did my father have, thrown out of his own country and dumped in Singapore? Born in Singapore, the Singapore government wouldn't be able to deport him to China. Correct?"

Shaking her head deepened the depression of the man sitting opposite her. "In 1946 the Singapore government could and did enact draconian legislation to maintain the colonial status quo, bureaucrats and puppets protecting a jaded Empire on which, referring to an old boast, the sun never set."

Alex draped a consoling arm around his mate's shoulders. "Huang Zhen's road would have been hard, bloody hard, but I'm certain he would have overcome everything thrown at him because of that special gene we seamen have down inside out gullets. We are above all survivors, Edward."

"Only I could believe that. Why the hell not the first ship to Liverpool, exposing those who inflicted this travesty on Liverpool families? Bringing down a cowardly, morally corrupt and bigoted system no better than the jackbooted fascists seamen fought and died in their thousands to defeat."

Offering her sympathy, her hand lightly brushed his arm. "If declared a Communist and a threat to the state and to escape impending deportation to China, your father might have crossed the causeway. May have even entered Thailand in the hope of joining a ship, though that is doubtful. So soon after the war he probably would not be welcomed in Thailand."

Edward had placed a lot of hope on the librarian recommended by the manager of a sleazy hotel, a distant cousin, her meticulously selected and copied government documents, to no avail. With a hangdog expression, he said: "Seemed so easy and straight forward in Liverpool, come to Singapore and dig around some archives and there it would be in the clear light of day, an open book on my father's life. Nothing. What more can I do? What is left, doing the rounds of the waterfront dives?"

"Which would be the last place I would look for him, and I know you do not mean it. By some chance your father slipped through the net on his arrival in 1946 your chances of finding his trail incredibly slim if not hopeless. If only you knew someone high in the police who could access files, search for a possible criminal record."

"Murder or bank robbery?"

"Not so dramatic, but despair and anger can drive a man to extremes. Even in those early post-war years the Singapore government would have needed some premise for deportation to China of Chinese landed on their shores from the United Kingdom, any pretext to satisfy their paperwork and tick the appropriate boxes. Being Singaporean Chinese his deportation would need legal grounds, no matter how flimsy, then again we refer to Singapore in 1946."

"Could I make an application for information from the Singapore police?"

The Chinese Seamen's Children

"Highly classified. Then again if you presented your father's birth certificate, written depositions from prominent persons in politics, church leaders, community activists, proof of deportation from the United Kingdom, yes." Then she smiled, again touching his arm. "Sorry it is so complicated, Mr Huang."

"Edward, please call me Edward."

"Edward," she acknowledged with a sympathetic smile. "My department head is an important man in Singapore and knows people who can delve into government archives, probably even police files. Influential in Singapore's 1963's unilateral declaration of independence, a presumptuous act from a fledgling country which thankfully did not result in a British fleet sailing southward with guns primed. I'll see what I can do."

From the depths of despair, a glimmer of hope.

"Lunch would be nice, and I will bring Leon with me. Leon will not impose, he brings his own lunchbox with rice and fish." Her face suddenly creased with thought, adding: "We have people at the library who are experts at research, your elusive seaman father might prove to be a real person after all. Above all, do not give up."

Outside in the stifling hallway the frequency of the soft tapping, seductive whispering and feet shuffling outside their flimsy door grew in intensity.

"Maintaining the highest moral standards, we have run the gauntlet of a bevy of girls doing a thriving business in the foyer. First thoughts were we might have gate-crashed a convention of bar girls and their pimp, the pimp manning the front desk," Edward said.

Both had enjoyed dinner in a restaurant close to the waterfront, then before returning to their hotel a few Tiger beers in a small bar overflowing with Filipino seamen in a pre-mating ritual with a dozen near naked girls imported from Quezon City. Dressing to a more reserved code of modesty, the local competition were somewhat overshadowed by the flamboyant imports, though no less eager to negotiate with their shapely bottoms squirming in the laps of two white seamen perched on barstools.

"Not tempted?" he said with a grin, Alex having bought the girl on his lap a dubious and highly inflated rum and coke, then shooed her off with a gentle tap on her tiny bottom.

Alex watched one of the girls reach over a table to pluck a cigarette from the drooling mouth of a drunken Filipino; she might have been the most attractive girl in the bar, her miniskirt stretched tightly across the top of her thighs exposing a thin strip of black lace panties buried between the brown cheeks of her buttocks. "Not at all."

"Jennifer's really got to you, hasn't she?"

"If she'll have me I want to marry her, but please keep this between us, Jennifer and I haven't even talked about it."

Edward's barstool crashed to the floor, embracing Alex with a wild whoop and a bear hug. "Wow! My Katherine's even better than I first thought. Then again you two swooning over each other made me want to throw up. Katherine will be in raptures! Going to be difficult, but my lips are sealed."

More knocking sounded on the door, an eye peering through the keyhole which served no purpose; she crooned her name Fifi or something similar, a nice clean girl, big breasts and rippling pincers where a man most desired. Above all, her final sales pitch, cheap.

Edward knew by her expression; Huang Zhen left no trail of his life. Documentation of his arrival in Singapore in government files noted his name, ship and a date of entry, no more. Equally disconcerting, no record being among Chinese undesirables deported from Singapore to China.

"From the moment my father stepped off a ship in Singapore he ceased to exist, is that what you're telling me?" he said, stricken.

"Whatever your father did he did of his own volition and without

The Chinese Seamen's Children

drawing attention to himself." Susan introduced her fiancé who bowed his head and proffered a timid a hand; the total opposite of his effervescent partner, he concealed a deadpan face behind thick, horn-rimmed spectacles.

Alex ordered a pitcher of mango juice and two Tigers for himself and Edward who with the fingers of his right hand drummed a mindless staccato on the table. Remembering them from the previous day, the proprietor's wife checked her supply of ice and put extra beers in the refrigerator, a toothy smile of welcome.

Sweet and sour pork and combination beef and rice for Alex and Edward, Susan indicated somewhat sternly for Leon to take his lunchbox out of his briefcase. Edward's attempt to change her mind and let him order a meal failed, a stern rebuff her fiancé practised financial restraint essential to a successful and prosperous future.

"What about you, the woman's role?" Briefly, the barest hint of a smile tempered the despondency he felt.

"Mine will be the bearer of his children. Sorry, Edward. We tried."

"Suppose the only good thing to come out of this is there is no criminal record or register of death," he said resignedly.

"Huang Zhen crossed the causeway there might be records in Kuala Lumpur."

"Too far, too far. What is certainly a fact to which I must resign myself, my fixation has come to an end. Also I have to remove from my mind my father's driving will to return home, a desire which seems did not exist. Alex and I both agree he possessed the professional means even if it took years. Could have, but he didn't for reasons we will never know." Hanging his head, he chose his words carefully and uttered them softly: "While I wallow in self-pity I apologise to my mate subjected to a beastly place of abode, teeming with cockroaches, rats, lice and bed bugs, not to mention under permanent assault by a stable of harpies. To you, Susan, it has been a privilege to be in your company and I apologise for burdening you with my obsession."

She thanked the proprietor's wife for the extra large bowl of rice which accompanied their meals; Edward with no appetite, held up two fingers which needed no interpreting.

Relenting because of the large servings, Susan shared her meal and Edward's untouched food with her fiancé; his lunch would form the basis for the evening meal.

"What a bloody idiot I am."

Alex reached out to his friend. "No, you're nothing of the sort. Edward mate, if more men were like the son you are, the love you give your mother and the desire to find the truth, the world would be a much better place."

Their last night in Singapore their door, its only means of remaining shut a wooden wedge jammed under the bottom style, withstood a furious battering; not by the thwarted girls in the foyer painting their nails and applying thick layers of rouge and eye shadow, but Billie-boys from a gay bar down the street whom the girls informed in no flattering terms in room 102 resided two men who might be of interest. Truth, even after offers no real man could refuse, these two obviously besotted lovers continued to rebuff their services.

Between their beds a carton of Australian beer, Victoria Bitter purchased in the supermarket next door for four times its value in Australia, their last night together deserving a treat. Above their heads the fan still threatened its hari-kari vengeance on anyone foolish to tempt fate to regulate it, but forgotten as the two men sat on their beds, a bucket of rapidly melting ice, beer and camaraderie.

Times lengthened when both men lapsed into silence, Edward with sombre thoughts about his lost cause and Alex memories of a girl in Liverpool.

24

OUT OF THE SOUTHWEST the wind from the bay swept up the heavily timbered flanks of Mt Eliza, dissipating its force to retreat to the coastal strip as an inversion layer of cool air causing a wintry Frankston to fall a couple of degrees lower in temperature than chilly Melbourne to the north. For Alex the reality of being home set in immediately, a job; at least four months or more on articles on his next ship to be able to return to Liverpool.

Dismissed without even a second thought asking Jennifer to make Australia home; long separations in a foreign country no matter how British, separated from her mother, her career and the loss of lifelong friends. Ships without swinging systems to accrue leaves long enough to warrant the high expense of regularly flying to the United Kingdom, firmly in his mind the option of living in Liverpool and shipping out of Australia.

Seemingly though short leaves did not pose too greater problems for the growing number of seamen married in the Philippines and Thailand; he even knew an AB with a wife in Galveston, Texas. First he would ring his father and thank him for renewing two lengths of rusted guttering and a section of downpipe. Not only that his father replaced a half dozen weatherboards affected by dry rot, priming and matching the topcoat paint near perfect.

Not forgetting his caring neighbours the Moorlands whose surveillance of his mailbox resulted in the two neat stacks of mail on his sideboard; Laura slipped a note through the rubber band she used to bundled the mail she needed to talk with him later on a matter of importance.

Standing at the window looking out over the white-capped waters of the bay, a grey overcast sky threatened rain; though these massed cloud banks rolled in from the Southern Ocean and not the Irish Sea, the dreariness reminded him of another sky, Jennifer so far away.

On the current market he wondered what price his home would bring, maybe $100,000; converted to an unfavourable exchange rate not conducive to purchasing a similar property in the United Kingdom, but a substantial start. Thoughts never far from his mind this home and what it symbolised. Two people above and beyond the bounds of parentage who gave a son an advantage in life that placed him far ahead of others destined for a lifetime of debt.

Turning from the window he paced the room, so many things to do but a quandary of what to do first; a rough guess his body recognised the time as early morning, but in Frankston the hidden sun dipped low on the western horizon. Laura, true to her word, a plate of chocolate chip muffins in one hand, hurried around the back, knocking on the screen door. Startled, her expression turned to a worried grimace. He looked awful! No meat on his bones! She had heard ghastly English food consisted mostly of baked beans and greasy fish and chips, no wonder.

"Gallivanting all around the world, look at you," she chastened. "Deathly pale and nothing of you. Before you expire though there is something you need to know, shame on you, Alex Nielsen, leaving behind a broken heart."

"Laura, my mind is a mess at the moment. Ask me what day it is I would get it wrong. What are you talking about?"

"Tuesday, so there. Our Roxanne."

Roxanne! Roxanne had never entered his mind! "Laura, did Roxanne tell you I asked her to come to the United Kingdom with me?"

"No, she didn't."

"Also she has a new job with high status value? She suffered muscular problems flying long distances? Oh yes, I think she thought it time to move on as well."

"So embarrassing when young people speak so frankly of matters that should be left in the privacy of the bedroom. Curious, I asked her about postcards and she said you had got what you wanted, then dumped her for conquests on the other side of the world. Hid it well, the poor girl heartbroken."

"Good god! Conquests! Laura, believe me I did not dump our Roxanne as you refer to her. Have you given it a thought she might have been looking for sympathy, regret rejecting my offer? As for getting what I wanted, a perfectly natural act of nature between two people of the opposite sex, or the same sex if you're that way inclined, is sharing. I must be wrong, not how Roxanne sees life."

"Dear me, young people speak so frankly. Naive me with high hopes the chemistry might work between you pair, set the headstrong girl in the right direction so to speak. She can be a little wild, though she is very young and yet to settle down." Pausing for breath, she pulled a sour face. "Then being an observer of your ceaseless comings and goings at all hours, what chance would a spirited girl have of having a natural relationship. Such a waste, you made a handsome couple."

"Yes, such a waste," he said, now wide awake and thoroughly depressed.

Booked to Sydney on the evening train departing Spencer Street, baggage checked from Frankston, and with the afternoon free he made a decision and having made it felt a sense of relief. Still smarting from Laura's false assumption of his dumping Roxanne, he finally convinced himself this brief segment of his life should be relegated to the past. She might be home or working; leave a message, some meaningless and quickly forgotten words.

Knocking on the door he waited a full minute before he heard shuffling and muttering in the hallway, the door warped on its rusted hinges opening begrudgingly. Encountering her in the street he would not have known, her face and body more bloated than when he had first been introduced, but he remembered her name. Clinging to her arm a twig of a young girl swayed back and forth as if caught in a draft in the hallway, her thinness bordering on anorexia, skin so transparent and taut she might have been a cadaver. Both drunk, she did not recognise him.

"Sheila, is Roxanne home?"

"Who the hell are you? If you're selling something we don't want it."

"Alex Nielsen. Roxanne, is she home?"

She drew the girl closer with a protective arm around her impossibly small waist, two jutting hip bones from which hung a nylon petticoat; her shirt unbuttoned to the waist exposed a sunken chest ridged with rib bones and he wondered if he misjudged her sex. Her lover cupped a bony buttock, leering at the intruder in her doorway. "Snotty bitch don't live here anymore. Amy here does, right, Amy?"

Amy, incapable of speech, lost her eyes somewhere in the back of her head.

With a sense of relief he asked another question, not caring if she answered it or not. "She live close?" Take a step back now and walk to the gate, the pointless reasoning for wanting to see Roxanne painlessly concluded.

"Uppity bitch's too good for us now. Though still a raving case, slut can't get enough of it."

"Does she live around here?" he repeated. End this, turn and go, an episode in his life concluded.

"Who'd know, who'd care? Got a fancy bloke, looks like a poof if you ask me. Brags he's in television, no one's ever seen him so she's lying. Strutted off with him and her things."

From somewhere in her head two dull eyes reappeared, Alex

wondering her age and did those she attached her life to like a limpet realise she suffered a serious affliction. Did anyone care?

Sheila in her befuddled brain visualised a spurned and shattered lover, and with gleeful pleasure twisted the knife. "All the time boasting the poof's hung with a big dong. Best she's ever been stuffed with, hundreds she reckons."

With relief he closed the gate behind him and hurried down the street to the railway station.

Alex booked into the Steelworks Hotel, a pile of bricks and brewery tiles at the top of Wentworth Street. One of three thriving hotels in Port Kembla's main thoroughfare, the distances apart no more than an inebriated man thrown out of one could stagger with fewer abrasions and bruises to the next. Because of their geographic location, the hotels needed little imagination to identify; Top Pub, Middle Pub, Bottom Pub.

Port Kembla nestled beneath the shadow of the Illawarra Escarpment, a towering upheaval of rock and dense vegetation formed in the Tertiary Period 200 million years ago, at its base a thin coastal strip. From seaward the escarpment presented a brooding mountain range topped with two prominent sentinels, Mt Kembla and Mt Ousley. Hidden valleys and jagged ridgelines within the escarpment featured geological wonders of spectacular natural beauty; rain forest, waterfalls, sheer cliffs brooding over small coastal towns smothered in choking pollution spewed from its industrial handmaiden, Port Kembla.

Every minute of every day the Port Kembla steelworks disgorged into the atmosphere a cocktail of gases and steelmaking particulates, in its concentrated form suspended along the foothills of the escarpment in a long red cloud. Existing in a shroud of toxic gases and flint-like particles it seemed improbable any living organism could survive, its poisonous tentacles driven by southerly winds even reaching Sydney forty miles north.

Unabated, the deadly miasma pouring from a forest of smokestacks, vents and blast furnaces, for no apparent reason environmentalists could pinpoint failed to destroy the escarpment. One theory a high rainfall continually inundated the range, raging streams staining the sea red. Testament to survival against almost insurmountable odds, Port Kembla thrived and as the suffering victim of its industries, rarely complained.

Port Kembla also came under siege from another nemesis; on the high side of Wentworth Street a concrete chimney soared so tall it cast a forbidding shadow down the middle of the street, gathered about its buttressed skirts asbestos clad iron roofed workers' cottages.

Those of a cynical mind the zinc smelter chimney reminded them of a giant finger making a profound statement to its contemptuous minions far below. Close inshore a fleet of anchored ships rolled in lazy Pacific Ocean swells, loaded to their marks with iron ore, limestone, lime sand, iron pellets and dolomite, others riding high out of the water chartered to load steel or coal mined from under the escarpment.

Closing its doors at 7:00 pm the Steelworks Hotel afforded some respite for its temporary lodgers between ships in need of undisturbed sleep. The Commercial Hotel, the Middle Pub burdened with a more risqué reputation, offered to patrons a cavernous lounge with a blaring juke box and an equally loud local band on Saturday nights. The Bottom Pub, the Port Kembla Hotel, Guinnery's to the locals, more family oriented and conservative, avoided by most seamen.

Where Wentworth Street commenced its steady rise to meet the feet of the zinc smelter chimney a wine bar engaged in a flourishing trade, a dark hole in the wall with a distinctive sour odour, some said of vinegar. Lighting posed no problem there being none except a bare bulb in a batten holder above the cash register. Wines dispensed from barrels and flagons, an occasional bottle, cheap and abundant, origin and vintage vague, clients could only guess at what ravages their stomachs suffered on ingestion. Rumours were its owner came

The Chinese Seamen's Children

from Eastern Europe, a plentiful source of amenable labour recruited by Australian Iron & Steel, who toiled like automatons with large brooms and shovels within the concrete bastions of the iron ore and coke berths, known throughout the steelworks as redskins.

Alex's room, spacious and spotlessly clean, accommodated four single beds and a mirrored dresser, an uninterrupted view over Wentworth Street to No. 2 jetty. Breakfast chanced in the hotel's dining room, if not liquid because the doors opened at 7:00am, usually rested heavy in the belly all day. Some preferred a stale meat pie heated in a small warming oven in the public bar, as a last resort a packet of crisps or peanuts.

Holding his attention a ship anchored in the lee of Toothbrush Island, a wash of water exploding from her port hawse pipe as she shortened cable. *Iron* on her massive bows as she swung to face the breakwaters; *Iron Newcastle*. There would be jobs in her relieving or permanent, coal for Japan or lightship to an iron ore port in Western Australia. After discharging iron ore she could load in Port Kembla or sail a hundred miles north in ballast to her namesake port. Another option, Queensland ports for steaming coal to feed Japanese power stations. Long voyages, long leaves.

Entering the Wentworth Street shipping office and his eyes growing accustomed to the gloom, he studied the engagement board marked in thick white chalk: *Iron Newcastle* 1 AB rel. 8 weeks? The question mark and rel. shipping office code for relieving and an additional thirteen weeks long service leave if agreed by the relief.

Below that and the only other job for the day: *Lake Barrine* 1 greaser relieving 6 weeks. The *Lake Barrine* on the black and tan run held no interest; coke for Whyalla, back loading iron pellets or iron ore for Port Kembla or Newcastle. Glancing around the near empty shipping office he saw two seamen sitting on a bench against the wall seemingly more interested sharing a racing form.

On the surface the atmosphere in the shipping office might have portrayed to an observer unfamiliar with maritime manoeuvrings a false sense of disinterest in the seemingly mundane affairs conducted within its sterile walls, ignorant to the strong undercurrents never far from the surface. Contrary to a fair and just system of employment an elite element waited in the background with bags packed, waiting a call to proceed directly to the offshore or a foreign run job.

These well known identities around the various waterfronts generously gave their time in the pursuit of keeping their union strong and on course. Making their sober presence known around the pubs where officials drank did nothing to lessen the employment prospects for these militant and articulate selectees. Their goal a stratum of specialist seamen to rise above the rabble, those with the mental capacity to throw iron ore impregnated hatch boards, spread tarpaulins and wage battle with forests of derricks. More than willing to sacrifice remaining leave entitlements to fly overseas to pick up tenders and new tankers, the occasional bulk carrier for the southbound trip only.

Almost 10:00am a few latecomers strolled in the pickup, feigning disinterest, a cursory look at the engagement board and because of their names lower down the roster relaxed; a buzz around the Port Kembla pubs persisted a tender docked in Hong Kong would soon be picking up, probably at the end of the week with no men on the Sydney roster.

Some bizarre tales originated in this cramped office where seamen at times reluctantly signed their names to ships articles. Of bad discharges, suspensions, loggings, exclusions from the industry, criminal charges and outright insanity. One such case gained notoriety when the tyrannical master of the *Lake Torrens* sought the authoritative opinion of the shipping master as to how he should punish a recalcitrant seaman. Full and just retribution for being absent from his station at sailing time, discovered by the apprentice sent to check missing heads drunk and unconscious in his bunk. Could the master charge him with desertion in addition to the logging and instant dismissal?

Himself a merciless disciplinarian, the shipping master thought not; the man's union would fight the charge and win. The shipping master defined desertion as the absence of a seaman and personal effects from the vessel at the time of sailing.

Acutely thin with a face likened to a weasel and a prominent hooked nose, the master and the shipping master, his physique and temperament that of a Viking, debated the matter in a professional matter behind the shipping office counter heavily engraved by the thumbnails of allocated seamen. Cowered on the other side, unshaven, smelly, the wretched creature in question awaited his fate with fatalistic resignation.

Wilful dereliction of duty punishable by six month suspension from the maritime industry? Again a ruling in the negative, his union with one member on the marine council garnered a lot of influence on those who decided these matters. Whatever the punishment against the drunk eventuated no one bothered to find out, though the seaman in question held court for a considerable time in the Top Pub telling all who would listen how he told the shipping master and old man of the *Lake Torrens* to get stuffed until it closed and he fell out the door.

Obviously bored, the shipping master intoned the roster of nine ABs, Alex at the bottom. Those sharing the racing paper shuddered in tandem as did another propped against the far wall, though not with rejection on the verge of delirium tremens.

"Nielsen?"

Without hesitation. "*Iron Newcastle*. I'll take the long service leave, too."

First question asked the BHP agent, her next port?

"Anchoring after discharge for a few days waiting for a Greek and a Panamanian to clear, then coal for two Japanese ports, light ship Dampier.

Twenty-one weeks!

25

ENTHRALLING BY SOME SEAMEN of more imaginative and creative minds having endured extended periods at sea, endless routines of work, drills, suffered sunburn and frostbite in a single voyage, that a yellow mangrove winglet bobbing on the outgoing tide in a muddy river is a marvel of creation and worthy of note. That this seed dropped from a stunted crown in the cycle of recreation of a not particularly attractive tree could engross a seaman to follow its bumpy progress along a ship's side would probably be of interest to the medical profession dissecting human behaviour.

Dropped in a cycle of reproduction in the shallow upper reaches of the north arm of the Hunter River, the ship low in the water as it passed on its journey to the sea, the *Iron Newcastle*. The seaman engrossed Alex Nielsen letting go the tug at the break of the focastle head informed by the second officer his relief would be on the wharf at noon, and to attend the Newcastle shipping office at 2:00 pm.

Overhead the banshee shrieking of electric brakes alternatively clamping shut on polished iron wheels, violent whipping and flaying of black oil soaked wires, the gaping maws of enormous grabs almost spanning the hatch, assailed with an almost maniacal intent the holds of the *Iron Newcastle*. Meaningless to Alex, his long relief including a prolonged strike in Port Kembla followed by a lengthy queue

The Chinese Seamen's Children

in Japan. Beside his bunk a photograph of Jennifer and Chloe, their smiling faces insulating his brain to the realties he and his fellow shipmates in the scheme of life no more than prisoners, some fortunate with early release. Encapsulating a seaman's existence a famous writer wrote life at sea could be likened to serving time in prison with the added risk of drowning.

From the 1950s six months on a ship roughly averaged the length of time at sea for most seamen burdened with commitments, and for those who dwelled in waterfront pubs and packed their gear in cardboard cartons possibly four ships or more in a year, a tally hardly worth mentioning when breasting the bar of pubs close to the shipping office. Early in the 1960s brought government administered stabilisation and regular leave, then followed swinging systems, tankers and specialised ships with two crews.

Acceptance into the Port Kembla Iron-boat clique, Port Kembla and Newcastle its heartland, now complete after surviving six months with his sanity intact, a feat worthy of boasting breasting the bar of the Top Pub. Among the many fallen he had overcome adversary in various forms. Crews out of Port Kembla and Newcastle who normally manned Iron-boats did so in conditions akin to marshal law. Shunned by the cream of their profession, those selected for oil rigs, tenders and tankers as mere muscle both in brawn and brain, capable of throwing 1200 hatch boards and spreading tarpaulins akin to circus tents, manning ships down by the head with drunks and the mentally impaired.

Utter monotony broken only by Jennifer's long letters received in Hay Point, Newcastle, Port Kembla, Port Hedland, Dampier and Japan. Letters read and reread during the lonely hours of twelve to four anchor watches. Taking two days to write a reply, pouring out his heart on paper. Excruciatingly slow weeks passed as did the months, the *Iron Newcastle* a well run job with a contented crew. Continually sunk to her marks with 160,000 tons of iron ore or coal, immaculately maintained and manned with Australians in a shipping environment motivated by greed, violence and merciless exploitation.

The *Iron Newcastle* competed successfully and profitably in a cutthroat world of substandard ships and mercenary shipowners because of the sound business principles of her steelmaking owners and the professionalism and commitment of her fully unionised crew.

Facts apprehensively observed anchored off the iron ore ports, the rarity of the Australian flag while ships registered in Africa and Panama with low paid and exploited crews shed their rust, pumped their engine room bilges, and dumped their plastics and garbage in the turquoise coastal waters of Western Australia.

Troubling thoughts of what the future held shared with a young second officer over a pot of tea on the twelve to four at 2:00 am, gently rolling in an oily swell with the lights of Port Hedland tiny jewels flickering in the east along a barren and desolate coast. Joining a queue of ships at least another week at anchor before loading for Newcastle. Memories now as he saw his taxi weave its way slowly through a group of wharf labourers returning from lunch, climbing the flattops of steel plate and coil being loaded on a Panamanian for Hong Kong.

Observed through the steelworks perimeter fence, heavy wire mesh strung with coils of rusted barbed wire, chaos seemed to be the order of the day, the steel wharf with a bank of electric luffing cranes loading from double and triple shunted flattops. Idling locomotives, stores trucks, ship repairers, road tankers, an army of seemingly leaderless men occupied in a dozen different professions. Parallel to the wharf separated by a road jammed with internal and external traffic, coated in inches thick iron ore and cinder, stood three brick and tile administration offices and canteen. Two trucks with meat and dry stores for the *Iron Newcastle* backed under the stern, another with deck stores tempting obliteration passing under the gantries where the bosun and two ABs stood by forward.

Now relegated to past memories, replaced with exhilaration having served his self-imposed sentence with a fine crowd of Port Kembla and Newcastle seamen, accepted now as one of their own. That in itself tribute to his mindset to adjust to a way of life routine to these men, the mundane operation of bulk carriers on long passages, weeks at anchor and the minimum time in port.

The Chinese Seamen's Children

Paying off and a night in a city hotel. Dinner on the company, lobster or a filet mignon, he thought as he threw his gear in the boot of the taxi. Then he would ring his girl.

With thoughts of Jennifer little did he know of what lay ahead and about to consume him.

Flights to the United Kingdom were heavily booked, family reunions and expatriates returning home for Christmas. Sympathy abounded in the office of the Frankston travel agent, a few seats available with Olympic Airways to Athens with connections, though it might take him a week to arrive in London, hopefully with his baggage.

Luck! A cancellation on a British Airways flight departing December 23rd. Separated from Jennifer for so long, a week would make little difference in the full leave he would spend with her in Liverpool.

When he rung she dropped the phone, the dangling handset picked up by her daughter who chastised him for upsetting her mother, and would he please hurry and come home to pacify her. Also he might be pleased to know his best friend would be home and he should make an effort to speak with him, finally a plea she and Grandmother were at their wits end what to do with Mother's moods.

Regaining some composure Jennifer tried to carry on a normal conversation between sniffs and blowing her nose. What he said to her flustered mind a blurred jumble; a seaman in high paid employment, member of the Commonwealth of Nations, white if that scored kudos with United Kingdom immigration, and assets which would not make him a liability on the British welfare and medical system. Verifying Edward's homecoming, his last words before he hung up something he wanted to ask her and would do so when he held her in his arms, enough for her to blubber and for him to put down the phone on the verge of tears himself.

Wayne Ward

Frankston to Melbourne, a boring train journey, familiar stations designed by railway architects of the previous century; red brick, terracotta chimney pots with wisps of smoke in winter, iron roofs, ornate metal lace and iron columns. Trains passed each other in this busy rail corridor in a steady stream of electric traction on broad gauge rails, boom gates, flashing red lights and bells barring the flow of traffic in both directions.

Flinders Street, railway architecture of an era long past, an imposing edifice to which the older inner suburban railway stations of Melbourne strove to emulate, dominated the inner city with its imposing clock tower and patina dome, rising supreme above all on its dominant site on the banks of the Yarra River. Aloof from its younger progeny to the north and west where the city sprawled in treeless isolation over the hot, windy and flat coastal plain; graffiti spattered, gouged perspex, mutilated advertising hoardings and pilfered dispensing machines.

Alex planned to have lunch in Little Bourke Street, pay his union dues and visit a military disposal store for a thick roll neck sweater for winter Liverpool. With these thoughts in mind he let himself be caught up in the flow of humanity, a mass outpouring down the broad steps of Flinders Street station, halted by a bank of traffic lights and pedestrian signals permitting multiple crossings. Two probationary constables stationed on the Princess Bridge Hotel kerb, their stern and official countenances concealing their nervousness, sufficient to thwart habitual light jumpers.

Normally he would have taken the train to Spencer Street one station north of Flinders Street, the country train terminal and less congested; for men on the Melbourne roster an easy walk, also closer to the waterfront pubs to meet with old shipmates. Thinking about it

The Chinese Seamen's Children

he rarely needed to come to the city, though a visit to Little Bourke Street for a Chinese meal made the trip worthwhile.

Gifts with an Australian theme for Jennifer and Chloe, definitely not native animal fur. Jennifer's mother and Katherine as a thank you. Myers department store, throw himself on the mercy of an understanding salesgirl for advice, skimpy lacy underwear for his girl.

Walking up the wide thoroughfare of Bourke Street he joined the yearly pilgrimage of families to the city to gaze upon with awe the windows of the big department stores bedecked with glittering stars and spangles, tinsel and crepe, pine trees and snow, without exception a portly figure of a jovial Santa Claus. Myer's theme this year eclipsed them all, even the ever popular Nativity, a northern hemisphere winter bathed in the glow of the aurora borealis, Santa Claus in company of his elves pouring over a huge book with the names of every child in the world.

Left turn where Bourke Street intersected Russell Street, a half city block then right into a narrow thoroughfare aptly named Little Bourke Street, Chinatown, a destination he knew well, Corrs Lane. Melbourne's Chinese district, a history reaching back to when the first Chinese poured off ships from China to pan alluvial gold in the 1850s, a thriving community amid the concrete and glass of the towering city skyline. Many of the current Chinese population could trace their lineage to those hard working miners who gravitated to the city when the gold ran out and set up businesses, others arriving in Australia through various sources, some legal, some not.

Little Bourke Street, a thoroughfare barely two vehicles wide, continually jammed with two-way traffic, from early morning until late at night an eardrum piercing resonance of horns and truck sirens, shouting and abuse from pedestrians scampering for their lives. For those with local knowledge walking became the only rational choice, impossible to find a parking space amid barrows and trolleys, entrepreneurs with their wares strapped to their backs and chests.

Lunchtime Little Bourke Street resembled a flash flood of office workers emptying from their towers, a quick and cheap meal before soaking up fifteen minutes of sunshine in Parliament Gardens. Diners could choose from all the cuisines of China, served either on damask with genuine silverware or hastily wiped oilcloth with massed produced chopsticks. Alex's choice, Corrs Lane, and if need be the kerb for a seat.

Those with long memories would ask those with even longer recollections when had the dim sim vendor first sent up his business in an apse in Corrs Lane, a lane so narrow two men could barely pass without brushing shoulders. No one really knew and no one really cared. Bathed in perpetual twilight, no ray of sunlight ever penetrated old Melbourne masonry that rose ten storeys either side of the lane, the dim sim vendor visible as a spectre in a smoky haze issuing from charcoal braziers under two large stainless steel steamers.

Like a beast of burden he pulled a cart, a high sided square box on bicycle wheels; icebox, water container, two bags of charcoal and bedding if he grew tired after selling his day's delicacies. With the tyres pumped up hard the cart also gave him instant mobility, the ability to flee when word passed like wildfire through Chinatown Melbourne City Council health inspectors were on the prowl.

Customers were offered a repertoire of gutsy songs, a surprisingly strong voice for an old and wizened man. Sucking in a large breath, he would expand his small chest and let out a roar, stamp his feet and sing. Alex thought his voice awful, more a continuous shout, but it seemed to give the old man greater stature, a fire in his eyes.

No excuses for the lack of seating, not even an upturned milk crate, one choice only to sit on the kerb to eat his soft noodle wrapped pork parcels dipped in a tangy, salty soy sauce. No serviette, no utensils, fingers only to devour the steaming hot morsels that continued to stew in their own succulent juices in greaseproof paper lined bags, large enough to hold six dim sims.

Mouth-watering ecstasy, the dim sim vendor with nimble fingers and a mind steeped in Chinese culinary excellence, had perfected an icon from his homeland so addictive people flocked from all over the city to stand patiently in a squalid lane. Wait with more patience while

The Chinese Seamen's Children

an odorous old man used tongs to extract singularly dim sims from a steaming mass of pure white casings about to split at the seams. In addition to a sumptuous meal came the bonus of a raucous song which no one understood.

To his addicted public he offered no name, no markings on his cart. In fact Alex could not recall ever hearing the man speak, only sing and stamp his feet in time with the rhythm of his mantra. Some wondered about his age, probably eighties, though that might have been unfair, his leathery skin the result of hard outdoor labour in his early years.

Even with the din of the city in the background he could hear the old man's voice as he turned out of Little Bourke Street into Corrs Lane; the dim sim vendor lambasted another old Chinese in a torrent of high-pitched screeching that could only be abuse, his foot stamping causing his cart to vibrate.

Seeing an approaching customer he spat at the man, once, twice, three times, reverting to a phlegm filled mouth of English. "Get away with you! Useless piece of shit! Off with you, I have a customer to attend to!"

Covering his ears with his hands, his victim edged to a safer position with his back pressed hard against a wall of masonry. Alex wondered if the old man could pay for his food.

"Do you need money?"

Dressed shabbily he looked a derelict and this mystified Alex because Chinese were not usually objects of visual poverty. Judging his age as old as his adversary, an impression formed in Alex's mind he possibly lived around the Queen Victoria Markets where an army of street people blended with no one the wiser. Also to earn a pittance for a bottle of wine unloading produce trucks at night.

"Are you broke and hungry?" Alex persisted.

Attempting to render his victim senseless on bluestone paving, the dim sim vendor threw a wild haymaker easily missing the intended target, postponing a song to unleash another verbal barrage of Chinese.

Alex had no choice but to act in the old man's defence, shielding him with his body, pushing him out of reach of the dim sim vendor preparing another assault, muttering what could only be obscenities under his breath.

"Stop! Bloody pair of you are old enough to be stuffed and displayed on the mantelpiece!" Gone his appetite for dim sims, out sympathy half dragging the old man to the mouth of the lane and into Little Bourke Street, one last look at the dim sim vendor furiously recharging his braziers with fresh charcoal and shouting a few bars of a new song.

Not overly clean with rows of identical green laminated tables and metal chairs, the restaurant suited his purpose. Alex asked the old man what he wanted to eat, receiving no response except a sullen and downcast face.

"How about chicken chow mien and special fried rice?" Why he bothered with this obvious ungrateful old man, the compassionate factor now worn thin, he found difficult to comprehend. "Okay, why do two senior Asian citizens go at each other's throats in a lane, albeit what I saw a one sided affair? There I am minding my own business anticipating the best dim sims in the world only to find myself sharing restaurant food with a bum definitely on the nose."

"Why are you sharing your food?" he uttered his first word.

"Maybe in my gullible mind you gave me the impression you might be hungry, assuredly broke. Get knocked back for a feed?"

"Starvation is preferable to eating what that traitor purports to be food."

"Someone dressed in the contents of a ship's ragbag is a food critic?"

"Clothes are not the man."

"Many would disagree. Couple of blankets in a doorway your home?"

Studying at the nearby Royal Melbourne Institute of Technology, the young Asian waiter tapped his pencil on his order pad. "Chicken chow mein and special fried rice to share," Alex said.

"No, I do not sleep in doorways."

"Sorry. Like a beer?"

"Tea. My name is Shen Kang, yours?"

"Alex Nielsen. Why the confrontation in Coors Lane?"

"My rage is justified, a sergeant in the Red Army taking offense with a traitor, a man who swore allegiance to the Kuomintang. A captain devoid of remorse forcing the youth of China to kill their fellow Chinese."

"How do you know this?"

"Because the traitor sings with great pride swelling its puny chest songs of the Kuomintang. Stirring words of the courageous Kuomintang marching victoriously through China, rousing the peasants to take up arms and stand by their exultant side."

Their food arrived with two smaller side plates, the portions huge. When Shen indicated his benefactor take first serving, Alex spread a bed of fried rice on his plate, topping it with the main dish.

"Please forgive me, I am ignorant. Thank you for your kindness, comrade."

Alex put down his fork. "What did you call me?"

"Comrade. Do you take offence?"

"Mr Shen, you offer me no greater proof of acceptance. Thank you for the compliment."

Both men ate in silence, the old man obviously hungry but eating slowly to savour each bite. Alex's curiosity got the better of him. "So there ends up in a grotty back lane in Melbourne an old Kuomintang captain, so what? There must be thousands of Chiang Kai-shek's army spread throughout the world. Only his elite would have fled with him to Taiwan plus those he needed to crush the locals and set up government, the rest dispersing to wherever opportunity arose. Have to admit, you Chinese blend in no matter where you are in the world."

"In their tens of thousands the Kuomintang disintegrated, mass desertions throughout the land when the army of liberation prevailed, though a hardcore of Chiang Kai-shek's retreating armies remained by his side to make their 1949 invasion of Taiwan a military success. Scattering like vermin throughout the world, one who will end his days in Melbourne."

"Running dogs and lackeys."

"Are you are familiar with the term?"

"Running dogs and lackeys are raised regularly at our union monthly stop work meetings in reference to the Liberal Party."

"Have you read of the civil war?"

"Bits and pieces about Mao's Long March, not much."

"We fought our own people and there lies an even greater tragedy than invasion."

"Throughout history the Chinese have been ill-treated. Mate of mine whose Chinese father served as AB on British ships out of Liverpool in the last war received for his loyalty deportation. Might have even got a double whammy with two deportations. It mattered nothing to the authorities his marriage to a British girl and their child. In fact the British government intended declaring his family aliens as well."

"Liverpool, Blue Funnel Line?"

"Alfred Holt, you know the shipping company?"

Shen's eyes almost pleaded to be allowed to scrape the last of the fried rice on his plate; Alex pushed both plates almost in his lap. "With no fond memories working down the hatches of those ships with tall blue funnels in Shanghai. After much thought my plans were carefully calculated, food and water for a long sea voyage, except a nosy officer in a white sailor suit found me on his rounds. Thankfully we were at sea."

"Stowed away?"

"For Australia around the time of the Korean War, weary of conflict. Alfred Holt certainly got their passage money out of my scrawny body, impressed in the boiler room with a wheelbarrow feeding coal to my sweating fellow countrymen. All too frequently times I thought I would not survive. Fed scraps from the galley and given no sympathy from my fellows who possibly saw me as a threat to their job."

"What happened when you arrived in Australia?"

"Nothing. Suppose there being so many of us in the boiler room and on deck I think the captain forgot me. The Korean War I never saw as a threat to China, unlike 1937 when China fought a vicious Japanese enemy. Though I did become apprehensive when United Nation forces reached the Yalu River. Of a highly disturbed and dangerous American warlord in the field who wanted to fight China on home soil. We were young soldiers, small pockets of poorly armed troops loyal to the liberation of China, with an oath of fealty to destroy the hated Japanese and banish the Kuomintang and hail Mao Zedong the leader of Communist China. Mao gathering his forces, bands of resistance fighters joining together to form armies.

"Killing Japanese for me and my comrades an act of retribution, satisfying and extracting a toll for their barbarous invasion of our country. Though the more I confronted the Kuomintang forces, sometimes young peasants whose voices had not broken, terrified and retreating, the more disillusioned to killing I became. Though not those who did their posturing from far in the rear and who ordered the youth of China to premature deaths so as to maintain their corrupt grip on power."

Thoughts of a veteran trimming coal from bunker pockets to recalcitrant fireman, expected to pay due homage to engineers, caused Alex to smile. "How did a freedom fighter adjust to being a lowly trimmer? Those white engineers would have been something to behold, not to mention the abuse from the firemen blaming you for bad coal."

"I accounted for nothing, a small inconsequential man pushing a wheelbarrow to dump coal at the feet of an equally insignificant man. What happened to your friend's father?"

"Deported to Singapore he simply disappeared without trace except for a single letter home. Strong willed and damned by a black mark against his name, a militant unionist. Undeniably, a man with a profile the government or shipping companies found unacceptable."

"Would he have taken up arms against the Kuomintang?"

"Huang Zhen landed in Singapore, not China."

"Singapore, Shanghai, Hong Kong, it made no difference. Singapore the first step in a journey home. True of the Chinese of Singapore, many succumbed to the mesmerising call of China calling for its children to liberate her. Also many forcibly returned to their ancestral home. Your Huang Zhen would not have been alone succumbing to his roots."

In the company of this old man he felt a camaraderie, an aged warrior fallen on hard times. Who had fought two enemies so violent and brutal later generations would cringe with disbelief at the suffering and grief of their forebears. Some Chinese sources would put the figure of dead from Japanese occupation at thirty-five million.

Plates wiped clean, Shen poured the last of the tea, both unwilling to end the conversation.

"Huang Zhen could have eventually returned to the United Kingdom because of the fact he had a British discharge book. Those lowly trimmers you shared your barrow with, the firemen you dumped coal on the plates for, every man on that ship issued with a British discharge book. Able to join ships of any flag, their discharge books as important as trade indentures. It classified a man a seaman, a British seaman."

"Huang Zhen may have seen his deportation as an opportunity to escape his commitments."

"So many things could have happened. Even crossed the Singapore causeway to join Chin Peng fighting the British in Malaya, but his family are of a mind there would have been impelling reasons for him to return to Liverpool."

Shen's eyes narrowed, "Chin Peng, my you are a knowledgeable young man. Hatred can be a force a man has little control over or down which twisted path it drives him. Chin Peng, he could have followed none better, a true leader of men betrayed by religious beliefs in a country dominated by Islam."

Both ignored the waiter fidgeting nervously under the tight-lipped prompts from the owner to remove their plates with haste, new customers backing up in the doorway.

"Mr Shen, I am up to my ears in things I have to do and not much time before I fly to the United Kingdom to ask a girl to marry me, but would you have lunch with me again?" With so much to do before his departure, he thought the request odd, an unnecessary trip into the city tomorrow. His only reason a niggling at the back of his mind he might possibly be in the privileged company of an extraordinary man.

"Thank you for suffering an old man with no more than faded memories of great battles to offer a lunchtime companion."

"Same time here tomorrow?"

Shen did something of a rarity, a physical contact with another human; he reached out a hand from a frayed cuff of a tattered jacket and touched Alex's arm. "No, comrade, meet me where we first met. Once more I wish to listen to the refrains of the Kuomintang minstrel. Only the victorious are allowed that dubious privilege. Also I have some items that might interest you."

———

Waiting at the head of Corrs Lane, the dim sim vendor entertained in fine voice; today he added an impromptu drum to his stamping feet, banging a large aluminium pot with a wooden spoon. Where exactly the voice and banging originated became even more difficult to define with a fresh pitch of charcoal smouldering under his steamers filling the laneway with acrid smoke.

From the outthrust chest of a soldier of another era came the rousing song of a despised enemy likened to a virulent disease befouling the beloved homeland, of his fellow believers encamped on a mountainous island in the South China Sea. Of the Kuomintang shouting their vitriol at the despised Communist regime across the Taiwan Strait, ready and willing to return to liberate China from the forces of indoctrination and enslavement. Supported by powerful allies from the democratic nations who recognised the Kuomintang as the government of China, victory would be assured.

Alex quashed a craving for dim sims; firstly he did not want to upset his new comrade by fraternising with the enemy, secondly their meal yesterday comparable to any first class restaurant in the city at half the price. Sitting at a table both men could face each other, ignore the aggravated waiter and the ferocious scowls of the owner over the exceptional long time it took to eat their meal and sip their fragrant tea. Shen also promised to bring with him something of interest.

Caught in the rushing lunchtime crowd he saw the frail figure of the old man approaching, wondering again why he wanted to meet on enemy territory. Walking with small calculated steps, his slow almost mechanical progress made him an easy target for people to bump, muttered apologies, sometimes abuse. None aware this warrior close to shuffling and dressed shabbily marched in the shadow of Mao Zedong, and with the Red Army lived off the land and joined up with core remnants of the Long March escaping the Kuomintang. Fighting a war as bloody and as inhuman as any fought in the frozen steppes of Russia with no quarter given. Surrender unacceptable, death inevitable to both winner and loser.

Close to his chest he carried a varnished wooden box with brass hinges and a hasp locking mechanism; catching sight of Alex he acknowledged him with a brusque nod, brushing past to enter Coors Lane.

"Have you changed your mind about the dim sims?"

"No! My body has not survived a long life by eating poison dispensed by dogs!"

Concerned, he watched him merge with the haze of charcoal smoke; the lane unusually silent as the dim sim vendor drank water from a flask to quench his thirst, a noisy throat clearing in preparation of another song.

Shen's voice reverberated off the canyon-like walls of the lane, a vitriol of hatred and condemnation. Alex quickly closed the gap between them, fearful the two old adversaries would this time make physical contact. With equal rage and a voice close to shrieking, the dim sim vendor retaliated, searching for a weapon to strike his opponent down; he found his poker and brandished it above his head.

Shen recognised the threat to his person, also the danger to his precious wooden box in the face of the enemy, using good sense to retreat.

"Jesus, don't you pair recognise what you both are, senior citizens and retired combatants?"

Claiming victory for the brief skirmish, with a still raised poker, he hid behind his cart chortling the opening bars of a Kuomintang song to herald a battle triumph.

Alex guided the vanquished to the mouth of the lane, even more confused. "Now what the hell are you on about, that needless confrontation over something you should have forgotten years and years ago? Impress me? We could have easily met somewhere on neutral ground, but no, you wanted to shape up again with the Kuomintang."

Shen regained his composure, tapping the top of his box. "As always the Kuomintang grovel in the presence of greatness, what I hold close to my heart. I wanted my sworn enemy to sense China in his worthless bones, taste it in his twisted mouth, feel it pulsing through his veins and fall to his knees in supplication."

Alex felt only bewilderment.

Another student waiter directed them to a table at the rear of the restaurant where though unintentional the owner's line of vision from the kitchen focused not on the darker interior of the restaurant but the front door. "Tea, please, and we will order later. Thank you."

"Chinese tea is a cleansing agent, not only for the body but the mind," Shen said, watching the young student return from the kitchen with a battered aluminium teapot and two cups. First pouring from the pot pleased him, strong and aromatic, finally softening the grimness in his face.

Alex commented on the box on the table between them; dovetailed, its multiple coatings of varnish so thick it might have been shellac applied with a trowel. Shen opened the box and turned it at right angles; tarnished medals, a sepia photograph, dog-eared papers bound with ribbons frayed and discoloured through age, the folded front-page of a broadsheet newspaper and large denomination but worthless bank notes. Teasing the nose a mildewed odour of age; the collected life of another old warrior, Shen's friend.

Using the tips of his fingers to gently lift the photograph, he handed it to Alex who let it rest face up in his palm. Momentarily his breath caught and he glanced across the table. "Mr Shen, the man seated is that who I think it is?"

Leaning over the table to better view the photograph he nodded; ten serious faced men in loose fitting uniforms and cloth hats stared directly at the camera, gathered behind a man sitting at an impromptu desk spread with a map and tea making apparatus. Hazy but still discernible in the background what might have been a razed village. "According to my friend who is standing third from the left he always drank hot water, though his officers preferred tea. As well the names on the back are in his handwriting, a gift for service to his country."

Turning the photograph over, Alex frowned; the date and Chinese characters only slightly faded. "Beyond me, can't read Chinese."

"Japan lay in ruins across the sea, the Red Armies regrouped into a conquering force of liberation. Now the traitors who paid homage to foreign devils faced annihilation at the hands of the people."

Alex used a paper serviette to clean the table before placing the photograph down. "Foreign devils sound like running dogs and lackeys, Mr Shen."

"Still the country remained under the iron heel of the Kuomintang, more years yet to suffer before liberation." With equal reverence to the photograph he removed the page from the box and placed it on the table; varying shades of amber, lighter where folded, close to parting along the seams. Breathing softly with his eyes in a distant place, he informed Alex it recorded a Red Army victory of great importance, column after column, paragraph breaks highlighted with tiny five pointed stars.

"Kuomintang forces, 100,000 men, held the west bank of a broad and fast flowing river, fortified with armoured vehicles, tanks and artillery. In the skies their aircraft flew unchallenged, bombing Red Army units taking up positions along the eastern bank. Against this force the Red Army mustered a thousand men, halted in their spearhead advance by the river. Leading by example, their commanders orders were explicit, destroy the enemy so the main body of the army massing in their rear could advance."

"Against the Kuomintang's overwhelming superiority, a liberation army of a thousand?"

Nervously passing his pencil over his empty order pad, the waiter kept an anxious eye on the owner who had emerged from the depths of the kitchen for a survey of customers; Alex ordered the same meal as yesterday.

Shen allowed a fingertip to gently touch the page, Alex certain the man had stopped breathing. "This records a turning point in the war for liberation. Of a leader and his officers who survived for greater achievements. Soldiers who would sell their lives dearly, young men with the ancient spirit of China beating in their fearless hearts. Who won a great victory with the supreme sacrifice."

"Mr Shen, are you telling me the Red Army won?"

"Their leader commandeered a small fishing village along the river and ordered the dwellings demolished and the timbers used to construct rafts. Men toiled all day and night without food or rest to build their rafts, and before first light sent their strongest swimmers with messengers attached to their waists, followed by stout ropes to haul the rafts across the river."

Honouring great sacrifice a tale of magical qualities unfolded, a legend passed around campfires by weary men before sleep finally overcame them. Good triumphing over evil that with the years and in its telling by even more imaginative storytellers would magnify until heroes grew taller and of greater magnitude, deeds more daring and courageous. An epic of wondrous proportions.

Remembrance of reading a colourful and expensively produced Chinese publication of the Great Leap Forward which came as a supplement with the Communist newspaper, *Tribune*. Miles wide the Pearl River in flood, a boiling torrent of raging water and viscous mud washing entire villages into the sea.

Regardless and ignoring the dangers a ferry made its regular crossing filled with happy and contented workers going home, their long day at their lathes and machines ended with production quotas exceeded. One exceptionally excited young worker who that day had received a promotion and for his dedication a new wristwatch from the company manager, pointing with pride at the skeletal structure of a new power station, cried out in stricken anguish.

Overcome with excitement of sharing a marvel of a new and prosperous workers state, the young worker's wristwatch band broke, his recognition of efficiency and dedication to his workplace lost forever in the ferment of the river. From the bridge two decks above the master with steely eyes firmly fixed on the difficult passage ahead heard the pitiful cry, rushing to the wing and without hesitation diving into the water. Cheers rang throughout the ferry as the master almost at once broke the surface of the water, holding aloft in a fist of triumph the wristwatch, with bold strokes overcoming the murderous currents and whirlpools to have the joyful workers haul him aboard a hero.

"Won by men who scorned death. Men who hand-over-hand hauled their rafts across the river, with their battle cries echoing off the Kuomintang ramparts in the early dawn light, prepared to fight to the last man. Writhing with fear the Kuomintang had never encountered such ferocity, such heroic determination, their commanders unable to maintain discipline as their forces crumbled before the ceaseless onslaught, abandoning their weapons and fleeing."

Ordered reasoning found it difficult to comprehend the different strengths, positions and firepower of the two belligerents in such a one-sided military encounter, but it did not detract from the story the old man related with his eyes on fire.

The Chinese Seamen's Children

"Would you like to keep these in remembrance of those young soldiers?"

"What of your friend?"

"My friend's eyesight like mine is poor, an old body worn and spent not only from war but from the unforgiving land he worked as a child to manhood. This box and its contents will only gather dust under his bed, its destiny to be thrown out with the rest of his junk when he dies."

"Could you translate it for me?"

"Please understand it is an understatement my eyesight being poor."

"Where could I get it translated?"

Their food arrived.

Shen rubbed his hands together enthusiastically as his eyes passed over the feast. "There is a means available which I think you should investigate, the Chinese consulate. No doubt their staff would be highly interested in such a piece of history, the consulate not that far."

26

THERE ARE FEW WHO having been exposed to bureaucracy have not condemned it for its creaking slowness and political correctness taken to the highest level of righteous absurdity. Blank stares from behind bulletproof glass, support seeking glances at colleagues in the background, ears attuned to every word, the Chinese consulate.

Why he even contemplated having the items translated bothered him, so little time left before his departure. What did he care about a battle fought years ago in China? Shen had already told him what the paper reported. Put the newspaper and photograph in a bottom drawer until he returned from the United Kingdom, a simple decision reached without haste whether to go ahead or not with the translation.

She might have recently completed her high school studies, a minor overseas posting before commencing university leading to a diplomatic future; he felt his resolve melting, credulous for being here. No, he didn't believe that, Shen Kang had activated an intense desire to delve deeper into what might only be fantasy. Other thoughts a close friend might have something to do with this interest in matters Chinese. Not that he believe that either, chastening himself for searching for mundane reasons when there were none he could positively identify.

The Chinese Seamen's Children

Adjusting her spectacles, she commenced reading, every so often her eyes drifting to the photograph; her cheeks slowly turned crimson, her lips moving and he clearly heard the murmured words, the wonderment. Pausing, she looked up. "Excuse me, sir, is it impolite to inquire how this came into your possession? Also why you have brought it here?"

"Translation, and that's probably odd as who really cares about old stuff kept under a bed? As well I already have a fair idea what it says. Both came into my possession for the price of two meals and two pots of Chinese tea, as well as the company of someone special."

Pressing a buzzer one of three doors opened and two young men came to the counter. One picked up the page while staring at the photograph his associate turned over; like the girl both their faces flushed. "Are you aware of their importance? Who the men in the photograph are and who wrote on the back?"

"By what I am told by this old Chinese veteran it records a battle for a river in the civil war following the defeat of the Japanese. Against unbelievable odds young liberationists sacrificing their lives to allow their comrades in the rear to regroup and eventually cross the river victoriously, Peking within their grasp. About the photograph, one I recognised easily, the others, no."

Veneration filled the young man's voice. "No, that is wrong. It is an obituary."

Alex frowned.

"With great care it shall be translated, but would you grant us one favour? May we keep these? Would you bestow a great honour upon the People's Republic of China?"

"Yes. Yes of course."

One of the three noticed him glance at a large wall clock. "It will take us time to translate, it cannot be rushed. At least until late tomorrow afternoon?"

With no choice, he nodded.

Like so many others he experienced the ordeal of the daily commuter, parking his car, wondering if he had locked it, mistakenly parked in a time restricted area, continually rushing, continually glancing at his watch, finally catching the train to Melbourne. Well serviced with rail, Frankston trains ran every half hour in peak, every hour off-peak. Train travel far outweighed driving to the city, congestion with trams and buses and rare parking opportunities. Commuting also gave him time to think.

Tomorrow his parents planned an overnight stay, his mother to cook a pre-Christmas dinner including the Moorlands. Informing them of making a new life in the United Kingdom his parents at first greeted the news with scepticism. Nora Nielsen, a mother fretting about son ever committing to marriage, nursed a fierce maternal desire to pander grandchildren born and reared in Australia, not another world away. On the paternal side there were misgivings, the high cost of living in England and the unfavourable exchange rate between the two currencies, especially with Alex's earning capacity in Australian dollars.

Like an aggravated lioness with irritating cubs, his mother grilled him over Jennifer.

"Jennifer is a career woman, her Chloe I hope to make mine," he said. "Jennifer is what the writers of romantic fiction describe as an English rose, her skin satin and quite unlike the tanned hides of Australian girls. She speaks well and never completes a sentence with hey, or uses endearments like mate or endless you-knows." Then he hugged his mother and headed her in the direction of the kitchen. "Your tickets are a gift to thank you both for so much, and if we have difficulty arranging Westminster Abbey, we'll have to make do with a small chapel in Merseyside."

At first Alex could only stare at it in wonder, the consulate staff having gone to exceptional lengths with the translation and its presentation,

The Chinese Seamen's Children

the entire office staff in attendance when he stepped out of the lift into the foyer, visible to those inside the consulate through glass double doors. Expensively bound, the document amounted to twenty-five pages of cream marbled heavyweight paper, secured between endpapers of the flag of the People's Republic of China, protected by a clear plastic cover. Embossed on the flyleaf an enhanced image of both sides of the photograph.

Staff members gathered about to shake his hand, ignoring with polite smiles his plea that it should be Shen Kang's comrade receiving this adulation. With the handshaking complete, Alex began to feel his status among men near to godliness.

Where to find Shen, an old decrepit Chinese in a large city with many Chinese? The Queen Victoria Markets.

Concluding the day's trading the markets, acres of rusted iron roofs set on unpainted hardwood posts bolted into stained and broken concrete, looked as if a cyclone rendered the area a disaster. Row upon row of stalls gave the impression of growing from a bog of rotting cabbages, cauliflowers, overripe fruit, potato sacks laid over concrete to soak up water used to hose rotting detritus down the city's sewers.

Always present the putrescence of potatoes turned black, pulped pumpkins and rotting fruit, freshly slaughtered meats, hot curries, pungent spices, and the powerful aroma of coffee from Brazil. Women from Asia, India and Eastern Europe squatted on their haunches over boilers on gas rings as their menfolk swept and piled the refuse of the day into already overflowing dumpsters and garbage bins.

For a few quiet hours there would be a narrow window to reconcile the day's trading, eat and catch up on sleep before the first of the trucks from interstate and local farms began arriving to recommence the cycle. At this time of day there emerged an underclass with the need to fill their bellies with discarded food, later unload the trucks. Even with a large number of Chinese traders it should have been easy to locate Shen, none he asked answering in the positive. Some would think for awhile, shake their heads and point to a neighbour who understood English better.

Giving up finding him, he saw a small figure sitting in a doorway across from the markets separated by double tramlines and a raised concrete and railing mid-street tram stop; his intentions of having a beer in the hotel nearby, a tram to Flinders Street and the train home, postponed with a huge sense of relief.

"Mr Shen, can I buy an old Red Army veteran a beer, for certain a meal in the pub?" Sitting beside him he had to press hard against his hip to make room on the step.

"Thank you, no."

"An old warrior with a little time on his hands, there is something I would like to show him." To protect the document the consulate had supplied a soft leather satchel from which he withdrew the translation.

Shen held it in both hands, then raised it to his nose and sniffed deeply. "Originals have been kept, correct?"

"Consulate requested it. Mr Shen, I felt myself raised to deity status."

"Pleasing, also for my friend."

"Mr Shen, is there something I can do for you?"

With a weary smile he placed a remarkably steady hand on Alex's knee. "You have done more than enough already, Alex Nielsen. Not meeting in the circumstances we did, and I never seeing in you the man you are, history would have been the poorer."

"Money?"

"Thank you, but of little use to me. Look around, I live well with no fuss."

"Many would challenge that assumption."

"Does you future include children?"

"Yes."

The Chinese Seamen's Children

"Always look to revolutionary history for names worthy of your children. All I ask for giving you the opportunity to look into the past, a glimpse worthy of a good man."

"Thank you, I will remember that."

"Of that I am certain."

In the swaying carriage of the almost empty train he opened the folder and read in the dim overhead lighting. Consulate staff had been correct, the rural newspaper front-page had left the recording of a great victory to other more significant journals, the columns of text an obituary. Slowly, he read the names one by one of the martyrs.

Name after name after name after name …

Staring at the mirrored panel at the far end of the carriage, his eyes blurred, his breathing so shallow he might not have been drawing air into his lungs, forcefully swallowing the constriction in his throat. Station after station sped by as if the train reaching its terminal early would lengthen its period of rest, an immediate return to Melbourne it fate.

Familiar stations announced by bells and red flashing lights, the headlights of idling vehicles. Mordialloc, the beginning of the Mornington Peninsula, a gun barrel run to Aspendale, Edithvale, Chelsea, Bonbeach, brief glimpses through a grimy window of the beaches of Port Phillip Bay illuminated in silvery moonlight.

Frankston, crossing the traffic free Nepean Highway, a short walk down a deserted street, his car the only vehicle by the kerb. Turning over in his mind a mental calculation of time.

Edward's voice might have been in the same room. "Mate! Been expecting a call and let me tell you it's been hell trying to keep your secret."

Alex seemed mesmerised by the *Titanic* print on the wall, his eyes transfixed by the artist's capture of a vivid yellow sunset and sky, the sleek ship sailing at full speed into her last sunset. "Edward, I found your father …"